Deanie Francis Mill[...] Stephen F Austin Univ[...], and until she became a full-time writer she taught high-school English. She has written five previous novels of suspense (*Losers, Weepers*, also published by Headline, is her most recent) and numerous articles for publications such as *Writer's Digest*, *Good Housekeeping*, *Redbook* and many others. She is an experienced speaker and regularly lectures to writers' groups. She lives on a ranch in West Texas with her husband and their two children.

Trap Door

Deanie Francis Mills

First published in Great Britain in 1994 by
HEADLINE BOOK PUBLISHING

First published in paperback in 1995 by
HEADLINE BOOK PUBLISHING

A HEADLINE FEATURE paperback

10 9 8 7 6 5 4 3 2 1

ISBN 0 7472 4733 1

Typeset by Avon Dataset Ltd., Bidford-on-Avon, B50 4JH

Printed and bound in Great Britain by
Cox & Wyman Ltd, Reading, Berks

HEADLINE BOOK PUBLISHING
A division of Hodder Headline PLC
338 Euston Road,
London NW1 3BH

FOR MY MOTHER, MAYREE.

Aurore Dupin, the great feminist writer who wrote under a man's name, George Sand, so that she would be read and taken seriously, once wrote: 'You can bind my body, tie my hands, govern my actions. You are the strongest, and society adds to your power, but with my will, sir, you can do nothing.'

Thank God, Mother, you taught me the same.

Though I have tried very hard to bring the gorgeous region of the Davis Mountains of Texas and the towns of Fort Davis and Alpine to life, I did take a few geographical liberties for the sake of the story, which I hope the good residents won't mind.

None of the characters or ranches described in this book are meant to resemble any existing, past or present, with the exception of the Prude Guest Ranch, which is mentioned in passing.

PART I

ob ses sion, *n. (L. obsessio).* 1. originally; the act of an evil spirit in possessing or ruling a person.

Webster's 20th Century Dictionary,
Unabridged Second Edition

'Survival is all in the mind.'

Anthony Greenbank
The Book of Survival

Chapter One

She was very young, very sweet, and a completely shattered human being. Her blonde hair was shaped into a good cut, but she hadn't been taking care of it. All during the interview, she bit fingernails which were already ragged. Some seeped little bits of blood.

Cady Maxwell handed a tissue to the girl and she blotted a face already mottled by tears. 'It's all right,' she told the girl. 'We've got plenty of time.'

'I don't want to remember,' the girl whispered into her tissue.

'I know, honey. This whole thing has been very hard on you and you've been so very brave. But if you can give me a good description of the man who raped you, and I can put together a composite drawing that helps the police find him, then they'll lock him up and throw away the key. He won't be able to hurt any other beautiful young ladies like you.'

The girl gave a slow nod and Cady waited quietly. Some witnesses responded to gentle prodding, some retreated when pushed.

'I was going to wait until I got married,' said the girl, staring into space with emptiness in her eyes. 'I mean, I know that's not considered cool for a high-school senior, but it's the way I feel. Felt.' Tears washed up over her eyes and spilled down her cheeks.

'It's all right,' soothed Cady. Part of the job of being

3

a forensic sketch artist was being a counselor as well. 'There isn't a good man in the world who would blame you for this. In that sense, you are still a virgin. Always remember that.'

The girl pushed a strand of hair over her ear and said, 'He had a mustache, but I don't know if I can describe it.'

'Why don't you show me?' Cady handed her the *FBI Identification Catalog*, opened to the mustache page.

The girl bent her head over the page and, after a moment, pointed out an example.

'Okaaay,' Cady murmured, her hand working furiously. 'Now, why don't you describe his nose to me.'

'Just . . . normal, I guess.'

Cady sketched in silence for a while. 'Like this?' She turned her portable easel toward the girl.

'Ummm . . . his mustache was a little fuller over here.'

'No problem. We can fix that easy. You're doing just great. We're almost done.' She worked on the mustache. 'How's this?'

The girl's innocent blue eyes widened a little and then she looked away, pressing the tissue against her mouth. 'He put himself inside my mouth,' she murmured. 'And I can't get the taste of it out.'

With that, she whirled to the side of her chair and threw up.

The television newsmagazine host's well-practiced smile accompanied her famous lisp as she gazed into the camera and flawlessly read from the cue cards,

'Our next story on tonight's program is about a remarkable woman from Texas who has helped capture so many criminals that the Dallas Police Department has taken to calling her their "trap door". James Anderson has more.'

As the miracle of TV graphics took over, introducing the segment, Cady Maxwell groaned loudly and threw a handful of popcorn at the screen. 'Who told them that?' she demanded.

Bob Hall, a burly, barrel-chested Homicide detective, with what looked like one bushy black eyebrow over his forehead, gave her a wicked grin, which she rewarded with a peppering of popcorn.

'*Shshsh!*' begged Elaine Martinez, a trim, pretty sex-crime specialist from the Crimes Against Persons division. 'They're starting.'

Cady's face appeared in close-up, her light-brown shoulder-length hair streaked with gold, her serious, dark-brown eyes staring with characteristic somber intensity at the camera.

Roger Baxter, a tall, thin black cop from Robbery, said, 'Cady! Isn't that a huge zit right there on the end of your nose?'

'Am I going to have to pull my gun to shut you guys up?' demanded Elaine.

'No, but we can negotiate,' deadpanned Bob.

'. . . Maxwell's work has resulted in solved crimes on both *America's Most Wanted* and *Unsolved Mysteries,*' Anderson was saying, his handsome, chiseled face carefully framing his words. 'She is one of the country's most respected forensic sketch artists and skull reconstructionists. Hundreds of criminal suspects have fallen through her trap door after having been identified due to one of her sketches, and with the process known as "age progression", Maxwell has been responsible for the return of many kidnapped children to their searching parents.'

'Wonder Woman!' shouted Bob.

'Biggest damn zit I ever saw,' said Roger.

'Do you see this, boys?' asked Elaine, waving her gun in the air. 'It's loaded.'

'So's mine,' answered Bob, thrusting his pelvis forward.

'With what, blanks?'

Shouts of laughter and catcalls followed, drowning out portions of the broadcast. Cady and her friends had gathered in a back room of CAPERS (Crimes Against Persons), to watch the program on a small set. She had planned to see it at home, but Elaine had wanted her to do a sketch for the rape victim, who couldn't come to the police department until late. She hoped she'd programed her VCR correctly at home. To be honest, she was very nervous about how she would appear on this program. Cady considered herself part of a team in law enforcement and didn't think she deserved any more credit than did the investigators who put together a case. It was embarrassing to her to be featured so prominently, when these guys usually put in twenty years or more without fanfare. She was grateful to them for being such good sports.

'Maxwell gained prominence when she perfected a process of skull reconstruction known as two-dimensional,' continued Anderson. Cady was shown holding a human skull in her hands, saying, 'The normal process for skull reconstruction is to take the skull itself and build a clay model onto the skull which reveals the approximate facial features.' A hideously burned body, its charred face heat-swollen beyond recognition, was shown.

'Oh no!' cried Cady. 'I had no idea they were going to use that slide on the air!'

'Somebody's papa probably just lost his hero sandwich,' drawled Roger.

'In a case like this, it's impossible to make an accurate facial identification of the body,' the TV Cady continued. 'So what we do is, well, I know it sounds awful, but we sort of clean up the skull, add certain tissue-depth approximations, then take scale photographs of it.' The TV Cady laid a piece of sheer paper over the photograph and showed the TV audience how facial features could then be super-imposed by the sketch artist over the photograph.

'How do you know what color hair the body had?' asked Anderson, his dark eyes properly serious.

'Sometimes a few strands still cling to the skull. And we use anything that we find with the body – jewelry, whatever – to add to the finished picture to aid in identification. Once I had a model pose her hands, wearing the victim's rings. The victim was then identified by the family based on the photographs of the model's hands.'

'You didn't tell that ole gal where those rings came from, didja?' asked Bob, and grinned at her.

'Some of Maxwell's sketches of criminal suspects have bordered on the miraculous,' continued the correspondent. 'This sketch was based on the description given by a blind rape victim. And this one was done at the bedside of a critically injured police officer who could only nod "yes" or "no" to Maxwell's questions. One drawing was done from descriptions provided by a victim who had repressed the memories for over a decade. All resulted in arrests and convictions.'

'Ticker-tape parade!' shouted Bob, showering Cady with popcorn, and was promptly booed down by the others.

'The most satisfying work I've done is helping to find lost children,' the TV Cady was saying. She then demonstrated how she was able to 'age' a photograph of a kidnapped child by drawing that child as he or she might appear years after the abduction. 'In this case,' she said, 'the little girl was abducted by her non-custodial father when she was two years old. We were able to find her after ten years had passed.' Cady's sketches were shown, followed by actual photographs of the child at the time of her recovery.

'You *are* a Wonder Woman,' said Elaine.

Cady shook her head. Compliments in front of her colleagues made her uncomfortable.

'Perhaps the most famous of the trap door's cases involved the pursuit and apprehension of the so-called LoverBoy Rapist, who obsessively pursued his victims for days or even weeks before the assault by sending flowers and love notes anonymously. His last attack became violent when the victim was able to pull off the ski mask he'd always worn. But she survived the beating and was able to give a description to Maxwell, whose sketch was then used as the trap door to capture the LoverBoy.'

Congratulatory hoots and catcalls erupted around the crowded television set. Cady smiled. This was the kind of compliment that meant the most to her.

Still smiling, she was unprepared for the shroud of sadness that suddenly fell over her. If only her mother could have lived long enough to see this. It had been only six months since breast cancer had stolen her mom from her life and Cady had surely lost her best friend. For a moment, she held her eyes open extra wide to ward off a sudden onslaught of tears. Grief had unbalanced her, shifting raw emotions dangerously close to the surface. It made the work she did much more difficult. After all, it wouldn't be very good for a hysterical crime victim if the sketch artist suddenly burst into tears.

The face of the young rape victim, squirming in humiliation while Cady cleaned up the vomit, flashed into her mind and she released her emotions with a long, heavy sigh.

The segment ended. Cady pasted a bright smile on her face as her friends congratulated her and complimented her on the show. They were good people – the best – there couldn't be, she knew, anybody better to work with. While the others drifted back to work or over to the coffee pot, Cady sat for a while, composing herself. Her mother's death wasn't the only thing haunting her.

Without her mother around she couldn't confide this particular problem to a single soul, but the cold, bald truth of the matter was that Cady, at thirty-six, was weary to the bone. Through the years, she'd seen more ravaged bodies, more terrorized victims, more suffering families, than she could begin to count.

Day after day, she'd witnessed the horrible aftermath of violent crime. Deep, deep within her, in that secret place nobody ever saw, Cady Maxwell was afraid.

And unlike most people, who live daily with an unnamed fear in today's society, Cady, more than anyone perhaps, knew just exactly what there was out there to be afraid of.

I'll never forget the first time I laid eyes on Cady Maxwell. Normally, I don't watch those newsmagazine things because they're just too depressing, don't you think? But I do love old movies and I was switching around, you know, trying to find something decent to watch, when that lovely girl with the honey hair and the serious brown eyes flickered onto the TV screen.

I mean, I was instantly captivated. I thought, My God, she's beautiful! Everything about her was perfect – and so unexpected, too. I figured anybody who did what this woman did for a living would somehow have a face imprinted with the evil she confronted each day.

But not Cady Maxwell. She had spirit; I could tell that right away. And fire, and courage. Like a wild Mustang, yearning to be free.

I could tell because I could see yearning in her eyes.

Lord knows, I understood that yearning only too well. During my own unfortunate time of captivity, I, too, had burned to be free, to be happy, to be loved.

She was so gifted! Why, someone as good as her could be a portrait artist to the Presidents! Why should she waste her time drawing cons?

I knew right away that we were true soul mates.

I just knew it.

It's one of my little gifts, this ability to recognize true love instantly.

10

But this was like nothing I had ever known in my life, I can tell you that. I just felt this instant and powerful magnetism to the woman on the screen – I can hardly describe it.

Those eyes! They beckoned me.

Well, I just had to meet her. No question about it. Like all my passions, this one was instantaneous.

Oh, I had a great time imagining just how it would be. I even gave a great deal of thought as to how I would dress for the meeting. How would she best respond to me? Just from looking into her eyes on the TV screen, I could tell how sensitive she was. I knew her that well, that quick! In fact, from that moment on, I figure I knew her probably better than she did. It's another of my gifts, this ability to know someone just by looking into their eyes. So. I knew I'd have to present myself just so. I could see us . . . we'd smile at one another, and shake hands, and in that one connection, a thousand words would pass unspoken between us.

Then, once I could get her alone and could really talk and get acquainted, I just knew that she, too, would see the inevitability of it all. She would see how good we were together, how close we fit.

Oh, I was so certain that she would be good for me! It makes me sad to think of it now.

I remember that I was so excited, I jumped up and did a little dance. I was so happy! I knew I'd never sleep that night. This was the princess I'd been waiting for. That one person in the whole world meant just for me. God knew I'd waited so long, and been so alone . . . but never, ever again.

All I had to do was figure out a way to meet her.

*Considering my situation and all, I knew it would be
a real challenge, but it wouldn't present that much of
an obstacle. Nothing would.*

After all, this was Destiny.

Chapter Two

'What the hell are all these people doing out at eleven o'clock at night?' muttered Cady as she maneuvered her maroon Lexus at breakneck speed through the Dallas freeway system, trying to get home.

The Lexus was her one indulgence, her own little world of pulsing music that insulated her from the noise, heat, and pollution that was the city, and kept a small part of her separate from the madness that was her world.

Except that now, even that one indulgence was at risk. American carjackings, especially of luxury cars, had reached an all-time high; Cady could never even stop at a traffic light without glancing nervously around. As she slowed for the exit, she reached down and touched the formidable grip of the Beretta 92 nine millimeter she always drove with, just for reassurance.

Hell of a world, she thought gloomily.

Her apartment complex was in a nice North Dallas neighborhood and was populated mostly with busy-single or divorced workaholics who weren't there much more than Cady was. She didn't know any of her neighbors and turnover was high. She remained alert as she parked beneath a bright light and sat for a moment, looking carefully all around for anything that might be out of the ordinary. Then she locked the Beretta in the console storage compartment between the bucket front seats, set the car alarm, and hefted her heavy leather purse – heavy because it carried a loaded snub-nosed Chief's special .38 – and hurried across the parking lot to her door, keys in hand. Paranoia was an occupational hazard for anybody who worked in law enforcement for very long.

Cady's apartment was little more than a stop-off place to sleep and change clothes for work. She seldom ate there and had done little to decorate it in the seven years she'd called the place home. She kept meaning to though.

She longed for a cat. She liked cats and a kitten would be great company on some of her long insomnia-ridden nights, but she didn't think it fair to keep a pet all alone for endless hours while she was gone.

After flipping around with the remote until she found an old movie on TV, Cady wandered into the kitchen for a glass of wine. She was all wound up, restless. That poor, ravaged rape victim she'd interviewed had really gotten to her.

Cady walked into the living room and checked the double-bolt on her front door. Then she went all through the house, turning on lights.

Hanging near the light switch in one room was one of her mother's needlepoints, this one quoting Elizabeth Cady Stanton – the nineteenth-century American feminist and Cady's namesake: 'Nothing adds dignity to character as the recognition of one's self-sovereignty.' Next to that was a shadow-box containing buttons, a small placquard, and the coat hanger her mother had worn on her head when she'd marched on the nation's capitol to protect abortion rights. It had been her last great protest before her illness incapacitated her.

'What's the matter with me these days, Mom?' Cady asked aloud. 'Why do I feel so . . . dissatisfied . . . all the time? I mean, there I was on national television tonight – did you see me? – and somehow, it just doesn't seem to matter any more. Well, I mean, of course it *matters*, it's just . . . I don't know. I wish you could have seen that kid I interviewed tonight. I try to stay apart from it. Not get involved. That's what they say you should do anyway. But hell, it still breaks your heart, you know?'

And what if it didn't? said her mother's voice in her mind. *What would you be then?*

Cady paced back down the hall. She found herself talking to her mother a lot these days. Who knew? Maybe she was going nuts.

The wine didn't taste right and she left it sitting on the coffee table while she stretched out on the couch to watch Cary Grant star in a movie made fifty years ago, before he'd found his true comedic rhythm.

She was just beginning to doze when the blinking light of the answering machine on the end table beside the couch caught her eye, and she reached out lazily to play her messages.

'Hey Cady. Sergeant Sawyer here.' Cady groaned.

'How'd he get this number?' she asked aloud. His voice was slurred and, from the background noise, she figured he must have been calling her from a bar somewhere.

'Just wanted you to know that I saw you on TV tonight. I'm sho glaaad you captured all those bad guys all by your pretty little lonesome, while the rest of us poor bastards just shtood around with our thumbs up our butts.' There was a loud banging noise as the receiver was apparently dropped, then a dial tone, followed by several congratulatory messages from friends.

But Sawyer's message – the asshole – hit Cady right where it hurt. It seemed that the more notoriety she got, the more that insecure guys like Sawyer resented it. Which fed her own guilt that maybe she was taking a little too much credit, although she tried very hard not to.

There had been an implied threat in Sawyer's tone. For one thing, Cady's private number was unlisted and she gave it out to very few people. How had he gotten hold of it?

Wide awake now, Cady flopped over onto her back and stared at the ceiling.

It was going to be another long night.

The plan, when it came to me, was true genius.

All I had to do was witness a crime – or pretend to, anyway – and then when it came time to do the composite sketch . . . !

Of course, I knew I'd have to make a change or two in my appearance.

I loved making plans like that! It was like stalking someone in a way, but in a nice way.

Actually, the more I think about it, the more I dislike that word: stalking. I know about nutcase dudes who stalked celebrities or old girlfriends or whatever and blew them away at the end. Uh-uh. That wasn't for me, no sirree. For one thing, I'm no nutcase. And for another, I'd never, ever have done anything to harm

Cady Maxwell. Not then, anyway.

How could I ever harm someone I loved? After all, our relationship was much too deep for that. I have to laugh a little at that – 'our relationship' – all she had to do was figure that part out! I didn't think it would take her very long. She's like me. Intuitive. At least, I thought she was.

But. First things first. I made a list, and the first item on it was, order a dozen roses.

The Monday after the Friday-night broadcast, Cady was late for work. Her head hurt from lack of sleep, she had a run in her stockings, and the French braid she nearly always wore to work was already coming unraveled. As she stepped out of the elevator, Elaine Martinez was waiting.

'Great sketch on the rape suspect you did last Friday,' she said, locking step with Cady as she hurried down the hall toward her office. 'You know – the night your story was on TV? We got a bunch of hot leads. If we catch this guy we may clear as many as a dozen cases.'

'That's great,' said Cady, fumbling for her keys.

'By the way. Some guy tried to get in to see you this morning.'

'What guy?' Cady looked up from her bottomless leather bag.

'I don't know. None of us have seen him before. It was really weird. He kept saying he had to see you, but when we pressed for details he kept changing his story. We got rid of him.'

Cady stared at her friend. 'Elaine, that's scary. I mean, for God's sake, this is a police department. Can't we have any better security than that? He could be some freak who saw me on TV or something.' She shuddered.

'We didn't let him in, did we?' Elaine said. 'My, but we're testy this morning.'

'I'm sorry,' said Cady as she pushed open her door. 'I didn't sleep much last night.'

'I don't blame you. I'd be excited to be on national TV too.'

Cady didn't choose to correct Elaine. A lot of people had misconceptions about fame. They didn't realize how intrusive it could be, how constricting and sometimes even how frightening. In fact, she wouldn't have agreed to the interview at all if she hadn't considered it a good forum to help close some of their unsolved cases. Unloading her aching arms of various work-related paraphernalia, she picked up her *America's Most Wanted* coffee mug.

Cady's office was as crowded as her apartment was sparse. Books covering every aspect of criminal investigation, facial structure, bones and the skeletal system – especially the skull; forensic art materials from workshops and seminars; sketching materials; medical texts, and true-crime stories stuffed every shelf, nook and cranny. Carefully labeled files reached almost to the ceiling. Framed credentials from the FBI and other organizations hung willy-nilly, along with a few framed newspaper articles displaying her sketches on a number of high-profile cases. And, over in one corner, a comfortable chair stood, surrounded by things such as stuffed bears and other toys, a box of Kleenex tissues, and a candy jar, ready to comfort shaken witnesses. Cold drinks

18

were kept in a small refrigerator.

There were dozens of newspaper articles about her successes, hand-written thank-you letters from cops and victims, and other mementos of her success which she kept tucked away at home, in a scrapbook. Next to her phone was a framed photograph of her mother, arm in arm with feminist-activist Gloria Steinem at a rally. There was a huge stack of messages beside the phone. Cady set down her coffee mug and began sorting through them.

'I gotta go,' said Elaine. 'Work beckons.'

Cady nodded. 'See you later,' she mumbled, already distracted by the messages. Someone had apparently called several times without leaving a name or number. Apparently he didn't realize that, even if Cady were in her office, her phone calls were screened before being put through, due to the sensitive nature of her work. She never allowed phone interruptions while interviewing witnesses for suspect sketches.

Out of the corner of her eye a ghostly figure loomed in the doorway, and Cady jumped. It turned out to be a huge bouquet of white roses with legs.

'What in the world?'

'Are you Cady Maxwell?' asked the roses.

'Yes.'

'These are for you.' The roses walked into Cady's office and lowered themselves to her small, crowded desk, revealing a skinny young man behind. 'Is there enough room?' he asked doubtfully.

'I think so,' said Cady, so dumbfounded she forgot to tip the guy. 'Thanks.'

He backed out slowly, leaving her to contemplate the flowers in bewilderment. They were truly exquisite, and so unusual – most people sent red.

There was no card anywhere.

The first person Cady thought of was Peter Stanton, the vice cop she'd been dating until recently. But he'd never sent her flowers then; why would he now?

It could have been her cousin Jackie, the closest thing to a sister Cady had, but it would be out of character for Jackie to send something this expensive without taking full credit for it. Besides, Jackie had recently quit work in order to stay home with a baby; they couldn't afford an extravagance such as this.

She felt someone watching her and, in the same moment, heard a deep drawl saying, 'I don't guess I could take the credit for sending those, could I?'

Cady looked up, and tried hard, if somewhat unsuccessfully, to hide her astonishment. After living in a glossy, self-conscious city and working daily among hard-core cops and cynical lawyers, this man looked like someone who'd just blown in on the West Texas wind.

Tall and craggy-faced, he wore a black-suede Western-cut jacket, an immaculate white Western shirt with pearl buttons snapped all the way to the throat but with no tie, plain Levis, boots, and a pearl gray Stetson which he removed with one hand, reaching the other out to shake hers. Piercing blue eyes smiled at her from deep corner laughter lines and a black mustache set off white teeth. He was not classically handsome – his nose was a little too big for that, his features maybe a little too angular, his teeth slightly crooked – but those eyes! There was an almost hypnotic irresistibility about them. Maybe it was the rugged, care-worn face or the black lashes; whatever it was, this man exuded a thoroughly masculine sensuality that caught Cady staring.

As she tried to unglue herself, Cady noticed that the deep bronze of his complexion stopped right at the browline where the hat fit, leaving his forehead strangely pale. She'd seen guys in cowboy hats before, usually festooned with all sorts of feathers and snakeskins and vulgar buttons. Dime-store movie-cowboy stuff. But this was a man who obviously worked outdoors in a hat; he handled it easily and gracefully, removing it indoors like a gentleman should.

'I'm Zach Ralston,' he said easily, encasing her small hand in one huge one, in a grip so firm she tried not to wince. The palm of his hand was rough. 'We have an appointment at eleven?'

Tearing her gaze away from his, she glanced at the little clock on her desk. It was ten forty-five. 'You're, uh, early,' she stammered, shuffling through the messages on her desk until she found the one that read, 'Zacharia Ralston/shooting witness/eleven a.m.'

It would have been nice if someone could have let her know. Maybe then she wouldn't have overslept.

And for God's sake; if she'd known *Clark Gable* was going to show up, she'd have at least fixed her hair!

'If you need me to come back later . . .' He turned for the door.

'*No!*' she cried. He turned back. She felt her face grow hot. 'I mean, of course not. Uh . . . would you like some coffee?'

'Sounds great,' he said.

She rummaged around for another mug.

'I saw you on TV last week. Very impressive. Of

course, little did I know I'd be meeting you professionally a few days later.'

She found an old Dallas Police Department mug and blurted, 'You don't act like a victim.'

He raised his eyebrows.

'I mean, well, crime victims don't really want to be here. They don't want to think about what happened to them. They're usually real timid and stand around outside until somebody tells them what to do. You just walked right in.'

He nodded. 'Very interesting. Actually, I'm not a victim in this case, just a witness.' He shrugged. 'And I guess when you've been around as much as I have, you learn to handle a few things.'

'You're not that old.' She took his hat and placed it in a chair.

'No. Not like that,' he said gently, picking the hat back up and carefully placing it upside down. 'Otherwise the brim gets flattened out,' he explained, adding, 'And I'm forty-five.'

Only then did she notice the soft streaks of silver at the temples through his dark, thick hair. Hair a woman could get her fingers tangled in. Inwardly, she shook herself. *Evidently it's been a while since you had a good lay, ol' girl*, she thought wryly. Aloud, she said, 'Coffee's down here in the break room,' awkwardly pushing past him. To her surprise, he followed her. She noticed that his right leg had a slight drag to it.

'You're not from around here, are you?' she asked over her shoulder as he stepped into the break room behind her, *filling up the small room with his masculine presence*, she thought. *Shut up! Since when did your life become a paperback romance? Guy's probably married with six kids and one on the way.*

'Out in West Texas,' he said. 'The Davis Mountains. I ranch there, but I have banking business that brings me to Dallas occasionally.'

'The Davis Mountains?' *Pay attention.* She poured him a cup and handed it to him, assuming correctly that he liked it black. 'I've never been there.'

'Oh, you should,' he said. 'It's just about the most beautiful spot in the state of Texas. But then, I'm prejudiced.' He smiled.

Cady took a sip of coffee. Some dribbled onto her blouse. Crimson-faced, she dabbed at it with a paper towel, then led the man back to her office, showing him to the comfortable chair and struggling to concentrate on the job at hand. 'Why don't you tell me what happened, while I get set up?'

His first remark caught her completely by surprise.

'I thought I'd seen enough death,' he said. 'I thought I'd kind of got used to it, you know? But watching somebody die never gets easy.'

Chapter Three

As Cady set up her sketching materials, Ralston lapsed into silence. She sensed that his mind had drifted elsewhere, and she gave him a moment to collect his thoughts. From a drawer, she withdrew the thin soft-cover book entitled *FBI Facial Identification Catalog*, placing it to the side of her drawing paper. Sometimes she needed it to jog a witness's memory, sometimes she didn't.

'Mr Ralston?' she prodded gently.

'Please, call me Zach. And forgive me. After all this time, you'd think a thing would get easier to talk about. Hell, it just seems to get harder.'

Cady kept her face expressionless, and when he glanced at her it seemed to reassure him. 'Take your time,' she said. 'And don't feel bad. I can guarantee you that it doesn't get easier for anybody.'

He gave her a studied look, seemed to consider something, then said, 'Back when just about the only prisoners being taken by the Vietnamese were pilots, I happened to be one of the honored few infantry grunts stupid enough to get caught.'

With a start, Cady realized that Ralston was not talking about the crime he had just witnessed, but crimes from long, long ago.

He shrugged and went back into himself again. 'Eight of us guys went out on recon. I was the RTO –

25

that's a radio telephone operator – for the platoon leader. Monsoon season in the jungle. Impossible to see or hear anything properly. We almost walked right onto the VC. We opened fire and called in artillery but, hell, they were too close and there were too many of them. My radio took a direct hit, so we were without commo. We knew the rest of our company was behind us, but they were pinned down by the bullets going over our heads. Must have been a hundred VC.' For a moment he was quiet, pain flinching across his face.

'The platoon leader took it first. Lost his face right next to me. A grenade blew out the chest of another guy and the legs of another one. I was hit in the head – cracked my helmet wide open like a melon – and that's the last thing I remember before . . .' He sighed. 'Never could figure out why they dragged me off with 'em instead of just leaving me there. I guess they thought the guy with the radio might know something. Boy, did they ever fu— screw up.'

Cady sat in stunned silence. Before she could speak, he cocked his head at her and said, 'I have no earthly idea why I told you all that. Haven't talked about it in years. I don't know . . . maybe seeing that murder the other day set me off or something.' His smile was weak. 'Hope I didn't ruin your day.'

She said, 'If you can believe this . . . I've heard worse.'

His eyes gazed through to her soul. 'Yeah. I kinda figured that. Maybe that's what got me going.' He shook his head. 'Most folks who've known me all my life never found out what really happened to me over there. I never was one to talk about it much.'

She nodded. 'Cops are that way, too. People don't

have a frame of reference, you know? They think TV and movies are the real thing.'

'But the smell of blood . . . you can't hardly get rid of it. That's not something they can put on TV.'

An involuntary shiver passed down Cady's spine. How had they got talking like this?

She busied her hands, straightening her desk, something she'd never done before during a witness interview. Suddenly she blurted, 'The hardest case I ever had to do was a woman who'd been horribly stabbed in her own home. Her two little girls were witnesses. After the attacker left, they tried to help her by putting band-aids on her wounds. Band-aids! They stayed with her for hours while she bled to death, too young to know what to do next.'

In the silence that followed, horror and embarrassment consumed Cady. Never had she ever said such a thing to a witness. Had she lost her mind? What had gotten into her?

'Please forgive me,' she stammered. 'I don't know what I was thinking.'

'No! I'm glad you told me. This may sound strange, but it actually made me feel better. In a way, you work in a war zone too. Makes it so you know what I'm talking about.'

To a point, she thought, *but I've never actually been a victim of violent crime. Always on the outside, looking in. I can sympathize, but you can understand.*

He cleared his throat. 'Guess we ought to get started.'

'Right. Why don't you tell me what happened Saturday?' She wasn't about to admit that since she'd been running late today, she hadn't had time to read over the police report. The whole day seemed oddly out of synch, as if a different and unexpected Cady were suddenly popping out of her skin, making remarks and doing things that she was unable to control.

And before she could pick up her pencil, it happened again.

'Are you hungry?' she heard herself saying. 'Why don't we go to lunch. We can talk about the murder there, then come back here to do the drawing. I don't have another appointment until one.'

He lifted his eyebrows, and her mouth went suddenly dry. She had never done anything like this before. Ever. Not at work anyway. Not with a *witness*!

He said, 'Are you sure you have enough time?'

'Oh sure,' the wicked Cady-impersonator said. 'I can do a drawing very quickly once we get started.' That wife and six kids went right out of her mind.

'Well . . .'

'My treat,' the brazen hussy prompted.

'My mama didn't raise no fool,' he said with a grin. 'Let's go.'

TGI Friday's was a trendy fern-bar type of restaurant, popular with young professionals, and as soon as Cady walked in the door with Zach, she knew she'd picked the wrong place. Though he was a man easy in his own skin, he seemed out of place and uncomfortable amidst all the tony three-piece suits and glitzy make-up of the regular patrons. These were the kinds of people who ordered wine spritzers and vegetarian salads and worried endlessly about things like whether their home computer was outdated or if their weekend tennis game with the boss might be ruined by rain.

There wasn't a single cowboy hat or pair of boots in the joint, and people stared openly as Cady and Zach made their way through the room. They were seated at a small table with two chairs, and Zach didn't have anywhere to put his hat, so he extended one long leg and balanced it on his knee.

She wanted to apologize, but she wasn't sure what for.

'Good thing I wore my good jeans,' he said with a grin, as if reading her mind.

'I don't know any country and western places,' Cady stammered.

'What makes you think I'd like a country and western place?' he said, his eyes twinkling.

'The food's good anyway,' she said lamely.

'And the company's excellent,' he answered.

She prodded at the back of her head – giant loops of hair were falling down in all places. 'Excuse me a moment,' she said, and hurried to the restroom, where she brushed the whole thing out, then stared at herself in the mirror and said, 'You are a screaming idiot.'

A woman stepped out of a stall and quirked an eyebrow at Cady. Face hot, she returned to the table.

'Beautiful,' he said. 'You should wear your hair down all the time, let the wind run through it.'

'I guess there's lots of wind in West Texas,' she said, then stared at her salad plate. Oh God, this was worse than junior high.

'It depends,' he said seriously. 'The mountains aren't like the plains.'

'What are they like?' she said. *What are they like?*

29

What are they like? They're mountains, stupid!

Again, he seemed to take her question seriously. 'Well, they're not as high and craggy as the Rocky Mountains, but they're every bit as beautiful. And the stars ... you can't imagine. McDonald Observatory is located there, you know. If you've ever listened to National Public Radio, you've probably heard their Star Date segment.'

Of course. She knew that. She'd just forgotten. 'I've been meaning to visit the observatory,' she said.

'Then it's settled. You'll just have to come out and see me,' he said.

See me. He'd said, see me! A little thrill started in her chest and worked its way down to ... She took a sip of water. *Woah. Not too fast here, little filly. Don't forget the wife and six kids.* 'You said you had a ranch?'

He nodded. 'It's not that big,' he said. 'Only seven sections. We raise Quarter horses and Hereford cattle.'

We, she thought. *He said, we.* She swallowed. 'How much is a section?'

'One square mile. Six hundred and forty acres.'

She tried to multiply the amount in her head and failed. *Not that big? Who was this guy, J. R. Ewing?* 'How often do you come to Dallas?'

'Oh, every couple of months or so. I've got some investments I check out.'

'Do you ever ... bring your wife?' *Real delicate, Maxwell. Like a sledgehammer.*

He was smiling at her as if he knew exactly what she was thinking. Oh, those eyes ... Her mother would have called them 'bedroom eyes'.

'No wife,' he said. 'I was married when I went to Vietnam, but she divorced me and married my best friend while I was a POW.' At her stricken expression, he said, 'I couldn't blame her really. We were too young to start with and the marriage probably wouldn't have made it anyway.'

'You never married again?'

'Once. I was looking for love in all the wrong places, I guess. She disappeared before we'd been married a year.'

'Disappeared?'

'Just took off. Left a note. And that was that. When I couldn't find her after about six months, I divorced her. Been a confirmed bachelor now for, oh, fifteen years or so.'

'I was married once too,' she said. 'To a cop. It didn't work out.' Not after the one and only time he hit her anyway, but she didn't mention that.

'How did you ever get into such a gruesome business?' he asked.

Gruesome. What an odd choice of word. She'd never thought of her work as gruesome, but she supposed it might look that way to some.

'I used to do quick portrait sketches of people at amusement parks during summer vacations,' she said. 'When I got out of college, I figured out pretty fast that it's awfully hard to make a living with an art degree. I worked for a museum some, and got to dating a cop, and one thing led to another . . .'

'And you married him.'

'Yeah. Then I married the job.' She blinked. Yet another comment straight out of the misty blue. It was true though.

'Is it a happy marriage?' he asked with a soft smile.

'I love my work,' she answered. 'It's just . . .'

He waited.

'It's what it does to you.' She glanced at him for some signal that he understood what she meant and, to her relief, he nodded.

A most amazing man.

The waitress came and went and Cady lost all sense of other men – of anyone, for that matter – in the room. There was a quiet strength in this man that made her want to curl up in his lap. And a certain raw sex appeal that made her want to do a lot more.

He had a way of listening to her that was unusual for most men, and he had old-world manners that made some executives she knew look like clods.

It was with reluctance that she finally steered the conversation around to business; a furtive glance at her watch made it necessary.

'I guess I owe my life to this hat,' he said, lifting the Stetson and running his fingers gingerly around the rim. 'If a gust of wind hadn't caught it and blown it off my head, I might not be here.' He sighed, laughter lines melting into fatigue lines, and she wondered what bloody memories had been stirred up by the crime he'd witnessed.

'I was parked around the side of my hotel because it was quicker to get to my room that way than through the front lobby. My plane was late Saturday, and by the time I was settled in they'd shut down room service for the night. Pissed me off, but what can you do?' A fleeting grin crossed his face. 'When I stepped out of that side door, there was this brisk little breeze coming around the north end of the building and it just yanked that hat off and rolled it underneath about three cars. So I dropped to my hands and knees to fetch the damn thing, and that's when I heard arguing.'

'In the parking lot?'

'Right. I started to grab the hat and get the hell out, but something about the way the voices sounded kind of stopped me in my tracks.' He shrugged. 'You get certain instincts in the jungle that never quite leave you.'

She nodded.

'So instead I just crouched down behind one of the cars, and when I'd figured out where the voices were coming from, I raised my head just enough to see over the hood of the car. Hell, they weren't but about five yards away.' He shook his head. 'Man, it happened so fast. I mean, by the time I realized one guy had a shotgun, he'd raised it and fired, point-blank, into the other guy's chest.'

'It was dark,' said Cady. 'How well could you see the guy's face?'

'It wasn't that dark. They keep those parking lots pretty well lit in the nicer hotels. I could see his face like I see yours, and I knew in a flash there wasn't nothin' to do but hit the ground. If he'd have seen me, I'd be dead.'

'What happened next?'

'He climbed into a car that was parked there with the rest of them and drove off.'

'I take it you didn't get the license number.'

He shook his head. 'I've kicked myself like a damn fool ever since.' He rubbed his hand over eyes which seemed suddenly weary. 'I tried to give the guy mouth-to-mouth. It just bubbled right out of the hole in his chest.'

'I'm sorry.'

'The thing is, you can "what-if" yourself to death on a thing like this. You know. What if I'd gone for help instead of ducking like a coward?'

'Do you think you had time?'

'No way. But still . . . You think.'

'Well, what I always tell victims of violent crime is that, no matter what happened, if you are alive, then you did the right thing.'

He gave her a lopsided grin. 'That's kind of the same thing they tell a soldier who's been to war. You're a pretty wise lady.'

She smiled back.

The shrill noise of her beeper caused them both to jump.

'And a busy one too, I see,' he said as she got to her feet with an apologetic shrug.

It was Lieutenant Throckmortan, and he was pissed. 'Where the hell have you been, Maxwell?' Throckmortan was a steel-faced rule-thumper, and he always frightened Cady a little. The only thing that kept her from feeling like a naughty schoolgirl at the principal's office was that her usual workaholic hours more than made up for this present transgression, and Throckmortan knew it.

'Uh . . . interviewing a witness,' she said. Technically, it was true.

'Well, why the hell couldn't you do it in your office? Never mind. When can you be done with the sketch?'

'In less than an hour.'

'Good. We'll have a chopper ready then. There's been a godawful shooting out at one of the malls and

34

I don't want to have to fuck around with traffic. Anyway, this guy didn't do us all a favor and kill himself when he got done with his little party. He got the fuck clean away.'

She swallowed. Feeling a presence at her side, she turned and saw Zach standing nearby. He had thoughtfully already paid the ticket (though it was supposed to have been her treat), and was standing, hat in hand, ready to go.

'When did it happen, Lieutenant?'

'About ten o'clock this morning. You didn't hear about it on the news or anything?'

'I . . . was listening to my . . . tape deck.' She felt incredibly stupid. 'Do you need me any sooner? I mean, if you're using the helicopter . . . I could probably postpone this sketch.' She gave Zach a questioning look, and he nodded.

'No need. The scene's still pretty chaotic. Some of the witnesses are wounded and some still too shook up to work with an artist.'

'What about mall security?'

'It happened in the parking lot, just as they were opening up. No time for anybody to do anything.'

'Okay. I'll be in my office ASAP, if you need me.'

'Good.' He hung up.

'Is your life always this exciting?' asked Zach as they hurried toward the door, his long limping strides equalling two of hers.

'Only on Mondays.' It was a weak joke.

'Look. I was planning on flying back home tonight, but if you need me to hang around we can do this sketch any time.' They reached her car and he waited while she unlocked the door.

'No. Thanks Zach, but the LT said we had plenty of time.'

He grinned.

'What?'

'I haven't heard that term since 'Nam. LT. Means lieutenant.'

Though her Lexus seemed plenty comfortable to Cady, Zach had to fold up his body to fit inside, and had to take off his hat yet again because he was too tall. As she pulled out into traffic, he said, 'When you get through with this latest crisis, do you think you'll have time for supper? After all, we didn't really get to finish dinner.'

First, she almost wrecked the car, and then she wanted to scream. 'Actually, no. I mean, I'd love to have dinner with you, but I'm already so far behind today—'

He lifted his hand in dismissal. 'No problem. Maybe the next time I'm in town.'

When will that be? she wanted to beg. She liked the quaint way he said 'dinner' and 'supper' instead of 'lunch' and 'dinner'. She liked a whole hell of a lot of things about him. She was dying to ask when he'd be back in town.

But she didn't. Like any good professional, she forced the sexy cowboy out of her mind and concentrated on the job at hand.

But it didn't keep her from giving him her card, with her unlisted home phone number written on the back.

Chapter Four

'He had a cap pulled down low over his eyes, and he was wearing those kind of sunglasses that make mirrors, you know?' The woman raised a styrofoam cup of coffee to her lips. Her hands shook so hard that some of it sloshed out.

Cady waited. The woman was like spun glass. Her whispery voice worked its way down Cady's spine like cold fingertips, causing goosebumps. It was a voice that should have been comforting a crying pre-schooler, not describing violent bloodshed. Her manner of speaking was hesitant and uncertain; she often ended statements in a questioning way. She wore heavy, outdated glasses that were too big for her face and her straight, black hair gave her complexion a pale, ethereal cast.

The whole time, she stared at her lap, as if establishing eye contact would somehow make the memories even more grim.

'And ... he had a mustache.' She bit her lip. 'And he stood very still the whole time. It was like he was ... target practicing. He'd pick out what he wanted to shoot at, and then he'd aim, and then ...' She shuddered.

'So he didn't spray the parking lot with random fire?'

'Oh no. He was very deliberate.'

37

'And yet he didn't shoot you.'

'To my dying day, I'll never know why,' said the woman. 'Everybody was screaming and running and crying. Some were shouting NO at him and some were trying to hide behind cars.'

'What did you do?' Cady coaxed the witness to talk even as her expert hand rendered the cap and mirrored sunglasses onto paper.

'I just stood there. Like a rabbit caught in car headlights, you know? Just stood there . . .' A little sob escaped her.

Cady handed her a box of tissues. They were working in the cramped, airless break room used by mall security. Outside the door, cops of all shapes, sizes, colors, and badges combed the mall, looking for more witnesses, and others searched the parking lot for shell casings and any additional evidence they could dig up. Cady leaned forward. 'You said he had kind of a big nose, but not huge, right?'

The woman blushed. 'To tell you the truth, I really didn't notice what kind of nose he had. All I could see was the barrel of that gun, pointed right at my face.'

'I understand. That's perfectly normal. There's even a name for it: hyperamnesia. It means you can remember one detail – such as the gun – vividly, but the rest tends to be a blur. Don't you worry about it. We'll get it close enough.'

'It was just a second, too. I mean, he looked right at me and pointed the gun. And then he just turned away.' She dabbed at her eyes underneath the glasses.

Gradually, as Cady slowly and gently drew her out, the woman grew more comfortable with her. Eventually, she stopped shaking, but her voice still quivered. Cady did what she could to reassure the woman, mentioning that this man now had reason to fear *her*, because she could get him caught. Even so, Cady often had to ask her to repeat things; at times her voice was so soft Cady couldn't hear what she was saying at all.

When the drawing was done, Mrs Cooper seemed reluctant to leave the room, and Cady could understand that. The scene outside was still chaotic.

'Why don't I walk you to your car?' she asked. 'You've already given a statement to the police.'

'Oh, *could* you?' the woman asked pitifully. 'I know it's silly, but I'm still so afraid.'

'I know.'

'I mean, he's still *out there*, isn't he? What if he changes his mind after all, and comes looking for me?'

Cady touched Mrs Cooper's arm and, to her surprise, the woman embraced her and clung a moment while Cady comforted her, patting her back and making soothing noises. It wasn't the first time she'd been hugged by crime victims, but it always made her feel a bit awkward, as if her protective wall of objectivity had been breached. 'I don't think you need to worry about that, Mrs Cooper,' she murmured. 'He's probably getting as far away from this place as he can.'

'I hope you're right. Oh God, I'll never forget the look on that man's face as long as I live. It was so ... *cold*. With those sunglasses and all, it was like ice. Like he was looking right through me.' She shivered. 'I just can't seem to get *warm*, you know?' She cupped the fingers of each hand into the other, as if to warm them.

There wasn't much Cady could say to that. She checked with investigating officers to make sure the woman was free to go and then walked slowly with her out to her car.

'I feel so silly,' said Mrs Cooper. 'Thank you.'

'No problem. It's no trouble at all, and you've been a terrific help.' She squeezed the woman's hand, waved goodbye, and waited until she'd driven away before heading back to the break room to see what else needed to be done, dragging her feet wearily.

Fear. It was the one common denominator of anyone who survived violent crime. Even if they were unhurt, their worlds remained forever shattered by the simple, raw truth that, yes, it could indeed happen to them. It gave body and life to the nameless fear that stalked many modern urban dwellers. She wished she could do more for them than just give them a quick hug or a soothing word. They came in and out of the revolving door of her office, frightened, wounded little birds who might never find the courage to fly again.

Cady liked to think that the one thing she *was* able to do was give them back a certain measure of control over their lives. By coaxing them to provide a viable description of their attackers, she enabled them to take charge again and make some sort of difference which might result in justice if the criminal were caught and successfully prosecuted. Because the one single thing that every victim of violent crime lost was the sense of being in control of their own lives. Once that control was violated, their sense of self was never quite the same again.

Some recovered. Some did not.

* * *

It was after dark when the helicopter finally ferried Cady back to the police department. A slight spring mist had moved in, giving the city a faraway, otherworldly glitter and a Christmas tree of sparkling, haloed lights spread out for as far as the eye could see.

Cottony wreaths of cloud cloaked the top floors of the highest buildings. Twinkling lights, like golden beads strung together, coursed along the freeways through the mist. Cocooned in the noise and vibration of the chopper, it was as if Cady were benevolent royalty, surveying a magic fairy kingdom far below.

She wished she could stay aloft forever, where nobody had to stare down the barrel of a gun and into the icy gaze of a killer, in whose mirrored glasses they could see – reflected back at them – their own terror.

After that first meeting with Cady Maxwell, I was delirious with excitement. How lovely she was, how competent, how strong – she was magnificent! She was everything I'd dreamed she would be, and more.

And she HAD responded to me! Oh, it was glorious! Night after night, I'd replay our time together, running the video tape of it in my mind.

But. I could see that things were going to have to go slower than I had originally planned. She was like a gazelle, graceful, wild, and free. I couldn't push her; I'd have to LURE her.

Of course, that was the fun of it. It was like . . . matching wits with someone who was – at last! – deserving of it. Like a game. Or an intricate dance. Step and counterstep.

* * *

Although Cady's busy days tended to blur together, she calculated that it had been about a month since she'd met Zach Ralston, and the tall cowboy had still not called her, a fact which disappointed her a lot more than she would have liked it to. She'd thought he might let her know when he was going to be back in town, maybe arrange a date. But as the days went by without a call, she had to concede that she must have been far more impressed with him than he was with her.

One day she even went so far as to get his phone number from information. With shaking hands, she dialed, only to slam the receiver down when she heard his voice.

If you're going to act like a thirteen year old, she chastised herself, *why don't you just have Elaine phone him up and say, 'Do you like Cady Maxwell? She likes you.'*

Sometimes she fantasized that Zach had the same problem, because every night and on weekends she would answer her phone, only to have the person on the other end hang up.

Once, when she answered a knock at her door, there was no one there.

Kids, she decided. Playing pranks.

So, when another bouquet of roses arrived one Saturday afternoon – this one on her doorstep – Cady almost hugged the delivery boy in her excitement. She could just see Zach as she had that first day, standing in the door to her office, drawling, *I don't guess I could take the credit for those, could I?*

He must be back in town!

She dug through the bouquet for a card but, to her

consternation, there wasn't one.

The flip side to excitement – dread – welled up in her.

As if on cue, the phone rang. This time Cady waited for the answering machine to pick up and screen the caller for her. There was a sound of light breathing, and then a raw whisper, saying, *'Did you get the flowers? Do you know what white roses stands for? Purity. Just like my love for you.'*

She started shaking. It did not occur to her that this could be a genuine secret admirer, somebody who was simply too shy to confront her directly. There were just too many kooks out there, and she knew what they looked like; she'd done sketches of most of them.

Cady yanked up the receiver and screamed, 'Leave me alone you sick son of a bitch!' She slammed down the receiver and stood for a moment, her body prickling with goosebumps.

She'd done sketches of most of them.

Dry-mouthed, she put in a call to Samantha Sagar, a chief prosecutor with the Dallas DA's office with whom she'd worked a number of times. Samantha, a high-powered workaholic of the first order, was not an easy woman to track down, not even on a weekend. To her supreme frustration, Cady had to call a number of places and wait around for a couple of hours.

When the phone finally rang, Cady pounced on it without waiting for the machine.

'What's up girl? I hear you've had the bloodhounds after me.' Samantha's voice was honey-smooth. Cady knew it could be double-fanged when necessary.

She felt the pulse at her throat and struggled to remain calm. 'Samantha, could you give me an update on the status of Harley Jefferson?'

'Ol' LoverBoy? What do you want to know?'

'He got twenty years, right?'

'Right.'

'With good behavior, how much of that sentence do you think he'd have to do?'

'Maybe a third of it. Maybe less. It was his first conviction.'

'And we sent him up when, six, seven years ago?'

'Something like that. Why?'

Cady took a deep breath. 'Sam, do you think he could be out now?'

There was a long pause. Finally, Samantha said, 'I guess he could be, Cady. Want me to check it out?'

'Please.'

'Hey – are you all right?'

'I'm fine. I just . . . want to make sure the LoverBoy Rapist is still behind bars.'

'You haven't heard from him, have you?'

'Well, no. Not exactly.'

'Okay. I'll call Huntsville and check it out.'

'Thanks. And Samantha, if you don't mind, I would appreciate it if you'd send over a Texas Department of Corrections photo of him. Remember, I didn't testify at his trial.'

'Oh yeah. That's when you got your appendix out, right?'

'Right. I was scheduled to testify but you guys managed just fine without me. Anyway, I need an updated photo.'

'Those things are hard to get and, besides, it's been a while. His appearance could be quite changed.'

'Still . . . I'd feel better.'

'Right. You got it.'

Cady had to wait all day to hear back from Samantha. It was, after all, a weekend. The apartment was growing cold and dark, and she was going around turning on lamps when Samantha called.

'He was paroled six weeks ago, Cady, to Greenville, Texas, where his mother lives. His PO says he's been a good little boy ever since.'

Greenville wasn't that far from Dallas.

'Are they watching him pretty close?'

'Sounds like it. They make unexpected visits to his home and the construction job where he works. So far, he's been clean as a whistle.'

Cady's fingers felt cold. She thanked Samantha and hung up, then she adjusted the thermostat to turn on the heat.

She knew the LoverBoy's pattern only too well.

It always started with roses.

Chapter Five

It took me a while to figure out what the beautiful Cady Maxwell's problem was. She was entirely too self-reliant. She didn't think she needed anybody.

But she did. She had needs she didn't even know about.

From the very start, I'd felt the chemistry between us. She felt it too – that was obvious enough. I knew that our minds were in perfect synchronization, so why, WHY didn't she understand about the roses?

Because ... she didn't WANT to understand.

She didn't want to understand for the simple reason that she didn't think she needed anybody in her life. Miss Independent!

I had tried to be nice with her. Gentle. Subtle. Romantic.

And she'd called me a sick son of a bitch! Why would she say a thing like that? Didn't she realize that my love was perfect, my love was pure, my love was ... my love ... How could she torture me like that? How could she be so blind?

She had within her grasp a love to tempt the gods!

And yet, she wouldn't listen to her own heart; if she did, she'd KNOW who it was on the phone and who had sent the roses. After all, I shouldn't HAVE to tell her. She should simply intuit the vibes that I sent to her each and every day – just as I had picked

47

up her vibes from the first moment we met. Hell, from the first time I ever saw her. I knew our love was too pure, too powerful for the ordinary.

I was going to have to show her, and I didn't like what I was going to have to do. It hurt to think of it. But, sometimes, it's necessary to hurt the ones you love.

It's like disciplining a child. You don't like to spank the child – it hurts you more than it does them! – but you do it for their own good, to make them better people.

It was the only way she would be able to see how very much she needed me – how much we needed each other.

And once she realized that I was there to meet all her needs, I figured she'd throw herself into my arms, and we would kiss long and deep and endlessly, and I'd caress her toes and suck her fingers and touch her body in places that would make her cry out for more, and . . .

Well, it's a little embarrassing to admit this now, but sometimes, just thinking of her like that, I would . . . touch . . . myself, you know, just like our bodies would do together one day, and I'd cry out her name . . . Cady . . . Cady . . . beautiful Cady . . .

The attack was swift, brutal, and unexpected. One minute, Cady was standing on the doorstep after having worked late – a bag of groceries in one arm and dry cleaning slung over the other, unlocking her door and pushing it open – and the next, she felt a powerful shove between her shoulder blades which sent her staggering.

As if in slow motion, the sack of groceries went spiraling out of her arms, spewing tomatoes and french bread and lettuce. A bottle of wine hit the floor and shattered – just as her front door slammed shut behind her and she heard the imprisoning click of the deadbolt.

It couldn't be happening! Not her worst nightmare!

Her gun. She had to get the gun. Her leather purse was all tangled up in the crook of her arm with the plastic dry-cleaning bag. She tried to reach the gun with her other hand, when a fist grasped her hair and yanked her to her knees.

The apartment was pitch black. She hadn't known she'd be working late, or she'd have left a light on.

But there wasn't time to think.

In the next moment, her attacker, swinging from behind her, landed a punch to Cady's cheekbone which sent her reeling, shaking loose the purse. She felt something split open just under her eye, and warm liquid ran down her face.

Never in her life had she been hit like that.

As Cady landed face-down on the carpet, staggering to get up, the intruder jabbed a savage kick to her back. She fell to the floor and curled up in the fetal position.

She was kicked in the head.

Everything was happening in dream-like sequence, a dark misty blur of blood and pain. She tried to make out her assailant in the darkened room, but could see nothing more than a dim shape.

He was going to kill her.

She had to fight!

With a swift roll to the side, Cady scrambled across

the floor to her bag. She managed to grasp it to her just as a hard kick landed underneath her right armpit. Cady screamed in pain.

Her arm and hand went instantly numb, but Cady fumbled anyway for the gun . . . *the gun! For God's sake, get the gun!* Her hand bumped against its cold hard reassuring surface, but she couldn't seem to get her fingers to wrap themselves around the grip.

She plunged her left hand into the bag instead, closed it around the grip, yanked it out and fired. The recoil bucked her wrist painfully. Muzzle-flash strobed through the dark, blinding whatever night vision she had accumulated, while the deafening boom reverberated through her head.

The shot went wild.

She'd never fired a gun with her left hand before, which made it even harder to control, and in the dark and terror and confusion and pain— She fired again, but she couldn't see and she couldn't hear over the ringing in her ears – everything was a daze. She emptied all three remaining rounds of the five-shot snub-nose toward any dark shape that loomed in front of her – and she kept clicking the trigger even when all the bullets were gone. But it was too late – he'd seen her coming and had leapt around behind her again or something. It didn't matter anymore anyway because something hit her head and Cady, quite literally, saw stars.

She wasn't out for very long but, when she felt herself coming to, the first thing she noticed – even before the pain – was that she couldn't move.

Oh God, was she paralyzed?

She wiggled her toes and they were fine, so that wasn't it . . . Then she realized she was tied up, face to the floor, her hands bound securely to her feet. Duct tape over her mouth nearly suffocated her.

And if she moved her head, she felt something choke against her throat.

Widening her eyes, struggling to notice detail – *anything* – that she could describe later, Cady suddenly realized that her right hand was free.

And that her attacker was straddling her body, the weight of his legs pressed securely against Cady's ribcage.

What was he going to do?

Had he raped her already? She felt no pain . . . down there.

He was going to rape her now.

Slowly, she turned her head to the side. The carpet burned her cheek. Heart pounding like a jackhammer, she waited.

The one thing Cady had learned through interviewing crime victims was that each case was different. Some assailants could be talked out of more violence; some thrived on their victims begging for mercy.

Before saying anything, Cady wanted to find out which type held her pinned to her own floor.

Then she realized how foolish that was, since she was gagged anyway.

The gunshots. Surely someone had heard and called the police. Then she remembered that it was Friday night on a Memorial Day weekend; most of the young professionals who lived there had already left the city as fast as they could pack their bags. Coming in, she'd noticed that the parking spaces for the apartments on either side of her were empty.

A soft gleam from the partially opened blinds in the living room reflected off something solid and heavy next to Cady's head. As her eyes finally focused in the darkness, Cady was able to make out what it was – a tool box.

Her cop mind kept overlaying her victim mind with thoughts like, how much does he weigh? How tall is he?

Why had she not been able to make out his face at all? A ski mask, maybe? What *kind* of ski mask?

Why was her right arm lying out to the side of her body? Why hadn't he tied *both* her hands together?

Could she reach the tool box? Grab a weapon?

She was trying desperately to think how to fight, while on her stomach, tied up, with only one hand free, when the lid of the tool box clanged back.

Cady's whole body jerked.

He reached inside and, through the dim glow from the blinds, she could see what he held in his hand.

A hammer.

Then, taking hold of her small right wrist in one gloved iron grip, he began to spread the fingers out, one by one.

Horror, unlike anything Cady had ever imagined, electrified her body. Screaming wildly against the duct tape, she yanked free her right hand, flailing it, while her body kicked, twisted and fought with every ounce of adrenaline she had.

She was choking, screaming, retching, fighting for her life.

She managed to upset the seat the attacker had on

her back, but when Cady scrunched her knees up in a desperate attempt to crawl away, she felt a yank on the rope tied like a noose around her throat. Gagging, struggling not to black out, Cady reached up her right hand and grasped the ski mask – against all reason, because she knew that if she *saw* him, he would kill her for sure. But she had to know, she *had* to, if it was the last thing she did, by God, she'd look her own killer in the eye.

The attacker fell to the floor with her in a deathlock.

The rope around Cady's neck jerked again. The familiar night-time shapes of her home around her tunneled into blackness, leaving only a pinhole of consciousness as, at last, her grip on the ski mask loosened and her hand – against her will – fell free.

Roughly rolling her nearly inert body over and straddling her once again, her attacker pinned down her weakened right arm at the wrist and picked up the hammer.

'NOOOOOOOO . . .'

It was a mute, hopeless scream, torn from her soul and ripped from her lungs, battering fruitlessly against the wet sticky tape that jailed the word, while Cady watched, with her last conscious breath, as the hammer came smashing down.

Not once, but five times.

She didn't make it past the third finger.

Chapter Six

Consciousness came before vision. The blackness behind her eyelids gave way to the murky, liquid grayness of very early dawn. The walls of the room swayed in and out rhythmically, keeping some sort of hypnotic beat to the pain.

She had never in her life known pain such as this. The pain had a life and a body of its own, a fanged creature which gripped her entire body in bloody talons, clutching her tighter with every jaw-clenching wave of nausea and dizziness.

Thoughts scampered through her brain in nightmarish flits, never standing still long enough to make any sense. *This is my own bedroom Where is my purse I have to go to the bathroom Am I late for work Mom will come by in a little while I must have had a nightmare It hurts it hurts it hurts Did I make my bed before I went to sleep Why am I wearing this nightgown Mike never liked it anyway Mike doesn't live here anymore I think I'm going to throw up Can I make it to the bathroom I have to call my boss I don't think I feel like going in to work today When is Mom coming over Oh yeah She's in the hospital What happened to me Oh God it hurts so bad but I don't think I could hold down any aspirin My hand what happened to my hand my hand my hand . . .*

She could barely turn her throbbing head on the

pillow to gaze at the huge contraption that was her hand. At first it looked like a boxing glove, but that was silly – of course it wasn't a boxing glove. It was a towel, all wrapped around her hand, which was propped up on a pillow.

She couldn't feel her hand; it was as if it wasn't there at all.

Slowly, clutching the side of the bed with her left hand, so that she wouldn't fall off, Cady let her gaze slide around her as best she could, but she still couldn't see very well.

She was dressed in the white-satin peignoir her mother had given her as a bride so many years before. Her ex-husband, Mike, had tastes which ran more for the black see-through numbers with the snaps in the crotch, so the peignoir had hung in the closet longer than Cady could remember.

Now she was dressed in it.

She was lying on her back in her own bed, propped up on pillows, with the satin peignoir arranged just so over the sheets. Her right hand, which she could not feel, was swathed in a towel and propped on a pillow at her side. Conveniently placed right beside her left hand was her telephone, the one which usually rested on the nightstand to the right.

There was a cloying scent in the room which seemed vaguely familiar to Cady. With infinite slowness and care, she managed to raise her head a couple of inches off the pillow, blinking and straining her eyes to see in the brooding pre-dawn dimness.

She was covered in a snowdrift of white rose petals.

The horror of memory slammed into her with such overwhelming force that she barely had time to turn her head to the side before vomiting.

Something was wrong with her jaw. Opening her mouth to keep from choking on her own bile sent a lightning bolt of pain through her head. Choking, sobbing, strangling, she clutched at the telephone with her good hand and punched 911.

With every move she made, the pain grew even worse. She couldn't talk. It was almost impossible to move her jaw and her tongue seemed to be swollen. When she tried to give her name, it sounded like, 'Caahey Naxhell'. By repeating it over and over to the patient operator, she was able to get out the words, 'Help. Hurt. Police.' Fortunately, her address had already appeared on the dispatcher's computer screen.

The woman's calming voice, warm and concerned, became Cady's lifeline as she waited for help to arrive. She had no way of knowing how much time had elapsed since her attack, and she was utterly terrified that her attacker was nearby – maybe still in the apartment.

The stench of vomit and the overpowering smell of fear mingled with the sweet scent of rose petals gagged Cady and she retched, clutching the phone with white fingers.

She couldn't take her eyes off her right hand.

If she tried to close her eyes, she'd see the hammer, swinging, smashing down. The room began to spin. Violent trembling overtook her.

Cady cried for her mother.

The officers had to break down the door, which had been left locked. A frightening noise otherwise, it brought great relief to Cady and to the 911 operator.

The first patrol officer to enter Cady's bedroom was

Ralph Potinsky, a gruff, red-headed tenderheart Cady had known since way back in her married days. He was followed closely by a young rookie she'd met a few days before, Rudy Martinez, one of Elaine's cousins.

Both men stopped in their tracks. 'Oh my God!' said Rudy, and then he broke into tears.

Cady didn't need a mirror to see just how bad she truly looked.

Ralph hurried over to the side of the bed and gently pried the phone away from her left hand. After reassuring the operator that the police had arrived, he hung up the phone, took Cady's hand in his big freckled paws and said, 'Don't you worry, sugar. The cavalry's here.' To the rookie he barked, 'Get outside and direct the ambulance!'

Cady tried to talk. She tried to say, 'I couldn't get a description,' but it sounded like, 'Ah cou geh a deschrishion.'

Miraculously, Ralph understood. 'That's okay, sugar. Don't you worry about that right now. We're gonna get you to the hospital real quick and you're gonna be fine.' He glanced around, his sweeping gaze missed nothing. When he looked back into her eyes, there were tears in his own. 'The door was locked, sweetie. Did you let the guy in?'

Painfully, she shook her head.

'Did you know him?'

Again, she shook her head, relieved that he was not afraid to ask her the questions they badly needed to know in order to be able to track down a vicious assailant who was still at large.

Sirens sounded, growing closer.

58

'You think he busted in?'

She said, 'Not me dewn at door.'

'He knocked you down when you were coming in the door?'

She nodded. The room sloshed around. She tried to grit her teeth but the pain made her think twice.

'So he hit you from behind? Was it dark, sugar?'

She nodded, whimpering.

He petted her hand – the only place, it seemed, that wasn't injured. 'I'm sorry, sugar. I gotta ask this stuff while I got the chance.'

'Okeh,' she managed.

'Could you get a take on how tall he was? Maybe about how much he weighed?'

Miserably, she shook her head, and in his eyes she saw mirrored her own frustration: *the sketch artist who couldn't see her own attacker.*

The sirens loomed, then stopped. There was a great bustle at the front door, a painful, blinding flash as somebody turned on the overhead light, and then help arrived in the form of crisp, busy professionals in white shirts who quickly gathered around her bed.

'What's the deal with the hand?' asked one man of Ralph. He was a short, wiry man who moved with quick surety.

'Don't know,' Ralph answered. 'It was like that when I got here.'

'You fix that hand up?' the man asked Cady.

She shook her head. The Emergency Medical Technician shot a look over her head at Ralph. Ralph said, 'This one's not domestic. She didn't know the guy.'

The words hung in the air for a split second, as

everyone in the room took in the white satin peignoir, the swathed hand, the rose petals, the battered, broken body on the bed.

No one said anything.

While one efficient woman took Cady's blood pressure, speaking soothing words to her, Cady watched as the man who had spoken to Ralph began to slowly unwrap the towel from her hand. She noticed that his eyes were very brown. Then she found herself staring with dark fascination at what he was doing.

A plastic bag packed with ice had been affixed to the injured hand with adhesive tape, the towel, wrapped around it. Much of the ice had melted.

'This ice has been on here for way too long,' the EMT mumbled. He yanked off the tape.

'I want that stuff,' commented Ralph. 'Might help us catch the bastard.'

The EMT nodded, removing the dripping contraption with slow, methodical movements.

Ralph gasped.

Cady stared.

What she was looking at was not a hand. It was a misshapen pulp of mangled flesh, blood, and bone, already swollen to three times its natural size.

Because she still had no feeling in the hand, it was not really a part of her. At first, her brain refused to accept what her eyes seemed to be seeing.

This was not happening.

It couldn't be happening.

Not to her. Not to Cady Maxwell, the respected forensic artist.

The artist.

The artist.

The artist.

The screams began deep in her diaphragm and fought past her injured jaw to escape; raw and primeval, out into the room and over the startled heads of all the cops and emergency technicians crowded there.

The screams took possession of her body, driving it to kick and flail and strike out at the very people who were there to help, people who couldn't possibly understand that whatever they were doing was wasted, that all their efforts were doomed, that everything she had ever worked for had been smashed with a hammer into a bloody mess.

She didn't feel the prick of the needle, but she knew when her muscles went limp and the screams died away and, at long blessed last, blackness descended and took her away from the stench of horror and into the peace of oblivion.

Chapter Seven

From the sheltered doorway of an apartment across the street and two doors down from Cady Maxwell's, I watched as they loaded her into the ambulance and took off, sirens screaming, into the gloom of a cloudy dawn.

Oh, how I hated to leave her! It felt as if my very soul had been ripped out! You can't believe how frustrated I was. I thought I might go mad, waiting to see if she was all right! I mean, I'd wanted to call 911 myself, but I was afraid that they would some day be able to match my voice with the recorded conversation.

I had done what I could for her, and it broke my heart. Of course, I'd wanted her to need me all right, but I was still shocked by the starkness of her bloody, battered body when I turned on the overhead light. How vulnerable and helpless she'd looked – how broken!

How could that have happened?

It frightens me sometimes to think of how easy it is to lose one's self-control. I don't like to ever lose control of myself, for obvious reasons.

When I was trying to brush the blood out of her matted hair, I'd whispered, 'I'll kiss it and make it better.' My mother used to say that to me all the time when the other kids would beat me up.

I used to wear a mustache then, and I got into the habit of stroking it whenever I was trying to think – like, how I could arrange a meeting in such a way that my presence would seem natural.

The last thing I wanted to do was frighten her.

Cady awoke in the humming velvet darkness that was a hospital room at night, to find her mother standing at the foot of her bed.

'Mom!' she cried. 'I'm so glad to see you! I didn't think I'd ever get to see you again!'

Her mother smiled, and Cady felt bathed in the warmth that was her mother's love. She wanted to cry but she couldn't remember why. 'I miss you so much,' she said. 'I want to come and be with you.' For some reason, she felt this particularly strongly – an overpowering urge to leave her skin and join her mother. She tried to get up from her bed, but her body seemed weighted and heavy.

Her mother laid a hand on the lump that was Cady's leg under the covers. Cady could feel an almost electrical current running from her mother's hand into her own body. 'My precious child,' said her mother. 'It is not yet time for us to be together. You still have much to do to fulfill your purpose.' She smiled again.

'What purpose?' asked Cady.

But her mother was beginning to fade, her image melting into the shadows.

'Mom! Don't leave me! Please!' Cady wanted to leap up and throw her arms around her mother's neck, but she was unable to move. 'Mom! You have to tell me what my purpose is! MOM!'

But her mother was gone and Cady was alone.

There was so much she had wanted to say to her mother, so many things she'd wanted to ask.

But the dragon sleep had already taken hold of her body and was dragging her into a cool, dark cave where there was no pain.

'I don't know if we can save the thumb. The metacarpal tendon's practically useless. It's virtually severed and the nerve damage is extensive. And I don't even want to *talk* about the abductor pollicis brevis muscle.'

Cady opened her eyes and followed the soft, low voice of a man in a white coat with a stethoscope hanging out of the pocket. He was talking to another man who looked just like him except he wore glasses. They were standing at the foot of Cady's bed – where her mother had stood before – and were looking at a chart and talking quietly as though there were no one else in the room. She wanted to say something, but she couldn't move her jaw, and her brain was hopelessly fuzzy. Her whole body, in fact, felt somehow blurred and out of focus, almost as if it too were vanishing as her mother had done. It was as though she were there and yet not there at the same time.

The things they were saying did not bother her.

'I don't know how many operations it will take to repair the damage to the other fingers, either. The lumbricales muscles and the flexor tendons are smashed to bits. No matter what I do, movement's still going to be limited. And that thumb – I'm afraid that if we don't remove it, she'll be in excruciating pain from it for the rest of her life.'

'When should we reduce the morphine?'

'As she regains consciousness more and more. I don't want to have to deal with an addiction problem here.'

'You're aware, of course, that this patient is an artist? Some kind of police thing.'

'Well, yes. If it weren't for that, I'd have taken the thumb already, in the first surgery. But under the circumstances, I think she deserves a say-so before we act.'

'I agree. Besides, if you took that thumb without asking her, you'd be a prime candidate for a malpractice suit.'

'Don't think I don't know that. Hell, my insurance premiums are eating me alive as it is. They go any higher, I'll have to give up my speedboat.'

'But not before giving me a ride.'

They chuckled quietly.

Cady closed her eyes and went back to sleep.

A loud, clattering crash brought Cady awake.

'Well, shit, Martinez. Just drop the goddamn flowers all over the floor.'

'Fuck you, Hall. At least I brought flowers.'

'Where'd you get 'em? At a traffic light?'

A word made its way out of Cady's dry lips. 'Hey,' she croaked.

The two detectives whirled around like marionettes.

'You're awake!' cried Elaine.

'Way to go, Martinez,' said Bob Hall, pushing his big body around a corner chair so that he could stand next to Cady's bed by the wall – the side where her good hand lay pristinely on top of the covers. 'How ya doin', sweetheart?' he asked gently, touching a sausage finger to Cady's forehead.

'She can't talk, moron,' said Elaine. 'Her jaw's wired shut.'

Cady was so glad to see her friends. She wanted them to tell her all about how things were going at the office since she'd gotten hurt the day before.

'You've been out a long time, girl,' said Elaine. 'We've been by to see you every day this week.'

Week?

Surely they were mistaken. She couldn't possibly have been in the hospital a week. She shot Bob a helpless look, as if to say, *Tell me she's wrong*, but he was smiling and nodding.

'You look . . . great,' faltered Elaine, glancing away.

Liar, thought Cady miserably. *A week! She'd lost a whole week out of her life!*

'We miss you down at the cop shop,' said Bob. 'You gotta get well and come back soon – that artist they got stinks.'

Elaine shot Bob a warning look over Cady's body.

Cady struggled to get out the words lodged behind the wires. She managed to say, 'Ketch hin?'

'What honey?' Elaine leaned closer.

'Ketch hin?'

Elaine shook her head sadly. 'No, I'm sorry. We haven't caught the guy yet, but the whole division – hell, the whole *department's* looking, you can bet that.'

'Don't you worry, sweetheart, we'll catch that bastard and hang him by his balls,' added Bob. Elaine nodded agreement.

Cady felt exhausted.

'They said your gun had been fired – all five rounds,'

said Elaine. 'What I don't understand is how on earth you missed him.' She looked expectantly at Cady, as if anticipating an answer. 'Me, I'd have blown his head off.'

'No, you'da blown his balls off,' commented Bob drily.

They laughed.

Cady stared from one to the other. The implied criticism hung in the room.

They're blaming me for not killing him, she thought in disbelief. *They think it's my fault that he got away*.

Her memories of the attack were sketchy at best. In her dreams, and in her odd waking moments, the only thing she could ever see was that hammer, smashing down.

Self-doubts assailed her. *Maybe they're right*, she thought dismally. *Maybe if I'd fought harder or aimed more carefully or done something differently, I wouldn't have wound up so badly hurt*.

'Ran into Peter Stanton the other day,' said Bob. 'Your old flame? He said that at least you kept the guy from raping you. That's one good thing.'

Unless he was planning on raping me and I made him so angry that he decided to take that hammer instead and . . .

As if on cue, a steady throbbing that extended all the way up her shoulder set in from Cady's heavily bandaged hand. The pain medication had worn off. She wondered if they'd let her have more, or if she'd have to wait an hour, like before. She didn't know if she'd be able to bear that. The last time, she'd wound up crying like a little kid. She closed her eyes.

'Well, we better clear out,' said Elaine. 'You look

totally crapped out. We just wanted to come by and cheer you up.'

'Yeah,' said Bob, giving her good hand an awkward pat. He hadn't once looked at the bandaged hand. 'It's good to see you lookin' better.'

Better?

Suddenly, Bob and Elaine couldn't seem to get out of the room fast enough.

They never came back to the hospital to visit Cady again.

During Cady's eternally long stay, she did have one welcome visitor: Jacob Goldberg. His name was famous all over the United States as one of the most colorful – and successful – defense attorneys in the country, but to Cady he was simply a good friend . . . and her mother's lover.

He had an Ichabod Crane body and a wild thatch of Einstein-like white hair. His sunken, permanently sad eyes and big, expressive hands had held many a courtroom spellbound as he'd pled for the rights of underdogs of all shapes, colors, and sizes through the years in a booming, evangelistic voice.

But when he came to see her, he had little to say. He just sat next to her for the longest time, holding her good hand against his wet cheek.

Cady's cousin, Jackie Cox, was a plump little blonde with dancing green eyes. Unlike Cady, who'd grown up in a quiet house of women (she'd lived with her mother and grandmother), Jackie's family was a big and boisterous gaggle of boys who spoiled their only baby sister with gleeful abandon. She liked to come over to Cady's house for the quiet and Cady liked to visit hers for the noise. They had made a good match.

Jackie had retained most of the weight she'd gained with the baby, and this seemed to preoccupy her, as did her 'perfectly magnificent' first-born son who, it seemed, nursed relentlessly all day and cried all night.

Cady knew that Jackie's chances to visit were all too rare, and she forgave her old friend for her seeming inability to talk about anything beyond the trials of first-time motherhood and the miracle of her baby. But one day, as Jackie's handsome husband, Tom, jounced and jiggled the baby down in the lobby, she blurted out a remark about the attack which had obviously been bothering her a great deal.

'Hey, Lib,' she began, using a nickname she had bestowed on Cady years before, due to her mother's feminist activities, 'there's something I just don't get. As paranoid as you are, on account of the weird work you do all day and all ... well, couldn't you *see* the guy comin'? I mean, how the hell could he just come up behind you like that?'

It was not the first time, nor would it be the last, that Cady was to discover how even dear friends could manage to reinforce her own nagging self-doubts with well-intentioned remarks that sometimes hurt worse than her injuries.

'Would it help you to know that these reactions are very common?' a woman who'd been sent around by the police department had asked her. The woman was a Violent Crime Victim's Advocate, and had come to visit Cady to inform her of various services which were available to her. Tall, mahogany-skinned and calm, she had explained to Cady that most people, no matter how well meaning, simply couldn't handle it when someone close to them became a victim of violent crime. It was too scary, too close – after all, it could have happened to *them*. The best way most of them could cope was to either find some way to blame the victim (after all, *they* wouldn't have been so foolish), suffocate the victim with overprotectiveness, or stay away entirely.

The result was an almost unbearable sense of isolation and loneliness.

And there was no medication for that.

Once the morphine was out of her system, nothing else came close to alleviating the pain from her hand. She no longer slept all the time. In fact, sleep was something she prayed for during the endless lonely nights.

As the rest of her body slowly healed, her hand was operated on twice more. Both times she refused to let them take her thumb. The attack had stripped her of enough. She was not going to allow it to mutilate her as well.

Meanwhile, she had plenty to keep her busy. She had to learn to dress herself one-handed (with her left hand, at that), and go to the bathroom, and spread butter on toast, and sign her name, and a million other things.

Worst of all, she had to learn to live with pain.

Some days she didn't want to do anything but lie in her bed and watch shadows creep across the ceiling; she didn't even want to think, really. She just endured. Other days she wanted to die. She even cursed her attacker for not killing her in the first place, but vivid in her memory was the strange 'visit' she'd had from her mother. Was it a dream? A drug-induced hallucination? Or a supernatural phenomenon for which there was no explanation?

Cady didn't know, but she believed what her mother had said: that it was not time yet for her to die and that she had not yet fulfilled her purpose. This was the only thing, sometimes, which kept her from seriously contemplating suicide.

At least until the day she finally was released, the day she'd been dreading, the day she had to go home, four weeks after she had been admitted.

All those days up until then had merely been suspended animation. Daily life in a hospital was so removed from the real world that, at times, Cady could move along within the strict boundaries of rigid routine and pretend that none of it was actually happening.

But once she was at home, amongst her own things, there would be nowhere to hide from the stark reality of her new existence.

This, she dreaded more than anything.

Rudy Martinez showed up in a patrol car to drive her; Cady suspected that Elaine had sent him. Cady would have preferred to have Elaine take her home – she desperately needed a friend to be with her – but a stubborn perversity had kept her from calling Elaine and asking. She was hurt. She wanted Elaine to think of it herself.

Still, she had to admit, in some ways Cady had been isolating herself from her friends as much as the other way around. When people did visit, she now felt apart from them, as if she were floating around somewhere up above, watching herself watch them. Detached. Separate.

Maybe they sensed it, and that's why they pulled away.

The apartment was cold. To Cady's great shock, it quickly became apparent that nobody had thought to straighten up the place for her. Everything was exactly as the paramedics had discovered it on that brutal morning: living-room furniture was overturned; bullet holes gaped from the walls and couch and one chair; her dry cleaning still remained in a pitiful crumpled bundle on the floor; moldy french bread, a black head of lettuce, stinking tomatoes, and a broken bottle of wine lay in a pool of purple; and the sticky white powder left behind by the fingerprint people was everywhere.

And of course, there was the blood: rusty brown droplets and splatters and pools of it on the carpet and furniture and walls.

Too stunned to react, Cady entered her bedroom. The sight of her bed staggered her. Crushed, bloodied, blackened and wilted rose petals covered it in a macabre shroud.

A sick weakness flooded her body. Cady hurried into the living room, where Martinez waited awkwardly by the front door, and collapsed into a chair.

'Are you all right?' he asked, looking as if he'd rather be anywhere on earth than where he was.

'C-could I have a drink of water, please?' she asked.
'The glasses are in the cabinet over the sink.'

'Sure.' He rushed into the kitchen, glad to have something to do.

She took the glass in her left hand and gulped down the water.

Never had she felt more alone, sickened, and frightened.

'I'm sorry, ma'am,' said the nervous rookie. 'I only marked out for an hour and it's been an hour and a half.'

Please, please don't leave me, Cady begged with her eyes. 'Of course,' she said. 'You go on. I'll be fine.'

'Would you like me to call someone to come over and help you?'

Who would you call? she wanted to say. *All my friends are at work.*

'No, that's all right. You go on. I'll ... get busy cleaning up this mess.'

'Well ...' he gave her a doubtful look. 'My sergeant might get pissed if—'

'It's quite all right. Really.' She forced a smile through her sore jaw.

'Okay.' He jiggled back and forth from one foot to another for a few moments, then gave her a shy smile and headed for the door.

'If you need anything ...'

'I'll know who to call. And hey – give my best regards to Potinsky. Tell him I don't know what I'd have done without him. And ... thank you for everything, Rudy.'

His smile this time was brilliant.

And then he was gone.

Cady hurried over to lock the door behind him.

Then came the fear, stark and powerful, slamming into her with all the force of her attacker on that terrifying night.

In the hospital, she'd been spared from confronting its skeletal presence. Constant intrusions by nurses and orderlies and volunteers and chaplains and visitors, combined with the humming daily efficiency of the hospital itself, had insulated her.

She was pitifully unprepared for this.

Thoughts scampered through her mind like so many rabbits. *He could be in the apartment right now. After all, she hadn't asked Rudy to check. She'd wanted to, but she'd been embarrassed, thinking he would think her silly.*

Stupid!

What was she going to do now?

Her gun was no longer in her purse – the police had taken it as evidence.

Then she remembered the Beretta.

Trembling now, and without looking back, Cady let herself out of the apartment and jogged over to her car.

The keys. She'd forgotten the goddamn car keys!

That meant she had to go back into the apartment and get the keys out of her purse.

She couldn't. There was no way she could go back into that apartment.

But she had to. What else could she do? Without her car keys, she couldn't even drive away.

Her hand was beginning to scream in pain, causing her whole arm to ache. Cradling it in her left hand, she slowly made her way back to her apartment and stood in the doorway, careful to look back over her shoulder and all around for anyone who might be lurking there.

No one.

Heart pounding, mouth dry, she stepped into the living room, spied the purse on a nearby table, and upended it, too frightened and impatient to dig around for the keys.

Her good hand closed around them.

This time she sprinted for the car, surprised and upset by how unbelievably weak she was; she had to stop, panting, and walk the rest of the short way.

She unlocked the door.

I can just drive away, she thought. *Go somewhere. A hotel, maybe. Or even the police department.*

Encouraged, she slid into the front seat, reaching over the steering wheel with her left hand to insert the car key into the ignition on the right side of the steering column.

She couldn't make it reach.

Stunned, she sat for a moment as the implications of her situation soaked in. *She couldn't drive!*

Her breath began coming out in short gasps.

Calm down. She had to get hold of herself.

Okay. So she couldn't drive. Not yet anyway. She'd figure it out in time. After all, if paraplegics could drive, why couldn't she?

Taking a deep, calming breath, she fumbled around in an awkward pretzel position, retrieving the Beretta from the console. Until she regained the use of her right hand, she'd just have to get used to taking a little more time with things she used to take for granted.

She locked the car and headed back to the apartment building, gripping the semiautomatic pistol in her good hand.

This time she wouldn't miss.

Walking deliberately back into the apartment, she left the door ajar so that she could get out quickly if she had to, or maybe call for help from someone (trying not to think about the fact that no one would be around in the middle of a work day). Then, standing back carefully, as though she were about to expose a rattlesnake, Cady kicked open each cabinet and closet door. She held the gun in front of her, alarmed at how heavy and wobbly it was without the other hand to support it.

The bed. She was going to have to search under the bed.

Stomach cramping, Cady stood, wrestling with her terrors like so many savage dogs.

What if he was armed? What if he was watching her right now from his vantage point?

What if he had a hammer with him?

A loud *creak* sounded right behind her.

Crying out, she started violently. The extra-wide grip of the Beretta made it difficult for her to disengage the safety lever with her small, awkward left hand. Fumbling with the gun in her panic, she watched in horror as it slipped from her hand and fell to the carpeted floor with a muffled *thud*. Whirling around, she dropped to her knees, grasping frantically for the gun . . . and put her hand right on the hard leather toe of a cowboy boot.

Still trembling, whimpering, and groping for the gun, Cady glanced up.

Towering over her, a look of total bewilderment on his face, was Zacharia Ralston.

Chapter Eight

She couldn't seem to stop trembling and found herself too weak to get to her feet, so she cowered there while Zach glanced at the horror that was her bed, the wreck that was her home, and the shadow of the woman that once was herself.

Cady reached up her good hand for a lift but Zach didn't take it. Instead, he knelt down to the floor in front of her, which made him only slightly taller, since most of his height was in his long legs. 'You won't find those boogers under the bed,' he said softly, 'because they're all up here.' He touched a gentle fingertip to the side of Cady's head.

Those simple words hung quietly for a moment in the room between them, then settled with downy warmth over the cold and wretched emptiness that had yawned over Cady's heart ever since the attack.

'You *understand*,' she marveled. Then, to her great frustration, she burst into tears.

Zach leaned back on his heels and pulled Cady into his lap as if she were a child, encircling her with his solid arms and pressing her head against his chest.

Never had she felt more comforted than she did by the steady *thu-thump* of his heart against her cheek.

Most of her friends, fearful of somehow hurting her arm or worse, had held her at arm's length when they'd come to see her. She'd been kissed in her hospital bed, but no one had gathered her in their arms and allowed her the supreme luxury of being cuddled, of having the demons chased away.

'I hate crybabies,' she blubbered, sobbing against his shirt.

He chuckled, and she felt the rumbling deep in his chest. 'I won't tattle,' he said.

'I know you won't believe this,' she mumbled, 'but this is the first time I've cried since—'

He nodded, his chin moving against her hair. 'You were afraid that if you ever once lost control, you'd never get it back again.'

She pulled back and stared into the depths of his blue eyes. 'How did you k-know?' she hiccoughed.

He shrugged. 'When I got released from the POW camp, and got out of 'Nam, and flew home, and hugged everybody at the airport . . . I was standing there on the tarmac, giving an interview to a reporter when all of a sudden the dam broke.' He grinned at himself. 'Bawled so hard the guy finally slunk off, too embarrassed to do the story.'

She smiled. It wasn't so very hard after all.

Zach groped in his pocket for a handkerchief, which he passed to Cady, then he got to his feet and tenderly pulled her after him. Arm firmly around her waist, he led her into the living room and settled her on the couch.

'This is pathetic,' he said, gesturing angrily at the mess. 'Haven't you got any friends who could have cleaned this up for you while you were in hospital? How could they have let you come home alone and face this?'

She tried to defend them. 'I guess they just didn't

think of it, and they're awfully busy—'

'Bullshit.' His eyes crackled. 'They're gutless wonders, is what they are. They couldn't deal with it. People make me sick sometimes, especially yuppies.'

The sudden shift in Zach's mood surprised Cady. 'My friends aren't yuppies,' she said with a weary sigh.

He knelt down and began to pick up the moldy bread and putrid salad vegetables.

'You don't have to do that.'

He stalked off into the kitchen, in search of a plastic garbage bag, and found one before Cady could shout where to look. He returned armed with paper towels and spray cleaner.

The spilt groceries and broken wine bottle were dispensed with quickly. Scrubbing at the wine stain vigorously, he said, 'I hate the city.'

Cady didn't know what to say. On the one hand, she wanted to argue on behalf of her friends, but on the other, Zach had tapped into some strong insecurities of her own. After all, what *were* friends, if you couldn't depend on them to be there for you when you needed them?

'Mom would have been here,' she said suddenly. 'And Nanny, and Aunt Ruth.'

He stopped scrubbing and looked at her, waiting.

'But.' She took a deep breath and let it out slowly. 'Aunt Ruth moved away last year and bought a condo on Padre Island, and Nanny and Mom are dead.'

He pursed his lips in sympathy.

'Nanny died a couple of years ago of heart trouble and I lost Mom six months ago – or is it seven, now? To breast cancer.'

'I guess this hasn't been your year,' he said.

'No.' Telling him had made her feel better somehow. 'What about your dad?'

She shrugged. 'No dad. He and Mom never married. She didn't believe in marriage. Said it was legally sanctioned slavery for women.'

'Feisty lady.'

Cady grinned. 'You don't know the half of it. Anyway, when she got pregnant, he took off. She said good riddance or some such thing and moved in with my grandmother – that's Nanny. Nanny was about as typical a grandmother as Mom was a mother. She taught me how to play poker and how to take my whiskey neat.'

'My kinda gal.' He was smiling at her and she smiled back.

'I think Mom pictured us some kind of Amazon family, you know. Facing the world happily without men.' She giggled. 'She never did figure out why I kept hanging out at Aunt Ruth's with my cousin Jackie.'

'Why did you?'

'I guess because they had what I considered to be a "normal" home – mother and father and lots of kids, a cat and a dog. Just what I always wanted.'

Those eyes. They seemed to stare right through to her soul and beyond.

He said, 'So . . . is that still what you want? A normal home with mother and father and lots of kids?'

Her face flushed hotly. She did not – could not – answer him.

Cady stretched out the full length of her body and wiggled her toes. If there were actually a heaven where good people went when they died, she was sure that this would be the first stop-off on the journey: soaking in a steaming tub of scented bubbles, surrounded by flickering candles, with the sounds of Kenny G's incomparable sax wafting out of the portable CD player.

Zach had set the whole thing up for her. She hadn't even mentioned to him that showers were the only thing available at the hospital, and those had been damn near impossible to maneuver because of the elaborate contraption of bandages on her arm. And she hadn't said that she'd probably never be able to completely relax in a tub like this without him outside the door to chase away the 'boogers', as he called them.

She hadn't had to say anything. He'd understood it all.

So, if there was a heaven, and God did send down guardian angels to watch over those who were in trouble or suffering, then she definitely had one with her right now.

The soothing water actually seemed to take the edge off the pain in her hand and arm, even though she was unable to get them wet. It had not occurred to Cady that any kind of tension tended to exacerbate her pain, and that by simply relaxing her mind and body, she was actually relieving much of her own discomfort.

That Zach had shown up on this particular day seemed a miracle almost beyond comprehension. A coincidence, he'd said. He'd gotten into town on business and had gone by the police station to see her. Elaine, who'd heard all about the sexy cowboy, had been only too happy to fill him in on Cady's ordeal and direct him to Cady's apartment. (Bless her.) Cady had no doubt an urgent phone call from Elaine would ring in shortly. She'd be hungry for all the details.

But there were some things that Cady would tell no one, for there was no one she knew who could comprehend the simple power of the fact that Zach *knew*; he'd *been there*. She didn't have to explain anything to him – he didn't even press her for lurid details of the attack the way everyone else had. He didn't seem to want to hear about it at all, which was a tremendous relief; most people, she'd discovered with a shock, were actually rude voyeurs. He had not second-guessed her or questioned her judgement about that night's events. 'As long as you are alive,' he'd said with an ironic lift of an eyebrow, 'then whatever you did was the right thing.'

She scooched her body down deeper in the tub and closed her eyes. The bubbles were almost gone but the water was still deliciously warm. She wondered if Zach would understand if she conked out and slept for a while after her bath.

Of course he would understand, she mused. Zach understood everything.

CRASH!

Cady sat straight up.

SMASH! CRASH!

Needle-claws of fear raked her body and goosebumps popped up.

TUMBLE-THUMP CRASH!

She stood up too fast; wooziness seized her and she grabbed the tiled wall of the bath with her right hand.

A lightning bolt of pain reminded Cady that she shouldn't do that. She plunked down on the edge of the tub, water pouring off her body onto the floor.

CRASH! The bathroom door rattled.

Her heart pounding like a jackhammer in her chest, Cady fumbled with a towel, dropped it, grabbed it to her as best she could – then stood there, frustrated because she couldn't open the bathroom door and hold onto the towel at the same time.

Clasping the towel under her armpits as best she could, Cady opened the bathroom door and hurried out, grasping helplessly as the towel started to slip, wondering (too late) where she'd left the Beretta.

Amidst the shambles that had been her living room, Zach was pitched in a life-or-death struggle with a man almost as big as he was. Unlike the neatly choreographed fist-fights of TV and movies, this was what most real fights were, a tight clinch of two bodies, slamming as one against walls and furniture.

The man's appearance was fierce and frightening. Oily dark hair hung to his shoulders. A large pentagram dangled from one ear. A black goatee further contributed to his satanic appearance, along with a couple of nasty tattoos on both forearms. His tight jeans were faded and his Harley Davidson muscle shirt stretched over a powerfully pumped chest.

'*You shit-kicking moron!*' he screamed. '*I told you – I'm a cop!*' He stretched a massive forearm around Zach's throat.

Zach reached back a big boot and tripped the guy. They fell to the floor together, smashing a small table.

'*And I said show me some goddamn ID!*'

'*You boot-licking asshole! I'm undercover! I don't have any ID! AHHHHHHH!*' He screamed as Zach yanked off the earring.

Just as Nanny had taught her, Cady put her two fingers between her lips and let out a loud whistle.

The towel fell to the floor.

Both men immediately stopped, panting and gaping like playground schoolboys.

Cady crouched down, grabbed the towel, and attempted to cover herself with as much dignity as she could muster under the circumstances, which wasn't much.

'Zach,' she said, 'I'd like you to meet Peter Stanton, a ... friend ... of mine. Peter, this is my friend, Zacharia Ralston.'

Chapter Nine

While Cady struggled into her clothes, she strained to hear what the men were saying in the front room, but soon forgot as she tried, for the first time, to hook a bra one-handed. She was almost in tears from the frustration of it when she heard a timid knock at the door.

'Cady honey, you need some help?' asked Peter in a muffled voice.

'No, that's all right.' She slumped forward in exhaustion.

'C'mon,' he said in a loud, clear voice. 'It's not like I've never seen you naked.' He pushed open the door.

'Get out of here!' she cried, cheeks flaming. 'How dare you!'

Ignoring her, he leaned over, hooked the bra in a flick of his fingers, then sauntered out, closing the door quietly behind him.

Impotent rage welled up inside her. With a furious kick, she sent a wastepaper basket skidding across the floor, wishing it was Peter's head, and not even sure why. Was it because he had laid some sort of primal claim on her in front of Zach, or because she really had needed his help?

Her closet was sadly barren of the button-up blouses she needed for dressing with her cast. She found an oversized tee shirt, but pulling it over her head was painful and by the time she was dressed, she was worn out. It had been a long day.

But two men waited for her in the living room.

Mustering up as much dignity as she could, Cady walked into where the men sat, as far away from each other as the small room would allow, making feeble attempts at conversation. They had made some effort to straighten up the signs of their fight, but a woman's touch was sorely needed and she had an almost overwhelming desire to be rid of them.

'You okay?' asked Peter.

'Yeah,' she said, and added grudgingly, 'thanks.'

He nodded.

Cady had a sudden urge to laugh. Here was Peter Stanton, looking for all the world like a hulking Hell's Angel reject, and Zach Ralston, who looked as though he ought to be living someplace with a name like 'Tombstone'. And they were both acting like boys waiting to see the principal.

'What happened here?' she asked Zach.

He shrugged. 'I went into the kitchen for some cleaning stuff, and when I came out I found this guy skulking around.'

'*I was not skulking!*' cried Peter. 'I still had a key to Cady's apartment, that's all, and I thought I'd come check things out.'

'Since when do you have a key?' demanded Cady. 'You gave that key back to me.'

He grinned. 'Not before copying it.'

She stared at him. 'You sly son of a bitch! Give that to me right now!' She held out her left hand and he meekly placed the key in it. 'I can't believe you did that,' she added, stuffing the key in her pocket. 'And

88

anyway, what's with this get-up?'

He struck a pose. 'It's my junkie persona. Like it?'

'What, junkies never wash their hair?' She was angry and somewhat unnerved. Things had been pretty heavy between her and Peter until she'd made the discovery that they had absolutely nothing in common but uncommonly good sex. Still, it had never occurred to her that he would have made a copy of her house key.

'Well, you wanna hear about the LoverBoy, or not?'

Peter's intention had obviously been to surprise her, but to Cady it felt more like a fist right to the stomach. Her fingers tingled and her knees buckled. She plunked down to the sofa.

Zach instantly got to his feet, shoved Peter aside, and knelt in front of her, taking her good hand in one of his. 'You idiot,' he said to Peter over his shoulder. 'Her hands are like ice.'

He had such a big hand and it felt so comforting. She smiled at him. 'I'm all right.' He squeezed her hand and let go, returning to his seat. She appreciated the gesture. It didn't make her feel crowded. She said, 'Go on, Peter.'

With a disgusted glance in Zach's direction, he said, 'You know the little bastard's out on parole, right?'

She nodded.

'Well, I've had him under surveillance the past week or two. It's a loose personal thing. I mean, it's not a police assignment or anything.'

She understood what he was saying. He'd been taking time out from his undercover work to check out the LoverBoy on his own time and without his superiors knowing he was doing it. She felt a rush of gratitude for him and, while she was at it, took in the bulging arms that sprang from the muscle shirt. The man did keep in shape. Uh-huh.

'I've been checking around. It's pretty easy, looking like I do. Nobody suspects the cops and this guy isn't exactly rolling in friends, if you know what I mean.'

Her heart began a jumpety-jump in her chest. 'Did you find out anything?'

He pursed his lips. '*Nada*. He's been a good little boy, staying in mommy's house since he got out of the joint. But I have a feeling that if we'd been watching him the night of your attack, we'd have seen him slither out one of those windows like the snake he is.'

Disappointment, coupled with the old frustration, squeezed Cady's throat. She swallowed, then heaved a sigh.

'I'm sorry, baby.'

The affectionate term, and the manner in which he said it, was unmistakeably intimate. Something about it bothered Cady. After all, they'd broken up. Did he think he could just show up while she was in a weakened state and stake a claim?

There was no doubt she was still attracted to him but the relationship was doomed; surely he knew that?

She was still struggling with how to respond to Peter when Zach got suddenly to his feet and reached for his hat. 'I guess I'll shove off now,' he said. He turned for the door, avoiding her eyes.

'No!' She jumped up and followed him. 'I mean, there's no need for you to go, really. We haven't even had a chance to visit.' She turned and glared at Peter, who was watching the whole thing with a sardonic smile on his devilish face.

'Well, I need to be getting back. I've got some business to wrap up before I leave town.'

She felt crushed. 'When are you leaving?'

'In a day or two.' He looked down at her with those liquid blue eyes and she wanted to melt right at his feet.

Damn Peter Stanton!

'Don't leave town without calling me, okay?'

He hesitated, glanced over at Peter, then said, 'Okay.' Then he touched a long forefinger to the tip of her nose and left.

She felt abandoned.

Turning slowly from the door, she narrowed her eyes at Peter. 'Happy?'

He gave her his best junkie 'duh' look. 'What do you mean?'

She stomped over to the couch and plopped down. 'You know exactly what I mean. Not only did we break up, what, two months ago? You never even came to see me in the hospital.'

He shrugged. 'You know me and hospitals don't get along.'

Her jaw dropped and she had to remember to close it. Of all the selfish, immature, ridiculous remarks she'd had to endure since the attack, this was one of the lowest.

She didn't even dignify it with a reply.

'Besides, I told you, I've been checkin' out the LoverBoy.'

She unclenched her teeth. 'I appreciate that.'

He moved over to sit beside her. 'Don't be pissed.' He put his arm around her and pulled her stiff body into its crook.

'Ow.' She adjusted her arm. She wanted to make him feel as bad as she could.

It didn't work. Without warning, he was kissing her, his full lips and soft tongue probing her mouth as though they'd never been apart.

Cady's reaction was instantaneous and uncontrollable. She flailed, kicked, bit, and screamed, fighting as if for her life.

At first, he sat like a stunned and unmoveable rock, enduring her assaults even as he was pulling away from her.

She couldn't stop. She pounded his thick chest and arms with her small left fist; kicked and shoved his big body with her feet.

'Jesus, Cady, whatsa matter with you?' Peter scrambled out from under the attack and towered over her, panting and bewildered.

Sobbing, she curled up into herself on the couch.

'If you didn't want me to kiss you, all the hell you had to do was say no,' he said, his face darkening with self-righteous anger. 'I ain't no damn LoverBoy Rapist.'

Overwhelmed with shame, confusion, and her own terrifying rage, Cady could say nothing.

Peter stalked out and slammed the door.

She sprang up and locked it behind him and, as she stood there, this . . . thing . . . she'd been trying so desperately to control seemed to bubble up from somewhere deep within, scorching her with fear and pain and frustration and the hot, bitter volcanic fury that wanted to scream, *WHY ME?*

She wanted to throw something or hit something and, for want of anything better, attacked the bookcase, flinging volumes right and left, as hard as she could, again and again, until the shelves were barren, the floor littered, and her insides hot, empty, and exhausted.

But it didn't help.

Her arm still throbbed its useless message to her like a neon VACANCY sign: You can't draw . . . You can't work . . . You can't . . . You can't . . . You can't . . .

Still shaking, Cady dragged an afghan off the back of the couch and collapsed on it, pulling the soft blanket over her shoulders and knees. Sleep pulled her into that dark place where she didn't have to think anymore . . .

The ringing of the phone jarred Cady awake to a dark, cold apartment. Panicky for light, and hopeful that it might be Zach, Cady fumbled for the lamp and yanked up the receiver without waiting for the answering machine to screen the call. 'Hello?'

For a moment no one spoke, and Cady's heart went cold. Then she heard her name in a whisper that sent dead fingers of fear down her spine.

'Cady . . . beautiful Cady . . . Why, why would you be interested in anybody else when you know we are so right for each other?'

Chapter Ten

Well, it didn't take me long to figure out that something had gone terribly wrong, and it was all my fault! I'd waited too long to make my move. I had to be so damn compulsive, obsessing about every little detail, trying so hard to make everything perfect for our reunion when she got out of the hospital . . .

Hell, I hadn't counted on somebody else horning in on MY territory!

A woman as beautiful as Cady Maxwell could have anybody she wanted, and that's what was worrying me. She was vulnerable just then; I could see how her head might be turned.

I was worried about her. Something wasn't right. And I wasn't sure what to do, how best to approach her. I mean, I loved her so very much but, for some reason, she just didn't seem to appreciate it the way I had thought she would. The unfortunate incident that had occurred in her apartment was apparently making her skittish toward everybody.

I'd been watching her, and she hadn't gone anywhere in three days, not even to buy groceries. A couple of her friends had stopped by to see her, but she'd gotten rid of them pretty fast.

Just like a sweet little wild deer that only needed to be tamed.

When the answer came to me, it was so clear and

simple I knew it had to have come from God. There was no other explanation for such a stroke of genius.

I remember, I was dying to call her – all the time really – just to hear her voice again, but I knew I shouldn't, not when I had all those new plans to make.

I really shouldn't have.

But you know, I just couldn't help myself!

This . . . powerful urge or drive or compulsion or what have you, had just POSSESSED me. It was as if I had no control over myself.

I mean, I knew that I shouldn't call her. Really.

Still, I couldn't help wondering, what if somebody else was with her? After all, I couldn't watch her apartment twenty-four hours a day; I could only drive by every couple of hours or so.

I would get to worrying that maybe she had left with someone else or something.

I just had to know, that's all.

I had to hear her voice. Surely you can understand that?

Wheel of Fortune was on. Cady didn't like it as much as *Jeapardy!* but she didn't have the patience for cartoons today and that was about all else there was to watch, now that the soaps were off. At least, until her favorite program came on: old reruns of *The Andy Griffith Show*. It was so clean, so innocent. She wished she could step right through the screen and live in that pure, sweet time when nobody locked their doors and the sheriff's deputy carried a gun without bullets.

Though it was a bright summer day, she huddled in the afghan in her dim living room and stared at another impossibly skinny and glamorous starlet trying to sell her something.

Cady was feeling kind of hungry, so she reached out a hand and rummaged through an old pizza box for a spare piece of cold pepperoni.

She was out of Cokes, but she was afraid to leave the apartment and she didn't know any grocery stores that delivered.

She was also out of milk, bread, juice, and toilet paper. She could ask for Coke the next time she ordered a pizza, but the toilet paper was a toughie.

The phone rang and Cady jolted upright. The piece of pizza fell upside down on the floor. Heart pounding, she listened to her own voice asking for messages, then listened again to the faint breathing sounds on the other end of the line.

Cady wadded her miserable body into a corner of the couch, shivering beneath the afghan.

He was out there.

Wasn't it just a matter of time before he came back?

She whimpered, 'Why are you doing this to me?' knowing *he* couldn't hear, and waited until the line went dead, watching blindly as game-show contestants jumped up and down and clapped their hands like excited children.

She'd gotten her phone number changed to yet another unlisted one, but what good had it done? He'd still managed to find her.

Having worked with cops as long as she had, Cady knew that, even if she reported the phone calls, there was little they could do. He never stayed on long enough to get a trace, and she had no proof that the person who was calling her was also the one who

97

assaulted her. It was just a feeling, a dread that lay cold and clammy on the back of her neck.

And even if she did report it and they said, 'What else has he done to frighten you?' what could she say? *He sent me roses?*

Wheel of Fortune went off and *Jeopardy!* came on, but Cady didn't hear the answers or the questions. Her hand throbbed with each beat of her heart, as though its injury were fresh, as though it would never heal.

Maybe she should have let them take the thumb. What good was it doing her? Her hand was worthless.

She was worthless.

Why didn't he just come back and finish the job?

A sharp knock at the door brought Cady full upright, heart in her throat, clutching the Beretta.

Slowly, stiffly, she got up off the couch and peered through the peep hole in her door.

There was no one there.

Pulse throbbing in her ears, she waited.

Another knock sounded. Suppressing a violent start, she croaked, 'Who's there?'

'Zach.'

Cady peeked again and, sure enough, there he stood, tall and solid and real. Using what she could of her casted hand, she fumbled with the chain, stuck the Beretta under her arm to unlock the door, and swung it wide.

He blinked. 'Kind of a new style of marksmanship, wouldn't you say?'

'Oh.' She set the gun down on the cluttered coffee table, which still teetered on a leg broken in the fight between Zach and Peter. 'Come in. Er, it's kind of messy in here.' She retired to the couch, folded herself up, and pulled the afghan over her knees.

Zach closed the door and stood there a moment, taking the scene in; it was obvious that she'd been living virtually on the couch for a week.

Still wearing his hat, he quirked one eyebrow up at her. 'Feelin' kinda sorry for ourselves, are we?'

Cady's face went hot. 'You don't know what you're talking about!'

'Oh, I think I do.'

She picked up the remote and turned up the sound. Zach reached over and calmly turned off the set.

'What are you doing!' She reached for the remote but he got it ahead of her.

'I'm not fixin' to stand by and let you give up on yourself.'

'I haven't given up on anything.'

'Like hell you haven't! Look at you. You're a mess!'

'Oh yeah? Well, you try washing your hair with one hand!'

'Poor baby. You never heard of a shower nozzle you can attach to the faucet and hold in one hand? Or maybe even going by the beauty shop and having them do it?'

She set her jaw. 'You don't know what I've been going through.'

He crossed his arms over his chest. 'Oh, I think I have some idea. You think your life is over, that everything you've worked for is lost, that your whole reason for living is gone . . . is that about it?'

She narrowed her eyes at him. She was furious that he was not only right, but casual about it, as though her life were the plot of a B-movie.

'Fuck off,' she said crudely. After all, she *was* in a very bad mood.

'And what's with this?' he gestured toward the Beretta.

'It's for when he comes back,' she blurted, still angry about the other remarks.

He cocked his head. 'What makes you so sure he's coming back?'

'Because he's . . . been calling me.'

'*What?*' He knelt down in front of her. 'Talk to me.'

She bit her lip.

'C'mon.' He reached up and tucked a wayward oily strand of hair behind one of her ears. His touch was remarkably gentle for such a big hand.

She told him everything.

He took his hat off and smoothed his hair back in a gesture of frustration. 'Have you told your cop friends about this?'

She shrugged. 'There's nothing they can do.'

His eyes were tender. 'Poor scared little rabbit.' He took her in his arms for a minute, then pulled back and said, 'Well, that settles it. That just makes up my mind.'

'What?'

'You're coming home with me.'

'What are you talking about?'

'I've been thinking about it. I knew you'd be battling depression and anger and a bunch of other confusing feelings right now, and I knew you were all alone, but I didn't realize somebody's been harassing you.' He leaned forward and put his hands on her arms. 'Come back with me.'

'You mean . . . to West Texas?' It seemed as if they

were discussing a foreign country, or maybe even the moon. She'd never seen West Texas before but, if it was anything like the old western movies, it was a barren, formidable place.

An isolated, lonely place.

'I'm living in my folks' ranch house,' he said. 'They're gone now, and there's plenty of room. You can stay anywhere you want, do anything you want. It's a magnificent place. It'll give you the space you need to decide what to do with your life. You can heal there, I know.'

Those eyes. Those hypnotic, wonderful eyes. She looked down into her lap so that she could think.

After all, who did he think he was? He couldn't just come in and take over like this!

On the other hand ... here she was, right in the middle of the Big City, just as isolated and lonely as she'd ever been. She bit her lip.

'Are there any trees out there?' It was the first question that popped into her head.

He grinned. 'Wait 'til you see. There's no more beautiful place on earth.'

She leaned her head back on the couch and closed her eyes. She didn't like being pushed.

On the other hand, what else was she going to do? The police department had put her on disability, so there wasn't any work she could do. Her family were gone or otherwise busy with their own lives.

And she was really getting sick of watching commercials.

The phone rang again and Cady jumped, knocking the remote control off the arm of the couch.

Zach yanked up the receiver. In a deep, loud

military voice, he barked, '*HELLO?*'

After a moment he smiled at her. 'They hung up.'

She smiled back and, in that moment, the decision was made. 'How long should I plan on staying?'

With a graceful, playful little move, Zach twirled his hat on the tips of his fingers, then settled it on Cady's head.

'Just as long as you want, Cady-did,' he said. Then, holding her gaze in the magnet of his own, repeated softly, 'Just as long as you want.'

PART II

'In its early stage, love is shaped by desire; later on it is kept alive by anxiety.'

Marcel Proust

'The talk of sheltering women from the fierce storms of life is the sheerest mockery, for they beat on her from every point of the compass, just as they do on man, and with more fatal results, for he has been trained to protect himself, to resist, to conquer.'

Elizabeth Cady Stanton

'GBU CUL'
'God Bless You; See You Later';

Secret tapping code used by
POWs in Vietnam to
communicate between cells.

Chapter Eleven

Everything happened so fast. One minute it seemed, Cady had been wallowing in self-pity, barely surviving each day, and the next, she was having her mail transferred to Zach's rural address, stopping the newspaper, and contacting a friend who'd been wanting to leave her husband but who had no place to stay. They were compatible enough to room together when Cady came back from West Texas, and she wouldn't have to worry about leaving the apartment vacant in the meantime.

Then there was the matter of deciding what to pack and what to leave behind. Zach pitched in to help with this, and caught her sobbing over her drawing things.

'I've never gone anyplace without them,' she blubbered. 'Even if it's just a sketch pad and pencil.'

'Then I think you should bring them,' he said.

He had meant to be kind, but Cady's moods were still volcanic. 'Why should I?' she cried. 'What's the point?' And she swept her hand across the table, sending pads, pencils, charcoals, art gums, and easel tumbling.

Zach calmly stooped down and gathered them while she slammed dresser drawers with impotent fury.

She hated herself.

During the several days it took for Cady to prepare to leave, she tried to back out a time or two. Since she could hardly stand her own company at this point in her life, she had a hard time seeing how anybody else would want it.

And sometimes, during the dark nightmare-tossed, pain-filled nights, she found herself having doubts about Zach. He just seemed too good to be true and, the truth of the matter was, she knew very little about him beyond what he had told her himself. Once, when she was alone in the apartment, she called a friend of hers on the Dallas PD and had them run a computer check on him.

When it came back clean, she was so ashamed of herself she could hardly face him.

Up, down, all around . . . there was no controlling her emotions or her thoughts, which seemed to predominate in the extreme. She was either exuberant about the trip, or despairing about her life, or furious about some little thing or other.

Zach never responded to her emotional outbursts. Through it all, he moved like a stately ocean liner next to a bobbing tugboat. When he was there, he handled the intrusive phone calls masterfully and, when he was not, he often called her himself, just to make sure she was all right.

He made her sleep in her own bed again, while he bunked uncomfortably on a couch too short for his long legs. But still she slept restlessly, either awkward with the aching hand, or lying awake in nervous anticipation of her trip, or running away from huge black hammers in her dreams. Sometimes she would grieve privately for her mother, wishing so desperately that she could talk things over with her. As a result, they both awoke exhausted.

But when the day finally dawned that all was done and it was actually time to leave, Zach was as giddy as a schoolboy. He sang in the shower, teased her in the kitchen, and happily made arrangements to drop off his rental car. They would be making the trip in Cady's burdened Lexus.

Cady wasn't as sure about things as Zach was. She'd made the decision and she knew it was right for her, but she found herself strangely reluctant to leave the apartment, even though it had been such a source of terror and sadness for her. After all, it was still her home; she'd lived there for years, and she didn't know anything about this West Texas ranch place. She was a city girl, wasn't she? What would she do out in the boondocks with a bunch of kickers, listening to whiny crying-in-your-beer music?

On the other hand . . . what was she going to do here?

They loaded her car on a muggy pre-dawn Dallas summer day. While Zach hoisted the heavy suitcases as though they were empty, she clutched her pillow to her like a forlorn little kid and wandered the rooms, checking to make sure she wasn't leaving anything important behind. On an impulse, she grabbed down the shadow-box containing the things her mother had worn during the march on Washington and tossed it into the back seat.

Remember what Helen Keller said, came her mother's voice, clear in her mind, *'Life is either a daring adventure, or it is nothing at all.'*

Yeah, said Nanny, *fuck 'em if they can't take a joke.*

Cady broke into a smile. As Zach was passing her, heading back into the apartment, she reached out and

107

caught his hand. 'I'm ready to go,' she said.

He squeezed her hand and gazed into her eyes. 'I knew you would be.'

And she thought to herself, *uh-huh, uh-huh*.

There didn't seem to be a time of day when there wasn't traffic to be reckoned with on Dallas freeways. Cady was glad that Zach was driving, though she was far more used to whipping in and out of it like a character in some manic video game, accumulating points every time she made it onto the freeway alive.

When had the city gotten so crowded? How had the crime and urban blight managed to creep up on the residents? There was a time when Dallas liked to think of herself as the sophisticate in the country family of the big state of Texas; the glossy, cultured sister to the cowgirl Fort Worth, the hippie Austin, and the bawdy callgirl Houston, not to mention that Hispanic stepsister, San Antonio.

But no matter how often the city got cosmetic surgery or retouched her hair, she simply could not hide her own signs of aging.

Cady sighed, grieving for her job, missing it already. She was aware of the high turnover rate among police officers, especially in Dallas, many of whom left the force before even completing their training. Their families, fearing a premature funeral, often begged them to. Race relations in the department were troubled, and an unsympathetic city council often tied their hands in bureaucratic red tape.

Cady knew what the officers faced out there on the streets every day; she knew now, more than ever. But she had given many years of her life to helping those men and women do their jobs; it gave her a great feeling of satisfaction to know that one of her drawings had helped to put another bad guy behind bars. It was a stimulating, busy, rewarding life.

And now, it seemed, it was over.

Cady thought she had some idea what castration must feel like.

They circled the city. A hot yellow ball of a sun gleamed off the silver and copper edifices to commerce that had always struck Cady as phallic symbols. She barely caught a glimpse of the red-neon Mobil oil horse perched atop what had once been the city's tallest building, now dwarfed by progress. They cruised beneath the towering spike of the rotating restaurant atop the Reunion Tower of the Hyatt-Regency. Cady had never had the nerve to take the outside elevator up to it.

By seven-fifteen the traffic was bumper to bumper. Melting humidity and choking heat, exacerbated by exhaust and concrete, had already set in. The radio gave frequent helicopter traffic reports on which freeways to avoid due to wrecks. Zach seemed to have lost his good mood as they stopped and went, stopped and went. As they inched along, Cady saw people putting on make-up in their cars, eating breakfast, sipping coffee, talking on the phone, reading the newspaper, sorting through cassette tapes, and disciplining children; miniature homes-away-from-homes. She had done many of the same things in her own car; it had never before struck her as odd. Somehow, with Zach sitting stiffly in the middle of it all, things looked different.

As they moved into the linking byways that

connected the Dallas–Fort Worth 'metroplex' (once two big cities surrounded by numerous small towns and suburbs; now a sprawling behemoth of concrete and steel), traffic opened up a bit and Zach relaxed a little. They passed the massive Texas Stadium, home of the Dallas Cowboys pro-football team.

Sun-glinted planes circled overhead as they circumvented the enormous, teeming DFW airport. The freeways were lined with fast-food restaurants, gas stations, shopping malls, businesses, apartment complexes, and housing developments. So many people. There seemed no end to it.

It took them almost two hours to finally reach open country. Rolling grasslands dotted with cows opened up a horizon which had previously been hidden by buildings. Zach visibly stretched out, as if he could feel the room inside the car. He reached over and took Cady's hand. The gesture surprised her; after all, they weren't exactly lovers, they hardly knew each other.

And yet here she was, traveling all the way across the second largest state in the nation, to visit him in his home, 'for as long as she liked'.

Go figure.

'Tell me about yourself,' he said.

She shook her head. 'No. I want to hear about you for a change.'

He shrugged. 'There's not much to tell. I'm a country boy, born and raised. I have a sister who's a park ranger in the Texas Big Bend country. She's more adventurous than me – always has been. Likes white-water rafting on the Rio Grande river and rock climbing, all that stuff.

'Me, I like the quiet life. I studied range science in

college because I always planned to come back and run the ranch eventually. But Vietnam came along and, like an idiot, I volunteered.' He grinned at her. 'Wound up staying a little bit longer than I'd planned.'

'What did you do when you got back?' Radio reception was beginning to fade, so Cady selected Eric Clapton's 'Unplugged' tape. As soon as the acoustic blues guitar sounds began to fill the car, she said, 'Oh! I'm sorry. I didn't think to ask what kind of music you like.' And added, 'I don't have any country and western.'

He laughed. 'I love Clapton. Whatd'ya think, if it's not Conway Twitty, I stop the car?' After a moment, he said, 'I didn't do so hot when I first got stateside. My wife had left me, you know, and my mom died not long after I got back.'

'I'm sorry!'

'It's okay. She was only fifty-three, but I think that whole POW scene just wore her down, you know?'

She nodded.

'So I made real good friends with Johnnie Walker.'

'Who's that?'

He gave her a sideways glance and she flushed. 'Oh. The whisky.'

'I spent the better part of a year basically drunk. It was pretty hard on my dad, so I moved into this little shack out on the ranch, so that I couldn't hurt anybody but myself. And I did lots of hard thinking.'

She nodded. No problem understanding that.

'The main thing I had to do was forgive myself for livin'.'

'What do you mean?'

He was quiet for a moment, listening to Clapton's,

111

'Nobody Knows You When You're Down and Out'. Then he said, 'See, *I* lived. I saw lots of great guys who didn't. Lots of 'em.' His eyes began to water and he let go of her hand to wipe them. When he took her hand again, his fingers were wet. 'It didn't seem fair somehow, you know, to the other guys. I felt guilty, like it was somehow my fault that they didn't make it.'

She stroked his fingers with her good hand.

He cleared his throat. 'I had to realize that, sometimes, when it comes to survival, there's just plain luck involved. Say you miss a plane, and you're standing there cussin' yourself for missing it, when the damn thing crashes.' He concentrated on passing an eighteen-wheeler. 'It doesn't mean that God somehow singled you out, like all those other poor slobs weren't as good as you or something.'

'But what about that saying, "There but for the grace of God go I"?' Cady said.

He shook his head. 'It doesn't make sense. Why would a merciful God have grace on you and not on the two hundred people who didn't miss their flight?'

'Good point.'

'I had to work out that, first of all, it was plain stupid luck that I didn't get shot up any worse than I did. Otherwise I might not have made it. I had to stop blaming myself for the other guys' deaths.' He cleared his throat again, then stretched up his body to grope in his back pocket for a handkerchief.

He blew his nose. 'And second, I had to give myself some credit for not giving up. I mean, some guys gave in to the depression. It can just sap your will to live.' He glanced at her. 'You can never give up hope,' he said, his voice gentle. 'Hope is what keeps you alive.'

Cady looked out the window, avoiding his eyes.

'Anyway, those of us who hung in there, who fought it and who overcame, are the ones who made it. And once you've made it through something like that, you never take life for granted again. You have this sense of purpose.'

'That's what Mom told me!' Cady blurted. Then, horrified that he might ask about it and she might have to admit that her mother had given her this gem of wisdom *after* she died, Cady clammed up.

'Your mom was a smart lady,' he said. 'Cady . . .'

She turned to look at him. He had a rugged, handsome profile.

'I want you to start thinking of yourself as a survivor.'

She sighed. 'Why do I feel more like a failure?'

'You're just in transition. You'll find a new purpose for your life. But the most important thing to remember is you made it. You're alive. That's all that matters.'

'But I just feel half alive!' she cried, dismayed at the sudden tears which pricked her eyelids.

He took his gaze off the road and caught hers. 'All life is about death,' he said. 'You are just dealing with the death of your old life. You've got the opportunity now to build a whole new one.' He concentrated on the road again, and the hidden significance of the remark lingered in the air between them.

They stopped for lunch at a quaint little roadside diner just off Interstate 20, not far from Abilene. Made from a converted trolley car, the diner served cherry cokes and big, drippy hamburgers. They bought munchies and soft drinks for the drive and giggled over the food like two kids on a first date.

The big trees thinned out as they drove further west, but the sloping hills were dotted with mesquite and cedar. Towns were far-flung. Sometimes they drove many miles without seeing a gas station or rest stop.

They talked about all the things people talk about when they're getting acquainted: books and music, politics and religion, movies and old loves. Cady told Zach that she and Peter had broken up because they didn't have much in common; she left out the part about the good sex.

Zach turned out to be a thoughtful, well-read man who didn't seem to need many people in his life. His tastes were surprisingly eclectic and he proved to be better informed on some issues than many of Cady's busy urban friends.

The sun climbed over the car and began blazing through the windshield. It was hardest on Zach because he couldn't wear his hat in the low-ceilinged car and apparently didn't own sunglasses. Cady put on a pair of shades and fiddled with the air conditioning. There were very few available radio stations, and most of those were country and western. After a while she decided to leave one on and was surprised to find how country music had changed in recent years; many of the songs had folk or rock overtones to them, and some had lovely harmonies.

When they got into what Zach called 'sure-nuff West Texas', the landscape grew more barren, populated only with leftovers of a once-prosperous oilfield business. The view outside the window was very flat and scrubby, dissected with barbed wire and broken up with oilfield litter. The sun was absolutely blinding; when Zach got a headache, Cady took over and drove while he folded his long body into a sort of Z and dozed.

Cady didn't tell him just how exhausted she was; she had underestimated the toll a long drive would take on her healing body and aching hand. The further they traveled, the more uneasy she became – she had really had no concept of just how far away Zach lived; or how remote was the country. He had already told her that it was a hundred-mile drive to the nearest airport. She had registered the fact as so much trivia; the reality of that kind of isolation was another matter.

Zach took over the wheel again somewhere near the little town of Pecos. They had traveled some five hundred miles, with no end of Texas in sight. Cady caught her first glimpse of the mountains – blue hazy peaks in the background. Signs of more economic disaster showed up in tiny country towns: abandoned ghost-skeletons of once-thriving cotton gins; just as tragic, in their way, as empty factories in big Northern cities.

They turned south at Pecos and eventually cruised through the spring-fed village of Balmorhea. Balmorhea was a lovely surprise. Irrigation ditches ran right through town like sidewalks and there was a famous swimming pool that was said to be the largest spring-fed pool of its type in the world. Towering clouds shadowed them as they began their final trek, sheltering them intermittently from the merciless sun.

And suddenly, there were the mountains. No gentle

115

foothills led in ever-rising slopes to these peaks. Instead, rugged, cloud-shadowed purple crags stood guard over the Chihuahuan desert. Occasional tiny clusters of ranch buildings huddled in their shadows. Mean, inhospitable plants like Spanish dagger-yucca and the spear-like Sotol stood sentinel in the rock outcroppings.

Tough, sinewy cattle roamed open pastures through which the road wound – unprotected by barbed-wire fence so the cattle had right of way. Now and then the Lexus would rattle over steel-pipe cattle-guards that straddled the road. Sheer-faced cliffs provided magnificent thermals for eagles and hawks to ride high above, as the Lexus began its slow climb into mountains that Zach said were often too rough for roads; they could only be traversed on horse or muleback.

He told her that the mountains had been formed by volcanic eruptions millions of years before. The entire area was basically frozen lava.

Cady gawked.

There were precious few cars. Slanting sunlight pinkened sheer rock-faces and velvety green stretches which looked to Cady like waterfalls of rock. Purpling clouds swept the endless sky and spiked craggy escarpments. She saw virtually no houses and no sign of civilization.

Zach began to hum under his breath. His excitement was palpable. 'We're almost home!' he cried.

Ohhh myyy God, Cady thought. *What have I gotten myself into?*

Chapter Twelve

'Welcome to my home town,' said Zach, grinning like a schoolboy. They entered the tiny 'mile-high' village of Fort Davis, dozing now in the gathering dusk. Dirt roads meandered through the outskirts of town without much rhyme or reason. They passed a ramshackle building with the sign 'Hook or Crook Books' in the window. Nearer to the center of town, buildings had been restored to capture a rugged frontier flavor: Baeza's General Store, the Old Texas Inn with its imposing false front, and the stately old two-story pink limestone Limpia Hotel. A black hound dog with a patch of white on its throat yawned from the covered wooden front porch of the post office. The mountains, stark and shaded in the dimming day, loomed as a close backdrop.

Cady's stomach twisted. Of course she knew that Zach came from a small town, but the population of this place couldn't be more than a thousand souls, and it was entirely cut off from civilization as Cady knew it.

'This is a great town,' said Zach, oblivious to her silence. 'I'll show you the old fort later.' He steered the car off the main road and onto Highway 118 north. 'The Buffalo Soldiers were quartered here. They fought off the Apaches, who had a natural first-come-first-served claim to the mountains but tended to have a rather bloodthirsty resentment of white settlers.'

'The Buffalo Soldiers?'

'One of the Army's first black regiments. The Comanches called them "buffaloes" because of their curly black hair and because they were fierce warriors. To the Comanche that was a great compliment.'

Cady held back a sigh. She was exhausted and hardly prepared for the Grand Tour. Not that it would take long.

But the view soon seduced her. To Cady's surprise, magnificent trees lined the frequent streambeds – towering cottonwoods and various varieties of oak. Green meadows, slanted with shadow from the blue craggy mountains, were dotted with piñon junipers. The air conditioning in the car began to chill them. Zach turned it off and rolled down the windows. Cool, moist mountain air lifted the hair off the back of Cady's neck and whispered, *relax.*

Zach pointed out comical stripes on the sides of bald green hillsides where, he explained, the cattle grazed laterally.

Cady grinned. 'Reminds me of an old Pecos Bill fable I read once in school, about cows with two short legs on one side and two long on the other, so they could graze mountain pastures.'

Zach laughed.

Cady marveled at him. Gone entirely was the Zach she'd known in the city. Here, he seemed so completely in his element that virtually all the tension lines had been erased from his face, now there were only laughter lines in the crinkles of his eyes.

The road wound in and out and around the mountain peaks. There were no intersecting roads.

On one particularly steep grade, the junipers were painfully gnarled in formations that allowed them to cling to the side of the mountain. 'There's a survivor for you,' Zach said, pointing out one of the twisted trees.

The setting sun gilded the tops of the mountains in shades of royal purple and gold, while encroaching shadows blanketed the valleys in misty blue. At one point, Cady caught a glimpse of the McDonald Observatory, needlepoint white on one of the highest peaks.

'I'm afraid it'll be dark by the time we get home,' said Zach after a while, 'but I just had to take you on the Scenic Loop through the mountains.' He turned on the headlights.

They made a particularly tight turn and suddenly Cady sat straight up. Caught in the glare of the headlights perched on the side of the mountain in the curve of the road, were five blinding white crosses: one large, and four small.

'What . . . ?' She pointed at the crosses as they passed them by.

'They're called *descansos*, or resting places,' said Zach. 'It's a tradition out here, begun by Hispanic settlers. Wherever there is a fatal accident on the mountain, crosses are erected to honor the dead.'

'Then those . . . ?'

'A mother and four children.'

Cady felt suddenly cold. She rolled up her window. Death. In the midst of majestic beauty, here it was. There seemed to be no escaping it.

The mountains were shrouded in black when Zach

finally pulled the Lexus to a stop at the blunt end of a crunchy gravel road. At Zach's insistence, Cady had packed a jacket, but it was in the trunk with the rest of her things. She shivered in the unexpected chill wind which swooped down, ruffled her hair and whispered in her ear as she unbent her stiff body out of the front seat and stood, stretching her back.

Zach seemed uncharacteristically nervous as he fussed around in the trunk, gathering bags. 'Dang it! I asked True to leave on some lights. Old fart's gettin' more forgetful all the time.'

Loud baying interrupted him and two strange-looking dogs tumbled over one another to get to him; their fur was a black-speckled gray and their eyes a clear silver. 'These are Australian Blue Heelers,' he explained. 'Best damn cowdogs in the world. Kip, Mutt . . . meet Cady.'

Cady leaned over to pet the dogs but they cowed at her feet.

'They're just shy,' he assured her. 'Actually, they're not used to too many people but me handling them. They're workin' dogs, not pets.'

Cady stored that information in the Yet One More Thing To Remember file. She was already hopelessly lost; even if she wanted to leave, she'd never find her way down that loopy mountain road.

Zach slammed the trunk and, when the tiny light bulb was extinguished, they were eclipsed in darkness so complete that goosebumps popped up on Cady's arms. She'd never realized before how *light* the city was at all times. Even at night, a golden glow from thousands of streetlights arched overhead. This darkness was cave-like. The only sound came from the night wind, creaking and rustling through nearby trees.

'It's not usually quite this dark,' said Zach, close to Cady's ear, and she jumped. 'But the clouds are covering up the stars and there's no moon. Once the clouds clear, the astronomers will really have a field day. Or I should say, a field night.' He took her arm and steered her up a path which loomed white at her feet. 'They sleep all day, you know,' he added, 'so they can work all night. Watch your step.'

Their footsteps echoed hollowly on a wooden porch, and Zach pushed open the front door of the house without using a key.

He flicked on a series of lights which left Cady blinking. One illuminated the front yard, and Zach headed back outside for the rest of the bags, while Cady looked around, rubbing her cold arms.

The house was old – maybe a hundred years, judging from the hand-laid parquet floors and the richness of carved and darkly stained oak moldings, door facings, bannisters, and fireplace mantel. The walls were whitewashed plaster and, from the looks of them, it had been a while since they'd seen much white. Cady suspected that when Zach's mother had been alive it had been a beautiful home, but the ensuing years of male-only occupation had made a true bachelor's pad out of it.

Clutter dominated every nook and cranny. One marble-topped antique table was littered with check stubs, a tube of antibiotic ointment, a rusty horseshoe, an odd-looking rock, a pocket calculator, a cracked flashlight, and a split bag of stale Fritoes. A fine film of dust overlaid everything.

Zach banged through the front door, arms laden with bags. 'I'll put these in the front bedroom,' he said. 'Nobody uses it much.' He climbed the stairs, two at a time, making no effort to apologize for the mess.

Cady studied the room. Her artist's eye could spot potential, and an effort had obviously been made – sometime – to make it warm and inviting. Attractively framed Western artwork graced the walls. Vivid Navaho rugs and hand-stitched rawhide throw pillows adorned the brown leather sofa and chairs.

Cady wandered over to the fireplace. A stone hearth extended to the ceiling. Fresh kindling had been laid. Branding irons were mounted over the mantel. A bronze sculpture, depicting a cowboy, his horse and a calf hopelessly but comically tangled in a rope, rested on the mantel. A few yellowing snapshots, faded in their frames, were crowded over in one corner. She recognized a painfully thin, youthful Zach, a plump, smiling woman who must have been his mother, and a tall, craggy-faced replica of Zach. His dad, obviously. How sad, living in this house all these years without them.

Like the little table, the mantel was also stuffed with an unusual assortment of odds and ends: a couple of huge medieval-looking syringes, some duct tape, a dusty Bible, a tangled coil of barbed wire (rusted and very antique-looking), a stack of unopened bills, and a sock with a big hole in the toe.

Zach came rumbling back down the stairs and Cady turned to face him. She didn't want to look like the snoop she was. He came over to her and crouched down to start a fire, bringing the room to warm, glowing life. It felt good and Cady stretched out her hands. The bandage on her right hand was much more flexible and comfortable than the stiff cast it had replaced.

'You're a fool to leave now,' the doctor had told her angrily. *'You need to start intensive physical therapy. What are you going to do out in the middle of nowhere?'*

That was right after he'd told her, in a brisk, efficient manner, that she would never draw again.

'It's good to be home,' Zach said, oblivious to her preoccupation. 'I'm going to check and see if True fed the dogs. Be right back.' And he bounded out of the room, toward the back of the house.

Cady crossed over to the large, worn, and comfy-looking sofa, moved a pile of clean towels, and curled up. Slowly, she began unwinding the bandage. She might as well get used to looking at it. Besides, her hand was aching and she wanted to massage it.

The knuckles, gnarled like those mountain junipers, stood out at twice their normal size. Scars from the surgeries crisscrossed the fingers. Her thumb crooked over to the side and inward. She tried to make a fist and couldn't even come close. Nor could she flatten out her hand.

The word *talons* crept into her mind. That's what she had now instead of fingers. Talons.

And here she was, a stranger in a strange land. A guest in a house that shouted *MEN ONLY*. At the end of a twisted road that led nowhere.

The minutes stretched out and still Zach did not return.

Wind rattled the front door and sneaked in around the old windows, licking at Cady's neck and sending shivers down her spine. Nervously, she paced over to one of the windows and peered out through gauzy white curtains, but what was there to see? It was totally dark.

The full impact of Cady's isolation began to sink in. She was lost out here in the middle of nowhere with a man she really didn't know. Lord, *there weren't even any neighbors!*

A creak sounded from somewhere overhead, startling Cady. Hell, who knew? He could even be like that creep on the old Hitchcock film, *Psycho*, and have his parents stuffed somewhere, up in the attic, maybe.

She glanced around the messy room. Surely he had a phone around here someplace.

Oh sure. And who would she call?

And if she knew who to call, what would she say? *Help! I'm out here in the boonies in this creaky old house and I'm scared shitless. Would you please play some traffic noises for me?*

Where the hell was he?

Cady followed where she had seen Zach go before – through what must have once been a splendid dining room and now seemed a sort of de facto office overstuffed with a computer and piles of read-outs and books – and into a big chaotic kitchen. Though the dishes were carefully washed and the dishtowels folded, every other inch of available space was junked up with everything from a hammer and nails to old Thermoses, from scratched Tupperware to stacks of bank statements and aging junk mail. A massive fifty-pound sack of dry dog food leaned against one wall by the back door.

Cady opened the door. It led to a dark and shadowy

screened-in back porch. She crossed through it and peered out the screen door into the windy dark. 'Zach?' she called tentatively.

There was no sign of him.

Something fluttered against Cady's cheek and she squealed and jumped back indoors.

Heart pounding, she scurried back into the living room and huddled by the fire.

This was getting scary.

A sound came to her, drifting over the wind. A crying noise.

Cady frowned. What could that be? The dogs, maybe?

But no. This was not like the baying sound that the dogs had made. It was more of a moaning.

That's it, she decided. *I'm getting the hell out of here.*

Pausing to stuff the loose bandage in her handbag, Cady marched out the front door and hurried out to her car. She didn't know how the hell she was going to get down out of these mountains, but at least in her car she felt as if she had a small measure of control. She would get – or send for – her bags later.

The crying sound was even louder outdoors.

She climbed into the car and slammed the door.

No keys.

Where were her car keys?

Zach had them.

Fighting panic, Cady looked around at the claustrophobic darkness of the mountains on a cloudy night.

Yellow light spilled from one of the windows of the house onto the front porch, which Cady could now see was more a veranda.

She examined her options.

Then, clutching her handbag to her, she bolted back into the house, head down, trying to drown out the moans that came to her on the wind.

Once in the living room, she ran up the stairs and turned to the first door that stood open, splashing light from a comfortable, pretty bedroom. Her bags had been stacked on the bed, the headboard of which had been intricately constructed of welded-together horse shoes. An old-fashioned turnkey stood in the keyhole.

Cady sprang into the room, locked the door, and took out the key, laying it on an old trunk which served as a nightstand. Panting, she collapsed on the bed and looked around her in surprise. There was no clutter and little dust. A cheerful patchwork quilt – soft from much loving use – was spread over the bed. It was obviously handmade and looked quite old.

Lovely doeskin baskets, beaded and fringed in Native American motifs, hung on one wall. A yellowed antique map, depicting the early state of Texas, was framed on another. Candles in pine-cone sconces rested on the trunk, along with a pile of old books. She glanced at the titles. They were early printings of essays by Emerson, poems by Edna St Vincent Millay, and a leatherbound copy of Zane Grey's *Riders of the Purple Sage*.

Cady lay back on the generous pillows. This was a woman's room. She felt comfortable. She couldn't hear the crying up here, though the wind still pried at the windows. A space heater provided just enough warmth.

Reluctantly, Cady undressed and got into a gown

for the night. She would sleep here one night and then that was it.

By morning, Cady Maxwell would be history.

Chapter Thirteen

The first thing Cady noticed when she opened her eyes was that she had slept through an entire night. This was a miracle almost beyond contemplation. Never a sound sleeper anyway – a night owl from way back – Cady had been plagued by bizarre dreams and dark nightmares ever since the attack. Intermixed with the constant throbbing pain from her hand as well as her other injuries, Cady had counted her sleep by the hour. She would sleep maybe an hour and lie awake another hour. Or two.

A glance at her watch told her that she had slept a whopping ten hours since locking herself in her room the night before. She swung her legs out of bed, wincing a little at the cold hardwood floor on her warm bare feet, and peeked out the curtain at the somewhat scruffy green lawns, the narrow white gravel road, her Lexus, the trees, and the mountains beyond. The sky was a more brilliant blue than any she'd ever seen; all the colors were sharp, as though washed clean.

Sheepishly, she let herself out of the room and listened for Zach, but there was no sound at all except the slow ticking of a tall, imposing grand father clock which stood in the hallway. Cady found a modern bathroom across the hall and treated herself to a luxurious shower and, as the water poured down her back, she thought about her behavior the night before and was embarrassed.

Had all those weeks of being alone, haunted by the assault and not being able to work, made a paranoid out of her? Was she losing her mind?

Still, she thought as she soaped up her hair, *Zach* hadn't *come back*.

On the other hand, this *was* a working ranch. Maybe he found some ranch-thing or other to do. As one of her favorite comics, Judy Tenuda, liked to say, 'It could hyaappen!'

But on the *other* hand . . . what about that crying sound she had heard? Had she imagined it?

No. If a sound was imaginary, it wouldn't necessarily be louder outside, would it?

Okay. She stood, eyes closed, under the marvelous current, letting the shampoo flood out around her feet. Okay. Say the sound was real. What could it be?

How about . . . a mountain lion or some other kind of critter? After all, she was a bona-fide city slicker. There had to be some kind of explanation. All she had to do was ask Zach.

Just as soon as she made absolutely certain that he would not die laughing.

The towels were huge and fluffy – one of the benefits of staying in a man's house. So, okay, the decision not to leave – at least, not just yet anyway – seemed to have been made easily enough. Picking what to wear, though, was a toughie. She'd never been on a ranch before. What did cowboys/cowgirls wear, anyway?

She dug through her bag and found a pretty Western shirt she'd bought on sale at Sak's Fifth Avenue and which she had never had an opportunity to wear. It was crimson satin with a black fringe around the yokes and green cacti embroidered on the cuffs. It looked great with tight designer jeans stuffed into a pair of black suede boots.

Examining herself in the tilting oval full-length mirror, its glass wavy with age, she liked what she saw. She'd lost a great deal of weight since the assault and it suited her. The battle of the bulge had been a constant war for her since college, though she would certainly not recommend her particular diet to anybody else.

Emerging into the quiet tick-tock hallway, Cady turned toward the stairs, then found herself hesitating. On impulse, she turned back down the hall and wandered on creaking floorboards a couple of doors down from her own room, until she encountered what was surely Zach's room.

It had to be – the flavor was entirely different from any room in the rest of the house. The furniture here was fairly new – very heavy solid oak – and masculine, with an unmade king-sized poster bed – its posts square-cut and burned with various brands – and walls lined with bookshelves. She browsed through a few titles: texts on forage, grasslands, range conservation and the like; books on agribusiness and computer science; and a wide selection of everything from studies on frontier history to recent bestsellers. There was also a vintage collection of works by Zane Grey.

A couple of russet-and-white Hereford cowhide rugs (she knew the breed because Zach had pointed them out on the drive down), lay on the hardwood floor, and a magnificent Navaho blanket, woven in smoky shades of gray, sienna, and turquoise, was displayed on one wall. Thumbtacked on another wall hung a large map of the ranch. A couple of different pairs of boots were scattered in characteristic disarray around on the floor, and several cowboy hats in various stages of wear adorned a hat rack in one corner. A lap-top computer rested on a small desk, with teetering piles of magazines nearby. Cady glanced through a few copies of *The Cattleman*, *The Farmer-Stockman*, and *Livestock Weekly*.

Figuring, what the hell, I'm already here, Cady slipped into the adjoining messy-as-usual bathroom, noticing with interest that Zach apparently shaved with an old-style barber's brush rubbed over a bar of plain Dove soap and used regular Noxzema skin cream – not cologne or aftershave – afterwards. Even his deodorant was simple and unscented. She found that fascinating. There seemed to be absolutely nothing even remotely citified about the man.

Moving furtively now, afraid that Zach might show up any minute, Cady hurried from the bathroom, catching her foot on the phone wire as she went and dragging it with a clang onto the floor. She picked it up and, as she returned it to Zach's desk, was surprised to find the business card she'd given him (that seemed a lifetime ago now). It was turned to her phone number and placed carefully right beside the phone.

Now *that* was odd. He had never called her from the ranch. She knew because she'd waited eagerly enough in that month after they'd first met and before the assault. If he wasn't going to call her, then why keep her number by the phone? If, on the other hand, he kept the number by the phone, then why the hell hadn't he called?

Yep, he was a mystery man all right, and just as soon as she chowed down on some vittles, Cady reckoned she'd mosey on down to the corrals and see if she could rustle up that wrangler.

In contrast to its cluttered interior, the ranch headquarters that Zach called home was picture-postcard beautiful from the outside. All the buildings were gleaming white stucco with red Spanish-tile roofs. The pens, all constructed of iron pipe, were painted bright red to match. A craggy mountain face seemed to drop right off behind the cluster of buildings, sheltering a playful stream lined with trees that formed the color-mottled backdrop to the scene.

Cady filled her lungs with moist, clear mountain air and followed a clean gravel pathway toward the strange sounds of high-pitched whistles, yips, and whoops coming from someplace behind the largest barn.

An eighteen-wheeler with open sides was backed up to one of the pens. Amidst a fine cloud of white dust, the cowboys – aided by Kip and Mutt – were driving a collection of cows up a ramp and into the truck. It seemed like a carefully choreographed ballet; a man and horse would cut one cow from the small herd gathered at one end of the pens, then those chosen would gather at the other end, where Kip and Mutt would help guide them to the gate. A couple of cowboys there would spank a coiled rope, a jacket, or their hands against their dusty leather chaps and whoop the animals up the ramp and into the trailer. Cady leaned against one of the fence railings to watch.

Zach, dressed in faded Levis, a denim shirt, and a

worn denim jacket, rode the horse, a beautiful chestnut with a sandy mane and tail and a wide blaze down its face. Zach wore a red bandanna around his throat; but rolled up tight and worn more like a choker with a small knot in front, not triangular or bandit-style, as she'd seen before on TV or in movies. He wore wide leather chaps that covered his boots and spurs, but she noticed that he never seemed to use the spurs, as he and the horse dodged back and forth as one. With his cowboy hat pulled down low over his blue eyes, his face set in concentration, Cady thought that she had never in her life seen a sexier man.

And to think she almost blew it last night. Good thing he'd held on to those car keys. Imagine what he'd have thought to come back to the house and find her gone?

The sun was brilliant. Cady slipped on a pair of Calvin Klein shades. Maybe those cowboy hats weren't such a bad idea, after all. And as for her shiny red shirt ... From what Cady could tell, nobody wore anything fancy to a barnyard, and for obvious reasons. She glanced down at her black suede boots. They were already gray with dust and Lord only knew what else.

She felt just like Billy Crystal in the movie *City Slickers*.

The last cow to be shipped was loaded and the big truck doors fastened behind it. Zach dismounted and signed some paperwork for the driver while every single one of the cowboys silently gawked at Cady.

As the driver pulled away, Zach strode easily across the empty lot toward Cady, spurs jangling, reins held easily in his hand as his horse followed along placidly.

Kip and Mutt just glared at her, heads lowered with suspicion.

'Good afternoon, sleepyhead!' he cried with a big grin, pushing open a gate Cady hadn't noticed. 'Come meet everybody.'

Cady picked at a loose thread on her bandage and walked slowly into the corral. She felt as if she'd stepped onto a movie set. Fighting panic with humor, she told herself, *Now, if I could just be sure that one of these guys is a criminal, I'd be all right.*

Convicts and cops. That was her world.

'You look terrific,' said Zach, and smiled at her with those eyes.

Oh Lord, was he always this tall? He looked so rugged, so damn *right*.

'Cady, I'd like you to meet my top hand and oldest friend, True Strayhorn.'

A wiry little man, his sharpened features wizened by age, stepped out from behind Zach, removed his hat, and bobbed his head in a sort of bow. His thinning hair and brows were snowy. His eyes, like Zach's, were a knowing blue, his face leathered by years outdoors. He, too, was dressed in a faded denim shirt and Levis.

'I'd shake your hand,' said Cady apologetically, 'but . . .' She displayed her injured hand.

'I wouldn't worry about t'at.' He drawled so slowly she had to incline her head to understand. (Had it been that long since she'd heard a genuine Texan accent in Dallas?) True was grinning as he held up his hands. 'I got me a matched set!' And he displayed two hands so pitifully twisted by arthritis that the fingers actually faced backwards.

Cady glanced at Zach, who was rolling a toothpick

around the corner of his mouth. He winked at her. She wondered if he'd brought her here partly because of True.

'It's an honor to meet you, sir,' said Cady with all the dignity she could muster.

He put his hat back on. 'Any friend of Zacharia's is a friend o' mine,' he said. 'Anythang you need, you jist ask.' As he spoke, even the word 'ask' had two syllables.

'True lives in that house,' said Zach, pointing out a small building near the stream, about a hundred yards from the main house. The big barn had hidden it from view the night before.

'C'mon, Dusty, no need to hide,' said Zach to a lean freckle-faced kid with a huge lump of snuff stuck under his bottom lip, who'd been hanging back. To Cady he added, 'Dusty's True's nephew. He helps out every summer.' He leaned down and murmured, 'Country kid through and through. Bashful as the day is long.' Louder, he added, 'Dusty's a real bronc-rider in the junior rodeo, aren't you, buddy?'

The boy, who couldn't have been more than fifteen, ducked his head. True elbowed him. 'Your hat, son. You're in the presence of a lady.'

Cady started to object but hesitated when she felt Zach's hand press against her arm. The boy doffed his hat then, crimson-faced, spun on his heel and headed toward the barn.

Zach chuckled and turned toward the other man standing close by, whose gaze toward Cady was frankly admiring. Like the others, his face was sun-browned, but his dark features and black mustache gave him a Mediterranean look. His teeth were very straight and dazzlingly white. His long-lashed mahogany eyes traveled up one side of Cady and down another. 'Zach, ol' boy,' he drawled, 'you didn't tell us you'us hidin' somethin' this fine up at the house.'

'We just got in last night,' blurted Cady, unnerved by the man's stare. She'd been around long enough to spot a lady-killer on sight and she took an immediate, unreasonable dislike to the man.

'I saw you on TV,' he said, 'but it dang sure didn't do you justice.'

'Don't mind him,' said Zach. 'This is Joe Fenton. He's been day-workin' out here since I was a kid. Well, except for that brief oilfield disaster.'

He and Joe chuckled together.

'Anyway, he just came to work for us again, and it's good to have him back. We grew up together – even enlisted together.'

'Should'a got drunk instead,' said Joe, who still hadn't taken his eyes off Cady. Somehow, the fact that he didn't lift his hat made her more uncomfortable than the fact that the others did.

'We did tip a few brews in our day too, didn't we?'

'The tales I could tell.'

'Keep 'em to yourself,' scolded Zach with a good-natured grin. To Cady, he added, 'Joe was a real big help to my folks when I was a POW.'

'I was tryin' to git 'em to adopt me,' deadpanned Joe.

I'll bet, thought Cady.

'So, you're from Dallas, huh?' asked Joe.

Cady nodded, wondering how long she was going to have to stand here and make polite conversation with this man.

'TV said you's a crackerjack po-lice artist.'

'Yeah,' she said. 'I was.'

'How long you plan on stayin' out here?'

Cady shrugged. She felt Zach's hand, warm and sure of itself, in the crook of her elbow. 'She'll stay as long as she likes,' he said. 'I thought I'd show her around the Three Aces some, Joe. If you don't mind, I'd appreciate it if you'd gather up Dusty and get him to unsaddle Penny here.'

'Sure.' Joe took the reins and gave Cady a sly sideways glance. 'What, you don't want to see the place on horseback? It's the best way.'

'Uh—'

'Maybe later,' said Zach. As they left the pens, he stooped and began unstrapping the custom-made leather chaps that seemed to fit his crotch and rear oh-so-snug.

Cady said, 'You named a horse *Penny*?'

He glanced up with a grin. 'What'd you expect? Somethin' like ... *Wildfire*, maybe? Or ... what ... *Wind Dancer*? Somethin' more romantic?'

She rolled her eyes at his teasing. 'But ... Penny?'

'It's what he looks like, don't he? A brand-new shiny penny. That's his registered name, in fact, Copper Penny Loafer. I don't know about you, but I always get a little thrill when I find a brand-new copper penny.'

And I always get a little thrill when I look at you, thought Cady. *Uh-huh*.

138

Chapter Fourteen

'So ... where were you last night?' asked Cady as they headed toward the house.

'I could say the same for you, you know.' He glanced down at her.

'I wasn't the one who vanished into thin air,' Cady said carefully.

'I didn't vanish!' They climbed the back porch steps and he held the screen door open for her. 'I went to see if True had fed the dogs, and he told me about a sick calf in the barn, so we went to check on her. Then there were some problems with a few of the cows we were getting ready to ship ... You know. One thing sort of led to another.' He hung up the chaps on a nearby coat rack, opened the refrigerator door, pulled out a jug of Gatorade, unscrewed the cap, and upended it, gulping with the thirst of a man who's been working cattle in the dust since before dawn. Suddenly he stopped, lowered the jug, and said, 'Oh my God. I've got to get used to a woman in the house.'

Cady grinned. 'Don't mind me.'

'I'll get civilized. I promise.'

'I don't know,' she teased. 'I kinda like this touch of the wild.'

'Oh, you do?' He was standing close to her, and the sexual tension was sudden and unmistakeable. She wondered if he would try to kiss her. She certainly wanted him to.

It wasn't like when Peter had made his sudden move, pinning her to the couch and bringing back the attack so vividly in her mind that she'd almost come out of her skin trying to get away from him. That had been a surprise, aggressive move for which she'd been unprepared. Besides, she hadn't wanted Peter to kiss her.

Zach was different.

But he turned away from her instead, busying himself with returning the jar. 'So . . . uh, what was your excuse?'

'Excuse?' She was still sorting through her disappointment at not being kissed.

'For the vanishing act.'

'Oh. I was real tired.' It was the truth. Nearly.

'I wasn't gone all that long. Want some ice water or anything?'

'No, I'm fine. It seemed like a long time. I just didn't expect you not to come back, is all.'

He held open the screen door for her again. She passed under his arm, conscious of his closeness, of his incredible masculine-ness, dressed like he was in those sexy cowboy clothes. 'You'll have to get used to that, Cady. Things happen on a ranch all the time that are unexpected and take a long time to fix, like, say, an animal getting tangled up in fence wire or something. But I'll make a deal with you. I'll try to let you know before I disappear again.'

'I'd appreciate that.'

They climbed into a battered, dusty ranch pick-up which was parked out back, the keys left in it.

'Aren't you worried about your pick-up being stolen?' she asked.

'Out here?' He laughed. 'I figure, hell, if a car thief's gone to this much trouble to come all the way out here to steal a vehicle, let him have it.' He gave her a teasing grin.

The truck was in a worse mess than the house. It was a simple, un-airconditioned, four-wheel drive ranch pick-up, dirty white with a fading red interior. A thin layer of dust lined everything: the plastic-lidded coffee mug lying on its side in the seat along with a pair of wire clippers, and a couple of stained leather gloves with rips in the fingers. An empty Coke bottle rolled around on the floor. A Winchester 30-30 Model 94 was mounted behind their heads and a cellular phone was tossed carelessly onto the dash. Empty feed sacks were stuffed behind the seat and the whole thing smelled like a country feed store. It was not a particularly pleasant smell.

'Where are the seat belts?' Cady groped around in the crease of the seat. 'Don't we need them?'

He grinned. 'What for?' and took off in a cloud of dust.

Slowing down just past the barns, Zach whistled. Kip and Mutt came tearing out, and he stopped long enough for them to leap into the back of the pick-up before pulling out onto a bumpy ranch road and heading up into the mountains.

It wasn't long before Cady felt herself clutching at the elbow rest inside the passenger door – which was almost impossible with her bad hand – as they heaved up and down mysterious bumps and dips in the road and careened around the edges of cliffs. The dogs, balanced precariously with their front paws braced against the rim of the truck bed, lifted their faces to the wind and grinned like little kids on a merry-go-round.

Cady glanced nervously at Zach. He drove one-handed, his elbow crooked out the open window of the pick-up. 'You think this is tough,' he said, 'you ought to try hauling a trailer full of horses up here. And talk on the phone at the same time.'

She swallowed.

After a while, they came to a small clearing, where he parked. The dogs scrambled out and dashed into the underbrush, noses to the ground. For a moment Cady sat, collecting her breath, while Zach got out and walked to the front of the pick-up, where he stood, his hands stuffed in his back pockets with the thumbs hanging out.

She got out and went to stand beside him. She gasped.

The valley which was spread out before them took her breath away; sweeping green meadows, freckled with juniper and oak trees and dotted with cattle, stretched out to meet the crumpled blue mountains beyond, peaceful in the morning sun. In the center of the valley, a small stockpond reflected the turquoise sky. Nearby stood a windmill. A lazy white ribbon – the road – wound through the valley and beyond. Cloud-shadows crept across the fields. From somewhere up above came the melancholy cry of a hawk, echoing from ridge to ridge.

'Prettiest place in the whole world,' murmured Zach. 'I just had to show it to you from up here.'

'Zach, I'm . . . I'm speechless.'

He put his arm around her waist and gave her a squeeze. Standing there next to him, with the wind tousling her hair and the sun warming her face, some sort of magic began to work on Cady. It was as if a spell were being cast over her, and she didn't want to move or do anything to break it.

After a moment of quiet, Zach said, 'Let's go down.' Reluctantly, she headed back to the pick-up. Zach whistled the dogs back and they began the descent, which seemed perilous to Cady and merely fun to Zach and the dogs. In spite of the climbing sun, the mountain air was cool as it swept through the open windows.

A cool place in Texas in summer. Incredible.

The valley was, if possible, even more beautiful up close. They rattled across a cattle-guard and passed a sign which read, 'Loose Livestock'. Cady could see no fences. The summer grassland was lush. Zach explained that the mountains received much more rainfall than the surrounding Chihuahuan desert, making it ideal cattle country.

A buck and three does sprang up from a clump of junipers nearby and bounded away.

'Oh!' Cady exclaimed. She'd never been so close to deer before. She craned her neck to watch them leap out of sight.

Zach smiled at her.

He stopped the pick-up by the windmill and got out to check something or other on it while Cady wandered around in delight. There was an earthy, cedar smell to the air. The silence was vast and absolute.

Peace began to seep its way into her soul.

143

'Watch out for snakes,' called Zach.

She stumbled to a halt and froze, staring all around with widened eyes. Zach's laughter peeled out, and Cady had to smile at herself.

Eventually, they got back into the truck and traveled on down the road for a few miles. Gawking at the scenery, Cady didn't notice Zach's mounting tension at first. He seemed to sit straighter, and his relaxed, easy-smiling demeanor began to twist up into something that hit Cady with a jolt when she turned to him suddenly to say something.

The lines in his face were pronounced, his mouth grim. He seemed to be looking out at something beyond Cady's shoulder but, when she turned to see what it was, she noticed nothing at first.

'What is it?' she asked, but he didn't answer.

She looked again. At first she missed it. Then, out of the passing blur, she suddenly spotted a scarlet streamer of some kind, tied to a tree limb and lilting out in the wind.

They continued to drive and, after a while, Cady noticed another one. She also saw that there was now a barbed-wire fence to the right of the road. All the bright red streamers were tied to trees on the other side of the fence.

'Goddamn him!' Zach cursed, whipping the pick-up to such a sudden stop that the dogs took a tumble in the back.

He got out, slammed the door, and stalked over to the fence near a red streamer. Then, to Cady's shock, he began savagely kicking a leaning cedar fencepost, his blows so hard that the fencepost straightened.

Dumbstruck, she stared at this . . . stranger . . .

before her. She had no idea that Zach had such a fiery temper and had certainly never seen it displayed before. It was as if the man who had gotten out of the pick-up was an entirely different person from the one who'd gotten into it just an hour before.

Even the dogs slinked off someplace out of the way.

Spent and exhausted, Zach leaned into the fence-post, head bowed. Cady got out of the truck and went to stand warily by him. 'Zach . . . what's going on?'

'I hate that son of a bitch,' he said, his words almost a snarl. 'Greedy bastard's going to ruin this country. *Ruin it!*' He took off his hat and ran his hand over the top of his head.

Cady waited. In her early married days, she'd attended a few law enforcement classes with her then-husband. In one kinesiology class, the officers had been warned to watch for just such gestures of frustration as foreboding a violent outburst.

But this wasn't a class. This was a man who, just a few minutes before, had been standing with his arm around her waist.

When he looked at her, his eyes were stony. 'Rex Zimmerman. The third. He owns the RZ Ranch next to mine. We've got bad blood going way back.' A bitter grin passed over his face. 'My granddaddy won this place from his granddaddy in a poker game.'

'Are you kidding?' Cady thought such things only happened in movies.

'Why do you think it's called the Three Aces?' The grin faded. 'It's just as well. The old drunk had mismanaged the place so bad he couldn't even pay taxes on it. And his grandson is no better.'

She pointed at a crimson streamer. 'What are these things?'

He scowled. 'Surveyor's markers. For the damn bulldozer crews.'

'What are you talking about?'

'Zimmerman's got a get-rich-quick scheme that's supposed to make him a millionaire and pay off all his gambling debts. He's having his place divided into two-acre plots, you see. To sell to all the city slicker snowbirds who drive through here once a year, fall in love with the scenery, and think they want to live in the mountains.'

'Are you talking about a housing development?' Cady wasn't sure she was hearing this right.

'Oh no. Nothing so crass. No . . . see, this is a *country-living* thing. Anybody who wants to can own a couple of acres of the mountains. That way they can come out here and build their little ticky-tacky houses or bring out their mobile homes and trailers to spread out all over Zimmerman's half of the valley.'

Cady was shocked. She had assumed that Zach owned the whole valley. She hadn't noticed the dividing fence from up on the mountain top.

The thought of this splendid, solitary place filling up with people, noise, traffic, and pollution was almost too painful for *her* to bear. She couldn't begin to imagine how it felt to Zach.

Hollow-chested, she followed him back to the pickup and they rode the rest of the way back to ranch headquarters in silence. Zach's change of mood had been so sudden and so violent that Cady felt just as excluded now as she had felt included only moments before they reached the fenceline.

He dropped her off unceremoniously at the house. 'You'll be all right alone for a little while, won't you? I have some things I need to do.'

'S-sure,' she said. What else could she say?

He seemed to notice her bereft expression then, because he softened somewhat and said, 'When I get back, I'll take you to lunch in town. Give you the Grand Tour.'

She gave him a weak smile. 'Okay. I'd like that. I need to do a little shopping anyway.'

'Souvenirs?'

'No. Boots and denim shirts.'

He grinned and winked and drove off, and she was left even more bewildered.

The house seemed empty and unwelcoming, when just a couple of hours before, she'd been standing right here in the kitchen, flirting outrageously with Zach. Why did life always have to be so goddamned complicated, anyway?

Dejectedly, she headed up the stairs. She was going to get out of this damned stupid Sak's Fifth Avenue cowgirl shirt and get into something practical.

Dressing and undressing were still big chores, so it took Cady a little while to get into some faded jeans, a black Dallas PD tee shirt, and sneakers. She was just headed downstairs when the phone rang.

For a moment, Cady hesitated. After all, this wasn't her house.

It rang again. She hurried back upstairs. It could be Zach, calling from the pick-up. On the third ring, she lifted the receiver. 'Hello?' She waited. 'Hello?'

She hung up. Must be a wrong number.

She had reached the bedroom door when the phone

rang again. She picked it up before it could ring a second time, and said with just a trace of annoyance, *'Hello?'*

That whispered voice, when she heard it, weakened her knees and slammed her heart against her ribcage. It said, *'I've got you right where I want you.'*

Chapter Fifteen

'Oh my God,' she said. 'How did you get this number?'

'Cady . . . beautiful Cady . . . don't you know?' I asked her. 'Haven't you figured it out yet? You and I are one. Soul mates. Nothing can ever separate us.'

She threatened to call the police.

I said, 'And tell them what?'

'Th-there are stalker laws on the books in the state of Texas now, you know. What you are doing is harassment. I can get you arrested.'

I thought that was pretty funny. I may have even laughed a little. I asked, 'Get who arrested?'

There was a long pause. I could almost feel her mind working. God, she was so intelligent. I admire that in a person. Especially one so beautiful as Cady.

'You're looking awfully thin,' I commented. 'You need to eat more nutritious foods.'

I heard a slight gasp.

'Yes, Cady. You can never get truly away from me,' I told her. 'You and I are one. You are a part of me. Surely you sense that? I know you must realize it by now. C'mon. Admit it.'

'Can't you just leave me alone?' As I recall it, her voice had little sobby noises in it.

I begged her not to cry. I told her that I'd never do anything to hurt her.

'But you already have!' she cried. Oh, I remember

149

*how I wished I could hold her right at that moment
and soothe her tears. I could almost feel her trembling
against me.*

*'The city is a dangerous place,' I said. 'I'm glad
you're living in the mountains now. I can look after
you here so much easier.'*

'No. NO!'

*'Don't resist me, beautiful Cady. Our relationship
is so much more powerful than you realize. Can't you
feel it? Just open yourself up to it. The "us" you see,
transcends anything of the "you" or the "me". The "us"
is a thing apart. You must know that.' I mean, what
more could I say?*

*I could hear her crying. 'If I were with you right
now, I would kiss it and make it better,' I told her. 'I
would kiss it and make it better.'*

Cady slammed down the receiver and fled the house,
running toward the barn, screaming Zach's name.

Old True came hobbling toward her from the stalls
as she entered the barn. 'What's all this ruckus?' he
asked, placing his backwards fingers on her arms.
'Didje come up on a snake or somethin'?'

'Where's Zach?' she cried, trembling violently from
head to foot. 'I need to see Zach.'

'He ain't here right now.'

'Please.' She pushed his hands away. 'I have to see
him.'

'I reckon he'll be back directly.' He squinted at her.

Dusty came jogging up behind him and stared,
asking a one-word question: 'Snake?'

'No.' Her knees felt much too weak to support her.
She looked around and spied a hay bale. Hurrying

150

over, she sank onto it as though it were a small island to a drowning swimmer.

True and Dusty exchanged looks.

Cady put her face in her hands and sobbed, her shoulders heaving. Her injured hand began to throb again. 'How could he find me here?' she blubbered. 'I can't believe he found me here!'

'Who found you?' True dug out a spotless, frayed, and carefully folded white handkerchief from his back pocket and held it out to her in one of his twisted hands.

She took it gratefully, and made a monumental effort to pull herself together. She was not given to public displays of hysteria, but this thing had caught her off-guard. In the city, she always had her game-face on, so to speak. She never knew when something might happen and she was always tensed and ready for it.

But this. Here, in this place, she felt safe, peaceful.

It was a violation.

Suddenly, she was filled with rage. How *dare* he invade her . . . her *mind*.

'*Goddamn him*,' she whispered, twisting True's handkerchief into a wadded ball. 'Goddamn him.'

She looked up into the old man's puzzled face. 'Please forgive me, True. I didn't mean to cause a . . . a ruckus.' She heaved a shaky sigh.

'Don't you worry 'bout t'at none. Th' important thang is you.' He narrowed his shrewd eyes. 'Somebody been botherin' you?'

She shuddered. 'The man who did this to me.' She held out the bandaged hand. 'He's been . . . stalking me. He . . . he found me at Zach's house.'

151

'Whatd'ya mean, he found you?' asked Joe, who had just entered the barn. 'I ain't seen nobody around here.'

'He called me. At Zach's house. Just now.'

'You mean, he called you from Dallas?'

'I don't know. True – he acted like he was here. In the mountains somewhere. Watching me.'

'No way he can watch you out here,' protested Joe. 'There ain't nobody within miles o' this place.'

True's wrinkled face set into hard lines. 'Anybody tries to git to you out here, young lady, they got to go through Zach first, an' Joe here . . . an' me.' He pulled his bent body up straighter, and it occurred to Cady that he must have been quite something in his youth, in spite of his small stature.

She gave him a weak smile. 'Thanks, guys. I'm sorry I acted like such an idiot.'

'What's going on here?'

They all turned to see Zach standing tall at the entrance to the barn. Nobody had heard him drive up.

Cady got to her feet and walked over to him. 'I'm afraid I gave the guys a fright,' she explained. 'They've already forgiven me for acting like a fool.'

He frowned. 'What happened?'

She swallowed, feeling suddenly weak all over again. 'He . . . he called, Zach. At your house.'

'What?' He glanced over her head at the other men and Cady read something there that she couldn't interpret – some kind of man-signal – but whatever it was, the atmosphere suddenly crackled with it.

He put his hands on her arms. 'What did he say?'

'I – I don't remember everything. I mean, I was in

such a state of shock. I never expected—'

'Give me the gist of it, Cady.'

'Well . . . he . . . he acted like he was *here*, in the mountains. And like he had been watching me.'

'Watching you?' He narrowed his eyes as True had done. 'You've only been here one night, Cady. He must be bluffing. Trying to scare you.'

'But if he has your phone number, then he knows where I *am*!' Her voice rose with a fresh wave of panic. 'There's nothing to prevent him from coming after me.'

Zach took Cady tightly into his arms, pressing her close. She realized then that she was still trembling. Her knees were still weak and she leaned against his solid, reassuring frame. 'I didn't mean to act like such a baby,' she said, her voice muffled against his chest. 'It's just . . . I never expected it here, Zach. It scared me so bad.'

He stepped back from her and tilted her chin up with his finger, looking her directly in the eye. 'You listen to me now. You are perfectly safe, Cady. There is no way that son of a bitch can ever get to you here. If he did, I can guarantee, one or the other of us would blow his damn head off.'

'You got t'at right,' affirmed Joe.

'Amen,' added True. 'Even Dusty's got a little .410.'

'That's a shotgun,' added Zach.

'I know!' said Cady.

'Did you bring that Beretta?'

'It's still in the console of my car.'

'Why don't you keep it in the house, by your bed or something. I've got all kinds of firearms, but I think you'd feel more comfortable with one of your own.'

A heaviness shrouded itself over Cady. She'd had a few sweet moments of such innocence, living in a house where they never locked the doors, not having to think about things like being afraid.

Her own little private *Andy Griffith Show*.

Now, with one phone call, it was all shattered.

How she hated him... *him*... whoever he was, for robbing her of her own peace of mind, for making her feel frightened and unsafe no matter where she was or who she was with.

He had no right.

Cady clenched her teeth and curled her one good hand into a tight fist.

He had no right.

Chapter Sixteen

As if to make her forget, Zach took Cady on the promised Grand Tour and, as he drove her through the seventy-five mile Scenic Loop (in his 'town pick-up', a fairly new two-tone red and white dual-cab GMC with power steering, tape deck, and air conditioning), he pointed out or mentioned mountains and creeks and valleys with names resonant of the great Southwest and its frontier history: Forbidden Mountain, Robber's Roost Canyon, Broke Tank Draw, Right Hand Creek, Bearcave Mountain, Sheep Pen Canyon, and Casket Mountain.

They did not speak of the phone call, as if by ignoring it, they might make it go away. As they passed Mount Locke, home of the McDonald Observatory, Zach promised to take Cady to a 'Star Party' one night. The observatory, he explained, was one of the few in the world which allowed public viewing from its huge telescopes. 'This is one of the darkest night skies in the world,' he bragged, and Cady had no trouble believing it.

They got out at a roadside ell overlooking the jagged, frightening Sawtooth Mountain with its sheer rock drop-off. Zach explained that the Davis Mountain range was originally named after former Confederate president Jefferson Davis, who had ordered the fort to be built to protect California Gold Seekers, settlers traveling Butterfield's Overland Mail Route by stagecoach, and others migrating down the San Antonio–El Paso Road, all of which were unfortunately situated just west of the Great Comanche War Trail and along the path of the Mescalero Apaches.

He spoke of the first white man to see the beautiful bubbling creek that tumbled through the mountains, so crystal clear he gave it the Spanish name, 'limpia', which meant 'clear'. And of the delightful discovery of a canyon covered with wild roses, truly an oasis for horseback explorers who had just survived a trek across the Chihuahuan desert. 'The creek is still clear,' he added proudly, and Cady wondered what it would be like to come from a place in which your family had dug in and put down roots, a place with a generational history reaching far beyond the suburban housing developments of most modern transitory settlers, who changed neighborhoods with each promotion and cities with every new job.

If you had a history, she mused, *you'd have a much clearer picture of just who you are*. Maybe that explained Zach's quiet self-confidence and decisiveness.

They passed the Prude Guest Ranch. 'Talking about survivors,' Zach said, 'the Prudes stood to lose the ranch if they continued simply raising cattle, so they created this incredible guest ranch and environmental study center out of it. What sets it apart from most dude ranches is that it is a fully working ranch.'

She smiled at his enthusiastic pride, and wished with all her heart that Rex Zimmerman would try something so creative.

By the time they reached town and ate lunch at the Limpia Hotel Dining Room, the phone call had assumed all the proportion of a bothersome fly in Cady's thoughts. Cady was surprised at the delicate white tables and chairs, the blue-flowered carpeting, the untreated wood paneling and giant beams from which hung dozens of bunches of dried herbs and flowers. An old-fashioned chalkboard proclaimed today's pie (Buttermilk), and Cady ate from a salad buffet which might have been served at a New England inn.

From the windows, she could see the old restored buildings across the street and the mountains looming so close the village seemed to be carved out of them. It was a popular place with the tourists, and Cady wondered if Zach were showing off for her; if he normally ate at some greasy roadside Mexican food place where the meals were cheap and tasted better than anything this side of Juarez. She was about to ask him when a man approached their table. Or was it a woman? Cady narrowed her eyes. A man, definitely.

An unlit cigar was clamped tight between his teeth, a grizzled, stained hat pulled down low over his eyes. A long, gray braid hung down his back. A plaid Western shirt strained at the buttons over his plump body, and a rawhide vest stretched over the soft shoulders. Worn Levis were stuffed into a scuffed pair of boots.

'How ye doin', Zacharia? I hadn't seen you in too long of a time!' *A woman*, thought Cady. *It* was *a woman.*

Zach smiled warmly. 'It's good to see you, Molly.

157

I'm surprised to see a girl like you in a fine establishment like this.'

She laughed heartily, a ruddy glow to her tanned cheeks. 'Don't worry, they's just about to throw me out.'

'*We were not!*' called the cook from behind the kitchen door.

Molly turned nut-brown eyes Cady's way. 'You must be that artist lady from the big city,' she said. 'No wonder Zacharia's been keepin' you all to hisself. You're too purty to expose to the town hooligans.'

'It's nice to meet you,' said Cady with a smile.

'I hear you got choused purty good. I don't blame you for comin' out here to heal up.'

Zach shook his head. 'Molly Maguire, I swear I don't know how you keep to yourself the way you do out on that place and still manage to know everybody else's business at the same time.'

'Yeah, the talent is to make it so nobody know's *my* bidness, see.' Her eyes crinkled into a grin. 'Y'all come see me sometime.'

'What, and get shot?'

She winked at Zach and made her way out of the restaurant.

'Talk about your basic characters,' said Zach admiringly. 'That old gal took over her ranch when her husband got killed, way back in the forties. She's run it all by herself ever since.'

'Doesn't she need help, er, shipping cattle and things?' Cady wanted to get the terminology right.

'She hires day-workers to help work cattle. Otherwise, she's happy as a tick just to be left alone. But don't let her solitude fool you. She knows what goes on in this town, let me tell you.'

'I like her,' said Cady.

They got up and made their way to the cash register. 'You could say women's lib got its start in the old West,' said Zach. 'It takes strong women to survive out here, even today. They work right alongside their husbands. The men know they can't make it without 'em.'

Cady had never thought about that before. She wondered what her mom would have thought of Molly and decided they'd have made great friends.

As they were leaving, he said, 'Hell, truth to tell, it was the women who settled the West. All the men did was push cows, drink, gamble, and shoot at each other. It's the women who brought churches and schools and children. In fact,' he added, chewing on a toothpick, 'it was the Western states and territories which first gave women the right to vote, and first elected women as mayors and governors.'

'From Ma Ferguson to Ann Richardson,' mused Cady. 'Mom would be proud.'

'You gotta see this drugstore,' said Zach, and took Cady for an old-fashioned soda at Fort Davis Drug. He browsed with her while she poked through pottery, antiques, and even hand-decorated cow skulls. Cady bought a small red rubber ball at one shop, but she wasn't quite ready just yet to tell Zach what it was for.

Outside the store, Zach was stopped by a very attractive blonde woman poured into skintight Wranglers and a tailored white Western shirt which showed off her tiny waist and slim hips. She placed blood-red nails gently in the crook of his arm, leaned

159

up to brush his cheek with a crimson kiss, and said, 'Zach! It's so good to see you again.' She gave Cady a cool, blue-eyed appraisal and said, 'This must be your new friend from Dallas.'

'Uh, yeah.' A ruddy flush appeared beneath his tan.

Cady stared at Zach. He seemed to have forgotten her name. She glanced back at the woman and said flatly, 'Cady Maxwell.'

The woman seemed oblivious to the awkward pause that followed. She had not removed her hand from Zach's arm. 'Well, Zach, aren't you going to introduce me?'

'Tammilee Sanderson,' Zach stammered. 'She's a . . . friend of mine.'

'I must say,' said Tammilee, 'that we were all surprised when Zach went off to Dallas on business and the next thing you know, he's brought a woman back with him!' She shook her soft blonde curls. 'And a TV star at that.'

'Well, not really . . .' Cady stumbled. She was infuriated at Zach. He had never mentioned a girlfriend to her. Not once. And clearly, he had not mentioned *her* to his girlfriend.

'You'll have to bring your new friend to the rodeo in Alpine this weekend, Zach,' said Tammilee. 'I'll be riding barrels. I can get you tickets.'

Cady was somewhat surprised at that. This woman appeared to be in her thirties, but she was still riding barrels?

'Thanks, Tammilee, but, uh . . .' Zach shot Cady a helpless glance but she was not about to help him with the situation. 'Maybe next time,' he finished.

'Well, it's been so nice to meet you, Cady. And Zach

– bring Cady out to the house sometime. I'm sure Mama and Daddy would just *love* to meet her.'

And still living at home, apparently. With Mama and Daddy.

The woman sashayed on down the street. Zach took off in the opposite direction, heading toward the bank. Cady had to trot to keep up with him. 'Very pretty lady,' she mumbled.

'I was going to tell you about her.'

'When? Before or after I made a fool of myself? Or should I say before *you* made a fool of *your*self?'

'Aw, hell, I don't know how to handle these things!' he cried. 'It's not like we were engaged or anything.'

'How long have you been dating?'

'About six months.'

'And you didn't bother to tell her about me?'

'I was going to.'

Cady's cheeks burned. She felt ambushed.

On the other hand . . . it's not like she and Zach were dating, either. What *were* they to each other exactly?

She had to sympathize with Tammilee. How would she feel if she'd been dating some guy for six months – a guy Mama and Daddy obviously liked – and the next thing she knew, he had another woman living in his house? Some woman she'd never heard of from another city. (A *big* other city.) The more she thought about it, the more she had to give Tammilee credit for her restraint. Cady felt lucky Tammilee hadn't raked out her eyes with those blood-red claws of hers.

She followed a silent Zach into the tiny bank and was astonished to see a genuine teller's grille, just like something out of an old TV western. When she exclaimed over it, he told her it was one of the few working banks which still had one.

Everywhere she went, people smiled and greeted her warmly. She didn't know if it was because they were always this nice, or because she was with Zach. Even the black hound dog with the white throat (his name was Hank, Zach said), followed them for a while, walking right into the bank with them.

As they were leaving, the door opened and a large man stepped in, amost colliding with Zach. His face was florid, his cowboy hat sweeping, his smooth suede Western jacket expertly fitted.

For a long moment, the two men stood in face-off, the air between them electric. Cady could see the muscles in Zach's cheek flinch. He spoke first, his voice low like a growl at the back of a dog's throat. 'You told me you'd hold off the surveyors for six more months, Zimmerman.'

The big man shrugged. 'I changed my mind.'

Zach's eyes sparked steel. 'You son of a bitch,' he breathed. Cady could see his right hand clench into a fist. She touched the iron muscles of his arm.

'Boys, take it outside,' said the teller, behind them. Cady didn't know if the bank clerk had heard the exchange between the two men or if she was just all too familiar with the tension between them.

Zimmerman touched the brim of his hat to Cady and stepped around Zach. Zach – trailed by Cady and Hank – left the bank.

For a moment, she took in the glowering mountains, the angry cowboy at her side, and the false-front frontier buildings, and felt as if she'd been caught in a time warp. She half expected to step into Baeza's

General Store next and buy a bolt of calico. Or for Rex Zimmerman to come out of the bank, call to Zach, and for the two of them to shoot it out in the dusty street. The sprawling city she had just left seemed so far away that it began to assume an otherworldly aura, hazy and unreal in her mind.

She slipped her hand through Zach's still-tense arm and felt it relax a little. He stretched his arm around her waist and gave her a squeeze. She liked the feeling. And she liked being with Zach Ralston, even though a day with him seemed shot full of surprises, from the meeting with Tammilee to the confrontation with Zimmerman.

Zach asked Cady what kind of clothing she needed, and after they clambored back into the pick-up, she began to realize just how small this small town was. There was no movie theater in Fort Davis, no video-rental store, no discount store, no department store, no fast-food restaraunt. There was one doctor in town and one vet (a female, he mentioned for her benefit), but no dentist and no hospital. For those luxuries, Zach explained, you traveled to Alpine, which was 'only' thirty miles away.

Alpine – an isolated mountain community of about 15,000 – boasted a small college, Sul Ross University, with its own outdoor theater and Southwestern museum. There was a Dairy Queen and a Pizza Hut in town. And there was actually a cinema with two screens. Alpine was a sufficiently sized town to handle most daily needs, Zach told her, but if you wanted a shopping mall or, say, an obstetrician or some other special thing, then you had to go to Midland/Odessa or El Paso, which were 'only' about two hours away in either direction.

A two-hour drive in labor. Sounded like great fun.

He took her to Alpine. Although the drive was 'only' thirty miles, it seemed longer to Cady because the scenery was so vast and barren, broken only by outcroppings of mountains. When they drove through the great empty desert and along the mountain roads and another vehicle would pass, Cady noticed that Zach would wave at the other driver and the driver would wave back, just like traveling pioneers who went for days without seeing anybody else.

There were no souvenir shops or 'Indian' outposts, no truck stops or fast-food places. Just a long winding ribbon of black road, its dotted white lines licked up beneath the pick-up in hypnotic rhythm. Cloud-shadows swept overland like majestic royalty, surveying their kingdom.

Cady bought boots, denim shirts, and a Levi jacket, at a place called Johnson Feed and Western Wear, which proclaimed that it sold 'Purina, Hay, Salt, Tack, Animal Health, and a Complete Line of Western Wear, Boots, Hats, Belts, and Clothing Men and Women.'

There, Zach bought her a white summer cowboy hat. 'Most women don't wear them unless they rodeo,' he said, 'but you just look entirely too cute to pass this one up.' Cady couldn't help but wonder how 'cute' Tammilee looked in one.

Most of the time, though, she was simply too wide-eyed and agog at the many different sensations there were to take in. Although they were new and some-times bewildering, she didn't find them unpleasant.

'You know,' she said during the long quiet drive home, 'I never really liked living in the city. I always knew there had to be something better somewhere, but I had no idea what. Or where.'

'And now?' he said, glancing her way with those too-blue eyes.

'Well, I'm just constantly amazed. You left your keys in the pick-up when we went into the bank!'

He grinned.

'There are so many little daily worries of city living that you just never have to think about here.'

'True,' he said, 'but we have little inconveniences that city folks never have to think about, too. Like distance.'

Sobering thought. Cady gazed out the window at the volcanic mountains, the arching blue sky overhead and the endless road before them. Could she stand the isolation?

It would be hard enough just getting along without Blockbuster Video! She smiled. On the other hand . . . *I'm not living here you know*, she told herself. *This is just a vacation. I can leave anytime I want.*

'Well, my girl,' said Zach, interrupting her thoughts. 'It's been a lovely day, but some of us do still have to make a living. Time for me to get back to work. You're welcome to come with me anytime you please. Otherwise, you're on your own for entertainment.'

'I think I can manage that,' she murmured. A clear mountain twilight was gathering shadows and smudging the mountains softly purple as they drove around behind the ranch house and parked. Cady followed Zach out to the barn.

'Hmmm. I guess Joe didn't go get the horses yet.' He glanced at her. 'Come with me. You'll love this.'

'Do I have to r-ride a horse?' she asked.

He laughed, shook his head, and led her to the ranch pick-up, where they bounced and jounced their way down another oblique trail. 'There they are,' he said, pointing out a small herd of about a dozen horses, grazing in the blue-green twilight haze. He climbed out of the truck, cupped his hand over his mouth, and let out a high-pitched whoop that would have struck bone-jangling terror in the heart of any frontier cavalryman.

A dozen chiseled equine heads lifted, watching him. He gave another loud call. Then, one by one, the horses began moving toward them in a slow, head-bobbing saunter.

'Watch this,' he said. He got into the pick-up and drove directly across the grass and almost behind the horses, then gave a short blast of the horn.

Electrified, they scattered to the winds, heads high, manes and tails flying in a multicolored blur, kicking up their heels in a mad race toward the barn; a picture of majesty and power and grace that brought sudden tears to Cady's eyes.

'*Oh,*' she said simply.

He grinned. 'Figured you'd like this part.'

They followed the horses in, and Zach began shutting certain individuals into separate pens. 'These are the boss horses,' he called to her. 'They'll hog all the feed because they can cow the younger ones.'

The rest of the horses gathered around various troughs, nipping and scuffling with each other like rowdy boys, waiting for Zach to pour in their supper of oats. He rubbed each one's forehead and called him by name, then walked around behind them, stroking their sides and checking, he explained, to make sure none of them had any cuts or scratches or sore feet.

It was quiet but for the horses' crunching and the occasional stamp of a big hoof. Zach led Cady up to the animals and let her pat them as they ate. They didn't seem to mind. They emitted a solid, comforting smell, a smell of the earth and sky.

Then, while Zach worked inside the saddle house on some tack, Cady sat cross-legged on the ground in front of the door, stroking Kip's fine head and watching the evening star rise slowly over the mountains. It started to grow cool, and Zach draped his big Levi jacket over her shoulders.

She felt a healing in her soul and, if she forced herself, she didn't even have to think about intrusive phone calls and ghostly whispers.

Surely that was from her other life. An aberration that would fade away in time, so that she may feel completely safe in a house where the doors were never locked.

'I'm gettin' hungry, how 'bout you?' asked Zach, lifting her easily to her feet.

She nodded.

'What're you thinkin' about?'

'Just how beautiful it is here,' she said. She didn't want to talk about the phone call. That was from another life. A rogue wave that would pass. She was convinced of it.

They ate sandwiches and drank cold sweaty beers on the back veranda, watching night cloak itself over the mountains. When they were finished, Zach led her (blindly, for she had no idea where to place her next step), out the back of the house to a spot he proclaimed dark enough to look overhead, and Cady lifted her gaze to the most spectacular sight she'd ever seen: the night sky.

The Milky Way splashed overhead, spilling into constellations Cady recalled from a space unit she'd done for a fourth grade science class. Zach stretched out on the grass and pulled Cady down beside him and they lay side by side as he pointed out this planet and that star. The air was black velvet and the stars crystalline, and if Zach had made the slightest move toward Cady she'd have ripped his jeans off faster than he could think. But he didn't so, unsure how he might react, she didn't either.

Still, even though it was cold and the wind was picking up, Cady was disappointed when they went inside.

In bed, she tossed and turned, thinking about Zach, her crotch pulsing, wondering when – or even if – he would finally make love to her. She wasn't above initiating sex with a man, but this man was different from any she'd ever known, and she sensed that he needed to make the first move.

Then, somewhere in the deep night, Cady heard a loud *thump*, followed by an inhuman wail.

Bolting upright in bed, she froze, goosebumps crawling over her body, listening in the throbbing darkness.

The cry, louder this time, came again.

It came from the direction of Zach's room.

Cady fumbled in the nightstand for the Beretta and eased herself into the hallway. The grandfather clock echoed in her ear as she heard another loud cry.

On bare feet, Cady slipped quickly down the

hallway and eased into Zach's room. A clock radio glowed red beside his bed: one-fifteen. Heart pounding, she stood uncertainly.

He cried out again – it was unmistakeably Zach's voice this time – and another loud *thump* reverberated from his direction, as though he had struck something in his sleep. Cady groped for a light switch and couldn't find it, but her eyes were fairly well adjusted because she'd been lying awake so long, and she could see there was no one else with Zach.

She laid the Beretta on a nearby bureau and crossed over to the bed, where she eased herself under the covers and stretched out beside him, cradling his head in her arms.

'Shhhhh,' she whispered. 'It's all right. Just a bad dream.'

She knew all about bad dreams.

Suddenly he stiffened in her arms and jerked his head up, looking wildly around. He was panting and the sheets were drenched with sweat.

'It's all right,' she murmured. 'You were having a nightmare. I'm here now. I won't leave you.'

His hand reached up and cupped the back of her head, pulling her down, and he kissed her full and hard. Her response was immediate; she arched her back into him and kissed him fully, probing his mouth with her soft tongue. He pulled her hard into his long body and she could feel the power of his erection and its urgency. She wrapped her legs around him and they tumbled from one end of the bed to the other, groping and touching and licking and sucking and kissing and holding and gasping.

He touched her hot throbbing velvet place and she

said, 'No, I want you inside of me.' And then he was. He filled her up so deep and so full and they rocked the bed against the wall in hard pounding thrusts. Then he pulled out, tormenting her, and reached down with his fingers, working her until she moaned and cried out. Then he plunged in deep and strong, still stroking her with his fingers, until the night and the dark and the she and the he were all mixed up and blended together, pounding and thrusting and rocking and nail-digging and crying and mounting and spiraling, until she was lost inside of him and two lonely souls touched and there was no beginning and no end.

And she knew, at that moment, that she would never leave him.

Chapter Seventeen

'It was that goddamned murder,' murmured Zach against Cady's hair. 'Seeing that kid get blown away really set me off.'

Cady was stretched out beside him, her head resting on his chest. He was stroking the soft hairs on her arm.

'I thought I'd got those dreams under control. Hadn't had one in years. Then that kid in the parking lot . . .'

'What do you dream?'

'That I'm back there. At the prison camp. And they're beating me or whatever. It's so damned *real*! Like it's happening all over again. Like it never quit.' He shuddered. 'It's that same hideous feeling of total powerlessness. Anybody who's been to war knows that feeling. And in the prison camps, it was just exaggerated.'

'You felt powerless when the boy was shot in front of you in the parking lot?' said Cady.

'God, yes.'

'I understand. I felt the same way when I was tied up.'

He squeezed her. 'I never dreamed I'd ever meet a woman who *could* understand,' he whispered.

'Zach, it wasn't your fault that the man in the parking lot got shot.'

'No, and it wasn't my fault that an eighteen-year-old kid who was walking in front of me stepped on a land mine, either. Or that one of my roommates in the camp made up his mind that he wanted to die and just quit eating. They weren't my fault, but *goddamn it! Why couldn't I stop them?*' He pulled away from her and sat on the edge of the bed, rubbing the heels of his hands against his eyes.

Cady got up on her knees and draped her arms around his shoulders. 'You said it yourself. Survival is a matter of luck – it was that kid's tough luck that he stepped on the mine instead of you – but, like you said, survival can also be a decision. The only power your roommate had was over his own mind and, once he made up his mind to die, then that was his decision. You weren't responsible for it one way or the other.'

He took her bandaged hand gently in his and kissed the palm of it. 'You have some decisions of your own to make,' he said.

Cady leaned her forehead against the nape of Zach's neck. He was right, but she much preferred speaking in the abstract to the personal.

She kissed the back of his neck, then ran her tongue over his shoulders until goosebumps broke out on his back. He twisted around and lay down beside her, surrendering himself to her kisses and caresses. She straddled him and arched her back until they both moaned, then stretched her body over the length of him and lost herself in the hot wet depths of his kisses. His climax, when it came, racked his whole body. Tangling his fingers in her hair, he gasped, 'Where have you been all my life, beautiful Cady?'

And she pressed her sweating breasts against him

and wondered the very same thing.

When Cady awoke, it seemed dreadfully early to her
– seven-thirty – but Zach had already been up and
gone a long time. They had talked or made love, it
seemed, the whole night. She wondered where he got
his energy. For a long while, she lay in the bed that
still smelled of the both of them together, then she
got up, took a shower, got dressed in one of her new
denim shirts – it wasn't faded yet, but it was a start –
and breakfasted on the sweetest, most delicious
cantaloupe melon she'd ever tasted. The label said it
was grown in Pecos.

Outside, the morning air was still dew-fresh and
she wandered down toward the stream out back. It
was a lazy little creek, barely there in some places,
but wet enough to support towering cottonwood and
oak trees, which creaked and rustled in the morning
breeze. Birds chattered noisily overhead as Cady
found a comfortable shady spot and sat down, pulling
the red rubber ball from her pocket.

Slowly, she unwound the bandage from her right
hand and placed it in a heap on the grass next to her.
Then she placed the ball in the palm of the crooked
hand and attempted to curl her fingers around it.

The pain was intense, and tiny beads of perspiration
popped out on Cady's upper lip as she gradually placed
the twisted fingers around the ball and, at last, gave
it a squeeze.

An infant could have done better, but it was a
squeeze, none the less.

Cady gathered up the bandages and stuffed them
in her pocket. Zach was right about decisions, and

one decision Cady had made was that she was going to regain the use of her wounded hand. Maybe it would never again be the same but it would be usable. Her method of therapy might not be sophisticated, but Cady vowed to keep squeezing that ball until the strength was at least equal to that of her other hand.

As for the pain, well, that was something she was going to have to get used to.

After working the ball until the pain became virtually unbearable, Cady turned and headed back to the house. She wasn't above taking a couple of aspirin when it became necessary. She'd give her hand a few hours' rest, then she'd exercise it again. And again.

She'd do whatever it took to make her whole again. It was the only way she had to regain the power over her own life that her assailant – whoever he was – had robbed her of.

But the pain was a second assault, and Cady was forced to lie down for a few minutes to rest the throbbing hand while the aspirin took effect. She despised her own weakness and vowed to overcome it.

The phone rang.

Zach did not own an answering machine, a fact Cady found curious, considering the amount of time he was away from the house and something she was going to rectify just as soon as possible. Heart pounding, mouth suddenly dry, she decided to let it ring.

Four rings. Five rings. Six.

Could it be Zach, trying to call from the pick-up? Would he be worried if she didn't answer?

Reluctantly, she picked up the receiver. 'Hello?'

'*I like your new blue shirt,*' said the now-familiar rusty whisper. '*Very sexy. I hope you wear it again.*'

Cady slammed down the phone. Trembling, weak-kneed, she sat down on the edge of Zach's bed and took deep breaths.

How could he possibly know she was wearing one of her new denim shirts?

Cady jumped to her feet and bolted from window to window, gazing out of each one, but all she could see were the distant mountains out front, the close mountain out back and, from some windows, the barns and outbuildings.

There was no sign of the men. Zach had said they were all going out to some distant pasture to repair fencing. Both ranch pick-ups were gone. Zach's 'town' pick-up was parked out back. No one was in it.

Cady paced up and down the upstairs hallway. No matter where she went, it seemed, she was a prisoner. And Zach was right. It was this feeling of power-lessness that made her crazy.

Could *he* – whoever the hell it was – have somehow followed her out here? Could he have followed Zach and her to Alpine? Could he have been there, watching, when she bought the denim shirts?

He couldn't possibly be watching her now.

Could he?

No. No way. Like Zach had said, he must be bluffing her.

But still. He knew about the denim shirt.

He knew about the denim shirt.

He must be following her. Had to be.

So . . . where was he now? At a motel? A guest at

the Prude Ranch? Or maybe... camped out somewhere at the state park, cellular phone in hand?

'*Goddamn you!*' she screamed. '*How DARE you invade my privacy! You... have... no... RIGHT!*'

The phone rang again.

Cady jumped, then hurried down the stairs, grabbed her purse, and headed for her car. If he was calling her from some remote place, then he couldn't follow her now, could he? So she would just leave and go wherever she goddamned well pleased. Maybe then he would lose track of her for a while, and then perhaps *she* would be in control. At least for a while.

It was a rushed, foolish plan but, at the moment, it was all Cady had.

'When do you think they're gonna get that SST built?'

Cady had been examining, somewhat in awe, the huge telescopes for sale at Fort Davis Astronomical Supply, when the door opened and a fresh-faced woman dressed in bibbed overalls and a University of Texas tee shirt came in. She wore no make-up and her fine blonde hair was almost as short-cropped as the 'Maggie' character on TV's *Northern Exposure*. And like the actress who played that part, this woman's face had an exquisite bone structure and sweet, high color in her cheeks.

The woman, who had been chatting with the proprietor for a while, joined Cady by the side of a twelve-foot monster with a price tag that was, to say the least, astronomical.

'I'm sorry?' said Cady. 'I'm afraid I don't know what an SST is. Is it some sort of weapon?'

The woman grinned. Her expressive gray eyes

sparkled. 'Yeah,' she said. 'A weapon against ignorance.'

The proprietor chuckled and shook his head.

'The SST is the Spectroscopic Survey Telescope,' she explained. 'UT's building it up at the observatory. It's an optical telescope designed for the spectroscopic analysis of light.'

'Forgive my ignorance,' begged Cady. 'But I was an art major.'

'Oh, sorry.' The woman giggled. Her voice was rich and throaty. 'Spectroscopy is the splitting of white starlight into its rainbow of colors. You do know that light is composed of many colors?'

'Well, yes.'

'With this telescope, they can analyze the light rays, whether they are absorption or emission, and learn their chemical and molecular composition.'

'Oh.' Cady smiled apologetically. It was fun to listen to this obviously intelligent woman, even if what she said made not the remotest sense to Cady, the art major.

'Please excuse my practicality,' said Cady. 'But what the hell difference does it make what the light's composed of?'

The woman caressed the telescope in front of them like a lover. 'Well, it means that we – meaning we heathen astronomers – can discover which stars pulsate and how stars rotate, their distances and ages, how many planets they have – all sorts of goodies. We might even get a glimpse as to how the universe was created.'

'It'll be one of a kind,' commented the proprietor. 'Eighty-five mirrors, each one thirty-nine point five inches in diameter.' His eyes glowed and the woman rubbed her hands together.

'It'll be a beaut, all right. Do you know when it's supposed to be finished?' she asked the guy behind the counter.

'Sometime this year, they say,' he replied.

'Yeah, and how long have they been saying that?' The woman shook her head and stuck out her hand. 'Well, my art-major friend, forgive us for all this boring talk. My name is Georgia Eldridge. I'm here for the summer, studying the stars, passing the time toward the light-years-away goal of achieving my doctorate.'

'Cady Maxwell. And my hand's kind of bunged up, so forgive me if I don't shake yours.'

'Jesus, what happened? A car run over it?' The woman took Cady's unbandaged, twisted hand in her own strong one.

'Something like that,' Cady mumbled. She really didn't want to get into it with a stranger.

Still, there was something about this woman that was so warm and likeable. Cady responded to her immediately because, the truth of the matter was, she missed her female friends. And, as long as she stayed on the ranch, she didn't know how she was supposed to meet others. 'Have you had lunch?' she asked.

'No, but I was just going to. Are you from around here?'

'Afraid not. I've only been here a couple of days.'

'Too bad. I was hoping you could recommend some little hole-in-the-wall place I hadn't tried. How about the Desert Rose? Have you been there?'

'No.'

'Me neither. Let's give it a whirl.'

'Sounds good,' said Cady. She felt as excited as a kid in a new school who'd just made her first friend.

Georgia proved to be a witty and amusing lady, completely relaxed in her own skin. She had not seen the television broadcast which featured Cady, explaining, 'I work at night,' but she was as interested in Cady's former occupation as Cady was in her work.

Cady didn't mention the assault or the threatening phone calls.

After lunch, Georgia insisted on taking Cady up to the observatory, although she protested. It made her feel guilty to go without Zach, but then he had told her that she was going to have to be responsible for her own entertainment, and it wasn't as if she were going to a Star Party without him or anything. Just a daylight tour. She'd come back, she promised herself, at night. With Zach.

The view from the top of Mount Locke was breathtaking. Cady stood, transfixed, as clouds dragged a rain curtain over a distant hill, then closer and closer, misting the peaks and valleys until cool raindrops swept over her upturned face and she ran, giggling, into the massive, white round building with Georgia.

Georgia turned out to be a capable and entertaining tour guide, explaining the purposes of the giant one hundred and seven inch telescope, and discussing the dire consequences of light pollution. She promised to see if she could squeeze Cady in on one of the public viewings for the larger of two telescopes, although the waiting list was months full.

At the souvenir shop, Cady bought a tee shirt with

179

the constellations upside-down on the chest, in glow-in-the-dark paint. She'd have fun wearing it in Zach's back yard. For Zach, she bought a couple of topographical maps of the mountains.

The afternoon was growing long, however, and Cady began to worry about Zach in earnest. After all, she had run out of the house without even leaving a note.

She tried to call him from a pay phone but there was no answer, and it had never occurred to her to ask for the number of the cellular phone in the pickup. She tried information, but the number was unlisted.

On the way down the mountain from the observatory, Cady grew confused and took a wrong turn. It took an hour – and one of the topographical maps – for her to get turned around and headed in the right direction. Even then, she was unfamiliar with mountain driving, nervous at every twist and turn in the road, distracted by the little white crosses that cropped up from time to time, bewildered by look-alike landmarks.

And of course, there was no place to stop and ask.

Night falls rapidly in the mountains, and Cady was already driving with her headlights on when she finally caught sight of Zach's distinctive red mailbox, jutting crookedly at the corner of his gravel road and the highway. She almost cried with relief. She was hungry, too, and her hand hurt.

She remembered to collect the mail. A handwritten note from the mail carrier told Zach that there was a package waiting for him at the post office. This frustrated Cady. If she'd known that, she'd have collected it when she was in town.

The house was dark.

Cady pulled up next to another car and bit her lip. It belonged to the Sheriff.

Cady got out of her car. The slate-blue twilight silence, coupled with the vacant look of the house, was unnerving. She looked around, and thought she caught a glow from the direction of the barn. She headed that way, hurrying a little, beginning to jog. Had something happened to Zach?

A thousand fears tumbled through her mind as she broke into a run. *That nut that was following her. He had shot Zach or something.* Stumbling a little, she rounded the corrals and raced into the barn, panting, trying not to cry.

She saw Zach first, standing tall, his hat pushed back on his head, his face contorted with rage.

Struggling to catch her breath, she stopped.

With a voice quiet as death, he said, 'Where the hell have you been?'

Slowly, she approached him and looked up into his eyes.

There was nothing there.

Chapter Eighteen

'I went into town. I – you said for me to make my own entertainment,' she stammered, smiling feebly up at him, feeling like a kid in trouble with Daddy.

'You couldn't be bothered to let anybody know where you were going? We've all been worried sick. True's been out on horseback all afternoon, lookin' for you.'

'I'm sorry.' Cady's face burned hot from the unexpected scolding. 'I called, but . . .'

His face was hard as cold granite. 'I called here at nine-thirty this morning, and there was no answer. When you still didn't answer after a couple of hours, I came home early for dinner, and there was no sign of you. All afternoon long, we worried that somehow that creep had gotten hold of you. I even called Dub, here.'

She glanced at the other man. He had a play-dough face and an iron-gray, Army-issue haircut. There was a little paunch over his belt buckle. His only uniform was the sheriff's badge pinned to his plaid Western shirt pocket.

'Dub Garner,' he said, extending a hand.

'Nice to meet you,' she mumbled. 'I would shake your hand, but . . .'

He smiled. 'Well, I was a damn fool to fergit about that. I saw you on TV. You're more than welcome in our little community.' He turned to Zach, his voice easy, as if he hadn't noticed the other man's barely concealed fury. 'I'll be goin' on now, Zach. I'm jist real glad she's all right.' He headed for the barn door, then turned back to Cady. 'You have any more trouble with that stalker feller, you jist let us know. Anythang we can do, we'd be glad to.'

'Thank you, Sheriff Garner,' she said. 'I appreciate that.' Cady hadn't expected professional respect this far from home, and she was grateful for it.

'You better call me Dub, or else I won't know who you're talkin' to.' He grinned at her, nodded at Zach, and left.

The barn was quiet until they heard the growl of his car and the scramble of the dogs in hot pursuit of it down the ranch road. Zach turned away from her, his back stiff as an icicle.

She touched his arm. 'I didn't mean to worry you guys, Zach. I just . . . I got another call this morning.'

He turned and stared at her. 'What'd he say this time?'

'He said, "You look really good in your blue shirt," or something like that.'

'Is that all?'

'*Is that all?* Zach, how could he tell what I was wearing?'

'Lucky guess.'

'Oh, please.' Cady was becoming angry now. 'The little worm's been following me, I know it. He had to know that I just bought these shirts.'

'Oh, I see. So the smartest thing to do is leave the house, *alone*?' He glowered down at her from the benefit of his height plus cowboy boots.

184

Cady wanted to hit him. She put her hands on her hips and glared back. 'I *figured* he couldn't exactly have watched me get dressed, right? So he couldn't have been watching me while I was on the phone. Ergo, I could leave the house and not have to worry about being followed.'

He locked her gaze for a long moment. '*Ergo?*'

She pursed her lips, trying valiantly not to break into a grin.

'Cady, I hate to tell you this, but nobody actually says "ergo".'

She clenched her teeth. 'Some people do.'

'Nope. Nobody does.' The lines in his face had relaxed and there was a twinkle in his eyes.

That did it. She broke out laughing, and so did he. He threw his hands up in the air. 'I love a woman's logic. Let me see if I've got this straight. "The cat's not watching the mouse, so the mouse is free to play?" '

'Something like that.'

'I admire you for being independent, Cady-did, but you're not all alone anymore. You're surrounded by people who care about you.' He paused. 'Just stop and think next time about, you know . . . about those people.'

'I will,' she said. 'It's true that I'm not used to thinking about anybody but myself.' Cady hated to admit to herself how relieved she was that Zach was no longer angry. Having the full force of his temper aimed at her was a frightening thing. It wasn't that she feared he might hurt her . . . It was more that she feared he might not love her anymore.

It was a stark realization. For a moment, Cady's thought processes were scrambled by it. *He's never*

185

said he loves you, she thought. In that same moment she knew, no matter whether he did or not, the truth was that she very definitely loved him.

It was a simple truth, but it was the most potent truth of her life.

She wasn't ready for it!

For one thing, she hated for him to have that kind of power over her.

'Earth to Cady.'

She returned his gaze. 'I'm sorry. What?'

'I said, tell me what you did today.' Picking up a bridle that needed mending, he sat on the edge of a hay bale and began fiddling with it.

She told him in animated gestures about meeting Georgia, and about visiting the observatory.

'I'm so glad you're making friends,' he said warmly. 'I want you to be happy here.'

A little thrill sliced through her stomach.

He lowered the bridle and caught her gaze. 'Do you think you can be?'

'What?'

'Happy here?' His eyes were shadowed beneath the brim of his hat under the barn's warm yellow lights.

Cady walked over to the hay bale and dropped to her knees in front of Zach. She put the twisted palm of her right hand against his warm cheek and whispered, 'More than I ever dreamed possible.'

The bridle fell to the straw-laden floor. He took her in his arms, his hand pressing her buttocks into the V of his crotch. She entwined her arms around his neck, and he lowered her to the musty, dusty, hay-scratchy floor beside the horsy-smelling bridle, in a dark little cave between hay bales.

The sound of spurs jingling and the clop-*clop*, clop-*clop* of a tired horse walking froze them. Cady struggled to get up but Zach held her firm, signaling her to be quiet.

'Ole Buck, it's been a long day, ain't it?' came True's rusty old drawl. 'I'd best go roust Zacharia and see what he knows 'bout the young lady.'

There was a slippery sound of a saddle and saddle blanket sliding from a horse, then a rattle as True removed the bridle. Cady started to giggle and Zach covered her mouth with a long, liquid kiss.

The *scoop* of a coffee can being plunged into a sack of oats sounded dangerously close to Cady's head. Zach responded by gently easing his hand down the front of her jeans. She caught her breath, heart pounding, frustrated at herself for not being more forceful at fending him off, but hopelessly aroused nevertheless. Then they heard the *pat-pat* of True slapping his horse's rear in an affectionate gesture of thanks, and the receding jingle of his spurs.

'We've got to go,' Cady whispered weakly. 'He's headed toward the house. He'll be worried.'

'He'll see your car. He'll figure it out.'

'*Zach!*' Her outrage didn't sound very convincing, not even to her.

He pressed his bulging jeans firmly against her, pulling her tight with one strong arm. The barn was shadowy and secluded and smelled of animals and leather and time and mystery.

That was all Cady was aware of, except for Zach's hands and mouth and body. She wanted to be a part of him – that was all she knew.

All she wanted to know.

* * *

In those early days of our love, I felt as if I'd taken a long cool drink from some magic potion. I was positively drunk from the headiness of it all: her scent, the sound of her voice, her touch, the funny little way she had of quirking one eyebrow when you said something droll.

Everything, it seemed, was a discovery to her; she had that awesome sense of wonder that makes you feel like a benevolent parent, showing a child something for the first time.

Since I was able to see her so much, I cut way down on the phone calls. But you can't be with a person every single minute of the day, so I'd call when we were apart, just to make sure she was all right. And to check and see if anyone else was with her.

When she bought the answering machine it was more difficult to get hold of her. If she left it on I'd just hang up. I hate those things.

I loved talking with her, but still, there was this great big part of myself that I could never share with her. Could never share with anyone. (WILL never share with anyone.)

So of course, I could never truly be myself. So many times I was tempted to break down and tell her – show her – everything, but I couldn't. She was still terrified of the person she thought of as a 'stalker'. I was afraid that if she knew it was me, she would get angry. I hated for her to be mad at me. I'd try to tease her into a laugh, which wasn't hard.

I should have known that it would be no time before she'd turn that vicious laugh on me.

She's not laughing now, though.

* * *

Cady had been living in Zach's house, and sleeping in his bed, for about a week before her innate sense of order drove her to begin straightening the place up. Keenly aware of her own sense of personal space, she hesitated to do anything that would make the man feel invaded. But surely, she hoped, he would not mind if she threw away that sock with the big hole in the toe. And put all the scattered tools and nails and related things into a tool box on the back porch. And cleaned out a cabinet to hold all the different plastic storage bowls. And put the horse-shot syringes and cow antibiotic salves and other medicines in a box marked, 'Veterinary Supply'. And threw away obviously unusable computer print-out sheets and placed the others in marked files.

Far from being angry, he was delighted with the results. 'This place hasn't looked so good since Mom was alive,' he said one evening, his eyes shining.

That was all Cady needed to hear. She attacked the clutter with a vengeance. There was one room Zach requested that she leave alone, and she was happy to do so. For the time being, anyway.

At times, she could hear her mother saying, *Lord, child! What have I done? Raised a hausfrau? Look at you cleaning and cooking. Where did I go wrong?*

It was ironic, she'd reflect as she rubbed oak bannisters with Old English furniture polish, that the daughter of one of the country's pre-eminent feminists would wind up cooking and cleaning for some cowboy out on a ranch in the middle of nowhere.

But she had never in her life been happier.

In spite of the pain, she used her right hand as

often as possible and, whenever she found herself sitting down for any reason, the small red ball was in her hand. She would knead and squeeze it until her poor knuckles turned blue, or until Zach gently pried it away.

He had bought an answering machine to screen phone calls and made sure that she could reach him or somebody else at all times. With the advent of the machine, the caller seldom said anything but, at the end of each day, the tape was full of hang-up calls.

It was a blot on an otherwise idyllic existence. There was so much to learn! Even riding horseback, which looked so easy when Zach did it, became something of a nightmare for Cady as she struggled to remember all the key points: squeeze with your knees, keep your heels down, sit straight in the saddle, hold the reins low, don't saw on the bit, and never feed a horse ice, as it causes colic. (She learned that the hard way.)

On some days, Zach would take her out with him while he rode a fenceline or looked for a lost calf. Fortunately for her, when riding Western, reins are held in the left hand (to free the other for roping, Zach said), and though she bounced around more than she would have liked, and lived in fear when the trail went up or down too dramatically, she cherished those days of warm buttery sunlight, cool mountain hair-fluffing wind, and the feeling that only riding horseback can give – utter freedom and kingly delight.

Once, they came upon a small pond upon which floated a small flotilla of ducks. Sitting horseback side by side at the top of a rise which sloped down to the water, they gazed for a moment, then Zach dismounted and skipped a small rock into the center

of the pond. More curious than frightened, the ducks
all swam of one accord toward the *plunk* in the water.
It looked like a mass boat race to Cady, as each duck
left a tiny V-shaped wake in the water behind him.
Scores of little Vs moved across the water, capped by
black and white dots.

The dogs romped along the shoreline, while huge
late-summer storm-clouds snagged distant mountain
peaks. A second rock seemed to sound an alarm, and
in unison the ducks rose like an enormous animal,
graceful and full of life, to circle above them and
disappear in a sweeping arc.

Moments like that made Cady's heart ache.

Though Zach didn't expect it every day, Cady took
to cooking a big dinner for the men on the days when
they had to be up especially early and work
particularly hard. They'd spill into the back door in
their sock feet, hang their hats on the rack, wash up
dutifully, and eat like horses at the trough.

Afterward, they'd all sit around Zach's dining table
(which had miraculously emerged from beneath the
blankets of computer read-outs), and swap stories on
one another. Nobody could tell a tall tale better than
old True. One of a vanishing breed – the old-time
cowboy who remembered driving the cattle to the rail-
head back when a day's pay was a dollar ('And boy, if
you had a dollar, you had money. Even if you had a
quarter, you wasn't broke.') – True would entertain
them until their faces were sore from laughing.

Afterwards, the men would stretch out all over the
living room like frat rats after a party, and sleep like
the dead for a brief while, before going back out into
the long day.

On those days, Cady made a real effort to overcome her instinctive dislike of Joe Fenton. She would talk and laugh with him like she did the others, and would even visit with him out in the barn sometimes when Zach had to be away. He seemed nice enough, even deferential, but his eyes told a different story to his surface conversation and country manners.

There was something predatory about his eyes that reminded Cady very strongly of every criminal she'd ever drawn. She was always careful not to become too familiar around him, and she never stood with her back to a wall.

The quiet evenings were Cady's favorite time of day. She'd heat up leftovers from dinner, or Zach would cook thick juicy steaks out back over a mesquite fire in a pit he'd dug, Indian-style. They would talk quietly as the day drew to a close. Sometimes they would make love on a quilt beneath the star-canopied sky.

Gradually the house, under Cady's loving care, took on a sheen and a glow. It began to feel more like Cady's home, and when Georgia dropped in one afternoon for a visit, Cady was proud to show it off.

'Good news, I think,' Georgia announced, rocker creaking on the front porch as she swigged her ice tea. 'My fellowship's been extended so that I can study the stars through the winter. So you'll be stuck with me a while longer.'

Cady was so thrilled she felt a lump in her throat. She'd become very close to her friend in the weeks since she'd arrived, and she'd been dreading Georgia's move.

'You're just about my only woman friend out here,'

Cady told her. 'I don't know what I'll do when you do leave.'

Georgia considered this. 'Do you ever get lonely out here?'

'Sometimes. I think if I had a "town job", I'd have more opportunities to make friends. One thing I'm learning about small towns is that their activities are centered upon children and the church. Of course, Zach and I don't have any kids, and neither of us is a regular church-goer, so it's hard.'

'The rodeoers hang out together.'

'Yeah. And the stock show people. And 4-H and Future Farmers – again, you gotta have kids!' She smiled.

'This must have been a pretty big adjustment for you.' Georgia sipped her tea and leaned back, watching the breeze toy with a ceramic wind chime Cady had hung on the veranda. It made a joyous, soothing sound.

'You know what's the hardest?'

'What?'

'The *traffic*!'

Georgia cocked an eyebrow at her. 'What are you talking about? There isn't any!'

'I know. That's the problem. People drive so *slooow* all the time. I'll come up on their bumper you know, and curse them, and then I'll think, "Hey, what's your hurry? You can drive from one end of the town to the other in five minutes!"'

'I know. And doesn't it blow your mind when you cash a check here?'

'You're not kidding! I keep hauling out all my credit cards and ID, and they stare at me and say, "I know you. You're going with Zach. I guess we can find you if we need you."'

'The distances drive me crazy sometimes. And if you don't have a satellite dish, forget it! TV is out of the question.'

Cady nodded. It felt good to have someone to talk to about her myriad adjustments. She never said anything to Zach because she didn't want to make him feel bad or worry him.

'Have you gotten to know very many of the local people?' asked Georgia, fishing ice out of her glass with her fingers.

Cady nodded. 'Some of them. They are kind and generous and honest, but . . .' She hesitated.

'Spit it out. I won't tell Daddy.'

Cady made a face at her friend. 'It's just that, well, those folks who were born and raised here, and whose parents were born and raised here, and who've never done much traveling – maybe they went off to Sul Ross or someplace not too terribly far away to college and then came right back – well, they strike me as . . . sheltered.'

Georgia nodded. 'I know what you mean. They can be so naive, and if they don't watch the news or keep up on current events, they can be so *limited*. Drives me crazy. I could never stay here, you know. Not when my research is done.'

'On the other hand,' said Cady, 'there are some folks who have come from the Big City, so to speak, like me, because they'd had enough of it all, you know? They're here because they want to be here. I'd like to get to know some of them better.' She stretched out her legs and crossed her ankles.

In spite of the adjustments, Cady found that something deep within her soul responded to the spirit of the mountains and the ranching life. The solitude and hard work and outdoors were good for her. And, without the distractions that city living can bring, she and Zach had grown more interdependent. Zach, of course, had friends but ranching was exhausting, all-day, week-round work, and Cady found that usually he was too tired to socialize on weekends, which suited her fine. She hadn't grown tired of his company yet. If anything, he was a constant surprise.

One evening, he hopped around like a little kid in the kitchen and said, 'Well, I guess you're all caught up with the house now. And I see your hand is really improving.'

'What do you mean, "all caught up"?' she teased, voice dripping with suspicion. 'It sounds like you let the house get trashed because you knew I'd soon be here to clean up for you, Oh Great One.' She genuflected before him.

'No groveling, please. Just throw money.'

She punched his arm with her good hand. Grinning like a mischievous kid who's just waiting for the preacher to discover the frogs, Zach took her elbow and steered her upstairs. 'Remember that room I asked you to leave alone?'

'And I was only too happy to do it, you slob.'

'Good. 'Cause you're not the only one who can organize things.' With a triumphant sweep of his arm, Zach flung open the door to a room at the end of the upstairs hall and snapped on the light.

Cady stood in the open doorway, mouth agape.

It was all here. All her things, lovingly arranged:

her easel standing near a northern dormer window, a table nearby stacked with all her art supplies, as well as some new things. Shelves held all her books on forensics and anatomy and drawing and criminal analysis. Her CD player rested on a bureau, with all her CDs lined neatly next to it. Even her mother's shadow-box hung prominently on the wall.

Just like Virginia Woolf had written: it was a room of her own, down to the last loving detail.

She was speechless.

'I had help,' said Zach, his words hurrying after each other. 'Your friend from the DPD, Elaine Martinez, sent me all the stuff from your office, and the lady who's renting your apartment now sent me the rest.' He stared at her silent form nervously. 'I've been watching you work that hand. I know you can draw again, Cady. I'm sure of it. And you don't have to do criminals! You can draw anything you want!'

Still she stood.

'You said once that you always wanted to do a children's book. You can write an animal story. We've got some good ones going on right in our own back yard.'

The words bumped into each other and stumbled to a halt.

Moving slowly, oh so slowly, Cady stepped into the room. She touched the virginal sketch pad which was propped on the easel with a shaking, knuckle-gnarled right hand. Removing the lid from a brand-new box of oil pastels, she put them close to her face and inhaled deeply of their clean, cool, unused scent. She picked up a mayonnaise jar from which sprouted dozens of sharpened pencils in every rainbow hue.

Like seeds planted deep in the rich earth, the room burst with the fertile ova of a thousand undrawn pictures, their colors stored in the pencils and pastels and paints like unknown gene patterns, just waiting to be birthed and nurtured into life.

By the hand of Cady Maxwell.

She turned to him, her face never more raw or vulnerable. 'But what if I can't?' she said, her words settling like dust on the muted rug at her feet. It was a struggle, getting the words out over the tennis ball in her throat.

'That's a decision you'll have to make,' he said quietly.

'Decision? What are you talking about? The doctors said I'd never draw again. What if my hand just won't do it?'

'The decision's not in your hand, Cady-did.' His voice was infinitely gentle and patient. 'It's in your head.'

She bit her lip.

'I've known quadraplegic artists who paint with their tongues,' he said. 'In the prison camps, they said we weren't to speak to each other. But we communicated all up and down the cells, to every prisoner.'

Zach didn't talk much about those days. Cady said, 'How?'

He reached over to the bureau and rapped sharply on it with his knuckles. Quickly Cady could tell a brief separation between each set of knuckle-raps.

'It's a code,' he explained. 'Based on a grid. Has to do with which number on the grid a letter appears.'

'How did the new guys learn the code, if you couldn't talk?'

'Lots of bleeding knuckles. Long hours on the wall.' He shrugged as though it were no big deal.

'And you still remember it?'

'The brain never forgets some things.'

She hesitated. 'What did you say just now?'

' "God bless you. See you later." It was the standard way we ended all communications.'

'Would you show it to me?' asked Cady.

This time Zach hesitated. 'Sure.' He picked up a black pencil and drew the grid on the sketch pad. 'See, it's easy really.'

'But it would take such a long time!'

'We used abbreviations whenever possible. Like that last message. I didn't spell out the words. I tapped, GBU CUL.' He gave her a wry grin. 'And anyway, it's not like we had anywhere else to go or anything else to do.'

She laughed, and the laugh caught in her throat. Zach was watching her. It was as if he had said, *It's not like you have anywhere else to go or anything else to do.*

Her palms were sweaty and she wiped them on her jeans. 'I was enjoying playing Susie Homemaker,' she mumbled.

'I know. But Cady-did, I didn't bring you out here so you could hide from yourself.'

'But I was really enjoying fixing up this wonderful old house!' She sighed.

'I know you were. And that's a part of you. A very lovable part as far as a man is concerned, I might add. But it's not the *whole* part.'

'That other part's dead,' she said stubbornly.

'That's your decision.'

'I wish you'd stop saying that!' She turned from the blue laser beam of his gaze and wandered over to the bookshelves, looking over the familiar titles, feeling that old nagging curiosity stirring within her again.

She didn't *want* to feel it! Not yet, anyway. But Zach was right. She was beginning to get "caught up" with the house. It was only a matter of time before the restlessness set in.

She shook her head and shot a sideways glance at him. 'You sure snookered me,' she said, using a favorite Trueism.

He grinned. 'Wasn't easy, either. I had to run you off to Alpine for groceries just to get the chance.'

'This is the greatest thing anybody's ever done for me, you know.'

'I know.' The smile spread.

Heart thumping, glancing first at her mother's shadow-box for courage, she blurted, 'So I guess there's nothing left to do but marry you.'

The smile vanished. 'What?'

Her ears began to ring. 'Well, I mean there's nothing else I can do with a guy who's so perfect for me, *but* marry him.' She stared at her feet, her mouth so dry she knew she'd never get out another word until he spoke.

In two steps, he'd crossed the room and taken her face between both his big, hard hands, his touch soft as a baby's.

'God, I love women's lib,' he said.

The ceremony was quick and easy, done at the courthouse in the Justice of the Peace's office, just one month after Cady's first tremulous night on the ranch. True stood in as a witness with the dog, Hank, looking on.

They decided to wait until winter and take a skiing honeymoon at New Mexico's Angel Fire. But they spent the night in one of the calico-quaint historic rooms at the Limpia Hotel. The owners hosted a small reception of Zach's closest friends and relatives and Georgia. They all toasted the newlyweds with champagne and got the word out on the grapevine, so that by the time Zach and Cady got home, they were swamped with well-wishers dropping by and calling and bringing casseroles and scolding Zach for keeping Cady such a good secret and for not having a big public wedding.

Even the obsessive caller seemed to back off for a while, as if giving Cady a break. Almost like a wedding gift.

For the first couple of blissful weeks, Cady's 'room' stayed pretty much as she'd found it. She wasn't quite 'caught up' with the house yet. (Or so she told herself.)

There was the still little matter of Zach's 'treasures'.

Every time he went out horseback or did any work on the ranch, he would bring home some little 'treasure' he'd found: a piece of rusty antique barbed wire, an Indian arrowhead, a chunk of petrified wood, a rattlesnake rattle, or just some pioneer discard that had worked its way up through several layers of soil.

Most of Zach's treasures were scattered over the house. Cady collected them and put them in a large cardboard box, but she wasn't too happy with that arrangement and made her way upstairs one day to the dust-choked, airless, spidery attic to see if she might find a trunk or something better in which to store them.

The attic turned out to be a treasure trove of its own, stuffed with relics of three generations of Ralstons, and Cady spent a whole sneezy, crawly morning up there, rooting through old photo albums and scrapbooks and high-school yearbooks and wedding books.

It was a luscious late-July day, ideal for attic-exploring. July was the Davis Mountain rainy season and outside, brooding clouds hugged close, mumbling thunder to one another and plunging the attic into a gray watery light of shadow and gloom.

Crouched close to the single window, Cady thumbed through one photo book after another. There was Zach at his first wedding, an impossibly skinny, Adam's-appled kid, really. The girl was pretty with her stiff, lacquered sixties beehive and Cleopatra eyes. They both looked like actors in a play that closed too soon.

Feeling like a guilty voyeur, Cady snuck glances at her watch and hurried through every single picture she could find. Thunder crawled closer and rattled the window glass.

Pictures of Wife Number Two were hard to come by. Apparently, one church wedding had been enough for Zach.

She did turn up one snapshot of him – a million years older than he'd been with his first wife – standing in front of the house with his arm around a petite, blonde who was also very pretty. Neither of them were smiling and Cady wondered if they'd ever really been happy.

She couldn't imagine that Zach had ever been as

happy with anyone else as he seemed to be with her.

She didn't want to think about it. She was jealous of the thought of any other woman in Zach's arms, even if it was fifteen years before Cady came along. A cloud scooted too close and clapped loudly at her ear. She jumped.

Rooting through some old, mouse-gnawed sweaters, dirty sweat dripping off her nose in the muggy room, Cady turned up a framed studio portrait which looked as though it had been Zach's second wife's high-school senior picture. It had that kind of youthful, posed look about it.

There was a crack in the glass, extending from one corner of the photograph all the way to the other, as if a line had been drawn right through her face. Cady couldn't help but wonder what would drive a young wife to disappear from her husband's life without a word. She must have been very bitter about something, Cady mused. Perhaps Zach was still drinking in those days, working through his own demons.

It was getting late. Premature darkness had set in with the impending storm. Zach would be home soon and Cady didn't want to be caught rooting through his past. Although it was true that she was a natural-born snoop, it wasn't exactly necessary that Zach know every single little thing about her, was it?

Wind soughed through nearby trees and creaked heavily against the roof rafters overhead. A few raindrops scattered across the window, dappling Cady's light.

Suddenly she noticed a battered, green Army trunk set over against one wall, almost lost under a towering pile of old clothes. Shoving off the clothes, Cady frowned at the padlock but grinned when she saw that it was not fastened. She pulled it off and the lid of the trunk fell over with a filthy *thud*.

To her delight, she found that the top tray had been filled with more of Zach's treasures, including a collection of antique medicine bottles that Cady instinctively knew could be quite valuable. She would clean them up, she decided, fill them with colored water and line them up in the kitchen window for the sun to shine through.

She lifted the top tray and placed it carefully on the floor beside the trunk. Rain hit the window in sudden, intrusive sheets, dousing the attic with a creepy chill. Cady shivered.

Then, as she glanced back into the murky depths of the trunk, her heart stood still.

Nestled in an old college sweatshirt, almost hidden in its faded folds, its dome glowing ghostly in the dim light, rested a human skull.

PART III

'Love cannot be much stronger than the lust to kill.'
Sigmund Freud

'No human being can give orders to love.'
George Sand

Chapter Nineteen

A cold trickle traced its way down the back of Cady's neck. Unconsciously, she glanced up to see if there might be a leak in the old roof, but the drizzle did not come from without, it came from within.

It was fear.

Cady had cradled many a human skull in her hands, but usually they had been withdrawn from heavy, meticulously packed boxes, usually marked, 'Medical Examiner's Office'.

She shivered.

Then, slowly, her own professional curiosity began to thaw the freeze and she reached in carefully with both hands, taking the skull gently by either side, and lifting it from the trunk.

Thunder beat against the window. Cady jumped, but she did not drop the skull.

She was moving in a sort of double exposure. There was the human part of her that recoiled from the find, wanted to trust that its presence here in this attic was entirely innocent, wanted, even, to slam down the trunk's lid and be done with it. Then, overlaying that, was the professional part of her that was dying to read the secrets every skull had to tell.

First, it was well bleached. This told her that the skull had lain out in the sun for a considerable period of time before being discovered, ostensibly by Zach.

Cradling the skull in her lap, she ran her hands butterfly-soft over the smooth, short brow ridges, then gently stroked the small mastoid processes – the pyramid-shaped promontories that projected behind each ear.

That gave her some idea as to—

'Ohhhh Cady-did, my love! It's a *grrreat* day for a nooner!'

Zach was home! His voice, full of teasing, drifted up to her from the kitchen far below. Could it be lunchtime already? At first, she didn't move, the skull still cradled in her hands while the truth took a moment to sink in. Gusts of rain sheeted the window.

'Where *arrrrrre* you?' He had bounded up the stairs and was searching for her in the bedrooms.

Hurriedly, she placed the skull back into the trunk and closed it. Then she sprang to her feet and inched her way as quickly as possible through the dusty clutter.

'Could I be disturbing the great artist at work?' He was entering Cady's studio.

'Cady! Where'd you go?'

Humidity had caused the small attic door to stick. Cady had to yank, and it squawked across the old warped floor. She ducked under it and tripped down the short, narrow stairway.

'There you are!' Zach turned from the door to Cady's studio.

She dusted at her jeans and attempted a smile. The double-exposure had not faded and she was confused.

'I *missed* you!' he said, sweeping her up in his arms. 'And I just *looove* a rainy day.' He kissed her with passion.

All she could see, behind her closed eyes, was the skull.

Zach pulled her shirt from the waistband of her jeans and cupped her breasts in hot hands. Then he took the shirt in both hands and ripped apart the pearl snaps. Cady gasped.

'I'm hungry for you, woman,' he murmured, kissing the pulse at her throat.

Her heart was pounding. Any other time, she'd have been plucking at his clothes as well, but something in her couldn't seem to respond.

The skull. It wouldn't go away.

He was unzipping her jeans and plunging his hand between her legs.

She flinched.

He knelt before her, cupped her buttocks in his hard hands, and buried his face in her soft furriness, his tongue probing hot and deep.

She groaned. The skull began to slip away. She tangled her hands in his thick hair.

He got to his feet, swept her up in his arms like a rag doll, and carried her into the bedroom.

It was a hard mountain late-summer rain. Waves of it drummed against the windows of Zach's muted, shadowy bedroom. (She still thought of it as Zach's room.) Gusts of wind alternately roared and whistled and blended with Zach's gentle snoring as he lay sprawled beside her in the big bed.

She could not sleep. The skull was back.

It whispered to her. *Let me tell you my secrets*, it said. It tugged and nagged at her and she could not sleep.

Finally, she slipped from beside her slumbering husband and tiptoed from the room, clutching her clothes to her like a prison escapee. Once out in the hall, she threw on her shirt and shoved her feet back into her jeans. In sock feet, she skulked back up the stairway to the attic and shoved open the little door, cringing at the loud *scrape* it made in protest.

For a long moment she poised, breath held, waiting to see if Zach got up.

This is silly, she told herself. *What am I hiding? Why don't I just ask Zach about the skull?*

Why indeed?

Okay, she thought. *I'll ask him. Later.*

Briefly, as she made her way back to the trunk, she wondered if he had somehow sneaked the skull back from the war, as some sort of macabre souvenir.

Considering what he had been through, and his state of mind at the time, she could almost understand such bizarre behavior.

She settled herself cross-legged on the floor in front of the trunk. Rain thundered against the roof, directly overhead. The storm sounded so much nearer here.

But her attention was already focused on the skull. Turning it about in her hands, Cady checked the teeth, which showed very few signs of wear. All the molars had erupted as well.

Cady's mind was racing. She thought she could hear the whispers of the skull's secrets herself, but she was not a forensic anthropologist, after all. She would have to refer to some of her books, and even then, she'd be operating on a best-guess basis.

'What are you doing up here?'

Lightning-jolts of shock needled through Cady's

body. She had not heard Zach climbing the steps to the attic. She glanced over her shoulder at him. He was stooping in the short doorway, bafflement etched on his sleepy face.

A thunderous blast of wind groaned through the rafters.

Zach's gaze dropped to the open trunk before Cady. He couldn't see the skull in her lap, but she saw him glance at the upper tray sitting beside the trunk. An expression she couldn't read flickered across his face, and it chilled her.

He came into the attic and stood, clad only in a pair of unbuttoned jeans. His chest and arms were an odd milky-white. The ruddy brown-red of his face made a V at the shirt-line of his neck and emerged again at the wrists. His large, veined hands were also tanned. Without his hat, his forehead was pale, and it gave him a boyish, vulnerable appearance. His head poked above one of the crossbeams of the attic and he had to duck under it to cross over to where Cady sat, still holding the skull in her hands like a nasty little secret.

'What are you doing, messing with my stuff?' he asked.

'I'm s-sorry. I was looking for . . . a place to store some things.'

'You could have asked me, you know.' His voice was brittle.

She took her bottom lip between her teeth. Thunder rumbled in the distance and the monotonous pounding of the rain seemed to slacken off somewhat.

Zach squatted beside her and leaned back on his bare heels. Gesturing toward the skull, he said, 'I see

211

you found ol' Apache Dan, there.'

'Apache Dan?'

'Well, that's what I call him, anyway. It's probably not politically correct or anything.'

She glanced at the skull in her lap and moved her thumbs over the short, smooth brow ridges. 'Where did you . . . get it?' she asked.

'It was after a big rain like this. I was out fixing water gaps and—'

'What's a water gap?'

'It's a fenceline that crosses a creek. In low water, the cattle could wander into the next pasture without it. After a rain like this, though, high water clogs it full of debris and sometimes breaks it. So when the rain lets up, you've got to go check water gaps.'

'Oh.'

'And ol' Apache Dan, here, turns up. I call him that because I figured he was a very old Indian skull. Maybe the creek washed through a shallow grave or something. The Southwest is checkered with them.'

'But you kept it!'

'Sure. Why not?'

'Well . . . don't you think we should tell the authorities? Maybe try and get it identified?'

'Nobody's going to identify a hundred-year-old skull, Cady.'

'But wouldn't the Indians want it back, so they could give it a proper burial?'

He made a snorting noise. 'You wanna open that can of worms? I mean, can you imagine the mess it would be? The Department of the Interior would claim it and then the state of Texas would claim it and then some museum would want it and then the Apache nation would pitch a fit and then along would come the Comanches . . . Forget it. He's fine right where he is. I pulled him out of my water gap on my creek. That makes him mine.' He grabbed the skull one-handed from Cady's careful grasp and tossed it into the trunk.

She flinched as if she'd been struck.

'Let's get some grub, woman. I'm starved.' Zach replaced the tray in the top of the trunk and closed it with masculine finality. He headed for the door.

Cady remained where she was. Something wasn't right about Zach's story. Something wasn't right, but she couldn't put her finger on what it was. She frowned.

'Are you coming?' It was a question, phrased like a command.

'Yeah,' she said slowly. 'I'm coming. You go on.' She caught his eye. His look said, *Keep the hell out of my stuff*, but he said nothing. After a brief hesitation, he ducked beneath the doorway and headed down the steps.

There was one thing she had to check. Just one thing. It had caught her eye in the flutter of an eyelash, and she just had to take one more look.

Hurriedly, she crouched before the trunk, opened it, and quietly laid the top tray on the floor.

The wind set up a mournful howl outside the single high attic window. It was there. Something she didn't want to see. Something she didn't want to face. Something that would change everything.

She started to put the skull back into the trunk. After all, Zach was waiting for her. He didn't really want her snooping around in his things – she could understand that, couldn't she?

But although she may be no expert in sexing and aging and attributing race, there was one irrefutable fact that Cady knew.

Drawn, almost helplessly, back to the skull, Cady took one more close look at the incisors.

And there it was. No bigger than the head of a straight pin, but there it was.

A filling.

Of one thing forensic anthropologists could be certain: Native Americans who lived a hundred years ago did not get their cavities filled at the dentist's office.

Chapter Twenty

The rain seemed to have passed, leaving the air oppressive and muggy. More storms were probably on the way. Cady felt a little cloudy herself as she replaced the skull in the trunk and closed the lid. Feeling suddenly old beyond her years, she pushed herself to her feet and shuffled wearily toward the attic door.

Nothing had changed, and yet everything had.

Briefly she wondered what would have happened if she had not had her own particular expertise, if she had not known the proper way to examine a skull. Would she have simply accepted Zach's explanation and left the mystery unsolved?

Probably.

But – in the twinkle of a tooth filling – her own knowledge had intruded into their lives and Cady knew that nothing was going to be quite the same again. This was not going to be a matter for a museum or the Department of the Interior or the Bureau of Indian Affairs or whatever to haggle over.

If only it could be that simple.

The presence of the dental filling brought the matter into the latter twentieth century in a hollow rush of years, slam-dunking the inevitable truth: this would now have to be a death investigation. In fact, the body may not have come from a shallow grave at all.

It could have been dumped.

Wait, she thought. *Don't jump to conclusions. A death investigation is not necessarily a murder investigation. This person could have died of natural causes and the body decomposed where it lay.*

Sure. It could hyaaapen.

She walked slowly down the stairs to the bottom floor, trailing her hand along the bannisters.

There was something else.

The matter of that other little, niggling worry, gnawing away at the back of her mind.

She didn't want to think about it.

Cady lingered in the living room a moment. She could hear Zach in the kitchen, opening and closing the refrigerator door, whistling softly to himself. She felt a pressure in her chest, so constricting she had to take a deep breath, and even had trouble doing that.

Why are you so worried? she thought. *You don't know anything for sure. Let Sheriff Dub figure it out.*

But if it *was* a murder, then why was the body left *here*, on the ranch?

He found it in a water gap, she thought. Cady didn't really want to examine all the implications. After all, she'd found the skull – not lost in a mountain cave somewhere, but hidden in her husband's Army foot-locker.

She chewed her bottom lip. Something didn't feel right. Something so dark, so mysterious, that Cady didn't even want to *think* about it.

'Cady? What's wrong?' Zach stood close to her. 'You feel all right?'

She searched his eyes, then turned away. She

216

couldn't stand this. She sat heavily in a dining room chair. Staring at her hands on the glossy table, she blurted, 'Zach, I don't think it's an Indian skull.'

'What? What are you talking about?' He came into the room and stood, looking down at her. He was still holding a mayonnaise knife in his hand. The mayonnaise was globbed on, just the way he liked it. She looked away.

'I saw a filling in one of its teeth.' Her voice was dull, quiet. 'Such things don't exist in hundred-year-old Native American skulls.' She decided to say nothing about her fear that the skull might belong to a murder victim.

'You must be mistaken, Cady.' He gestured with the knife.

'No.' She studied the twisted configuration of her injured hand on the dining table. It was getting stronger, and hurting less, but it still looked like hell. Probably always would.

He turned and walked into the kitchen. She waited, and when he didn't say anything after a while, she got up and followed him. He was staring out the window over the kitchen sink, his half-made sandwich forgotten on the cabinet nearby. He did not look at her. 'So what are you saying?'

'I'm saying that, well, I think we need to turn it over to the sheriff.'

'Why?'

'So that he can begin a formal investigation.'

'I see.' He turned away from her. 'Is this absolutely necessary?'

'It's an unexplained death, Zach.'

'You mean it's unexplained to *you*.'

'What's that supposed to mean?' Her voice grew sharper.

He shrugged. 'Mountain streams sometimes take detours through the years. Flood through spots they hadn't touched before. So a grave was disturbed. Things like that happen. People out here mind their own business. It's not necessary to call in the cavalry.'

'Call in the— Zach! You can't believe that!'

He turned toward her. His eyes were cool, ice cool. 'Can. And do.' He gestured toward her hand. 'I told you you'd start to get restless. You just want an excuse to get back into the game.'

Her cheeks flushed hot. 'I do not!'

'Aw, c'mon Cady. You led an exciting life for a lot of years. There's nothing out here to compete with that. Now you've found your very own mystery. So go on! Call the Texas Rangers! Call CNN! Have a ball!' He threw the mayonnaise knife into the sink with a clatter.

'What are you talking about!' she shouted. 'You've got the head of a probable murder victim upstairs in your attic trunk and you want to hang on to it like some kind of souvenir?'

All color drained from Zach's face.

Shit! Cady thought. *How could I have said such a thing? How could I have lost my temper like that?*

'What do you mean, "the head of a murder victim"?' asked Zach, his voice so deadly still the words seemed to hang in the air between them like a spider web.

'Nothing,' she said. 'I just lost my temper. I didn't mean anything.'

'No. You meant something, all right. I just want to know what the hell it was.'

'Nothing,' she insisted. 'I just . . .' her words trailed away. The look on his face was frightening her. 'Zach, I didn't mean anything.' She reached out to touch his arm, but he drew it away as if her hand were electrified.

'Don't lie to me,' he said, so quietly she could barely hear the words. 'Don't you ever lie to me.'

She swallowed, trying to collect herself. Something had gone dreadfully wrong and she wanted so badly to make it right. 'I . . . I don't know that it's a murder victim's skull,' she said finally. 'I just thought it looked like it might be.'

'I see.'

'There are . . . ways you can tell.'

'I forget,' he said slowly, 'that you're the expert.'

She glanced away, miserable.

Abruptly, he brushed past her, heading for the door. She stood helplessly, watching him pull on his boots. What a glorious day they could have had together if only she had minded her own damn business! She hadn't opened that trunk looking for storage space; she'd opened it in order to snoop into Zach's past.

Just like Pandora.

'Don't you want your lunch?' she asked.

'I'm not hungry.' He shoved his hat on his head and reached for his duster. Once again, with the long, waterproof coat over his denim clothes, he looked like an old-time cowboy who'd just stepped in off the frontier.

Reaching for the screen door, he gave her a long, mystifying gaze, and said, 'You do whatever you want to, Cady. Build a shrine to the damn thing if you want.

I don't care.' He stepped out and the screen slapped shut behind him.

'Where are you going?' she cried.

'I'm going to check water gaps,' he said, and his boots thunked across the veranda, down the steps, and he was gone.

Chapter Twenty-One

Cady went so far as to look up the sheriff's number in the tiny four-town phone book that served Fort Davis.

Then she put the phone book back in the kitchen drawer.

Pacing from one end of the house to the other, she talked to herself. 'What if Zach's right?' she asked aloud. 'What if it's really no big deal? Maybe it's not even a murder victim at all. Could be it came from a disturbed grave in a small family plot somewhere — maybe even from miles away. Say the family hasn't even missed it. Wouldn't they be better off not knowing that the head of their loved one wound up tangled up in some rancher's water gap miles away?'

She climbed the stairs to the second floor and paced that hallway, still talking. 'So . . . let's say I did call the sheriff. What would he do? He'd call in the Texas Ranger who serves this district.

'And what would the Texas Ranger do?' she asked herself. 'He'd take the skull and ship it to the Texas Department of Public Safety headquarters in Austin.

'And what would they do with it?' she postulated, gesturing boldly with her arm. 'They'd send it down to their Criminal Intelligence Division. And what would *they* do with it? They'd turn it over to their forensic sketch artist and, after checking with experts on sex, age, and things, that artist would do a two-dimensional skull reconstruction of it.

'Then what? Well, they'd take that drawing and reproduce it in their Missing Persons Clearinghouse Bulletin and in the Texas Crime Information Center computers. They might even put it in the FBI's National Crime Information Center computers to see if any law enforcement officers anywhere had a missing person whose description matched the drawing.'

Cady wandered into Zach's room and flopped back onto the bed, still disheveled from their afternoon revelries and his nap. Staring up at the ceiling fan, she thought, *I could do that.*

Maybe not the part about registering it with the NCIC and TCIC, but the first part . . . the two-dimensional skull reconstruction.

Hundreds of little objections began voicing themselves like unruly children in her mind. She didn't have access to the scale photography, for one thing. But that was the least of her worries.

She would have to draw again.

What if she couldn't do it?

Even worse: what if she could and the drawing wound up being a dead ringer for some missing person?

What then?

On the other hand, she thought, *what if it doesn't? Think what a relief that would be.*

For who?

For me.

That was the bottom line, after all. Cady would not rest until she learned the identity of the skull.

But why, *why?*

She couldn't help it. The skull spoke to her. It said, *Let me tell you my secrets.*

Emotionally drained and exhausted, Cady began to drift. From somewhere in the misty recesses of near-sleep, she heard Nanny's voice in her mind, saying, *Yeah, and you know what curiosity did to the cat.*

But it was too late.

Chest heaving, gulping air, Cady ran through the darkness, stumbling, grasping for support that wasn't there. He was getting closer and she couldn't run much longer. She tried to scream for help but the words clogged in her throat, even though she opened her mouth wide and strained with all her might.

Something hard shoved her between the shoulder blades and she tumbled forward, dropping the bottle of wine she clutched in her hand. It shattered and, in slow motion, splattered blood-red droplets all over the floor. They twinkled and gleamed black in the blue moonlight which streamed in from the front windows.

Cady tried to scream again but he was on top of her. She fought, but he was too strong, too big, and then there was the hammer! It was enormous, bigger than he was! But she dodged and kicked and struggled. The hammer struck the floor nearby and shook the house. It went up again, like the swing of a pendulum and, as it was sweeping downward, Cady saw that it was going to hit her right in the head.

'NOOOOOO!' she screamed, flinging her body to the side, ripping off his face mask as she did so. The hammer shattered the floorboards right by her ear and swung up again. This time it was a regular-sized hammer, but he had it in his hand, reaching over his

*head to strike her with it, and when she flung up her
hands to protect her face, she saw, she SAW!*

It was Zach.

'NOOOOOO!

'NOOOOOO!' Her own screams woke her. Her arms
were still flailing in the air, her heart pounding in
her ears, her breath ragged in her dry throat.

'Oh God, oh God,' said Cady, struggling to sit up.
The room was suffused with the gloom that precedes
darkness. She snapped on the light, trying to force
reality upon herself.

Of all the horrible dreams Cady had suffered since
the assault, this one was by far the worst. The image
of Zach's face, twisted and terrible as he swung the
hammer toward her head was branded into her mind.

Trembling, she held her arms close to her body and
took deep breaths.

Zach. Why would she ever dream such a thing?

Her skin was clammy and she shuddered. *It didn't
mean anything*, she told herself. *It was just a terrible
dream. You were upset about finding the skull and
the fight with Zach. That's all.*

She glanced at the clock and groaned. She'd been
asleep for hours. She got up and headed downstairs,
turning on lights as she went. The house was still
and dark. There was no sign of Zach.

Cady stepped out on the veranda and strained to
see if the lights were on in the barn. There was no
one.

Her stomach growled. She hadn't eaten anything
since morning. Zach would be hungry too. Earlier,
she had thawed out a couple of steaks and put them
in the refrigerator. Cady glanced out the window over

the sink again. Heavy, depressed gray clouds brooded overhead, clinging to the mountains like moody drunks.

She put the steaks in the broiler and popped a couple of potatoes in the microwave. Then she made a salad, drinking a beer and munching as she went along.

Cady rehearsed an apology to Zach. 'I didn't mean to hurt you,' she'd say. 'Maybe I did jump to conclusions. I won't call the sheriff.' She would not mention that she was going to do the reconstruction herself.

As her mother would say, What he didn't know wouldn't hurt him.

Cady put some soft music on the stereo, lit some candles, and set the table in the dining room. Every few minutes, she'd look out the window toward the barn again, but there was still no sign of Zach.

When the potatoes and the meat were done, Cady ate her salad, too hungry to wait. Then she wandered out on the veranda and watched for Zach some more.

An hour passed. Cady ate the rest of her supper and blew out the candles.

Another hour crawled by. Cady fixed a plate for Zach and put it in the microwave. Then she washed the rest of the dishes and cleaned up the kitchen.

The rains came back, sweeping mean and lusty against the side of the house. Cady lit a fire in the fireplace and curled up on the couch in front of it, alone and very frightened. He must have had a terrible accident.

At ten o'clock, she pulled on her own boots and huddled inside one of Zach's old dusters. Outside, the rain lashed her face and she pulled the duster up over her head like a turtle shell. She sprinted down the pathway to the barn and beyond, toward the little house by the stream.

There was a light inside one window, a flickering light like a television set would make. Cady pounded on the door. Dusty opened it, looking very young in his sock feet. Beyond, she could see True, struggling up out of a nap in his favorite recliner.

'Have you seen Zach?' Cady asked, her voice etched with anxiety. 'He didn't come home for supper.'

'He went to Alpine with Joe,' said Dusty. True had got to his feet and was hobbling over to the door in that bow-legged gait arthritis had forced upon him. 'I thought you knew,' added Dusty.

'No,' she said, feeling foolish, angry, hurt, and sad, all at the same time.

'Anythang wrong?' asked True. 'Come on in here and warm up.'

'No thanks, True. I just . . . Zach didn't tell me he was going to town. I was worried.'

'He an' Joe had some kinda bug up thar asses,' said True. 'Come on in here, girl.'

'Thanks, but I'll just go on home. Thanks anyway.'

He nodded, and his blue eyes saw right through her. She turned away and stumbled through the blinding rain toward the house.

Feeling thoroughly wet, cold, and miserable, she hung up the duster and turned on the fire beneath the tea kettle. She removed the supper plate from the microwave, covered it in aluminum foil, and placed it in the refrigerator.

Cady was even more frightened now, and for

different reasons. Zach had never done anything like
this before. Had she driven him away?

The phone rang and she lunged for it, certain it
had to be him.

'Hello?' In the background, she could hear crowd
noises and loud country and western music.

The hoarse whisper, when it came, seemed to suck
Cady dry of what few reserves of strength she had left.

'Do you know where your husband is?' he asked.

It was long past midnight when Cady heard the pick-
up churn up the road to the house. She lay awake in
the big lonely bed, her hands folded across her
stomach, heart thumping. The rain had stopped and
the night was still as death. Men's voices drifted up
to her window, which was open now to catch what
moist breeze the rain had left behind. A pick-up door
slammed.

She heard the slap of the screen door downstairs
and the growl of the truck as it worked its way back
down the muddy road. The clink of the refrigerator
door. Lights snapping on and off. A loud stumble and
a curse.

After a while, her husband's heavy steps creaked
the floorboards as he climbed the stairs. The hardwood
floor groaned and cracked as he came down the hall
toward the bedroom.

She'd left on a small lamp on the nightstand, with
a red nightgown of hers draped over it to mute the
light. The room was suffused with a whorish glow as
Zach loomed, sheepish and big, in the doorway.

He reeked of beer and stale cigarette smoke and
cheap perfume.

From across the room, Cady could spot the crimson lipstick smear on the breast of his shirt.

She turned away from him and pulled the covers up to her ears.

Chapter Twenty-Two

For the first time since Cady had stepped foot on the ranch, Zach slept late. His big body was flung across the bed, mouth open and drooling, stubble ragged and rough, eyes dark-ringed, hair disheveled, snores echoing off the four corners of the bedroom. Standing next to the bed, gazing down at him, Cady didn't see much of the tall, dark, romantic, dashing cowboy who'd stolen her heart so quickly such a short time ago.

Cady had no desire to intrude upon Zach's hangover, and eased downstairs to make herself a cup of hot, black coffee. She wasn't feeling very well. The heavy, dream-tossed afternoon nap had stolen any rest the night might have held for her. She'd lain awake beside her errant husband, listening to the storms subside and the rafters drip, nearly until dawn, before falling into a sort of exhausted catnap. Her head ached, her stomach was queasy, her eyes were grainy and tired, and her heart felt like a lead anchor in her chest.

Wadding herself into a corner of the couch, Cady huddled beneath an old afghan and sipped the coffee. Faded gray light filtered through the gauzy white curtains, but not enough to dispel the shadows that lurked in every corner.

Cady didn't know what was going on with Zach

but, deep in her heavy heart, she knew she had to accept some responsibility for it. For one thing, she'd been cocky about the skull. She was a reconstructionist, not a forensic anthropologist. Her job was to take what clues they gave her and try to piece together the mystery. When Cady found the skull, she'd tried to provide her own clues, and the truth was, she could be very wrong.

Except for one thing. The skull did not belong to a century-old Native American. Of that she could be sure. Beyond that, well, it took years, and the examination of hundreds of skulls, to be able to do anything more.

But she knew.

Deep, deep down inside, Cady knew she was right.

On the other hand. If she were going to do this properly, she'd have to get confirmation from an expert before beginning her reconstruction. It was the procedure she'd use if she were doing this for any law enforcement agency.

Cady set the coffee on an end table and curled up on the couch, her head propped on the cushiony armrest, the afghan pulled up to her ears. Her favorite forensic anthropologist was Dr Karl Gustav, at the University of Texas in Austin. Cady's mother had taught women's studies at the university and Cady had grown up in Austin. She known Dr Gustav for many years, and he had helped her before.

She could air-express the skull to Dr Gustav. He could examine it and do the scale photography she needed. And he would not ask a lot of questions about it. That was the most important part. He'd hurry, too, if she asked him.

230

But having a plan of action did not make her feel better. If anything, Cady felt worse. She wished she'd never found the damn thing in the first place. She wished with all her heart she'd minded her own business.

Just like Pandora, who – against express orders – had opened the trunk and let out all the world's troubles, Cady had opened a trunk and set off a shockwave from which her raw, new marriage might not recover.

Could it be that Zach's behavior the previous night had been some sort of throwback to those early, post-Vietnam, pain-filled days when he'd drowned his troubles in booze? That, somehow, her insistence on solving the mystery of the skull and bringing in the authorities had sent him reeling into a past over which he'd had no control?

Her stomach was churning and she stretched out flat on her back on the couch, taking deep, slow breaths to calm herself.

On the other hand – and this was the *really* painful part – why . . . *why* would Zach get so upset over her discovering the true identity of the skull? Why should he feel so threatened by that?

A wave of nausea swept over her and she gritted her teeth. Maybe he *had* brought home a skull from the war. There had to be all sorts of rules and regulations preventing such a theft. It could get him into plenty of trouble. Maybe that was it.

But he said he found it in a water gap. Here. On the ranch.

Cady wondered if she should go into the bathroom and try to throw up. She never should have drunk

hot coffee on an empty, nauseated stomach. Maybe
that was it. Maybe she just needed to eat something.

She got to her feet and made her way, somewhat
shakily, to the kitchen, where she nibbled on a dry
cracker. It seemed to help, so she ate three. But she
still felt so very tired. She curled back up on the couch,
beneath the afghan.

The phone rang and Cady lunged for it. The
answering machine was set for four rings, which
would most assuredly wake Zach, and she wasn't
ready to face him just yet.

'Hello?'

'I'm bored, how about you?'

In spite of herself, Cady smiled. 'Hi, Georgia.'

'There's not much astronomers can do on cloudy
nights except a bunch of frustrating computer work.
I say, who needs it? So, now I'm all caught up on my
sleep, I thought I'd come by and visit, if you can stand
the company.'

Cady thought about Zach, asleep upstairs. It could
be awkward. Glancing out the window, Cady noticed a
scattering of sprinkled droplets on the glass. More rain.

She still had some thinking to do before she
confronted Zach about last night. And she very much
needed a friend, a woman friend, to ground her and
take her out of herself.

'Tell you what, Georgia. Why don't I come to your
house instead?'

There was a brief hesitation. 'Well, the place is
really trashed. I don't think much about housework.'

'Who does?'

'Oh, don't give me that. You've made that old place
positively glow.'

'Yeah, but you should have seen my apartment when I was single.'

Georgia laughed. 'Well, you're still a newlywed. There's plenty of time for him to get to know the *real* you!'

It was funny, but too close to home at the moment for Cady to laugh. 'Why don't you give me directions to your place?' she said. She was starting to feel better already.

After she hung up, Cady felt well enough to eat a couple of pieces of toast. She labored over a note to Zach. Finally, she wrote, '*I thought we could use a little thinking space. I've gone to visit Georgia – her phone number's at the end of this note. I'll be back after lunch. I love you. Cady.*'

She didn't want him to think she was in a rage about his late-night indiscretion; on the other hand, she didn't want him to think it didn't matter, because it did.

Cady rubbed her aching head. God, this relationship business was hard. In the years since her divorce, she'd forgotten *how* hard. Now that specter rose up to haunt her.

Had she failed again? Already?

Heaving a sigh, she gathered up her things. She wanted a hot shower but was afraid Zach would wake up, and she really was not ready for that scene just yet.

Okay. She was running away. Again.

But she'd be back. That was the thing about marriage. You kept coming back ... until there was nothing left to come back to.

* * *

Georgia lived in a cozy, rustic, A-frame perched atop one of the highest mountain peaks in the area, with a spectacular view out of the glassed-in upper floor which housed the single bedroom and a bath. A large, handsome telescope was mounted in front of the glass wall, near a table piled with computer print-outs and books on subjects like astrophysics. The place was normally rented out to hunters, she explained to Cady, but the owner was happy to extend a lease to her, since her residency was not dependent on the seasons.

A cheery fire leaped and danced in the bulky wood-burning stove downstairs, which was offset beautifully by a back wall of stone extending to the hearth. Cady settled herself in a big rugged leather chair and hassock which were set at an angle to the hearth, while Georgia scampered about, gathering up scattered newspapers and other clutter.

'You don't have to do that, really,' protested Cady. 'The place looks fine. Sit down here with me and talk.'

'How about some hot chocolate?' countered Georgia.

'That sounds perfectly marvelous.' Cady's stomach had settled down, but she felt chilled by the damp, the unexpected cold, and the unrest in her heart. And her head still ached fiercely, in spite of the aspirin she'd taken before leaving the house.

She leaned her head back on the scrunchey leather. It was such a delicious relief to be with a woman friend again. There was always something so soothing and satisfying about female friends, who could make you laugh about things like cramps and men and pimples and being broke.

Georgia brought the cocoa in big hand-thrown pottery mugs, with sticks of cinnamon poking up through clouds of miniature marshmallows. She set a tray of chocolate chip cookies on a low table before the couch and said, 'Okay. I confess. The cookies are store-bought but, if you put them in the microwave for a few seconds, they taste homemade.'

Cady laughed.

For a few minutes they munched cookies and sipped the cocoa, and then Georgia said, 'Okay. So talk, girlfriend.'

'About what?'

'Don't be coy with me. I sense trouble in paradise. I knew something was wrong the minute you answered the phone.'

What could Cady say? How could she possibly explain the turmoil in her life without sounding more and more bizarre? She sighed.

'Just start at the beginning,' coaxed Georgia. 'Like, what the hell *really* happened to your hand, moving on to why you almost never answer the phone at your house, and concluding with what's going on with you today?'

Cady rubbed her head.

'Headache?'

She nodded.

'Okay.' Georgia got to her feet, arranged a few sofa cushions on the floor, and said, 'Lie down.'

'What?'

'I can fix it. Just do what I say, and nobody gets hurt.' She grinned.

Feeling a little foolish, Cady stretched out on the floor. Georgia began rubbing her shoulders with strong, practiced hands.

'Ouch!'

'Don't whine. I'm doing this for your own good. Now talk.'

It was easier, somehow, face-down on the floor, not having to establish eye contact. She told Georgia about the assault, and about the stalker. She wasn't quite ready to start talking skulls just yet.

'So let me get this straight,' said Georgia, kneading Cady's shoulder blades like bread dough. 'The creep's still calling you? Here?'

Cady yelped. 'I'm not a piece of hamburger meat, you know!' she cried. 'Yes. He's still calling me.'

'So run a trace.'

'He doesn't stay on long enough and, anyway, I don't think the local sheriff has those kinds of facilities. *Ow!* That hurts all the way down to my knees!'

'So, think how much better you'll feel when I'm done. What about the Texas Rangers? Or the FBI? You must have lots of contacts in the business.'

'I keep thinking he'll give up, you know?'

'Do you really believe that?' Georgia pounded the muscles on either side of Cady's spine with the sides of her hands.

After a moment, Cady said, 'No.'

'So? Why don't you *do* something about it then?' She got to her feet and, to Cady's surprise, stood on Cady's back and began walking, placing her bare feet carefully on either side of the spine. All the breath *whooshed* out of Cady's lungs and she heard a string of popping noises, like tiny muffled firecrackers. She felt a sharp, quick pain in her head and neck.

'Boy, you were strung out like piano wire,' commented Georgia. She stepped off of Cady's inert body and plopped down on the couch.

After a moment, Cady rolled slowly over onto her side, and then sat up, blinking at her friend. The headache was gone.

Georgia grinned. 'What can I say. It's a gift.'

'For a while there, I thought you were trying to kill me.'

Georgia's smile quickly faded. 'Not me,' she said. 'But honey, I worry about that psycho who keeps calling you.'

Cady shrugged. 'I figure, if he wanted to get to me, he could have done it by now.'

'That depends.'

'On what?' Cady helped herself to another cookie.

'On his plan.'

'What plan?'

'Cady . . . Do you think this guy would follow you all the way out here without having some kind of plan?'

'I don't know. I never really thought about it.'

'He's obviously obsessed with you. I don't think a few brief phone conversations and meetings with an answering machine are going to be enough for him. He's going to want more.'

Cady toyed with the cookie. She hadn't intended to get into this. After all, she tried not to think about the stalker – or whatever he was. Right now, her mind was pretty consumed with Zach and making things right with him. She put the cookie back onto the plate.

'I didn't mean to upset you,' said Georgia.

'It's okay.'

'I just think you need to face this thing head-on.'

Cady nodded.

'What does Zach think?'

Zach. Cady said, 'He thinks he can protect me.' *If he still wants to*, she thought. Suddenly, she missed him terribly. She wanted to see him and make things right. She wanted to feel his arms around her again.

She got to her feet. 'This has been wonderful, Georgia. I need to go though.'

A worried look crossed Georgia's face. 'Hey, I didn't mean to run you off.'

'You didn't. Really. I just have some . . . things I need to take care of at home.'

'Are you sure? I didn't mean to stick my big nose in where it doesn't belong.'

Cady patted Georgia's arm. 'I appreciate you being there to listen. It's just . . . well, to tell you the truth . . . Zach and I had a fight last night and I'd like to go home and make things up with him.'

Georgia nodded sagely. 'I *knew* something was wrong.' She walked Cady to the door. 'Drive carefully on these slick mountain roads. And let me know how things work out.'

'I will.' Cady smiled at her and headed for the car.

'And Cady?'

She stopped and glanced over her shoulder, car keys already in hand.

Anxiety lines creased Georgia's forehead. 'Just . . . be very, very careful about that guy, okay? I mean, he could be really unpredictable. Just don't take him for granted. I guess that's what I'm trying to say.'

'Georgia.' Cady smiled. 'I didn't realize you were such a worrier.'

Her friend did not return the smile. 'And I didn't realize you were such an innocent.'

An *innocent*? Of all the words Cady might have used to describe herself, *innocent* would certainly never have made the list. Not in the past twenty years or so, anyway.

She waved goodbye, climbed into the car, and headed home.

Home. How strange that sounded.

She was grateful for her friend. She *was* going home, and she felt much better than she had when she left.

All the same, she checked the rear-view mirror several times during the winding, mountainous drive, to make sure she was not being followed.

The house was empty when Cady got home.

She was disappointed, but not daunted. Her note to Zach had been moved, which meant he had seen it. She glanced around, but there was no note for her.

It was very muddy out. She pulled on a pair of boots and headed down the pathway to the barn. It was a cloudy, bereft sort of day that signaled the coming of autumn. She pulled her Levi jacket close against the damp chill.

Voices, raised in anger, slowed her steps.

'She didn't have no business snooping around where she didn't belong,' said Joe.

'I don't know what you're so upset about,' said Zach. 'It's my problem.'

'Maybe it is and maybe it isn't. What if she goes to the cops?'

'We'll just have to cross that bridge when we come to it, Joe. Shit, I wish I'd never told you in the first place. I had no idea you'd get so bent out of shape.'

'Yeah? Well, there's lots o' thangs you got no idea about.'

'What's that supposed to mean?'

'It *means* you got a bad habit of losin' control of your wives, is what it means.'

Silence crackled between the two men. Then Zach's voice drifted out to Cady, deadly quiet. 'You stepped over the line, Joe. If I was you, I'd step back.'

After another moment of silence, footsteps thunked across the wooden floor of the building and squelched into the mud, moving quickly away.

Cady's heart was thumping rapidly in her ears. Joe's words echoed in her mind: *What if she goes to the cops?*

And Zach's: *It's my problem.*

She swallowed, feeling sick again.

Slowly, she eased herself from behind the saddle house door, preparing to sneak back to the house and collect her thoughts, but her boot heel slid out from under her in the slick mud. Involuntarily, her hand flew out to grab the door, which banged loudly back against the building. Cady staggered to her feet, and looked up into the shadowed eyes of her husband.

Chapter Twenty-Three

'Cady! I thought you said you weren't going to be back until after lunch.' Zach reached down and took her arm, steadying her and helping her up into the saddle house.

'I just . . . wanted to see you.' She searched his eyes, looking for some sign that he knew she'd overheard his conversation with Joe, but his expression was unreadable.

There was a brief, awkward silence, then they both spoke at once, beginning, 'I'm sorry about—'

They stopped.

Zach said, 'I was a pig last night. I don't know what came over me. Maybe I'm just not used to being married. But I had no right to walk out on you like that.'

She picked up a slippery bottle of Neatsfoot oil and studied the label. 'Did you see Tammilee last night?' she blurted. The label was faded.

'I went to a club with Joe. We used to hang out there a lot. Anyway, Tammilee was there. We danced one dance.'

Cady set down the bottle and wiped her oily hands on her jeans. 'I'm sure she found it interesting that you chose to go dancing with Joe rather than with me.' She fiddled with a sheepskin cloth.

'I told her we had a fight.' He chuckled softly to

241

himself. 'She told me to get my butt back home.'

'How big of her,' said Cady, despising the note of sarcasm in her own voice. This wasn't turning out the way she'd wanted it to. The last thing she'd intended to discuss was Tammilee. Apparently, her own traitorous jealous heart had other ideas.

'Cady.' He reached for her arm and turned her about until she was facing him. 'If I'd have wanted Tammilee, I'd have married her. But I didn't marry Tammilee. I married you.'

'Maybe you should have.'

'What?'

'Married Tammilee.'

'Oh, for Chrissake!' He rolled his eyes. 'Tammilee Sanderson is a spoiled little daddy's girl who's had more husbands than I've had horses. I was never serious about her.'

'Was she serious about you?'

His gaze caught hers and held it. 'Only when she thought she couldn't have me.' He grinned.

She refused to grin back. The truth was, she was a lot angrier about his behavior than she'd realized. 'You can't just pick up and go honky-tonking whenever we have a fight, you know!' she cried.

His eyes twinkled. 'Honky-tonking?'

'Stop it, dammit! I'm furious with you! I was worried sick. I thought you were hurt someplace. I had to ask *Dusty* where you were! And you should have seen yourself when you got home last night. It was disgraceful, Zach!'

'I know.' He nodded. 'You're right. There was no excuse for my behavior, and I give you my word it will never happen again.' His gaze was long and sincere.

She pursed her lips. 'Okay.'

He picked up the sheepskin cloth and began buffing one of the saddles.

It was still not settled, and Cady knew it. His going to a bar with Joe was a symptom of the problem, not the problem itself.

After a moment, she said, 'About the skull.' She glanced at him. He continued to polish the saddle, taking great care with the pommel and skirt.

'I . . . I jumped to a lot of conclusions. About the skull, I mean. It would be up to an expert to tell anything for sure about it.' She didn't mention that she already had one in mind. 'There's probably no need to call in the sheriff.' *At least, not yet,* she thought. 'I didn't mean to push so hard and get you upset,' she added.

For a while, he continued working on the saddle. Finally, he said, 'Do what you think you have to do, Cady.'

She studied her muddy boots. Somehow, she'd thought that reassuring Zach about the skull would make everything right between them once more.

Now she found herself wondering if things would ever be right again.

Once Cady found that skull, things changed between us. For one thing, she started lying to me.

Oh, maybe not out-and-out LYING, but she damn sure started to withhold the truth.

I gave her every opportunity to let me know what was going on. We would talk and I would drop hints, you see. Try to trap her. But she was wary and very good at dodging.

The rhythm was off, somehow. I mean, she was still the same in many ways. We'd laugh and talk like always, just enjoy each other's company, you know, but I always knew she was holding something back.

I guess that's the first time I really started to doubt her.

As Cady was prying her boots off on the bootjack outside the back door, she could hear the phone ringing and the answering machine kick in with its spiel. In her sock feet, she passed through the kitchen and dining room to stand by the phone, the familiar dread shadowing her.

'Goddamn it, Cady! I refuse to hang up this time. I'm going to sit right here and talk until you pick up this godforsaken phone—'

She snatched up the receiver. 'Peter! It's so good to hear your voice!'

'Oh yeah? Then why the hell don't you answer the damn phone when I call? You know I hate these infernal machines.'

'Well, if you would leave a message instead of hanging up all the time, I could at least call you back, Peter.'

'Some messages aren't for machines,' he said, his tone at once serious.

Her chest tightened. 'What's wrong?'

'Nothing. Maybe. I don't know.'

She waited, fingering the cord with her twisted fingers.

'It's the LoverBoy. He's gone.'

'What do you mean, *gone*?'

'He took off a few weeks ago. Nobody's heard from

244

him and he hasn't reported to his PO.'

Cady sat down. 'What does his mother say?'

'She says she doesn't know where he went, either. She was upset when I talked to her. I think the old broad really doesn't know.'

'Did you put out an APB?'

'Hell, yes. NCIC, the whole bit. Don't worry, sweetheart, everybody's lookin' for the guy.'

'I've been getting calls out here, Peter.'

'Shit! How'd he know where to find you?'

'That's what I'd like to know.'

'What does he say?'

'Most of the time – as you know – we leave the answering machine on and he just hangs up. But a few times I've answered the phone myself, and he acts like he's out here. In the mountains.' She shivered. 'Watching.'

'Jesus, Cady.'

'Yeah. It's a bitch, all right.'

'Maybe you should come back here. I could keep an eye on you.'

'I can't.'

'Whad'ya mean, you can't?'

'I . . . Peter . . . Zach and I got married.'

She could hear the *whoosh* of his exhale. 'Geez, Cady. It would have been nice if you'd have let a few of your old friends know.'

'I'm sorry. I've been meaning to send announcements—'

'Forget it.' There was a pause, then he said, 'Is that cowboy good to you?'

She thought of the night before – maybe a little too long? – and said, 'Yes.'

245

'Because, if he's not, you just let ol' Pete know. I'll come out there and kick his ass.'

She smiled. 'Peter, about that last night we were together, you know, on the couch—'

'Hey. It's history. I was out of line anyway.'

'I was a little crazy then.'

'Whad'ya mean, *then*?'

They laughed a little, but the awkwardness was unavoidable. Peter said, 'I'll keep you posted on the LoverBoy thing.'

'I'd appreciate that, Peter.'

'You take care, sweetheart.'

'I will. You too.'

'Bye.' He hung up before she could say anything more.

Slowly, she replaced the receiver in the cradle and wandered around the big old house, picking up clutter half-heartedly. She had intended to stay outside with Zach, but he was in a peculiar mood and conversation between them was strained, so she left him alone to brood.

She wondered if she would ever understand his moods.

She felt no particular panic that the LoverBoy had split. Somehow she'd always known it. The ID photos she had were poor quality and Cady doubted that he looked anywhere near the same anymore. There were any number of ways he could have disguised himself by now.

Upstairs, Cady picked up the clothes Zach had worn the night before off the bedroom floor. She hated the way they smelled and hurried down to dump them into the washing machine, adding a generous measure of baking soda as she did so. She wanted to remove all traces of the scent of another woman from her house.

Then she went into the kitchen, and stood stock-still in the middle of the room, trying to remember why she'd come there in the first place.

But her thoughts were consumed with the LoverBoy. How long would he be able to hide himself in a town the size of Fort Davis without attracting attention? During tourist season, maybe for some time, but what about after? Autumn was approaching. After a while, wouldn't somebody notice the new guy in town?

Maybe. Maybe not. Could be he was camping out somewhere. Could you do that indefinitely? It was something worth checking out.

Something was happening to Cady and it brought her to a full stop in the living room.

She was taking control.

That was it! Now the shoe was on the other foot. Something had galvanized her. Maybe it was Georgia's warning. Or the phone call from Peter. Even the fight with Zach. Whatever it was, Cady was through being stalked.

The decision was made. Just like that.

This time, *she* would do the stalking.

Cady considered notifying Sheriff Garner, but decided against it. For one thing, he would immediately tell Zach, and Cady didn't want this added disruption in the midst of their fragile peace. He would only mount some sort of vigilante search, which would cause the chameleon rapist to instantly vanish into the surroundings.

And, even if she were able to convince Dub not to tell Zach, she still worried that if law enforcement suddenly started sniffing around, asking questions, the LoverBoy would smell them out before they ever found him.

She thought that if she could somehow find him first, then point him out to the law . . . well, it wasn't the best of plans, maybe, but it *was* a plan.

The first thing she did was call Georgia and tell her everything.

'Oh, how exciting!' she cried. 'A real mystery! You've simply *got* to let me help you. At least until the clouds clear up.'

'Whatever inquiries we make have to be very discreet,' said Cady. 'If he's here – and I'm sure he must be – and he thinks I'm on to him, he'll leave again and there'll be no way I can find him then.'

'Cady, let's think about this a minute. If this is the guy who attacked you in your apartment, then he must be very dangerous.'

Cady hesitated. 'Yes. That's another reason we must be very, very careful. He has raped and brutalized a number of women, and I'm convinced he's the one who assaulted me and did this to my hand.'

'Hmmm. This may be a rude question, but did you ever wonder why he didn't rape *you*? After all, that's his thing, isn't it?'

'Yeah, I've thought about it. I figured he must be after revenge. It was my drawing that ultimately helped to catch him. I guess he blames me instead of the detectives who arrested him.'

'Were either of them women?'

'No.'

'Well, that explains it.'

'Oh. I never thought of that.'

'So what do you think he's after now?'

Cady shuddered. 'I don't know. I don't want to know.'

'What I don't understand is, if he wants to harass and frighten you, then why doesn't he make threats or something? Why does he keep pledging his undying love?'

'I have no idea.'

'Okay – and this is a toughie – what about other women in the community? Aren't they in danger?'

Cady took her bottom lip between her teeth. Finally, she said, 'Ouch. Good point. I tell you what. Let's set a sort of deadline on our search. If we haven't found him by, say, the end of the week, then we let Dub know, okay?'

'One week then.'

'And Georgia? Let's not tell Zach that the LoverBoy has disappeared and may be here, okay? He worries about me enough as it is.'

'I don't know, Cady. If it were me, I'd want to know.'

She considered this. 'Okay. Let's just not tell him until I have some kind of conclusive evidence that the LoverBoy's really here. I mean, we don't know anything for sure right now anyway. There's no need to worry him just yet.'

'Whatever you say, partner.'

As Cady was hanging up the phone from talking to Georgia, she heard the back screen door slam shut and the sound of Zach scuffling the bootjack into position. Feeling buoyant and energetic now that she had a determined plan of action, she went through the dining room and into the kitchen to greet him.

He was standing just inside the door in his sock feet, his hat and duster still on. He had that little-kid look on his face again, and Cady marveled at how mercurial his moods really were.

'I've got something for you.'

'What?' She went to stand close in front of him. He was so tall and he smelled of the outdoors. Every day it seemed, no matter what had transpired the day before, she fell in love with him all over again.

From out of the voluminous folds of his duster, he pulled forth a small, scruffy kitten of indeterminate color, no bigger than the palm of his hand.

'Oh!' Cady's heart leaped in delight, but as she reached forth her hand to touch the kitten, she noticed that something wasn't quite right about it. Its little head was not triangular-shaped, like most cats'. It was more fox-like, with a long, un-catlike nose.

She peered closer.

The animal had no eyes.

Cady took a sharp intake of breath and looked up helplessly at Zach.

'The little eye sockets are fully formed,' he said, 'but, if you'll look closely, you can see that the eyes just didn't ever mature.'

'Poor kitty,' she whispered. The creature swiveled its ears in her direction.

'His mama's an old pro barn cat. She took real good care of him for about a month, but now his litter-mates are big enough to follow her out huntin', and he just keeps gettin' all tangled up in the brush.'

Zach fondled the tiny head with one big thumb, gentle as a feather.

'But . . . don't you think it should be . . . destroyed?' asked Cady with a shudder. 'It can't live a normal life.'

He shrugged. 'Who are we to make that decision? He's got as much right to survive as anybody else. Granted, he's pretty doomed outdoors, but I figured he'd be fine as a house cat. If you want to try.'

'What if he can't find his litter box, or his food, or . . .'

Zach smiled at her. 'I expect he'll make adjustments. Just like the rest of us.' He held the kitten out to her.

She took the frail little ball of fluff into her hands. The kitten was entirely trusting.

'You should have seen him sitting up in the middle of the barn, his face turned up, swiveling those ears – he looked like Stevie Wonder!' Zach chuckled.

The kitten turned its little face toward him and pointed its ears.

Cady smiled. 'Just like Radar – that character on *MASH*.'

'Right! He could hear the helicopters coming before anybody else.' Zach laughed. 'I guess the little critter's got a name.'

'Radar?' said Cady. She felt a tiny vibration as the kitten began to purr.

'You said you always wanted a cat,' said Zach. 'I figured you could learn something from this one.'

Her love for this man rendered her helpless. Cady leaned her head into his chest and he enveloped her in his big, safe arms.

251

* * *

Cady hummed softly to herself as she shoved open the attic door. Little Radar had proven true to his name, maneuvering his way around the kitchen using his whiskers, strutting his little paws out ahead of him like white canes. He quickly found his water and food dish and seemed unaware that he should be having any problems.

Maybe she *could* learn something from him.

Cady had come to the attic because she remembered seeing a shallow pan which would work very well as a litter box. She deliberately avoided looking at the green Army trunk in the corner. As she sorted through various piles of the flotsam and jetsam of family life, the pan finally turned up behind a decrepit old lamp. Perfect.

Brushing a few spider webs from the pan, she tucked it under her arm and tried again not to look at the trunk.

Leave it alone for now, she told herself. Things were finally beginning to get back to normal between her and Zach. The last thing she needed to do now was bury herself in the attic, examining that skull.

She headed for the door.

But she couldn't help one quick glance.

That's when she saw the padlock, clasped firmly in place, denying her access to the skull.

Chapter Twenty-Four

Cady set down the pan and edged closer. The padlock she'd first seen on the trunk, which had not been fastened, was now securely locked in place.

A frustrated little knot of anger formed in her stomach. Zach had told her he didn't care what she did with the skull, and then he proceeded to treat her like a child in front of a medicine cabinet, locking it out of sight. Her first impulse was to charge downstairs and confront him but, considering how his mood had lightened in recent hours, she decided against it. She didn't want to provoke another angry scene with him, didn't want to set off another mysterious brooding session.

When Cady got married, it had never occurred to her that she might resort someday to sneaking around behind Zach's back, hiding things from him, or lying to him. Now she found herself in a predicament women had faced for centuries: whether to lock a man head-on in a power struggle, or find a way to get what she wanted without such an uneven confrontation.

Thoughts of her mother tugged at her conscience, thoughts of all the wars she and her feminist sisters had fought so that women would have the courage to wage their own individual battles.

Cady hesitated. She loved her husband. She didn't want to do anything that might upset him or bring back unpleasant memories for him. But, in spite of what Zach said, this skull was not his private property. It had, after all, once been a living, breathing human soul with a history and an identity and, right now, it fairly begged Cady to solve that mystery and lay the matter to rest.

If she took the necessary steps to piece together the puzzle, would it be so wrong to do it quietly, without flaunting it in her husband's face? What would be harder, confronting him with the final results – and whatever consequences that entailed – or battling him tooth and nail every step of the way?

She sighed. 'Sorry, Mom,' she whispered, 'this is a battle I'm going to have to fight in my own way.'

She gathered up the pan and headed downstairs, where she made no mention of the padlock. Neither did Zach.

The rain stopped, but cooler air rolling off the mountains mingled with warm air from the desert, forming an eerie fog as the afternoon stretched toward evening. It helped teach Cady one of the first things a ranch wife learns, that bad weather is welcomed because it keeps the cowboys home. Since they'd married, Zach was often up before dawn, back for a couple of hours in the middle of the day, then gone again until dark. Sometimes she went with him on his various working jaunts around the ranch, but usually he left with the other men and Cady was on her own.

For the first few weeks, she'd been busy settling in and adjusting to the routine, but increasingly of late, Cady was seeing the wisdom of Zach's insistence that she re-establish her artwork and make a new life for herself outside of the house. What neither had counted on was that her interest would be renewed by the discovery of a skull in their attic.

As the mists pressed close to the windows, Zach read the weekly *Jeff Davis County Mountain Dispatch* and the daily *Alpine Avalanche*, both of which arrived in the mail a day late. He sat on the couch in front of the fireplace, his sock feet crossed at the ankles. Cady sat cross-legged on the floor at his knee, playing with Radar. She had discovered that he loved to hear the crinkling noise made when a piece of paper was wadded up, and when she tossed the balled-up paper across the hardwood floor, he would chase it and bat it around.

'He'd make a great mouser,' she commented, 'as long as the little guy keeps squeaking.'

Zach, hidden behind the newspaper, chuckled. Like most men, he liked to claim that he could read about one thing, converse about another, and think of yet another, all at the same time.

The dogs started baying outside, at just about the same moment that they heard the rumble of a pick-up surging up the drive and parking around behind the house. Only visitors who did not know them very well parked out front.

Zach leaped to his feet and headed through the dining room. Cady lagged behind. She was jealous that someone had intruded on her quiet afternoon with her husband. Especially after the trouble they'd been having. Radar abandoned the wad of paper and scampered along after their footsteps. She stooped and picked him up.

Zach glanced out of the window over the sink, and his whole demeanor changed. His back stiffened, he cursed, and then hurried into his boots. Cady glanced out the window just in time to see Rex Zimmerman emerge from behind the wheel of his big black pick-up with the RZ brand emblazoned on the side in red. She groaned.

Zach stomped out of the back door, across the porch, and down the steps. Obviously he did not want to invite the man into the house. Cady put Radar down and followed as far as the back porch screen door. Zach had his back to her, but the men's words carried to her clearly.

'Cute trick, Ralston, removing all the red surveyor's markers from the valley.' Zimmerman turned his head to the side and spat a brown stream of tobacco.

'I don't know what you're talking about.'

'Oh, really? It's just the kind of childish thing you'd do. What, you think we couldn't figure out where to put 'em back? You're not only a liar, you're stupid to boot.'

'I didn't touch your goddamned markers. Now get off my property.' Zach's hand clenched into a fist.

'A fucking liar.' Spit. 'A fucking *stupid* liar.'

Zach threw the first punch but, clearly, Zimmerman had been expecting it. He deflected the swing with his upper arm and socked a punch to Zach's midsection that doubled him over. Then he grasped Zach's head by the hair and yanked it down to smash Zach's nose into his knee. Zach dropped to the ground, blood gushing.

As Cady watched through the screen-door grid in the blurred dim light of the fog, the whole thing took on a dreamlike feel of unreality. Zimmerman pulled back a monumental fist.

Moving in what felt like slow motion, Cady hit the ground in a single leap, running barefoot through the mud. She flung her body onto Zimmerman's back, pummeling his head with her fists. He pulled her off with one hand and flung her across the yard like a bothersome bug. She fell to her knees in the middle of two furiously barking dogs and sprang back up just in time to see Zach charge Zimmerman like a mad bull, knocking him to the ground in a flail of fists and spit, mud and blood, and brown tobacco juice.

For a second, Cady froze as her husband became a half-crazed stranger, his face twisted and wild, fists a blur as Zimmerman's head plopped back into the mud and his jaw went slack.

'*Zach, stop it!*' she screamed. '*Zach, you'll kill him!*'

Propelled by the knowledge that Zach had somehow passed into a demon world in which he had no self-control, she sprinted over to his pick-up and removed the rifle from the gun rack, which she fired over her head.

The gunshot sliced through the fog and echoed off the mountains.

Panting, Zach seemed to crumple inside himself. He rolled off Zimmerman's body and wiped his bleeding face with the sleeve of his shirt.

Zimmerman was moaning, his head swinging from side to side. The door to True's house was suddenly flung open, and he and Dusty sprinted down the path toward the house. Cady's hands were shaking so hard she could barely hold onto the gun. It sagged toward the ground.

'Dusty, git that gun 'fore she drops it,' commanded True as he reached them. 'Zacharia, you all right?'

'Just get that carcass the hell off my place,' said Zach, pushing himself slowly to his feet. 'Before I kill him.'

True nodded. 'Dusty, I'm on'a take this feller on home. You foller along in my pick-up.'

The boy, his face crimson, scrambled to obey. They helped Zimmerman to his feet.

'If I's you, I wouldn't come back here no more neither, you got t'at?' said True as they loaded Zimmerman into the passenger side of his black pick-up. He nodded and leaned his head onto the dash.

True went around to the driver's side. 'And I'd thank twice afore I pressed any charges, understand?' He slammed the door of the truck.

Zimmerman was still folded over in his seat. He had not closed his door. Then they all heard the swoosh of tires and looked up through the mist to see Georgia pull up into the drive. Nobody knew what to say or do, so they all just stood in place while she got out of the car, peered at Zimmerman, glanced over at Zach, then Cady, and said, 'Oh shit. I guess my timing rather sucks, doesn't it?'

'You wouldn't believe what folks is sayin' all over town,' commented Joe over Cady's shoulder as she peeled potatoes in the kitchen sink the next day.

'I mean, there's hardly a soul left in Jeff Davis county who ain't heard about the fight.' A toothpick jutted out of the corner of his mouth, and he worked it with his lips. 'Zach's the sentimental, odds-on favorite for a rematch.'

'Doesn't Rex have any friends?' Cady asked. She

was reluctant to be drawn into the conversation and felt uneasy alone with Joe behind her. The other men were gathered in the living room, waiting on dinner. The quiet murmur of their voices drifted through the dining room. She wished Joe would join them.

'Nah. Nobody likes the son of a bitch. Not even members of his own family.'

'So he has a family, then?'

'Jist a sister. She lives in Midland.'

Cady glanced over her shoulder and rinsed off the potatoes. 'What does his sister think about the sub-developments?'

He shrugged. 'Aw, she hates it, same as ever'body else. But she ain't got no say in the matter. His daddy heired the whole place over to Rex.'

'Primogeniture,' mumbled Cady, filling the pan full of sliced potatoes with water.

'What?'

'Nothing.' She carried the heavy pan to the stove.

Joe stepped back out of her way, but not so far that her breasts didn't brush briefly against the front of his shirt. He grinned at her.

She ignored him.

'Ol' Sammy Benson heard that Rex and Zach pulled guns on one another.' He raised his eyebrows.

Cady dried her hands on a dish towel. 'Not true, Joe. You know that.'

'And over at the post office, I heard that you shot at Rex and missed.'

'Oh, for heaven's sake!' This was Cady's first experience of small-town gossip, and she was unprepared for its speed and rampant progression from the truth.

259

'And another feller over at the bank said he heard from a guy at the drugstore that Zach invited Rex over jist to have it out with him once and for all.'

Cady frowned. 'I hope you set him straight.'

'I don't know,' he said. 'Did he?'

'God almighty, Joe!' she cried. 'You know better than that!' The voices in the other room quieted. Cady picked up the knife she'd used to cut up the potatoes and threw it into the sink with a rattle.

One corner of his mouth quirked upward. 'Maybe so, but it's more fun to watch you git all riled up.'

She stomped away from him, breathing deeply to calm herself. She hadn't wanted to cook anyway – just the smell of food made her want to throw up – but the men had worked hard and expected it.

She was beginning to despise Joe.

'By the way,' he commented, his voice casual, 'Zach tells me you made a little discovery up in the attic.'

'Yeah,' she said, keeping her back to him. 'I found pictures of his ex-wife.'

She gave him a rolling-eyed glance over her shoulder, then turned to look at him a little more closely.

He'd gone yellow-pale beneath the ruddy tan, and turned away from her before she could read the expression in his eyes.

Cady tried to stay away from town altogether, hoping that the excitement would die down and the gossipmongers would find somebody else to pick on. In light of recent events, she and Georgia decided that it would be best if Georgia showed the LoverBoy's picture around town with a nice little story attached, so that Cady would not attract any more attention to herself.

In the meantime, Cady rummaged through Zach's drawers and jeans pockets like a thief, looking for a key that would likely spring the padlock. On the fourth day after the fight, she found it. While he showered downstairs, she removed the skull from the trunk and put it into a box, which she hid temporarily behind some junk. She replaced the padlock, locked it, and raced downstairs to put the key back where she'd found it – her emotions a confused mess. She hated herself for all the skulking around, but she also hated the fact that her husband had put her into this position in the first place.

The next day, she shipped the skull down to Dr Gustav. She mailed it from Alpine and, in a move which surprised even herself, took out a post office box there for him to return the skull. *It would hardly do*, she told herself, *for the mail carrier to bring it down to the house some afternoon while Zach was home for dinner*.

At least, that's what she told herself.

In the days following the fight, I sensed another change in Cady. Not just the lying and sneaking around. Something more. She seemed preoccupied somehow, not as quick to laugh. She lost the thread of a conversation and was awfully defensive if you tried to tease her.

That's when I figured out that she must have been plotting against me.

I couldn't let her do that, you see.

After all, I still loved her. I didn't want to lose her!

I had to get her attention somehow.
Surely you can understand that.

On the Saturday morning after the fight, Cady lay awake, trying to decide whether or not to get up. She still felt lousy most of the time. Zach told her that flu bugs generally made the rounds about town after a spell of bad weather and that she ought to stay in bed and get some rest. He'd been exceptionally quiet as he got up in the pre-dawn hours, trying very hard not to wake her, then left without leaving a note. She wasn't sure whether he was with the guys or not.

She dozed for a couple of hours, dreaming fitfully, and when she awoke she felt worse than ever. An oppressive heaviness weighed down on her, as if every limb were tied to the bed. Her chest was constricted so tight she couldn't take a deep breath. She couldn't seem to warm her hands and feet, no matter how tightly she scrunched up her body under the covers. There was a dull ache to her head and her stomach felt like a lump of clay.

It was a sense of dread.

A crack of sunlight spilt through the side of the drapes. Sunlight! *The clouds must be breaking up then*, she thought. Perhaps that's what she needed, to sit out in the sun for a while. She'd been cooped up too long. She was beginning to imagine things.

Cady forced herself out of bed and padded downstairs in her gown. Radar greeted her at the foot of the stairs with the little trilling noise deep in his throat that he reserved for Cady. She picked him up and cradled him in the crook of her arm as she passed through the dining room and kitchen and out onto the veranda. She pushed open the screen door and gazed out toward the sun-dappled stream.

Cady's breath caught in her throat. An ancient tree, most of the branches long since dead, was covered with vultures. Grasping the boughs with gnarled talons, they perched, long, scraggledy wings outspread as if frozen in a macabre dance of death.

If True were here he'd say something infinitely sensible right now, Cady knew – something like, 'Them ol' buzzards is jist dryin' out their wings after all the rain.'

But True was not around, and this was not a day for being sensible.

It was like an omen.

Her stomach churned and she hurried back indoors to the relative gloom of the house, setting Radar down near his food dish and making her way back to the couch, where she stretched out flat on her back and gritted her teeth.

Something was wrong. Something was very wrong.

Cady told herself she was being foolish. Told herself to forget about the vultures and eat some dry toast. Told herself to go back to bed and sleep it off.

She wondered where Zach was.

That was it, then. Something terrible had happened to Zach. She knew it. She *knew* it.

Don't be silly. Nothing's wrong. You're being neurotic.

She couldn't help it. She picked up the phone and dialed Zach's cellular phone in the pick-up. After four rings, she hung up.

Could be anything. Could be he's on horseback and far away from the truck by now. Could be nothing.

She made herself choke down some dry crackers. Took a shower. Tried to read. Dozed.

Waited.

The noon hour came and Zach did not return home. Cady had prepared a stew, and she ate a little of it while she waited. *It's not the first time he's been late at dinnertime*, she told herself.

She peered out the window toward True's place. But the house was not readily visible from the kitchen window and she couldn't tell if he and Dusty were back or not. Maybe she should call.

Not just yet, she told herself.

Joe lived in town and drove out to the ranch each morning to work. His pick-up was not parked in its usual spot near the barn this morning. Very unusual.

Around one o'clock, the phone rang. Cady snatched it up, hoping it was Zach.

Crowd noises in the background. A ringing cash register. 'Cady?'

'Georgia? Where are you?'

'I'm in town. Listen, girlfriend, I've heard some news here in town, and I figured you'd appreciate it if I was the first person to tell you.'

Cady's heart went cold. She swallowed. She knew it was bad, knew it already, didn't want to hear it. She waited.

'Rex Zimmerman's dead. Somebody shot him this morning. His wetback hand came tearing into town, looking for the sheriff. They say he was too scared to stay on the place, you know, and call for help . . . Cady? You there?'

Chapter Twenty-Five

It took a moment for the reality of what Georgia had said to sink in. Cady sat heavily on the couch and took a deep breath. The first thing she said was, 'You mean Zach's okay?'

'What? I didn't say anything about Zach. I said—'

'I heard what you said. It's just . . . I've had this awful feeling all day that something terrible has happened to Zach.'

Rex Zimmerman was dead. She repeated that in her mind. The memory of the mud and blood and spit of last week's fight was still so vivid that she simply could not accept the fact that the man was actually dead.

'Are you sure this is true, Georgia? You know how gossip spreads. Stories grow.'

'I heard it from the guy who runs the Limpia Hotel. He was at the courthouse when the wetback came running in, rattling Tex-Mex so fast even the Mexicans had trouble understanding him.'

'Do they know who did it?'

'I don't know. I don't think so. They're questioning the wet.'

Rex Zimmerman was dead. For the first time, Cady began to consider the implications of this. If Rex were dead, then his sister stood to inherit the ranch. And she'd already gone on record as saying she opposed the two-acre ranchette program.

So the valley was saved.

'My God,' breathed Cady.

'What?'

'You don't think . . .'

'Don't think what.'

Cady felt a little prick of fear in her heart. She couldn't say it, and she prayed no one else had thought it.

'Whatwhatwhat?'

'Nothing.'

'Oh, I *hate* it when you do that! C'mon, tell me.'

'It's nothing, really.' *Nothing,* she thought, *except . . . Could my husband be capable of murder?*

It was after two before Zach rumbled down from the mountains, hauling a dusty trailer. Cady immediately left the house and jogged down to the barn to see him. Weary lines etched his face as he unloaded his lathered horse from the trailer.

Cady leaned up to kiss him and followed him to the barn, where he unsaddled his horse. 'What took you so long?' she asked, watching the dogs leap tiredly out of the pick-up and hurry over to the water troughs, where they lapped and lapped.

'A mama cow and calf got separated up in the mountains. Took one hell of a ride through the brush to get 'em back together again and put 'em where I wanted 'em.' He placed the damp saddle on a mock-horse barrel, then took the sweaty, hairy horse blanket and laid it upside-down on top of the saddle to dry out. A sweat stain in the shape of a saddle remained on the horse. Zach removed the bridle, patted the animal on the neck, and hung the bridle on a nail. The first thing the horse did was lower his ponderous body to the dusty ground and roll vigorously. Zach leaned down to unfasten his chaps.

'I have some news,' said Cady. He glanced up at her, removed the chaps, and hung them on another nail. 'Rex Zimmerman's dead.'

'What?' He whirled to look at her.

'Somebody shot him.'

His eyes, beneath the brim of his hat in the shadowy saddle house, were clouded, the expression impenetrable. He turned away from her, took off his hat, and rubbed his hand through his hair. 'When?'

'Sometime this morning. One of his hands – a wetback, they say – ran into town to get the sheriff.'

He swiveled toward her and said, 'Zimmerman had a wetback?'

It was not what she expected to hear. 'Well, yeah, apparently. I mean, it's obviously illegal, but I don't know what difference that makes.'

'I thought all his hands were helping the Rocking A work cattle today. That's where I sent Dusty and True and Joe.' He turned away again, mystifying her. 'I'd have gone myself, but I saw this cow yesterday. Her bag was really full, and I knew if we didn't find her calf soon, it would die.' He leaned his hands against one of the mock-horse barrels, his head lowered between his shoulders. 'How'd you find out?'

'Georgia called me from town.'

He was quiet for a moment. 'Do they have any idea who did it?'

'No.' She approached her husband and put her hand

on his tense shoulders. There was nothing else she could say.

Though Zach usually came home at noon ravenous, he only picked at his stew. Then he stretched out on the living room floor on his back, with only a sofa pillow beneath his neck, and fell into a deep sleep. His exhaustion had a finality to it that disturbed Cady. She wondered if she had passed on a flu bug to him. She almost hoped that's what it was.

She sat for a long while, watching her husband, thinking about him. Radar lay in her lap and she stroked him absently.

Could a man gentle enough to rescue a blind kitten be capable of cold-blooded murder?

Could he?

No, she decided. *No.*

And that's all there was to it. She was being paranoid. Period.

Zach was still asleep on the floor when the dogs began barking to the sounds of a vehicle pulling up in the drive around the house. He did not wake up.

Cady glanced out the window and felt the old constriction in her chest. It was the sheriff. He was accompanied by a sturdily built, clean-cut man wearing brown trousers, a pearl-gray Stetson, and a plain white Western shirt. Pinned to the pocket was the simple silver-peso badge of the Texas Rangers.

She met them at the back door and invited them in. At the sounds of their voices, Zach stumbled to his feet and trailed into the kitchen, hair disheveled, eyes sleepy.

'Sorry to disturb you folks,' said Dub, removing his

hat and extending a hand to shake with Zach.

'No problem, Dub. You caught me napping.'

'I'd like to introduce ya'll to Jeff Jenkins. He's the Ranger from Alpine. Serves this county and a bunch others. Anyway, he's come out here to help me today.'

'Come on in and sit down,' said Cady, her own voice betraying her nervousness. While she might not know a great deal about ranching, one thing Cady Maxwell did know was law enforcement officers. The purposeful look in Dub's eyes, and the quiet, steely gaze of the Ranger was unmistakeable to her, and it made her ill at ease.

'Wish I could take a little snooze right about now myself,' said Dub.

'Would you like a glass of iced tea?' asked Cady.

'That'd be jist fine, thank you.'

Cady hurried into the kitchen and made a glass for each of them. She didn't know about Zach, but her mouth was dry.

When she returned, the sheriff was exclaiming over Radar. 'Now don't that beat all?' he said, taking a glass from Cady. 'Little feller acts like he knows jist what he's doin'.'

'He's memorized the layout of these rooms already,' said Cady. 'We just try not to confuse him by putting things like laundry baskets in the middle of the floor.'

Dub chuckled. He watched as Radar sniffed his way over to where Cady sat and pulled himself up onto the couch to sit next to her. 'He doesn't jump up on things because he has no way of knowing how high they are,' she explained, taking the kitten into her lap. 'So he climbs up and jumps down.'

'But he doesn't know how far down it is either, so

he always takes this huge leap,' offered Zach.

Dub smiled, shook his head, sipped his tea.

And that was about all the conversation anybody could think of for a moment.

Finally, Dub said, 'I came to ask a real big favor of you, Mrs Ralston.'

'Oh, please, call me Cady.'

'Cady. All right. Nice name. Not Katie, right?'

'Right. I was named after Elizabeth Cady Stanton.'

Dub blinked, and Cady realized he had no idea who that was. She leaned forward. 'What can I do for you?'

'Well, I guess you folks have heard about Rex Zimmerman. Town this size, it's all anybody's talkin' about, I expect.'

Cady nodded.

'Well, thang is, we got us a witness to the shootin'.'

'Who?' asked Zach sharply.

Cady glanced at him. He said nothing more.

'Ol' Rex had him one o'them illegal aliens, a wetback. Guy was hidin' in the barn when the trouble started, but he saw it happen through a knothole in the wood. Imagine that. Anyway, he panicked. Man didn't even know how to dial 911, course, it wouldn't a done him any good anyway, since we don't have that service out here in the boonies. He's illiterate – couldn't read the phone book, didn't know how to call for help, so he jist came runnin' into town. I thank the further he drove, the scareder he got.'

Cady knew what was coming. She studied the melting ice in her tea glass.

'Now, I know about how you got injured and all back in Dallas, Cady, and I hate to ask you this, but we sure could use some help gittin' a composite sketch done o' this suspect.'

'The artist we normally use is out of town,' offered Ranger Jenkins. 'When Dub told me you were living here now, I couldn't believe our luck.' He smiled. He didn't look quite so steely, after all.

Cady glanced helplessly at Zach. She had not picked up a pencil since the assault. There was no way of knowing if she could even do what they were asking. Zach gazed back at her, as if to say, 'It's your decision.'

Heart pounding, she held out her gnarled hand, unconsciously studying it. 'I haven't done this since . . . I left Dallas,' she said.

'We realize that ma'am,' said Jenkins. 'But we're pressed for time.'

He didn't have to tell Cady that the longer they waited to begin a serious search for the killer, the colder the trail got. She sighed. 'I'm pretty rusty,' she said lamely, unwilling to say what was really screaming through her mind: *What if I can't do it? What if I can't do it?*

Jenkins caught her eye. 'It doesn't have to be the Mona Lisa.' There was a slight note of impatience in his voice. Like most cops, he wanted to get on with it. All this socializing, with Radar and the iced tea, had probably driven him crazy.

Her mouth was dry again, but her tea was gone. She crunched some ice. 'Okay. Just let me run upstairs and get my things.'

Relief lit up the officers' faces. Cady glanced at Zach. He was not looking at her.

She hurried upstairs. Her hands were shaking as she gathered up the sketching materials, the *FBI*

271

Facial Identification Catalog, and the other tools of her trade and stuffed them into the battered old leather carryall she had at one time never left home without. How strange it felt to be doing this again, and yet, it was as if she had never left. She felt a little thrill of excitement, and a twinge of nerves.

It's my decision, she thought. *I can do this. I know I can.*

She ran a quick brush through her hair and put on a black cotton blazer over her jeans and white tee shirt. She figured that would be professional-looking enough for Fort Davis. Besides, the officers were waiting.

Downstairs, the three men were standing in the living room, chatting about that favorite country topic: the weather. Cady lifted her face to Zach for a quick kiss. 'I don't know when I'll be back,' she said.

'We'll brang her home safe an' sound,' said Dub. He and the Ranger headed for the back door. Cady stepped after them, but Zach touched her arm. She turned back.

'Go get 'em, tiger,' he said, his eyes strangely hollow. 'And just remember one thing: I love you.'

Suddenly, and without warning, that creepy feeling of dread which had plagued Cady all morning long shadowed her once again.

She searched her beloved husband's eyes, trying to read them, and saw only a stranger gazing back.

Cady was led to and left in a small room in the county courthouse. A window overlooked a courtyard shaggy with trees. Gazing out the window, Cady could see Hank, ecstatically accepting pats on the head from a tourist. The door opened and in walked Molly Maguire, unlit cigar clamped firmly between her teeth.

'What are you doing here?' blurted Cady in delighted surprise.

'Hell, they needed an interpreter. None of the Meskins wanted to do it. Like I got nothin' better to do.' She plunked her thick body down in a folding chair, rocked back, and propped her boots up on the scarred wooden table. 'This better go fast. I got a windmill needs fixin'.'

'I should be done in less than an hour,' Cady said, and immediately wondered if her hand would work as fast any more. She made a tight fist with it and squeezed.

'Reckon them fangers is still up to it?' asked Molly, her hawk eyes missing nothing.

'I hope so.' Cady gave her a weak smile.

'Hell, if that old fart True kin bridle a horse, and him so twisted up hisself, then I figger you shouldn't have no trouble.'

'He's quite a character, isn't he?'

'None like him. Only don't tell him I said so.'

The door opened, and in walked Ranger Jenkins and a very frightened, very dark little man, who twisted his wide-brimmed hat around and around in his hands. Jenkins showed him to a chair beside Cady and leaned against the wall, arms folded across his chest. The little man glanced over his shoulder at the Ranger with wide, white eyes.

'Jenkins, if this here feller ain't under arrest, then git the hell out of here. We don't need you, and you're scarin' the shit out of him.' Molly thunked the chair down to the floor with authority.

Cady almost swallowed her tongue.

Jenkins frowned mightily at Molly, glanced down at the little man, and shrugged. He left the room, closing the door firmly behind him.

Cady flipped to a clean sheet on her pad and smiled reassuringly at the man. 'What's your name?'

'*Como se llama?*' asked Molly.

'Pablo Romero,' he said, so quietly they could barely hear him. Molly reached into a breast pocket and withdrew a cigar. She leaned over and handed it to Romero, who grinned broadly. She spoke rapid Spanish, he nodded, and stuck it in his mouth without lighting it.

Cady picked up a pencil in her right hand. It dropped to the floor and rolled underneath the table. Face hot, she reached under the table and groped for it, giving herself a split second to calm herself. She sat back up and placed the pencil in her right hand again.

She couldn't hold it. Somewhat desperately, she tried again, but with her thumb crooked out and to the side, the pencil had no prop. She took her bottom lip between her teeth and tried again. It still wouldn't stay.

Romero shifted uneasily in his seat.

Cady dropped the pencil again. Tears of frustration pricked behind her eyelids as she stooped to pick it up.

'Here, try this,' said Molly, taking the pencil from Cady. 'Stick it between your fangers, like this.' She jammed the pencil into Cady's hand.

It stayed.

Cady stared at her hand. *I can't do this*, she thought. *I can't.*

In the back of her mind, she heard Zach's voice saying, *It's your decision.*

She cleared her throat. Without looking at Romero, she said, 'Could you tell me a little something about the man? Was he white or Hispanic or black?'

Molly translated, listened to the man's answer, and said, 'White.'

Cady gestured with her hands, around her face. 'Do you remember the shape of the man's face? Let me show you.' While Molly's Spanish rattled behind them, she showed Romero the general face shapes as set forth in the *FBI Facial Identification Catalog*: oval, round, triangle, rectangle, long.

He studied the pages and tapped on the one marked, 'long'.

Hesitantly, bracing her hand against the pad to keep it from trembling, Cady began sketching an elongated face shape, using very light pencil strokes. She expected to be erasing a great deal.

She asked what color hair the man had. Romero said dark, and added that the man had a mustache.

While Romero pored over the catalog pages detailing eyes ('squinting', 'deep-set', 'close-set', 'wide-set', and so on), Cady worked on the hair as he had described it. Finally, he chose two different photos of eyes that resembled those of the man he'd seen shoot Rex Zimmerman.

Although the pencil felt strange and unfamiliar, gripped, as it was, between Cady's fingers, her hand seemed to have a memory of its own, moving swiftly across the page as though it had never left. Her old sureness of touch was lacking, a confidence matter that she was going to have to work on, but her skill remained strong. Her heart leapt within her.

The nose was more difficult for Romero, possibly because he had only really noticed the mustache. He was also unsure about the brows, for the man had been wearing a cowboy hat. He had no trouble pointing out the mustache type in the catalog.

So intent was Cady on the physical mechanics of putting pencil to paper and rendering a sure likeness to match the witness's description, that she did not at first notice anything amiss.

It wasn't until Molly gasped that Cady pulled back from her almost cramped inspection of the drawing to see what was wrong with Molly. When she glanced back at the picture, as if seeing it as a whole for the first time – and not just as separate features – Cady's stomach went stone cold.

No. It couldn't be. She was just being paranoid again.

She stopped drawing for a moment, waiting on Romero to describe the mouth and chin. Usually she worked nonstop, touching up this portion or finishing that, while a witness pondered.

This time she waited.

Finally, he pointed out the pictures in the catalog and gestured with his hands – speaking rapid Spanish to Molly – showing Cady what the rest of the face looked like.

Cady's breath began coming out in little shallow gasps. She wanted to quit drawing right then, snatch the paper off the pad and rip it into shreds.

She wanted to burn every pencil she owned and never draw again.

Because there, right in front of her and for all the world to see, was a beautifully rendered Cady Maxwell sketch . . . of her husband, Zacharia Ralston.

PART IV

'I do believe it was love which first devised the torturer's profession here on earth.'

Titus Maccius Plautus

'Take hope from the heart of man, and you have left a beast of prey.'

Oida (Marie Louis de la Ramee)

Chapter Twenty-Six

At that inopportune moment, the door swung open and Ranger Jenkins entered the room. He did a double take at the drawing, and then said, 'Ma'am, this looks an awful lot like your husband.'

Cady nodded, afraid to say anything.

'Do you think you could have made some kind of mistake? Like, maybe you were thinkin' about him or something?'

'Thar's been a mistake made here, all right,' boomed Molly, 'but she didn't make it.'

He left the room and came right back with Dub in tow. Dub studied the drawing with crinkled brow, then said, 'Cady, do you think this man knows Zacharia?'

She shrugged. 'I don't have any way of knowing.'

Lips pursed, Dub nodded. Finally, he said, 'Well, hellfar and brimstone.'

'You gonna haul Zacharia in here and arrest him?' demanded Molly of Dub. 'You do, and thar'll be a lynch mob form outside, and it'll be for *your* neck.'

'Of course not,' said Jenkins. 'We'll need to do a line-up first, and get a positive ID from Mr Romero. I'm sure Mr Ralston will be glad to cooperate with that. And we'll want to ask him some questions, anyway. It's no secret in this town that he and Zimmerman had a feud going way back.'

'I'll grant ye that the killer might *look* like Zacharia,' insisted Molly, 'but thar's no way that boy's a killer hisself.'

For the moment everyone had forgotten Cady, standing sick and miserable in the corner.

A fear so deep it had no name had gripped her heart in cold hands. She couldn't imagine Zach killing anyone, but then, *they* hadn't seen the look on his face when he was pummeling Rex Zimmerman senseless in the mud and fog. *Get his carcass off my property*, he had said, *before I kill him.*

She thought about how late he'd been getting in for dinner that day, how exhausted he and the animals were, his strange behavior when she told him Zimmerman was dead, how disturbed he'd been that there'd been a witness. *I thought all his hands were helping work cattle at the Rocking A*, he'd said. *That's where I sent True and Dusty and Joe.*

She thought of all these things, but said nothing.

'Well,' said Dub, studiously avoiding looking into Cady's eyes, 'I guess we need to run you on home.' Jenkins took Cady's drawing and steered Romero out of the room by the elbow.

Moving like a robot, Cady slowly gathered up her things. Dub held the door for her and, as they headed down the hall, Molly's voice echoed down to them, 'Jist don't you fergit, Dub Garner, thar's some folks in this world need killin'.'

Zach came out of the house, hatless, looking rumpled and familiar and dear, and met them as Dub drove Cady up the lane.

I've betrayed him, Cady thought. Her eyes filled

with tears and she blinked them rapidly away. She'd only been doing her job – no more, no less – but somehow, she felt a grave responsibility for the outcome.

Worse, she felt doubt, and that hurt more than anything.

Zach opened the car door for her, helped her out, and took her things. She tried to smile at him and couldn't.

Dub got out and leaned his elbows on the roof of the car. 'We got us a little problem here, Zacharia,' he said. The eyes of the two men met across the expanse of the automobile. 'That witness seems to thank whoever shot Rex Zimmerman looked a whole helluva lot like you. We're gonna need to ask you a few questions.'

Zach's gaze dropped to Cady's and he searched her face.

'I'm so sorry,' she blurted, and her voice broke. Against her will, a tear crept down one cheek. He put an arm around her and squeezed her tightly against him. She could feel his big heart thumping reassuringly against her ear. 'It's all right,' he murmured. 'It's not your fault.'

His arm around her was as safe and solid as it had ever been, but so very much had changed in such a short time.

'Just let me get my hat and my wallet, Dub, and I'll come along with you.' He headed into the house, with Cady following closely behind. Dub, out of respect and trust, waited outside.

As he headed toward the bedroom, where his wallet rested on the bureau, Cady began to babble. 'Molly

Maguire was translating, and I was just concentrating on face parts, you know, eyes and ears and things that he picked out of the FBI ID Catalog. I didn't even notice it looked like you, Zach, until Molly pointed it out.'

Stuffing his wallet into his worn back pocket, Zach said, 'I don't blame you, Cady. I'm just glad you were able to draw again.'

'Oh, Zach.' She felt the tears again, big ones this time, and she struggled not to lose control. It was the last thing he needed.

He picked up a comb and ran it through his hair, stooping to see in the mirror. 'I guess I'd better change my shirt,' he mumbled. 'Sweaty as I got this morning.' He rummaged in the closet for a white Western 'town' shirt.

Watching him toss the denim shirt in a bundle in a corner of the room, she said, 'I don't understand what's going on.' She bit on her bottom lip. 'I don't know why this man thinks you shot Rex.'

He pulled himself up to his full height as he fastened the pearl snaps on the crisp white cotton shirt, stared her square in the face, and said quietly. 'Do *you* think I did it?'

She had not expected the question, did not have an answer ready. Cady didn't know *what* she thought.

He read her hesitation and, to her horror, a hardness came into his eyes. 'I see,' he said, tucking in the shirt and connecting the silver buckle on his dress belt. 'So much for my wife believing in me.' He brushed coldly past her and headed down the hall toward the stairs.

'*Zach! Wait!*' she cried. She hurried after him. 'Please.'

He stopped and looked back at her.

'I love you,' she said, fighting to hold back the floodgates.

'Don't you see?' he asked gently. 'It's not the same thing.' And he turned and strode through the living room.

Numbly, she followed.

As he was putting on his good hat, he said, 'You'll have to tell the guys what happened and make sure Dusty knows to bring in the horses and get them fed. And somebody'll have to come out later and pick me up.'

'I'll pick you up, Zach,' she said helplessly, but he had already gone out the door.

The men returned from the Rocking A ranch just a few minutes after Zach and the sheriff had left. Cady was an emotional shambles. There'd been no time to get her thoughts collected, to face the reality of what was happening to them and deal with it. *So much for my wife believing in me*, Zach had said.

And that was the question. *Did* she believe her husband had murdered a man?

In the hundreds of times that Cady had sat across from shaken witnesses and done composite sketches for them of their assailants, there was never any question about believing them. She — and the officers who distributed the sketches — believed that the criminals they sought were represented there. She'd never seen one convicted on the basis of her sketch alone, but the sketches usually put the officers on the right track and, once the perpetrators were found, then other evidence tended to follow, sometimes even a confession.

The trouble was, Cady was used to thinking like a cop, not like a wife.

That nervous little man had never wavered. He seemed to know what he was looking for, for the most part, and once he found it in the ID catalog, he'd seemed satisfied with her rendering.

Could Zimmerman have been shot by somebody who bore an incredible resemblance to her husband?

What were the odds of that happening? Especially in a town as close-knit as this one. Wouldn't they have run into one another at some time, or been mistaken for one another by the local townspeople?

She was still wrestling with these thoughts, still struggling to maintain self-control (though very tempted to just give in to the despair she was feeling), when the ranch pick-up and long, four-horse trailer rattled down the road past the house and around to the barn.

Heavy-hearted, Cady wandered slowly down the path to where the men were unloading their tired horses out of the trailer. As they hollered hello and went about the business of unsaddling their mounts, it occurred to Cady that they hadn't even heard the news yet.

She positioned herself in the door of the saddle house and said, 'Guys, I have some bad news.' They stopped what they were doing and stared. 'Rex Zimmerman was murdered today. Shot. A wetback saw it happen and he ... he thinks the killer might be Zach. Or somebody who looks a lot like him,' she hastened to add. She left out her part in the whole ordeal.

'What?' Joe tipped his hat back on his head. 'You got to be kiddin'.'

'I wish I was. Zach's with Dub right now, answering some questions.'

'Shiiiiit,' he said, kicking a rock with his toe.

'They don't think Zach did it, do they?' asked Dusty anxiously, his young face glowing with sweat and red from the sun.

'I don't know,' said Cady. 'They're just asking him some questions right now, I think mainly because of the fight last week.'

'Thar ain't no dang point in them wastin' thar time with a innocent man,' said True. 'I know him and he'd never do such a thang.'

True believes in Zach, Cady thought guiltily. *So does Molly. But he couldn't get his own wife to support him when he needed it most*. She glanced away from True's penetrating gaze and stepped down from the saddle house door.

Silently, the men finished unsaddling the horses.

'Oh, Dusty,' said Cady. 'I almost forgot. Zach said for you to remember to go get the horses and make sure they're fed this evening.'

'He did?' gasped Dusty. True and Joe turned and stared. 'I never got to do that before.'

True said, 'Son, I reckon he feels you've earned the privilege.' He didn't smile, but his eyes twinkled.

'Oh, man,' said Dusty. He disappeared into the barn while the other men parked and took the pick-up loose from the trailer.

When the boy didn't come out after a minute, Cady followed him into the shadowy, sneezy recesses of the big building. From over in a dark corner, she heard a muffled sob. She tiptoed toward the sound and found the boy sitting on a hay bale, hunched over his knees, his face in his hands.

'Dusty?' She stepped closer. 'What's wrong?'

He shook his head and turned away from her, wiping furiously at his nose with his sleeve. 'It's all my fault,' he mumbled.

'What is?' She put a hand on the thin shoulder blade that stuck out from his back like a little wing. She'd seen the kid eat like a horse, but he worked hard and carried not an ounce of fat on him.

He murmured something else.

'What?' She waited. 'C'mon, it's all right.'

'I did it,' he said.

Her blood ran cold. 'Did what, Dusty?'

He gulped and took a shuddering breath. 'I tore all those surveyor's markers off the trees, down in the valley. I did it. That's what started this whole thang. That's why Rex came over here and picked a fight with Zach. That's why this whole thang happened.' He stifled a sob. 'And he's trustin' me. He's trustin' me to go git the horses, and it's my fault he's in so much trouble.'

'Oh, Dusty.' Cady let out her breath in one relieved *whoosh*. 'You can't blame yourself for this. It's not your fault. There's been bad blood between those two men going way back. Hell, if Zimmerman wanted to pick a fight with Zach, he could have come up with most any excuse.' In her voice, she could hear the beginning of a West Texas twang.

'Really?'

'Really. And Zach would never trust you with such an important job if he didn't think you could handle it.' She could almost see the tension unwinding from the back of his neck. How vulnerable he looked, sitting here in the dark, hiding his fears. Still just a child, really. She patted him on the back and said, 'Well, you better go get those horses and take care of them.'

He nodded, and Cady turned away and walked out of the barn, leaving the boy-man with his dignity.

Back in the big, hollow house, evening was gathering its haunches beneath itself and crouching, ever-vigilant, as Cady fed Radar and forced a sandwich into her jittery stomach. She couldn't tell if the gloom which seemed to follow every move she made came from the house or from her.

She couldn't get down the last of the sandwich and opened the back porch door to toss it out for the dogs. A movement, high above the mountain crags which hulked near the ranch buildings caught her eye.

Vultures, circling in a slow lazy spiral on out-stretched wings and updrafts, moving in concentric circles, around and around high over the mountains, searching, searching.

She slammed the door and, hands shaking, gathered up her purse and the car keys for the Lexus. She would go to Zach, wherever he was, and wait there. Anything was better than this.

The phone rang. Her heart leaped. Maybe it was Zach, calling to tell her it was all a great big mistake and he was free to come home.

She picked it up on the second ring, too anxious to wait for the machine.

The voice was almost a hiss. '*Whatever you do, my beautiful Cady, don't you ever forget about me.*'

Chapter Twenty-Seven

She did not panic. She said, 'Who are you?'

'You know who I am. In your heart, you know.'

'Why are you doing this to me?' She sat down and took a deep breath.

'Because I love you desperately, but you don't seem to realize yet that you love me in the same way.'

'How can I love you?' she said, and risked, 'I don't even know you.'

There was a slight hesitation, then a soft chuckle. *'Oh, very good. You, my beautiful Cady, are so smart. You thought you could get me to tell you who I am, didn't you?'*

Cady didn't take the bait. She said, 'If you're so crazy about me, why don't you show yourself?'

'And why don't you open your eyes?'

'What does that mean?'

'For an artist, you can be so blind.'

'Then I already know you? Is that what you're saying?' Her heart began a slow pounding in her throat. She waited.

There was a *click*, followed by the dial tone.

Cady allowed herself a small smile of triumph. This was the first time the stalker had hung up on *her*.

She was getting stronger, and he knew it. Perhaps that frightened him. Maybe it took away his sense of control over her. Which was just what she wanted.

Her little smile faded to a small frown. *Could* she actually *know* her stalker?

No. It couldn't be. Cady didn't know anybody who would be capable of this kind of harassment.

At least, she didn't think she did. Of course, in her line of work she was used to seeing many people who were not what they seemed: the priest who molested children; the banker who raped; the coach who robbed.

She flashed back to the living nightmare she had experienced, of waking up in her bed, covered with white rose petals, beaten senseless, her drawing hand mangled. Whoever was watching her, calling her, following her, *stalking* her, was also capable of nearly killing her.

Was there anyone Cady knew who was actually capable of such a thing?

Which brought her back to the present, and the car keys she still gripped in her hand.

And her husband, accused of murder.

Cady was stunned to find the courthouse empty and dark, locked securely against the night. She stood for a moment beneath wind-whipped trees, bewildered and lost, like Dorothy who suddenly finds herself in Oz, without a clue as to how she got there.

Exhaustion tempted her to just walk away, to get in the car and escape from her ever-more-complicated life, but she ignored the temptation and dragged herself over to the warmly lit Limpia Hotel, to ask the owner if he had any idea where everybody had gone.

There was no jail in Fort Davis, he informed her.

Matters as weighty as murder had to be settled over in Alpine.

Hollow-chested, hands shaking, Cady made her way back to the car for the drive to Alpine. *No jail in Fort Davis.* That must mean that they intended to put Zach in jail.

This can't be happening, she told herself as she headed down the empty, black highway, cold fingers gripping the steering wheel, her car headlights boring fruitlessly into the velvet darkness. *They can't put Zach in jail. He didn't kill Rex Zimmerman.*

Or did he?

She despised herself for her own doubts. He was her *husband*, for God's sake.

For an artist, you can be so blind, the disembodied voice had said to her. Had she been blind? So love-sodden that she hadn't realized the man she was marrying could be capable of deadly violence?

How well did she really know him?

After all, they'd gotten married so quickly. She bit her bottom lip. Had she just grabbed onto the first security she could find after the assault? Had moving out here and marrying this cowboy been some big elaborate subconscious plan to escape her own fear?

Had she made a terrible mistake?

Her stomach turned over and she opened the car window, gulping fresh cool mountain air.

The unlit highway was blacker than black. *The darkest night sky in the world,* Zach had said. Cady felt foreign, separate, as if she were some alien creature hurtling through space in a time capsule toward an unknown destiny.

You never belonged here in the first place,

whispered a mean little voice in her head. *This place isn't you. It's a B-movie Western, and you just happened to stumble onto the set. You ought to pack up your pencils and get the hell back home.*

She shook her head, as though doing so would clear the spidery thoughts from the cobwebs of her mind.

What home?

She had thought her home to be at the ranch, with Zach Ralston, the man she had married, the man she didn't know.

Dub Garner was gentlemanly and apologetic. 'I'm sorry, Cady,' he told her when she finally caught up with him at the Alpine jail. Weary lines pulled at his face. 'Romero positively identified Zacharia as the man he saw kill Rex.'

'But . . . was he *sure*?' she asked, fighting the panic which was rising up inside her.

'I'm afraid so. The man seemed to have no doubt at all.'

'But . . . how much could he see through a knothole?'

'He saw enough, I reckon.' He took off his glasses and rubbed the rut they'd made on his nose.

'I can't believe this is happening,' said Cady.

'I know how you feel. It seems that way to me, too.'

Her thoughts were a jumble. She struggled to sort them out. 'Well, can't they release Zach on his own recognizance, or something? Has he called a lawyer?'

Dub replaced the glasses, which slipped right down into the rut. 'He's called his lawyer in Midland, but the guy's a civil lawyer, not a criminal one. He said he'd come out tomorrow, but jist 'tween you n' me, I'd git Zacharia somebody else. I don't thank this guy knows much about what he's doin'.'

Cady nodded, feeling again that dreamlike sense of unreality. 'Can't I take him home?' she pleaded. 'You know he'll show up for any hearing or whatever.'

'I know that, Cady. Ever'body knows that. But we got to follow correct criminal procedure here, no matter who it is. Zacharia's got to wait for his preliminary hearing tomorrow. The judge'll decide then about bail.'

'I didn't bring him anything from home,' she mumbled, half to herself. 'I just assumed I'd be taking him back.' She shook her head. 'It never really occurred to me that he would be arrested.'

'Hardest thang I ever had to do,' said Dub bitterly. 'Dang near cried.'

She touched his arm. 'I'm sure Zach realizes that, Dub. I know I do.'

He sighed heavily. 'I know he an' Rex hated each other, but I never thought Zacharia would ever be capable of killin' the man.' He looked away from her.

He's given up on Zach, she thought. *He just assumes Zach did it.*

And what was he supposed to think? A witness had placed him at the scene, gun in hand, period. Not only that, but the whole town knew how Zach felt about Rex and he did stand to gain, in a sense, from Rex's death. She shuddered, remembering the first day Zach had shown her the valley; his rage at the presence of the scarlet streamers.

People had been convicted on less.

It seemed then as if every muscle in her body, every sinew, had suddenly taken on extra weight; it dragged at her and suffocated her.

295

'Can I see him?' Her voice was low and sounded pitiful, even to Cady.

Dub hesitated. 'Well, normally I'd have to say no, but you wait right here and I'll see what I can do.' He disappeared through a doorway and Cady sank into a hard wooden chair.

Her injured hand ached from the day's activities, the drawing and the driving. *Funny*, she mused as she rubbed on the hand, *after I got hurt, I thought my life was over.*

It was Zach, in fact, who had given her a reason to live.

Now she wondered if that life, too, were coming to an end.

Zach had aged years in the hours since Cady had last seen him. Dub had given them a small room in which to talk, while he waited outside the door. To her surprise, he brought Zach to her uncuffed, something that would never have happened in a big city. But then, she'd never have been allowed to see him in the city unless it was the scheduled visiting time.

Zach wrapped his arms around her and they clung to each other for a long time. She could feel her own body trembling against his, but Zach was steady. Only his eyes betrayed his own anxiety.

They sat down side by side in two of the hard wooden chairs and held hands. 'Did Dusty take care of the horses?' Zach asked.

She nodded. 'He was thrilled to be given the opportunity.'

Zach smiled. 'Kid's growing up.' He sighed and rubbed his hand through his hair. 'I'll need to talk to

True about the place. We've got a workin' comin' up. Some cows and their calves need vaccinatin'.' It was typical of Zach to be worried about the ranch above anything else.

'Don't worry.' She squeezed his hand. 'True and Joe and Dusty can take care of everything until you get out of here.'

He leaned his head back against the cold wall. '*If* I get out.'

'Of course you'll get out.'

'I don't know. They've got a pretty good case against me already.'

'Circumstantial,' said Cady, her legal mind taking over in spite of herself.

'They've got a witness.'

'Who saw the shooting through a knothole, for God's sake. A good lawyer could tear him apart on the stand.' She peered at him. 'You need a good lawyer, Zach.'

He shrugged. 'It doesn't matter,' he said. 'They're going to do what they want with me anyway.'

'*Zach!* I can't believe you'd say that.'

'Well, you ought to see things from my angle.'

Cady chewed on her bottom lip. She'd never seen him in such a defeatist frame of mind before. *Maybe he did do it,* said the wicked voice. *Maybe that's what he knows that you don't.*

Cady's hand throbbed and her head ached. Everything had happened so fast; she couldn't think, couldn't feel.

Dub tapped politely on the door and opened it. 'Sorry to bother you folks, but I need to be takin' Zacharia on back to the cell.'

To the cell. Suddenly, the full horror of Zach's situation dawned on Cady.

Here he was, a prisoner again.

Powerless.

The house was cold, dark, and empty when Cady made her exhausted way up the back porch steps and across the veranda. At the back door, she hesitated. It stood ajar. It creaked as she pushed it open and she snapped on a light switch as she entered.

The kitchen sprang to stark life and Cady blinked in the sudden bald light. For a moment she stood, trying to remember if she had securely fastened the door behind her when she left. She couldn't remember for sure, but the chances were good that she had not. She'd been in a hurry, after all. And she'd had that phone call on her mind.

She got herself a glass of milk out of the refrigerator and drank it at the sink, too weary to wash the glass. Then she headed through the shadowy dining room and into the dark living room. Faint light peeking through from the kitchen caught a glimpse of something ghostly and white that startled Cady. She flipped on the overhead light switch.

White roses, dozens of them, filled vases on the coffee table and end tables to overflowing, drooping petals prettily like teardrops, onto the dark polished floor beneath.

Chapter Twenty-Eight

Silence shrouded the house. Something creaked overhead. Cady's heart began a slow, heavy jerking in her chest. Something touched her leg and she cried out, jumping back and kicking Radar halfway across the floor in doing so. Murmuring apologies, she picked him up and cuddled him close to her, as much to reassure herself as him.

He had been in the house. Might still be, for all she knew.

The Beretta was upstairs, in the nightstand by the bed. Setting Radar down gently on the couch, Cady turned around and walked out of the house. Standing on the veranda in the wind and dark, Cady recalled ruefully that True and Dusty had gone to a Midland hospital to visit True's brother, who was dying.

With Joe at home in town, there would be no help for her.

She marched out the door and down the path toward Zach's ranch pick-up, intending to take down the Winchester 30-30 from the gun rack behind the seat and carry that with her while she searched the house.

It was gone.

That was strange. Zach always kept the Winchester in the pick-up. You never knew when a threatening rattlesnake or a rabid skunk made one necessary. She couldn't remember ever seeing the pick-up without it.

What could he have done with it?

In the house, upstairs at the end of the hall, was a locked gunrack, but Cady knew every slot in the gunrack was full, mostly with deer rifles and things that Zach rarely used. His dad had been a big hunter, he'd told her one time, but once Zach had returned from Vietnam, he said, he'd lost his taste for killing living things.

That's what he had told her. And now he was under arrest for the murder of Rex Zimmerman.

Cady sighed. Standing outdoors under billions of stars, listening to the wind moan through the trees, Cady looked around for the dogs. How could they have allowed an intruder into the house?

Do *something*, she thought.

At the moment, she couldn't stand the thought of stepping foot in that house again. Not now. Not with her husband locked up in jail and her living room full of those loathsome white roses. Not when she couldn't get at a gun, anyway.

She trudged back down the path to the house. The lights were still on downstairs, at least as far as the kitchen, so she went in, retrieved her bag, then left again.

Outside, she climbed wearily back into the Lexus and headed down the driveway toward the winding black mountain road.

'Oh no,' said Georgia when she opened the door. 'It has to be bad news or you wouldn't be here.'

'I'm sorry to interrupt your work,' said Cady, her

voice a bleak weary monotone. 'I just didn't know anywhere else to go.'

'Screw the work. Come in and talk to me.' Georgia took Cady's hand and led her into the rustic living room, where a warm fire flickered merrily in the wood-burning stove. 'Want some coffee?'

'No. I'm worn out and I don't want to be up all night.'

'Hot chocolate, then. Tell me what happened.'

Cady followed Georgia into the narrow kitchen which lined one side of the A-frame and sank onto a bar stool, while Georgia, on the other side of the bar, heated the cocoa.

'They arrested Zach.' It sounded incredible, saying it out loud.

'Oh, shit.' Georgia took down two mugs from the small cabinet over the sink. 'Why?'

'That witness identified him. It's partly my fault,' she said, and her voice broke. She leaned her face into her hands. Hot tears squeezed out between her fingers.

Georgia turned the flame out beneath the cocoa and came around the bar, where she perched on a stool next to Cady and put a reassuring arm around her shoulders. 'What do you mean? How can it be your fault?'

'Because, I did the composite sketch.' Cady put her head down on folded arms and wept.

Georgia's hand between her shoulder blades was warm and soothing. 'Oh, you poor kid. You can't blame yourself. How were you supposed to know the guy would describe your own husband?' Georgia went to fetch a box of Kleenex tissues, which she placed next to Cady's elbow. 'What a tough, tough day you must have had.' She stroked Cady's hair.

The gesture reminded Cady of her mother. Soothing.

After a moment, Georgia said, 'Cady? Do you think Zach really could have done it?'

'I don't know.' Cady blew her nose and dabbed at her swollen eyes. 'I just don't know. Sometimes I think that there's just no way, you know? I mean, he's my *husband*. And then other times . . .' She withdrew a clean tissue and held it over her face like a washcloth.

'Well, he did beat the crap out of Rex last week.'

'He nearly killed him, Georgia. That's why I fired the gun overhead.'

'You know, I hate to bring this up, but Zach *was* a POW and all. Maybe he's having some kind of post-traumatic stress thing. Maybe Rex just pushed him over the edge and he snapped.' Georgia went back into the kitchen, stirred the hot chocolate, and poured it into the mugs. 'You'll have to take it straight,' she said, pushing it across the bar toward Cady. 'I'm all out of marshmallows.'

Cady smiled weakly and took a grateful sip. Her friend hadn't said anything she hadn't thought herself, in the deep, dark recesses of her heart. She didn't want to talk about that aspect of Zach's nature: his mood swings and sudden rages. Not yet, anyway. After a moment, she said, 'I think maybe that guy was in my house tonight.'

'*What*? When?'

'When I went to Alpine to see about Zach. Dusty and True are out of town, and somehow he got into the house and put white roses all over the living room.'

'Holy shit, Cady! How'd he get past those dogs?'

'I don't know.' Cady's eyes burned. She closed them and pressed her fingers against the lids. 'That's why I came here. I didn't want to sleep in that house alone.' She yawned.

'Do you think he still could have been there? In the house?'

'I don't know. I didn't hang around long enough to find out.' She rolled her head around on her shoulders.

Georgia set down her mug. 'I'm glad you came. Jesus, Cady, you're so vulnerable out there now with Zach gone.'

Cady couldn't help an involuntary shiver. 'I have a feeling this guy knows that.'

'You better believe he knows it.' Georgia left the kitchen and started up the stairs. 'I'm sure he knows everything there is to know about you . . . Cady,' she said after a thoughtful moment, 'why didn't you call the cops?'

'What cops? Dub Garner *is* the cops, and he's in Alpine, busy throwing my husband in jail.'

'Oh. You do have a point there.' She headed up the stairs. 'I'm just getting you some sheets and things,' she called over her shoulder. 'I'll be right down.'

Cady slipped off the bar stool and wandered over to the couch, where she kicked off her shoes and stretched out, her head on its cushioned arm.

By the time Georgia got back, arms bulging with sheets, blankets, and pillows, Cady was out cold.

When Cady opened her eyes, only a small glow shone from the wood-burning stove and the room was chilly. Pale light peeped through heavy drapes which had been drawn across the expansive windows. She sat up groggily and stretched. A soft blanket had been tucked around her shoulders and the others placed neatly at the far end of the couch.

Cady knew Georgia would still be asleep. As an astronomer, she worked late into the night at her telescope, weather permitting. And last night had been crystal clear.

A frightening thought occurred to her: could she be endangering Georgia just by staying with her? The stalker seemed to know everything else she did.

Dismay, mingled with nausea and weariness, tugged at Cady's bones. She needed to get back home anyway. Looking back, she wondered if she had panicked prematurely at the sight of the roses, assuming automatically that the guy might still be in the house, refusing even to return there. She wondered if fatigue was making her panic now. Sunlight had a funny way of washing out old terrors and replacing them with common sense.

On the other hand, she had a pretty bad history with white roses.

Cady left a thank-you note on the bar and eased herself out of the house. On the way home, she wondered if stress had exacerbated that flu bug, if she should visit the doctor, maybe tank up on antibiotics. She would need to be strong in the coming weeks.

The men were tinkering about in the barn when Cady got back to the ranch. She knew she should talk to them right away, but she felt too shaky and weepy. And she didn't want to get into the thing about the white roses. What could they do about it now? Besides, they were upset enough about Zach's trouble. Added to True's sick brother, it just seemed like too much of a burden to put on the old man's shoulders – he would blame himself for not being there to protect her. She hurried into the house.

Like the night before, it was woefully silent, but this time, Cady ignored it. She walked straight through to the living room, where she gathered up the roses. Without hesitating, she stalked outside to the area at the back of the house where they burned the trash, and stuffed the roses into the blackened drums. She would burn them later.

Feeling better, more purposeful, she went back into the house and straight upstairs, where she took off her clothes and took a long, hot shower. Afterwards, trying to ignore their big, empty bed, Cady dressed in slacks and a blazer, dabbed some make-up on over the previous night's damage, and was heading downstairs for some toast when, out of the corner of her eye, she spotted Zach's shirt, wadded and tossed into a corner.

She picked it up and inhaled the scent of him. Longing and loneliness swept over her. After a moment, she went into the bathroom to throw the shirt in the hamper, when something else caught her eye. She pulled the shirt closer and examined it.

On the cuff of one sleeve were three tiny blood splatters.

Everything – even time itself – froze for Cady. This was the shirt Zach had been wearing when Rex Zimmerman was shot to death.

She stood there in the bathroom, holding her husband's shirt in trembling hands.

The phone rang. Cady jumped and let it ring. When the machine took over, the caller hung up.

She studied the blood spots. They were not stains which hadn't washed out. They were fresh.

Ranching could be bloody work at times – from castrating calves to doing veterinary work. Even slipping while sharpening that indispensable pocket knife could get blood droplets on a shirt cuff.

Cady knew the ins and outs of criminal investigation. She might very well be asked to hand over this shirt to law enforcement officers. DNA testing could pinpoint the source of the blood in a matter of a few short weeks.

But what if it wasn't innocent blood? What if it was Rex's blood?

Burn it, said a little voice. *With the white roses. Burn it.*

But no. They might find fragments of the burned shirt, then *Cady* might find herself under arrest as an accomplice to the crime.

Maybe it's not Rex's blood, she thought hopelessly. *Maybe it belongs to that calf who was separated from its mama, the one he said he'd been searching for in the mountains all morning.*

Maybe she should just turn it over to the sheriff. If her husband was innocent, what harm could it do?

Cady drifted down the stairs, the shirt clutched close to her heart.

If she truly believed in her husband's innocence, she would just hand the shirt over to the sheriff if he asked for it. Wouldn't she?

So much for my wife believing in me, Zach had said.

She looked at the bloodstains again, then reached

for her bag and impulsively stuffed the shirt deep inside it.

And if he's guilty, said the voice, *and you remove evidence of that guilt, and he comes home again to you . . . what will you do then?*

Moving like a robot, she fed Radar and gave him clean water. His litter box needed changing, but Cady was out of fresh litter. As if it were any other day, she made a note to get some in town. Life did, indeed, go on. One way or the other.

Then she squared her shoulders, slipped her bag over her arm, and went out to the barn to see True and Dusty and Joe.

As she had expected, they were horrified and outraged at Zach's arrest.

'Those sons of bitches?' cried Joe. 'They don't got no evidence whatsoever and they know it.'

'I'm hoping that's the way the judge will see it when he sets bail today,' said Cady, trying to sound confident.

'It's a travesty o' justice,' added True, his eyes watering. 'I cain't believe that anybody would suspect for even one moment that Zacharia would be capable of such a thang.'

Cady glanced away from his piercing gaze.

'We'll go with ye to the courthouse,' he added. 'Zacharia needs all the friends he kin git and, besides, thar ain't no need you going through this alone.'

'Oh True, I'd appreciate that so much.' Cady was ashamed of herself. It hadn't even occurred to her that the men might want to go to Zach's hearing.

'What time's it start?' asked Joe.

'Ten o'clock.'

'Dusty,' called True, 'let's go git cleaned up fer town.'

'I'll head on back to my house then,' said Joe, 'and you guys kin pick me up on your way to Alpine.'

True nodded, and the matter was settled. He and Dusty headed for the little house by the stream. Joe went to get his pick-up.

'One more thing,' called Cady. The men stopped and turned back. 'I can't find Zach's 30-30. You know, the one he kept in his ranch pick-up. Do any of you guys know where it might be?'

Dusty shook his head. 'No ma'am. Last time I saw it was at the fight, when Mr Zimmerman was here.' He turned back for the house.

Only True and Joe stood stock-still, staring at her. This time, Cady looked full into True's wizened old eyes and, to her eternal sadness, read the first tiny signs of doubt in their faded-blue depths.

Just then, a plain, cream-colored sedan drove up to the house and parked. Dub Garner and Jeff Jenkins got out, armed with a legal search warrant, good for every building and vehicle on the ranch.

Chapter Twenty-Nine

'I'm sorry about this,' said Dub as Cady handed back the search warrant.

'I was about to go back to my place,' said Joe. 'You don't have to search my rig do you?'

'It's technically a ranch pick-up,' said Ranger Jenkins. 'If you don't mind, I'd better take a look before you leave.'

'You're not gonna rip out the seats or anythang, are you?' he asked, worried.

'No,' reassured the Ranger. 'We're not looking for drugs.'

'What are you lookin' for?'

'I'd rather not say,' hedged Jenkins, sliding into the passenger side of Joe's pick-up and popping the glove compartment.

Dub lowered his voice and Cady inclined her head toward him. 'We're still waitin' on autopsy reports,' he said, 'but we found some 30-30 shell casings at the scene.'

Her heart jumped a beat.

'Now, if you don't mind, I'm gonna need your help in the house,' said Dub.

'Certainly,' said Cady. They headed toward the back door.

'You know, we'se in town before it dawned on me that Zacharia had changed his shirt yesterd'y,' said

Dub. 'I'm gonna need to see it.'

'Sure.' Cady's bag was still dangling off her shoulder. She wondered if the sheriff would notice as he followed her through the house and up the stairs toward their bedroom.

'How's that little blind kitty?' he asked politely.

'He's fine.' Cady went into the bathroom adjoining their bedroom and rummaged through the hamper. *Thank God I haven't done laundry yet this week,* she thought, pulling out a denim shirt Zach had worn the day before yesterday.

'He'd been in the brush, chasing down a calf all morning,' she said, wondering if her voice sounded as nervous as she felt. 'And he was all sweaty. You know how it can get. He just wanted to get cleaned up a little.'

Garner took the shirt from her and dropped it into a plain paper grocery sack.

Cady almost laughed. A country evidence collector.

'There's some more officers on the way to help us look,' said Dub. He touched Cady's arm. 'I hate this, you know.'

She nodded. 'I know.'

'Believe me, I'd be thrilled if we could find somethin' that would prove Zacharia was out chasin' that calf. This whole case has about made me sick.'

'We all feel that way. I can't quite believe it myself.'

'I know. I know.' He shook his head. 'When you watch 'em grow up, send 'em off to war, see 'em turn out to be hard-workin', decent men . . . well, you jist hate it when somethin' like this happens. Hell, this is Fort Davis. It *don't* happen, hardly ever anyway.'

Cady nodded, her heart aching with affection for

these people who had been so good to her since her move to West Texas – especially Dub, a decent man just doing his job.

City cops tended to get hard-boiled fast, full of suspicion and distrust, clannish to a fault, and quick to expect the worst of people. This was because a city cop saw, on the average, more crime and more of the worst of human beings in one week than Dub Garner probably saw in a year.

He was still willing to believe, like most small-town folk, that people were what they seemed.

'Guess we ought to start at the top and work our way down,' said Dub. 'Which way to the attic?'

Cady led him up the short stairway to the attic door, which opened more easily now that the storms had dried out. He stooped under the doorway and whistled under his breath.

'Dang. Feller could be in here all night.' He walked into the middle of the room and stood a moment, looking around.

As if magnetized, his gaze fell to the locked trunk.

'You got a key to that padlock?' he asked.

For a long, weak-kneed moment, as Cady stumbled her way back down the stairs to fetch Zach's key, she wondered what the sheriff would have thought of his old friend, if he'd pulled out the top tray of that trunk, and found a human skull nestled inside.

The murder of Rex Zimmerman was a test, see. I had to see if Cady really loved me. I had to find out where her loyalties lay.

It was the only way I could find out for sure if she was plotting against me.

I mean, I couldn't always tell when we were together. Sometimes she was just like always, you know? I would be absolutely convinced that she loved me after all.

Then, in the blink of an eye, her expression would change, or she'd make a casual remark, some little thing that seemed innocent enough on the surface but, when I looked at her, I could see her eyes were lying.

It got to where I doubted just about everything she told me. I wanted to trust her, I really did, but I just couldn't be sure.

She needed something to shake her to the bones, something to rattle her so badly that she would finally realize just what we meant to each other. I wanted her to run into my arms and beg me to forgive her for ever doubting me.

I had every detail all planned out.

But even the best-laid plans of mice and men . . . well, not everything always goes just the way you want it.

The bail hearing was short and disastrous. While Zach's civil attorney rummaged through papers, mumbled to Zach, and stumbled over his words, the prosecutor presented a convincing argument that, while Zacharia Ralston may not present an immediate threat to other people in town, he was a very poor risk for flight.

The judge apparently agreed and, to the astonishment of everyone in the room, including reporters from TV stations and newspapers in El Paso and Midland/Odessa, he remitted Zach to the county jail, to be held without bond.

They led him away to the hoots and jeers of a number of townspeople who had come to show their support. Cady was not given an opportunity to speak to her husband.

He threw her one despairing glance, over his shoulder, and then he was gone.

Cady returned from the dismal bail hearing to madness. Her new home, over which she had lovingly labored for so many weeks, was a shambles. The deputies from Alpine who had come to help Dub in his search had obviously done a thorough job. Drawers and closets had been dumped out, willy-nilly, on the floors and furniture. Couches and chairs had been moved, beds disassembled.

Her life had become a bizarre nightmare with no end.

And Radar was missing.

With increasing panic, she combed the house, calling for him and searching in the kinds of places cats liked to hide when they were frightened.

With all the traffic in and out of the house, he must have somehow gotten out.

It was a horrible thing to contemplate. A blind kitten, roaming the pastures, was doomed to a slow death of dehydration and starvation, if he didn't become a meal for some wild creature.

Cady searched around the house and down to the stream, calling for him everywhere.

She wanted to start screaming and never stop. It was as if the loss of the kitten had somehow rendered her incapable of handling the other stresses.

High overhead, vultures circled, watching and waiting.

Cady stood, feeling powerless, holding back hopeless tears. She heard the rumble of a pick-up pulling up behind the house to the call of the dogs and looked back. It was Joe. He saw her and began walking toward her. She was too dejected even to pretend nothing was wrong.

As he grew near, he slowed down. 'Hey there, missy, what's wrong? Is it Zach?'

'No. Well, yes. Of course it's Zach, but . . . it's Radar. He got out while the officers were searching the house and I can't find him anywhere.' She appealed to him, vulnerable as a child.

He came up and put his arm around her. 'Aw hey, is that all? Tell you what, why don't you go on in the house and git off your feet for a while. There ain't a inch of this place I don't have memorized in the back o'my mind. I'll find the little fart.'

'Will you?' She felt so tired, so *dependent*. She didn't mean to be but, the truth was, she had no idea where to begin to search for that kitten, who could have been gone for hours by now.

He grinned. 'Trust me.'

She sighed, nodded, and headed heavy-footed for the back door of the house. Inside, she made herself a glass of iced tea and stretched out on the couch, which sat catty-corner to its old position. She had no energy anymore, it seemed, and all she wanted to do was bawl.

She dozed a little, until pounding on the back door brought her to her feet. A glance at the clock told her an hour had passed. Cady went to the back door, and there stood Joe, grinning broadly, holding Radar in his big calloused hand.

Cady almost cried. (Again.) She took the kitten and invited Joe in for iced tea. Radar's fur was hot from the sun and he was panting shallowly. She set him down in front of his water dish and splashed in it with her fingertip so he would realize where he was. He began lapping thirstily, dipping his little nose in every once in a while and sneezing.

'You shoulda seen him,' Joe said with a chuckle. 'Goose-stepping through the weeds like a little Nazi. Never saw anythang like it.'

'How far had he gotten?'

''Bout half a mile. Purty good distance for such a little critter.'

'This means the world to me, Joe,' said Cady. The ice had frozen together, and she took an ice pick out of the drawer to unstick it. Without thinking, she used her right hand, and the ice pick slipped from her grasp and poked hard into the soft flesh of her left hand.

'*Ouch!*' she cried, dropping the pick. 'Of all the dumb things to do.' Blood oozed from the puncture wound and she reached for a paper towel to dab at it.

Joe got to his feet. 'Hurt yourself?' He reached for her hand.

'It's all right, really.'

'That's okay,' he said, taking the hand in his own. 'Just let me kiss it and make it better.'

And while Cady stared at the man, all the blood draining from her face, he looked into her eyes and said it again, 'Let me kiss it and make it better.'

The phone rang. Cady jerked her hand from Joe's as if it were hot and reached for the receiver without waiting through four rings for the machine. Her skin crawled. She was afraid to look at Joe and afraid not to.

Let me kiss it and make it better.

The stalker had said that to her once. She could remember it vividly. And, although she had no clear memory of it, she was certain he had said it to her another time as well.

Heart throbbing in her ears, Cady remembered the first day she met Joe, when Zach had told her that Joe had only recently started working for them again. Something about an oilfield job.

'H-hello?' Her hand was shaking so hard that she pressed the phone against her chin so that Joe wouldn't notice it trembling.

'Cady Maxwell, please.'

'This is she.' Joe was standing close by. Too close. She stepped to the side.

'This is the Alpine Post Office. We've got a package here for you from a Dr Karl Gustav?'

'Yes.'

'Ma'am, you need to sign for this before we can release it.'

'Thank you. I'll . . . I'll be there later this afternoon.'

'That'll be fine. We close at five.' The woman hung up.

Joe had not taken his eyes off Cady. 'What's up?' he asked casually.

'Just some . . . business I need to take care of. I . . . I need to leave pretty soon.'

'Sure. No problem.' He gestured toward the tea glass, still sitting on the counter, a couple of pieces of ice melting in it. 'I'll sure take you up on that offer for tea though, if you don't mind.'

Cady turned away and quickly filled the glass, which she handed to him gingerly, reluctant to touch his hand again. He drained it in one long gulp. 'Ol' Zach,' he mused, staring into the glass. 'Always was one lucky son of a bitch.'

'Not anymore,' said Cady, willing him out of the house.

'Guess not.' Glancing at Radar, he said, 'Thanks for the tea.' He turned to go. 'Keep an eye on that cat,' he said. 'He thanks he knows where he's goin', but he don't.' He gazed into her eyes. 'Like the rest of us, I guess.'

'I guess.' She struggled to calm herself.

At the door, he stopped. 'I'll check in on you from time to time. Wouldn't want you to git lonesome or nothin'.'

The look in his eyes chilled her. 'I'm fine,' she said. 'Thank you for finding Radar.'

'No problem. See you later.'

He left, and Cady slumped over the counter on trembling hands.

Could it be Joe?

She'd never liked him, never liked the come-hither look in his eyes. But Zach had always been around, a safe and solid wall of protection.

Now Zach was gone.

Cady hurried through the dining and living rooms and up the stairs to the bedroom, where she retrieved the Beretta from the nightstand. She tucked it deep in her purse, underneath Zach's bloodstained shirt.

Head swimming, Cady headed back down the stairs, her bag considerably heavier on her shoulder. She would get rid of the shirt someplace. It might not

317

make much sense to anybody else (though nobody else would ever know), but Cady felt as if she owed Zach that much.

Then she left, headed for the post office in Alpine, and the analysis from Dr Gustav, which, if her worst suspicions were confirmed, could put the final nail in her husband's coffin.

Chapter Thirty

Dr Gustav's report, when it came, was more damaging than anything Cady could have imagined.

But that wasn't entirely true, either. She sat in her parked car in the Furr's Supermarket parking lot in Alpine, the box containing the skull beside her on the passenger seat, clutching Dr Gustav's letter. The clean white page bearing the University of Texas Department of Anthropology logo shook in her hand. She leaned her head against the cool car window.

She *had* imagined just this very thing. All along, from the beginning, when she'd first run her fingertips over the skull's smooth surface, she'd wondered . . .

It was the kind of deep, dark mystery of the soul that the conscious mind protected one from until he or she was strong enough to handle the devastation such knowledge would wreak.

She read the letter again:

My dear Cady,

As usual, it was a delight to hear from you for, once again, you have presented me with a provocative challenge. I will tell you what I think; as usual, it is merely my opinion and you are free to use it as you see fit.

Cady could almost hear Dr Gustav's gravelly, slightly accented voice.

> *I concur absolutely with your conclusions that this skull is not that of a centuries-old Native American. In fact, it is most decisively not Native American at all but Caucasian.*
>
> *There are several features that could be indicative of a Native American skull. For instance, they tend to have forward-projecting cheekbones and somewhat flat facial features. And the eye sockets are more circular than Caucasian. I did not find these indications in this skull.*

Cady found herself nodding. That was what she had thought.

> *Now, there is one feature that can be counted on by forensic anthropologists to be present in at least eighty percent of Native American skulls: the maxillary incisors – the four center teeth in the upper jaw – have prominent ridges on the side nearer the tongue, called shovel-shaped.*
>
> *In this specimen, I found no sign of the shovel shaping. And, of course, as you mentioned, the presence of the tooth filling would place this skull solidly in the twentieth century.*

Cady almost smiled. The pedantic tone of the letter was so like Dr Gustav, who could never resist the chance to lecture.

> *Now, as to the approximate age of the skull.*

Judging from the degree of closure of the cranial sutures – the places where the various plates of the skull fuse together – particularly the sagittal, or top suture, this skull appears to be fairly young, say, mid-twenties. The teeth are another excellent indication. They show very few signs of wear and the molars have erupted as well – all of which confirms my hypothesis, something I am sure you noticed if you examined the skull closely enough to spot the tiny filling in the front incisor.

Cady rolled her head around on tense shoulders. Most of what Dr Gustav had said in his letter, so far, was no great surprise. Cady had suspected as much from the beginning. But it was still somehow disturbing to find her suspicions confirmed.

So, it would appear that we have here a Caucasian skull of a person somewhere in his or her mid-twenties.

The sex, in this case, was fairly easy to tell. Large brow ridges and robust mastoid processes would indicate a male. However, the brow ridges in this instance are quite delicate, the mastoid processes petite.

Now, granted, there are small, effeminate men whose features often resemble those of a woman but, in this case, judging from those factors, as well as examining the overall shape of the cranium and facial bones, I can be reasonably assured that we are dealing here with a young, Caucasian woman.

Somehow, Cady had wanted to believe that the skull had been some sort of macabre war trophy, or the remnants of a pioneer body, buried hurriedly during the long, brutal trek across the West. But Dr Gustav's letter removed that hope.

I can't say for sure how long this person has been dead. As you indicated in your letter, the skull is well bleached and therefore has lain out in the sun for some time. But if you will permit your old friend the luxury of a guess, I would say that this death occurred some time in the last twenty years, maybe even ten or fifteen years ago. Keep in mind that this is only a guess.

As you requested, I have enclosed the scale photography you will need to do a two-dimensional reconstruction. I left the skin-depth indicators in place for future reference.

As always, I will respect your desire for discretion.

My dear, if I have not said so, please know that I was terribly saddened by the death of your mother. She was a great lady, and a fine inspiration to the female co-eds on this campus, proving that one can, indeed, do whatever one sets out to do.

Come and visit me sometime. I am, as always,
Yours,
Karl Gustav, PHD

A profound sadness settled itself over Cady's shoulders. How she missed her mother.

She hadn't wanted to face it, hadn't wanted to think

of it. And then, with Rex's murder, she'd sent the thoughts out of her mind as neatly as she'd mailed the skull to Dr Gustav.

Out of sight, out of mind.

But it was there, hidden away like the skull; it was there.

The doubt. The fear.

Somehow, the body of a young, white female who had been dead only fifteen or twenty years had wound up on Zach's ranch. And the remains of her head had been in Zach's attic trunk.

He'd said he found it in a water gap. Maybe he had.

He'd also said that he did not kill Rex Zimmerman. Or had he? No, he'd never actually said that. He'd asked her what *she* believed.

Cady hadn't said what she believed at the time, but she had just taken elaborate measures to hide a blood-spattered shirt that Zach had been wearing the day Rex Zimmerman was murdered.

Why would she hide the shirt of an innocent man?

Cady dropped her head forward onto the padded steering wheel. Zach was in the Alpine jail, awaiting trial for Zimmerman's murder. She was his wife. Here she sat, in Alpine.

She should go visit her husband.

But she couldn't. Not yet. Not when the skull had one more secret to tell her.

She had to know that secret – it was almost out of her control now.

She had to know the secret . . . but deep, deep within, in that place which had no name, Cady feared that she already knew it.

* * *

The afternoon was drawing to a close as Cady turned the Lexus, at last, onto the ranch road and headed toward the house. The drive home had seemed interminable. All Cady could think about was getting to her studio and completing the reconstruction.

Before getting out of the car, she cast a furtive glance toward the barn. She didn't want anyone to know what she was doing. But there was no one about and she hurried into the house.

Cady could not remember if she had eaten that day. She'd skipped lunch for sure, but she couldn't be bothered with that for now. She took a Coke out of the refrigerator and ran up the stairs.

In her studio, she affixed one of the scale photographs to her drawing board with thumbtacks. Over it, she lay a sheer piece of tracing paper, which she taped at the corners so that it would stay in place.

By following the skin-depth indicators, the drawing of the outlines of the face was fairly simple to do. It was the facial features, such as the nose and mouth, that were a little trickier.

Cady frowned in concentration. The eyebrows fit, fairly neatly, along the upper rim of the eyesockets. The cornea was placed somewhere in the middle between the inferior and superior margins of the eye orbit. Absorbed in her task, she sketched rapidly, adjusting to the unusual grip of the pencil between her fingers. The angular desk lamp formed a circular pool of light over the paper as shadows slowly gathered in the corners of the room.

The nasal projection would be approximately three times the length of the nasal spine. While she drew,

Cady occupied her mind with meaningless little technical terms, such as the three types of skulls: Mongoloid, Caucasoid, and Negroid.

Somewhere in the bowels of the house, the phone rang. Cady ignored it. Lip thickness was determined by measuring the distance from gum to gum. She took her bottom lip between her teeth as she worked.

Mongoloid, Caucasoid, Negroid.

Hair style, length, and color would have to be a guess.

She made it blonde. Just for the hell of it.

Caucasoid. This was a Caucasoid blonde.

She worked longer than she needed to, filling in details as her imagination provided them, taking care to respect every angle and plane. Postponing the inevitable.

Finally, she stood up and stretched. Sharp cramps shot through the weary muscles of her damaged drawing hand. She rubbed it, gazing at the drawing, procrastinating the final moment.

Pulling the drawing paper away from the scale photograph was usually a thrill, seeing bone and tooth revealed as a human being who once lived and laughed. It was immensely satisfying, knowing that because of this particular skill, someone's nightmare of unknowing might finally be ended, so that the past could, at last, be remanded to the past.

But this time, Cady knew, the nightmare was only just beginning. Slowly, she pulled off the tape tabs that held the drawing down and gazed at the face before her long and hard.

She had to be certain.

Why, *why* couldn't she have left well enough alone?

Why couldn't she leave it alone now?

She had to know. She just had to, and that was all. The skull continued to seduce her with its whispers, *Let me tell you my secrets*.

Holding the drawing limp in her hand, Cady left her studio and groped her way down the darkened hallway toward the attic stairs. There was no hall light, but at the top of the stairs, she knew, was a light bulb with a chain.

Her throat felt as if it were swelling against the back of her mouth, strangling her. Holding onto the wall with one hand, she climbed the short stairway and reached up for the chain.

The light bulb cast bald, hateful shadows. Cady pushed open the attic door, opening a gap of light across the murky floor. Twilight haze glowed dimly from the high window, casting just enough dust-showered blue illumination for Cady to stumble her way to the corner where she had found the wedding books and photo albums of days gone forever.

Setting aside scrapbooks and yearbooks, her hand finally closed on the framed photograph she sought. A spider scurried over the back of her hand. Cady jumped, and the photo dropped to the floor with a crash.

Her shoe crushed a sliver of glass as Cady floundered for the picture and, as she picked it up, a small slice from the shattered glass of the frame pricked her finger.

She carried the frame through the cluttered, darkened attic until she could stand beneath the stark, slightly swaying light bulb, casting its deathly glow first over the portrait in one hand and then the sketch in the other.

As she stood in the ghostly shadows of the silent, accusing attic, she knew there could be no doubt. The face which stared so mysteriously from Cady's drawing eerily matched the face which smiled out from the smashed frame, a face now splintered and blood-smeared.

The face of Zach's ex-wife.

The realization imprinted itself on Cady's brain; no more whispery secrets to hide themselves from Cady's own thoughts; no more irritating little doubts to insinuate themselves into her dreams; no more traces of wondering when Zach said things like, *She disappeared fifteen years ago. When I couldn't find her after six months, I filed for divorce.*

And yet, here she was! Found, in his own attic.

It was Cady's last conscious thought, as the blood drained from her cheeks, her hands went numb, the drawing slipped from her grasp and floated like a spirit down the hall, the framed portrait spiraled to the floor, and Cady herself slumped to her knees and tumbled, end over end, down the stairs.

Chapter Thirty-One

Cady opened her eyes to the dismal, lonesome sound of the wind, howling down off the mountain like an enraged intruder, pounding on the doors and rattling the windows as if its sheer presence alone would be enough to allow it to bully its way into the house and frighten away all its occupants.

She lay crumpled at the foot of the short attic stairway, just out of reach of the light from the single light bulb. Everywhere else the house was black dark. Her entire body ached. One leg was numb beneath her, and her bad hand throbbed like a sputtering neon sign.

Bewildered, she sat up, rubbing a sore elbow and trying in vain to lift the deadened leg. She had to use her hands to straighten it out. Soon, hot needles scraped the inside of her skin as the circulation was restored to the limb.

At first, she had no idea how she had come to be deposited in a heap at the foot of the attic stairway, but a ghostly glimpse of a sheet of paper near her foot reminded her. She closed her eyes against the mental picture she would never forget of that shattered, bloody face next to her drawing.

The floor was cold. Cady shivered, listening to the wind cry and moan around the corners of the solitary old house. She had never fainted before in her life.

Perhaps that was why she'd not noticed the early warning signals and avoided the fall. Stupid of her not to eat.

She sighed. It seemed there were a number of unpleasant truths which she was having to face on this endless day, and one of them was that she was simply not well, and hadn't been for some time. She was going to have to go to a doctor and find out what was wrong with her. She couldn't go around somersaulting down stairways.

Heaving a weary sigh, Cady pushed herself tentatively to her feet and stood, swaying uncertainly. Nothing seemed to be broken, though everything felt bruised. She limped down the hall and into her bedroom, where she stretched across the bed on her stomach.

The phone rang, startling her. Heart pounding, she listened through four rings and the brief message.

'Cady, honey, are you there? Pick up, darlin', it's Zach.'

She buried her face in her arms, her body trembling, aching for him.

'Oh, I can't believe I missed you. This is the first chance I've had to call all day, and I won't get to call back ... I was hopin' you'd be able to come see me today.'

She began to sob.

'Uh, tell True I said the vet's supposed to be out next Tuesday to vaccinate those cows and check for cancer eyes and whatnot. He'll know what I mean.'

Her shoulders shook with each racking, aching tear, as if her soul were being sucked inside out. Emotions tangled with logic in a hopeless jumble.

'I love you, my darlin'. Sleep well tonight.'

Still weeping, Cady lunged across the bed and grappled in the dark for the receiver, shouting, *'Hello, Zach?'* But it was too late.

It was too late, it seemed, for everything.

If ever a human heart had truly broken, Cady thought she had some idea of what it felt like. It *hurt*, her chest actually ached, a sucker punch for which she had been unprepared.

It had taken Dr Gustav three weeks to get back to Cady with his report. It had been an eventful three weeks. Summer was waning. School had already started.

And her husband, the man she had pledged to cherish for the rest of her life, was in jail for murder – she had hidden his bloody shirt from the police – while all along, upstairs in his attic, had rested the skull-head of his previous wife.

Every common-sense sinew in her body *screamed* at her to leave him, to get out while the getting was good, to accept the fact that there was something terribly, terribly wrong here. Every cop-trained fiber of her being pounded home damning evidence, from his volatile moods and sudden rages to the missing 30-30.

It seemed she was married to a killer.

But the blood which coursed through her body failed to heed the warnings of muscle and sinew; it throbbed through her heart and tingled through her fingertips; it said, *I love him! Oh, God, I still love him!*

Deep down inside, in some inner core of her being, Cady simply could not accept that the same man who had nursed her back to health, the same man who had caressed her in bed with such delicate passion, the same man who'd rescued a blind kitten, could be a murderer.

But there it was: the evidence, versus her heart.

You're a fool, an idiot! she told herself. *Don't you know? Haven't you studied the criminal mind enough to realize that nobody manipulates women better than male psychopaths?*

Had she been that stupid? Had the assault rendered her so vulnerable and bruised that she'd been fair prey for a man who, like the vultures, seemed to benefit most from the deaths of those around him?

And there it was.

A fresh gust of wind screeched against the window, scattering tree leaves across the glass like scraping fingernails.

Cady had never asked how Zach's father had died, but his death had presented the ranch to Zach. The disappearance of his second wife had taken away an annoyance, and the death of Rex Zimmerman had removed a threat.

The three things criminal investigators searched for in any murder case were: method, opportunity, and *motive*.

Cady's heart was pounding. She knew she needed to eat.

Just pack up and go, she thought. *Just walk away.*

She could do it. She had money. For some reason — maybe subconscious warnings? — she'd never closed the savings account she maintained in a Dallas bank. Most of her earnings since the assault had been deposited there. She could leave in the night — maybe even outfox the stalker. Start all over again someplace.

Without Zach.

She couldn't imagine it.

It's not that I can't live without him, she thought, *because I can. It's just that I can't begin to imagine such a life.*

After the death of her mother, when her drawing hand was smashed, Cady had thought that the worst things that could ever happen to her, had.

But she'd been wrong.

Losing this man, and this life . . . that would, by far, be the worst. Or at least . . . losing the man she had thought him to be. Had she only loved a mirage, that had vanished upon closer inspection?

Lying on her back in the darkened bedroom, listening to nature's tantrums outside her isolated country home, Cady wondered, *How do you survive the worst thing that can ever happen to you?*

And she remembered what Zach had said, that survival could sometimes be a decision.

She had a decision to make and, again, Zach had put it into words when he'd said that believing in him was not the same as loving him.

Cady was going to have to *decide* if she believed in her husband, or not. If it was worth staying in for the long haul.

If she did not believe in him; if, instead, she chose to accept the evidence and conjecture and believe that her husband had taken another life, not once, but twice . . . then there was truly no reason for her to stay. It went too much against the grain of her steadfast belief in right and wrong, good and bad, the divine and evil.

She'd seen much evil in her life, beheld the aftermath of evil and what it could do to the victims it left behind. She could not – would not – live with it.

If, on the other hand, she *did* believe in her husband, rejected the indications of his guilt and decided that he could not have done this evil and was, therefore, worthy of this powerful love she had for him still . . . then she would stay. If that were the decision, then she would fight, not just for her own survival, but for Zach's.

And for the survival of their marriage.

Heart thumping, she lay on her back, listening to the wildness and savagery of nature unhinged as it beat against the house until the rafters moaned. It was a sound of vast lonesomeness. Of all the years Cady had lived alone, she'd never felt it more than now.

She stared, hard, up into the darkness toward the high old ceiling of the ranch house. She bit her lip, and she cried, and she dozed and dreamed of her husband.

During the pre-dawn, early-autumn hours, the wind gave up its frantic, frenzied attack, pulled into itself, and retreated, leaving behind the downy soft of quiet and a crystalline cold. Cady rose from her rumpled bed and left the house, walking through damp grass toward the stream.

On one side of the sky rose the sun, scarlet-blushed and fresh, melting over the purple tops of the hazy mountains; while on the other side, the harvest moon settled softly into the sky like a rose-flushed pearl nestled in crimson velvet, slipping peacefully into its rest behind the midnight-blue crags. Cady filled her lungs with dew-sweet morning air, watched the moonset with dry eyes, and made her decision.

And as the day made itself more comfortable, sitting up and rearranging its sunny folds over the blue mountains and heaving an Indian-summer sigh, Cady finally visited the doctor, only to learn that she was not sick at all.

She was pregnant.

Chapter Thirty-Two

The plan was working beautifully. At least, that's the way it seemed at the time.

Zacharia Ralston had been a problem for me from the beginning. At first, when Cady took off for West Texas, I figured it was an ideal chance for us to be together in a completely natural way. But when she up and married him like that, I was stunned. I mean, she'd only known the guy a few weeks. Not only that, but he was way wrong for her. Not nearly her caliber.

Well, I knew right away I was going to have to get rid of him somehow. What I didn't count on was Zach being so cooperative in implicating himself. I mean, I've known for a long time that the man is not all he's cracked up to be. It was so obvious – I can't believe nobody else could see it.

Even worse, Cady was supposed to be street-smart. If anybody could spot a con, you'd think it would have been her. He just had her blinded. Must be hell on wheels in the sack. What else could explain it?

Still, by this time, it did seem as if Cady was beginning to figure that part out, FINALLY.

So far, everything was going great. Zach was in jail and Cady herself had been instrumental in putting him there – which was a stroke of luck I could never have counted on.

I knew she was going to be mine soon. I could FEEL

it, you know? It was all I could do to contain myself.
And then.

Talk about a break. It happened one day when I was in her house.

Getting in Cady's house was simple. Usually I would approach the ranch house from a mountainous back road three-quarters of a mile from the stream which ran behind the Ralston house. I'd park there, then walk down the road. For the first half-mile or so, I made no particular attempt to hide, but when the road dipped down to within sight of the house I'd leave it, zig zagging through brush and boulders and juniper trees, slipping and sliding down half-hidden paths I had come to know. I remember that particular day so vividly. The sun was high overhead and I had to be careful not to be spotted; the old codger's eyes were hawk-sharp.

In the end, I abandoned the animal path altogether, hung down and dangled the last ten-foot sheer drop, then let go and landed softly in the mud of the stream. The dogs didn't see me at first but I wasn't worried; they were easily handled. At this point, I was at an angle to the barn. No one could see me if I was careful. It was the last few yards of lawn that were the tricky part, but even then, if someone accosted me, I had good reason for being there.

Just as I was headed across the yard, something caught my eye. There, in the barrels they used to burn trash. I had to look both ways before I could sprint over to them and look inside.

I'm telling you. It would've made you sick.

All those lovely white roses, thrown away! I couldn't believe it. They were wilted and sooty and just a mess.

I could not imagine what had gotten into the girl, and it pissed me off, but I was willing to forgive her because I knew she was under stress.

I forgave easily then.

Anyway, no trash had been burned yet, so I gathered up as many as I could hold and, craning my neck again to make sure no one was watching, I started toward the house.

Sure enough, the dogs spotted me and came barreling across the yard, baying like hounds from hell. But all I had to do was call to them softly by name, and when they saw who it was, they dropped their ruffs and came wagging up for a pat. I always had treats for them in my pocket. Then I hurried up the back porch steps to the veranda and across to the back door.

Imagine my surprise when I found the door locked. It had never been locked before. It had not occurred to me at the time that she might lock the door before leaving the house. Why would she do that?

Naturally that made things a royal pain. I had to make my way around the house until I found a small bathroom window which was cracked open a few inches. So much for security measures.

I had to push the roses into the room first, then wiggle in through the window, which was set high off the ground and not particularly easy to reach. Fortunately it was on the side of the house opposite the barn, so I didn't have to worry about being spotted.

The bathroom smelled of potpourri and scented candles. It was just like my beautiful Cady to make a home so welcoming. I couldn't wait for the day when she would make our home as lovely as she'd made this one.

Sometimes I didn't think I could wait another day.

I remember how thrilling it was to be so close to her, in such an intimate way, without her knowing. Arms full of roses, I went on upstairs and headed straight for her room, where I dropped the roses on the bed. I still couldn't believe she had thrown them away. She would learn that it would not be that easy to defy me.

Now came time for my favorite part. I had done this before, but it never lost its thrill. I opened the lingerie drawer and fondled her sweet soft underthings, caressing their silky smoothness, imagining them on her body, picturing myself removing them, one by one. As usual, it made me very excited. I always liked to remove one of the pairs of panties and keep it.

The bedroom was filled with the delicate scent Cady liked to wear. I loved to spray a little of her perfume on the panties, then crush them to my nose and just get filled up with the scent of her . . .

It seems silly now, looking back, but I was just so carried away with everything that I did a little dance around the room, wafting Cady's panties through the air like a flag. She was alone now, and soon she would be ready to fall into my arms, just as I had dreamed for so long.

Oh, I can tell you, it was heady stuff. I just fell back onto the bed amidst the roses with Cady's panties across my face. All I could think of was the word, SOON. Soon. It would all happen soon. I just didn't know if I could stand the wait.

I'm smiling now, as you can see, just remembering. Anyway, after a while I got to my feet, stuffed the panties into my pocket to enjoy later, and wandered over to Cady's studio. I loved that room almost as much as her bedroom, more even, because there was no presence there of the man she had so stupidly married.

That had been Cady's worst mistake, without question. But it hadn't stopped my plans any . . . just slowed them down a bit.

You can't begin to imagine how much I hated Zach Ralston at that point.

I didn't blame Cady for the betrayal. The bastard had taken advantage of her when she was vulnerable and had seduced her. A woman as brilliant and as beautiful as Cady Maxwell would never have married somebody like that if she hadn't been weakened by the attack.

She was beginning to come to her senses too, I was sure of it. It was just a matter of time before I would make my move and she would be mine forever.

I stepped into Cady's studio. On her work table was a broken picture frame. I picked it up. The glass was shattered, and there was a smear of blood across the bottom. It was a picture of a woman.

Thumbtacked onto the work desk was a photograph of a skull with little round things stuck all over it and, next to that, a drawing in the same dimensions that almost matched the photograph.

Very curious. It reminded me of something I'd seen on the television broadcast about Cady . . .

Just then, there was a sound below. I jumped and put the frame back onto the table. I strained to listen. Careless of me. I hadn't been paying attention, hadn't heard a car drive up. Was she home already?

I slipped over to the door and opened it a crack.

Cady's voice drifted up the stairs. She was talking to the cat.

In a heart-pounding blur, I was still trying to figure out what to do when I heard her footsteps echoing off the hardwood floors of the upstairs hallway.

Cady headed straight for the studio. She'd been in such a fog all day she'd been careless. It had occurred to her halfway to the doctor's office that she'd left the box containing the skull, the scale photographs, her drawing, and the portrait all out in plain view in her studio. She had no reason to suspect that anybody would go into her home and her studio when she wasn't there, but she was taking no chances. For all she knew, the police might come back for another search.

Opening the door, she crossed over to the work table, removed the thumbtacks from the scale photograph, and gathered up her sketch and the portrait. Wait. She couldn't handle it like it was. Putting everything back down, she removed the portrait from the shattered frame and dropped the frame in the wastepaper basket. While she was brushing grains of broken glass off the portrait, she caught a glimpse of something written on the back: 'Laura Lynn Baker, Alpine High School Class of '74'.

So, her name was Laura. A gentle, innocent name. And somebody had murdered her.

'Don't worry, Laura,' murmured Cady aloud, 'I'm going to find out who murdered you, and who killed Rex Zimmerman, and I'm going to see to it that they pay.'

Cady slipped the sketch and Dr Gustav's

photographs, along with his letter, into the box containing the skull. She needed a permanent hiding place for it, but her mind was a blank. She decided to put it in the storage closet until she could think of a better place.

Cady's studio was actually a converted bedroom, and the closet was cluttered with junk. She'd been meaning to clean it out but, with recent events, had forgotten it. She opened the large, walk-in closet. It was frustrating that such a big closet did not have a light, but she fumbled around at the back of it and found a spot for the box high on a shelf.

As Cady was standing there in the closet, the downy hairs on the back of her neck suddenly rose, and goosebumps swarmed over her body. She had a sudden, creepy sensation of somebody watching her. She leaped out and slammed the door.

Hands trembling, she stood in the middle of her studio, trying to shake the uncomfortable feeling that had come over her in the closet. It was so *weird*, like somebody was *there*.

'You're getting so paranoid,' she said aloud. 'Jumping at shadows.' She left the room and headed downstairs to the kitchen. The doctor had scolded her for not eating, so she would eat, already. She took down a can of Campbell's chicken and noodle soup, poured it into a bowl, and popped it into the microwave. Cady never diluted it because she liked the noodles best.

The back screen door opened and Cady heard cowboy boots thunk across the porch.

'Cady? You home?'

'Sure, True,' she called. 'Come on in.'

He stepped into the back door, hat in hand. 'How's Zacharia?'

'All right, as far as I know. I'm going to see him in a little while.'

He nodded, and looked down at the crumpled, stained old hat he preferred to work in. 'It don't look good for him, does it?'

The microwave beeped. Cady removed her steaming soup. She shook her head.

'I'd like ye to know somethin',' said the old man, pinning her with a sharp-eyed gaze. 'I've knowed that boy since the day he was born. Now, he an' Rex didn't have no use fer one another, that's true, but I can guarantee you that Zacharia would never take another man's life.'

'I know that, True.'

'Do ye? Do ye really? Cause he needs you right now to stand by him. He needs all of us.'

Cady's cheeks flushed. This was the closest thing to a reprimand she was ever likely to get from the old hand, and it stung. She *had* doubted Zach, in the beginning, and the old man missed nothing.

'In this world,' he went on, his slow drawl curling the words, 'there's hearts that's pretend, and there's hearts that's true. The pretend hearts'll smile at ye like they's your best friends, but they'll backshoot ye as soon as look at ye.'

She nodded.

'Joe, now, he's a pretend heart. Don't git me wrong, he'll make ye a good hand, but ye got to keep an eye on him. Ye cain't trust him because he don't allow you to. Soon as you do, he'll snooker ye.

'But Zacharia, he's a true heart, Cady. He's as good

a man as walks this earth, and anybody don't thank so kin come take it up with me.'

In spite of herself, her eyes filled with tears. 'People are talking in town,' she said. 'It's like they never knew Zach.'

He nodded. 'Some folks is like buzzards. They'll feed off the carcass of other people's troubles because they've made such a wreck outa their own lives. But the true hearts'll stand by Zacharia. You'll see.'

She blinked back the tears. 'I'm going to stand by Zach, True. I want you to know that.'

He gave her a gentle smile. 'I figgered you'd come around directly. City folks is quick to suspicion other people. That's cause they's too busy rushin' around all the time to learn how to tell the true hearts from the pretend.'

There was such immense comfort in just being in the presence of this man whose kind was fading as fast as nature's untamed wildness. True was the type of man who told time by the sun and stars, whose lifecourse traveled on the rhythms of the seasons. Life was simple and straight to such a man, not complicated by cynicism. 'Why don't you have some soup with me, True?' She indicated her bowl.

'Naw, thank ye kindly, though. The main reason I come up here in the first place is to tell ye that I've had some bad news. My brother died.'

'Oh, True! I'm so sorry!'

'Well, it's not like we wasn't expectin' it. He's been eat up with cancer for months, now.'

Cady thought rapidly. 'This isn't Dusty's father, is it?'

'Naw, naw. Dusty's daddy is my *baby* brother. This

345

here was my older brother. They was seven of us boys.'

'Can I do anything to help you?'

'Naw, I 'preciate it. But Dusty an' me, we got to go be with family and all. I thought I'd tell ye that we's gonna be gone for a week or so. Joe's gonna come live in my house while we're gone and look after the place for Zacharia.'

She and Joe, alone on the ranch.

'I could take care of things,' she said quickly. 'I could feed the horses and check on the cows, and if there was some trouble, I could call Joe and he could come out and look after it.'

'Naw, that's a good offer, Cady, but you need to be concentratin' all you got on Zacharia's plight. Git him whatever help he needs.'

'Okay.' Cady tried not to panic. She didn't want the old man to have any bad feelings about leaving her alone on the place.

'You'll be all right?' he asked, his piercing gaze missing nothing.

'Yeah, sure. I just miss Zach so much, is all.' She decided not to tell True about the baby, not when Zach didn't know yet.

'Let me give ye a phone number whar I kin be reached, if ye need anythang.'

'Okay.' She rummaged around in the drawer for a pad of paper and a pencil, and handed these to the old man, who calmly shoved the pencil between two gnarled fingers just as she had to do, and wrote down the information she needed in a cryptic, old-fashioned hand.

'Does Zach know about your brother?' she asked, watching his slow, painful scrawl across the page.

'Yep. He's got t'is number too.'

'We'll be just fine without you,' she lied. 'But I'll miss you both.' She touched his sleeve. 'I really will.'

He put the pencil down and smiled at her, cocking his hat over one eye like the rakish lad he must once have been. 'We'll be back 'fore ye know it,' he said.

Then he was gone, and Cady was alone.

Chapter Thirty-Three

While Cady ate her soup, she took the pad and pencil True had used and began to make a list. She titled it, *REX*. At the top of the list, she wrote, *eyewitness*. That was Zach's first, and most important, strike against him. Somehow, Cady was going to have to find out why Pablo Romero had positively identified Zach as Rex's killer. Looking back, there was something about that sketching session that was niggling at the back of Cady's mind . . . something that was not quite right about it, but she couldn't specify what it was. She would have to go over it in her mind again, and she would have to talk to Pablo Romero.

Next, she wrote, *blood on sleeve*. Okay. That would be easy enough to identify, if she had access to a forensics lab. Which she didn't. Anyway, it was too late; Cady had discarded the shirt, deep in a Hefty bag, buried in a dumpster somewhere in an Alpine alleyway. So now there was no way to prove that the blood was not Rex's. She wanted to kick herself, but there was no time for regrets.

Just below *blood*, Cady wrote, *missing 30-30*. Dub had already told her that a Winchester 30-30 had been the type of rifle that killed Rex. If Cady could find Zach's rifle, ballistics could prove it was not the same weapon which fired the fatal shot. Still, even the fact that the gun was missing looked very bad for Zach, as if he'd hidden the weapon after using it to kill Rex.

Beneath that, she wrote *Rex*. The man himself could provide clues as to who might want to kill him. Apparently, he had many enemies but, once the eyewitness had placed Zach at the scene, law enforcement had begun building a case against Zach, rather than following any other leads.

Next she wrote, *set-up*. Who would have the most to gain by setting Zach up? The killer, of course. Somebody who knew Zach and who had access to his pick-up.

For a few moments, Cady tapped the pencil on the page. Then, she drew a line down the middle of the page, and started a second list next to the first, titled, *LAURA*. If Zach was innocent of the murder of his second wife, then he had probably found the skull exactly as he said he had: lodged in a water gap after a storm. Cady doubted that it would do any good to try and find the rest of the body. Too much time had passed and scavenging animals had certainly scattered what remained.

If Cady were a real detective, she would start with the murder and make her way backward. She wrote, *When did Laura disappear? Who saw her last? What led up to her eventual disappearance? Did anyone search for her?*

Cady knew that if the sheriff or Texas Rangers had any idea that Zach's second wife had been murdered, they would slam the doors on Zach so tight he would never get out. She had wrestled that demon herself all night long, not to mention the doubts that had sprung up within her from the first time she had laid eyes on the skull. For one man to be anywhere near two murders during the course of his lifetime was almost automatic condemnation in the eyes of the law.

But they didn't know Zach. Not like Cady knew him.

Staring at the two lists, Cady began to wonder if there could possibly be a connection between the two murders.

Was it possible that the same person could have committed them both?

Crash.

Electrified, Cady froze. The loud noise had come from somewhere downstairs.

There's somebody in the house, she thought. But there couldn't be. She'd locked the doors and everything. And there were no vehicles near the house.

Heart pounding, she made her way timidly through the dining room and slowly into the living room. There was no sign of anyone.

Something flickered in the corner of her eye, from the direction of the downstairs bathroom. Cady's breath began coming in little shallow pants. Should she run upstairs for the Beretta?

Radar came stalking out toward her, trilling her name in his inimitable little language. Cady relaxed a little, swooped him up, and went into the bathroom. A bowl of potpourri which had sat on the back of the toilet had been upended onto the floor. The window was gaping wide open, curtains swaying softly in the breeze.

'Radar? Since when have you been able to climb up to the back of the toilet?' Cady crossed over to the window and looked out. She frowned. She could not remember leaving it open, certainly not this wide.

'Careless of me,' she mumbled, closing and locking the window.

Putting down the kitten, she stooped to clean up the scattered dried flowers and wood shavings. *He's an adventurous little guy all right*, she thought. *Before we know it, he'll be climbing up the stairs.*

Lack of sleep and exhaustion tugged at Cady. She longed to go upstairs and collapse onto her bed for a nap. But she dare not slow down or waste a single minute.

Cady sat down on the edge of the bathtub and put the palm of her hand unconsciously on her stomach. There had been no time to let the doctor's diagnosis sink in.

A baby.

The stress of Cady's mother's death, added to the assault, had caused her menstrual cycle to swing wildly. She'd even skipped a month after both events, so it had never occurred to her, not for a minute, that she might be pregnant.

Cady was glad she had decided to stay with Zach *before* she'd learned of the pregnancy. It made her decision more pure somehow, but now she was even more determined. She'd grown up without ever knowing her father, and she was damned if she was going to do that to her own child.

A child.

It was too incredible still, as if this were happening to somebody else, some other Cady who stood over to the side and observed. She had always longed for children, but had been far too busy in her career to even dream of having one outside marriage and, until Zach, there hadn't been anybody she'd wanted to marry. (Not since Mike anyway, and she didn't count him.)

It gave Cady even more compelling a reason than any other she could think of, besides the power of love, for her to see to it that her husband was set free.

She glanced at her face in the mirror. It was resolute, determined. Cady left the bathroom, collected her purse and keys, and left the house, locking the door behind her.

Zach's appearance had deteriorated alarmingly. He did not look like himself at all in the strange bright orange county jail inmate jumpsuit. His stubble was day-old, his face gaunt and pallid, and his forehead paler than ever. Even more frightening were his eyes. They were completely without life.

Cady's gut constricted as she embraced him in the small room set aside for visitation. A few other weary-looking inmates occupied the room, along with their worried wives and hyperactive children. The room smelled of perspiration, fear and defeat. A sheriff's deputy leaned against one wall and watched everything. A toothpick jutted from a corner of his mouth.

They sat across from each other at a plastic table with plastic seats attached to it that were too close for Zach's long legs, and she held both his hands. 'I'm going to get you out of here,' she told him quietly.

'Brought your trusty hacksaw, did you?' There was a flicker of light in his dull eyes, but that was all.

She squeezed his hands. 'I mean it. I'm going to get you another lawyer – a good one – and I'm going to find out who killed Rex.'

353

He shrugged. 'Whoever did it's long gone by now, Cady-did.'

She shook her head. 'Maybe not. Why should they leave? Nobody's looking for them.'

'That's true.' He glanced around, his eyes wary. 'Keep your voice down. The place has ears.' Before she could say anything else, he said, 'My sister, Sarah, came to see me yesterday. She said to tell you she was real sorry she couldn't go on to Fort Davis to visit you, but that this is the height of white-water rafting season – at least as far as the inexperienced tourist is concerned – and she couldn't get away any longer.'

'I'm glad she came, Zach.' Cady knew that Zach felt close to his sister, but Sarah had lived in the Big Bend for a very long time. Cady doubted that talking to her would help much. Still, she made a mental note to consider it if it became necessary.

She dreaded what was next, but she had to discuss Zach's case with him. Leaning forward, Cady whispered, 'Do you know what happened to the 30-30 you kept in your ranch pick-up?'

He shook his head. 'They already asked me about that. I have absolutely no idea. Last time I saw it, it was in the rack, in the truck.'

She leaned forward. 'Zach, do you have any idea who might want to frame you for Rex's murder?'

'Sure.'

Her heart leapt. 'Who?'

'Whoever did it, that's who.' He sighed with great weariness.

Cady leaned back. Everytime she saw him, he looked worse. 'Hey, big guy,' she said, tugging at his hands, 'you haven't given up on me, have you?'

He glanced up at her, then away.

'You've got to survive this, honey,' she urged. 'For us. You've got to make that decision.'

He rolled his eyes, but didn't say anything.

'That's what you've done, isn't it? You've given up.'

'It's open and shut, Cady. A kangaroo court. They'll put me away for life.'

'No. *No.* Zach, I love you. I *believe* in you. You have got to stay strong in here, you've got to believe that we will find a way to prove your innocence.'

His words were so bleak that they chilled her. 'I can't go through this again, Cady. I can't be a prisoner again. I just can't.'

This was serious. More serious than Cady had realized. For the first time, it occurred to her that Zach might be suicidal. She held tightly to his hand. 'If you can't do it for yourself, then do it for me.'

His eyes watered and he blinked. He stroked the back of her injured hand. 'Ever since I first saw you, I figured I would lose you one day.'

'What?'

He held up one hand. 'Even after you came out to the ranch with me, even after you *married* me, I always figured you would be lured back to the city by your job and all the excitement you missed.'

She began to protest, and he shushed her. 'That's why I locked that goddamned skull back into that old foot-locker. It was a stupid, childish thing to do, I know, but somehow I thought that if you couldn't get at the thing, you'd leave it alone. You wouldn't get back into the game. You wouldn't be seduced by the mystery and the fascination and the press attention and the good-lookin' single guys that used to be your job and your life.' He smiled, a slow, bitter, sardonic smile. 'I was just so afraid of losing you.'

'Oh, Zach.' Cady interlaced her fingers in his. She felt a twinge of guilt, but kept it to herself.

'I want you to leave me,' he said suddenly. 'All I've done is screw up your life. Go back where you belong. I won't fight it if you want to divorce me.'

She yanked back her hand as if his had burned it, and put her fists on her hips. 'Zacharia Ralston! Did it ever occur to you that if I wanted to go back to that old life all that badly, I'd never have married you in the first place? I happen to love you, you big fool, and I love the life we've made together.'

'I know that, Cady, but your work is important to you.'

'So? What makes you think I can't do both?'

His brow furrowed.

'Yeah. Did you realize that I could maybe freelance for various law enforcement agencies, if I wanted, and make as much money as I used to working for one department? I could still work for *America's Most Wanted* and *Unsolved Mysteries*, whenever they needed me. Or I could dump the criminal aspect altogether, at least for a while, and do that children's book. I've got all sorts of options, and they do not, I repeat, do not include leaving you.'

She took his hands again and forced him to look into her eyes. 'It's a *decision*. Just like the decision to survive, right? It's the decision to love, and to work at love, and to stick with it no matter what, for the long haul. The survival of a marriage, if you want to call it that. So, I decided. And now you're stuck with me.'

Though Zach's eyes remained dry, something flooded into them, something like a light. It was, as the song said, a look of love. He took her hands and kissed them.

'And besides,' she added, 'it would be pretty stupid of me to walk out now, what with being pregnant and all.'

His mouth gaped open.

'Incidentally, for future reference, I had already made the aforementioned decision *before* I found out I was pregnant.'

His eyes were sparkling. He said, '*Aforementioned?*'

'Aforementioned.'

'Nobody says, "aforementioned".'

They smiled broadly at each other.

'I can't believe it,' he said.

'Me, neither. But the doctor was certain.'

'Oh God, Cady. A baby! This is wonderful! I love you!'

'Then let's concentrate on getting you the hell out of here, all right? I ain't about to go into that delivery room all by myself.'

Cady tried not to notice True's conspicuously absent pick-up as she drove around behind the house and parked the Lexus. Hauling bags of groceries, she dragged her weary body up the back steps. The talk with Zach had taken more out of her than she'd realized, and she was still deeply worried about him.

She made herself a sandwich and watched a little mindless television, trying to unwind, trying to calm her thoughts. There was so much to be done, she hardly knew where to start. She kept the pad and pencil close by, and whenever she thought of another lead to track down, she'd make a note of it, until finally she gave up the pretense of paying any attention to the TV and turned it off.

Thanks to Daylight Savings Time, it was still light out, though growing dim, when Cady made her slow, tired way up the stairs for a shower and bed. The doctor had told her that she might have to cope with much less energy and that getting plenty of rest was important. Now she could hardly keep her eyes open. She flicked on the bedroom light, and stood rooted to the spot in the open doorway.

A white satin peignoir had been carefully laid out across the bed.

Dappled across the gown, the pillows, the turned-back comforter, and the sheets, were wilted, soot-stained white roses.

Chapter Thirty-Four

Something snapped inside her.

She could almost feel the breaking loose and the giving way, like a hastily constructed cage that bends and bows before the exploding power of its captive.

It had been there, ever since the assault – ever since her mother's death, really. It had been crouching inside of her, but she had tamed it, civilized it, taught it manners, and forced it to behave when provoked. With the assault, it had almost consumed her, but she had fought it back and been very proud of herself for doing so.

But now it came to full, rearing, bloody life ... this *thing*.

This rage.

Before she knew how it got there, the Beretta was in her hand, in her strong right hand, and she was roaring.

'You goddamn son of a mother-fucking bastard!' she screamed. *'Where are you? Are you hiding, like the slithering coward you are? Come out here and face me down and let us see just how tough you really are!'*

Kicking open closet doors, she flung aside clothes, then stormed from the room, hitting light-switches, slamming doors back against walls, shoving aside furniture with her feet.

In her studio, she banged back the closet door,

yelling, *'You want me? You come and get me, you sleazy little fucker!'*

Then her bloodthirsty gaze fell to the high closet shelf and, at once, all the fire inside her turned to ice.

The box containing the skull was gone.

The scale photographs, her forensic sketch, and the portrait of Laura Lynn, Zach's ex-wife . . . gone.

Heart thudding like a dull drum in her ears, chest heaving, Cady slowly lowered the Beretta and stared, *willing* the box to come back.

'Oh my God.' A wave of nausea lapped at the back of her throat, and she gritted her teeth to keep from vomiting. A moment before, she could have faced down the most deranged psychopath and set him cowering, but this was far worse.

This was power.

Now, whoever it was who could follow her every move, who could tell what she was wearing on a given morning, who could get into a locked house at will and fool the watchdogs outside, who left dozens of hang-ups on her answering machine all day long, *now* this person had power over her.

He could destroy her husband.

She cursed herself. How could she possibly have been so stupid as to leave those things in her home?

I was stressed and exhausted and sick, she told herself. *I wasn't thinking.*

But excuses no longer mattered.

Violent trembling overtook her. She thought of Zach. *I can't be in prison again*, he'd told her. And she'd promised to set him free. She had promised.

Only instead, she'd handed his fate over to the one

person who had the most compelling reason to want him out of the way.

In no time I had me a great little shrine built.

'Oh, Laura Lynn, you stupid girl,' I said (just like that, in a little sing-song voice), as I oh-so-carefully slipped the high-school portrait into a new brass frame. 'You should have known better than to marry Zach Ralston. Look where it got you.'

I carefully positioned the frame on its stand, next to the skull, which glared hollow-eyed at me from its place of pride in the center of the table. Those little eraser-head things all over it were an annoyance, but I left them on because you never knew when you might need them later. Cady's sketch was framed and arranged just-so on the left side of the skull. Each frame was turned at a precise forty-five degree angle, partially facing the skull and partially facing me.

Stunning effect.

On the wall behind the table, I took a scarf and some thumbtacks and made a lovely little draping over the whole tableau, fashioning it into, well, a shrine. Then, directly in front of the skull, I put a lit candle.

When I turned out the lights, it was absolutely perfect. I tell you, I could hardly contain myself! This was the best break – I couldn't have dreamed up anything better myself.

I'd been so patient, so very, very patient.

But it had paid off, and now I was certain she was ready. She had to see him for what he really was.

She had to know what a dim-bulb jackass she had married. Ralston was so far beneath her in intelligence and class it was laughable. He'd bumbled right into his own trap and was still too stupid to figure it out.

As usual. Only this time, the whole damn town was starting to realize it.

Soon, very soon, the scales would fall away from her blinded eyes and she would realize that I – not Zach – was her true soul mate, her life-song, her heart. She would come to me, her eyes brimming with love, and say, 'I've been such a fool.'

I pictured us making love over and over again. I could see it so clearly, could smell it, could FEEL it.

And the plans. I had so many many plans and dreams for us! Of course we would marry. I was sick of that place; I would take her someplace lush, someplace exotic, someplace feral. We would oil each other's bodies and play in the surf all day and make love beneath the palm trees to the sound of the ocean and the tropical breezes.

We'd have us a little cottage, and she would have a studio. We'd work together, side by side. Maybe I would write stories and she could draw pictures to illustrate them. I know some pretty good cowboy stories.

Because we were both so brilliant, the books would, of course, attract the attention of a New York publisher, and we would become wealthy. I figure the only distractions we would have from each other would be the intrusion of the press, who would be clamoring for interviews and pictures of us together. And Hollywood, of course, who would insist on doing movies based on our love affair. It would be a nuisance, but I figured we would deal with it. I knew our love was certainly strong enough to handle the stress.

Our love was strong enough to handle anything.

We could have had it all. It was right there in front

of us, so close I could practically feel it. She could have felt it too, if only . . .

You know, everything could have turned out so very, very differently, if Cady Maxwell had only listened to her heart.

I gave her every opportunity in the world, I really did.

It's her own fault things turned out the way they did.

But on that day, anyway, I still believed in her. I danced around my little shrine, wearing a pair of her panties (how else could I get so close to her?), dreaming of our future together, and listening to a tape of 'The Ocean's Relaxing Surf'. It was turned up real loud, so that the room was filled with the noise of pounding waves. Then, I stretched out on the bed, face first, and began moving slowly, rubbing my crotch against the mattress, panting at the touch of her underwear against my skin, picturing her beneath me, moaning and crying out MY name. And then . . .

Wait. This is getting a little too personal.

I think it's time to change the subject.

When the pounding on the back door came, Cady sat straight up. She was sleeping in the lovely little room that had been her first home here. It was a front bedroom, so the hammering on the back door seemed far away, but that made it no less frightening in the dead of the night.

She was sleeping in one of Zach's white Western shirts, which came down to mid-thigh. She groped around for a robe but couldn't find one. Of course, it would be in the other room. The pounding was so insistent that she forgot about the robe and hurried downstairs as she was, the Beretta clutched behind her back, hitting light switches as she went.

Radar was dashing confusedly from one side of the kitchen to the next; loud, intrusive noise frightened him. She spoke a soothing word to him and glanced out the window beside the door.

'What do you want, Joe?' she called through the locked door.

'I gotta talk to you,' he shouted. 'It's important. Zach sent me.'

At the sound of her husband's name, Cady's heart lurched. She unlocked the door and stepped back a few paces.

Joe sauntered in, his cowboy hat cocked up on the back of his head, grinning lazily at her. He reeked of whiskey and carried a bottle of Jack Daniel's with him.

'Jist thought I'd come check and see how you's doin',' he drawled. 'Thought we might have us a sociable little drank.' He reached into the cabinet over the sink as if he owned the place and pulled down two glasses.

'You're drunk.'

'And you're smart. Here. Have a shot o' Jack Black.' He held out a glass.

'No, thank you.'

He scowled. 'What do folks like you drank? Champagne? Brandy? One o' them little apper-tifs?'

'I don't drink at all,' she said. *At least, not for the next seven or eight months.*

'Mebbe you need to. Might loosen you up.' He knocked back the bourbon, then hers, and poured himself another.

'You said Zach sent you.'

'Yeah. I did say that, didn't I?'

She sighed. 'What do you want, Joe?' Moving a few steps back from him, she leaned against the refrigerator.

'Like I said. I jist wanted to talk, is all.'

'It's the middle of the night.'

'Not really. You jist went to bed early. I noticed all the lights was out a long time ago, and I said to myself, "Self, that ol' gal needs a party." So here I am.'

'I don't need a party. I need for you to leave.'

He studied the bottom of his glass. 'You know, I'm a purty loveable guy, if you'll jist give me half a chance.'

'I'm tired, Joe. I want to go back to bed.'

His eyes lit up. 'Now, there's a happy thought.'

She rolled her eyes and pursed her lips.

'Why don't you like me?' he whined. 'I never done nothin' to you.'

She didn't say anything. She was trying to figure how to get him out the door without shooting him.

'Laura Lynn liked me.'

Cady's whole body went cold. 'T-tell me about Laura,' she said, trying to appear calm.

'She was purty, like you.' He upended the bottle and drank from it. 'Like I said, Zacharia always was one lucky son of a bitch.' He stared up at the ceiling. 'They never got along. Never shoulda got married in the first place. All they ever did was fight.' He glanced back at her. 'She run off, you know.'

'I know.'

'I don't even thank Zach noticed. He's drankin' purty hard back in those days. I guess he figgered, good riddance.'

The light from over the kitchen sink haloed Joe,

casting his face in shadow. She strained to read his expression, but couldn't.

'Yep, the women always wanted Zach. Hell if I know why. I cain't see that much dif'ernce between us, can you?'

Cady shrugged.

'I mean, I'm a good-lookin' guy, ain't I?'

'Sure, Joe,' she mumbled. *Keep him talking.*

'I kin ride same as him, and rope, and dance. Only dif'ernce I can see, is that Zach's rich, and I'm not.'

She shook her head. 'Zach's not rich, Joe. Surely you know that.'

'Oh, but see, there's where you're wrong. Zacharia Ralston's got *land*, purty girl. He's got land. And that makes him rich. And he didn't do a damn thing to earn it, neither. Jist came to him, on a silver platter. Me, I work my butt off, but the women, they all flock to Zach.' He took another long swallow, and held the bottle up to the light to see how much was left.

'Laura Lynn Baker now, she shoulda been mine. I'm the one that first spotted her at the rodeo dance that night. It was me she danced with first. It was me she put the move on. Ever'body there knew it too. Then she laid eyes on Zach, and that was that.' He sighed. 'I don't even thank she liked him. Jist married him 'cause he's got land. It ain't fair that Zach gets all the good women.'

He plunked the bottle down on the cabinet and eyed Cady up and down. 'You look sexy in that shirt. Bet you don't got nothin' on underneath.' He took a step toward her.

'Get away from me, Joe, I mean it,' said Cady,

staring him down. 'Go back to your own house and sleep it off.'

In one quick step, he had her pinned against the refrigerator. She could feel the Beretta cutting into her back, but she couldn't pull her hand free.

He pressed his hard body against hers, prying her lips open with his wet ones, suffocating her with the smell of liquor, pawing at her breasts.

Cady struggled against him, which only served to excite him more. He arched his crotch hard up against hers.

Cady managed to turn her body ever so slightly to the side, which freed her gun hand. In one swift move, she shoved the barrel of the Beretta hard against his genitals and seethed, *'Get off me, you son of a bitch, before I blow your balls into the next county.'*

He froze. Lifting shaking hands into the air, he stepped slowly back and said, 'Jesus Christ, woman!'

She supported her right hand with her left and said, 'Now get the fuck out of my house and don't you ever come back.' She released the safety and cocked the weapon. 'The way I feel tonight, you're lucky I didn't kill you.'

His Adam's apple bobbed as he swallowed. She gestured with the gun. He jumped and began backing toward the door. 'We, uh, we don't have to tell Zach about this, do we? I didn't mean anythang, you know. I's drunk.' He stumbled.

'Yeah Joe? You were drunk, huh? Were you drunk when you killed Laura Lynn Baker? I'd just like to know.'

Chapter Thirty-Five

The blurted question hung between them, surprising Cady as much as it did Joe. She certainly hadn't planned on this, but there it was. She had no choice now but to go with it.

In the white light of the kitchen, all color bleached from Joe's face. His Adam's apple bobbed again. 'W-why would you ask me a thang like that?'

'Did you make a move on her Joe? Huh? Just like you did me? And did she fight you Joe? Like I did? And did you strangle her to death? I just want to know.'

'I d-don't know what you're talkin' about. I thank I'm gonna be sick.' He whirled and vomited into the kitchen sink.

Cady's stomach hadn't been too solid in recent days either, and this almost got to her. She swallowed and ground her teeth together, hard. 'Turn the faucet on and rinse it down the sink,' she barked. 'Hurry up. It stinks.'

He splashed cold water on his face and did as he was told, groping for a dishtowel, which he pressed to his face. Finally, he said, 'Laura Lynn disappeared. I don't know what you're talkin' about.'

'I think you do, Joe. I think you know what happened to her. I think you've known all these years.'

'I don't.' His face was tinged a sickly olive.

Underneath his tan, his complexion was pasty, and his forehead was sweaty.

She took a menacing step forward, still pointing the loaded, cocked gun at Joe's midsection. 'Did you even bother to bury her Joe? Or did you just dump her down in some gulley for the buzzards to feed on?'

'I thank I'm gonna puke again.'

'You do and I'll shoot you.'

'I don't know what happened to Laura Lynn.'

'You do know, Joe. You killed her.'

'I didn't.'

'You murdered her, you lying son of a bitch, and I can prove it.' Actually, *that* was a lie, but it was a trick often used by the cops to pry confessions from scum just like Joe. She figured it was worth a try.

'How? How can you prove it?' He wiped the dishtowel across his forehead.

She gave him a mystifying smile.

'You cain't,' he said. 'You cain't possibly prove it. It's been too many years.'

'Too many years since what, Joe?'

He stared at her, his eyes hollow cigarette burns in his face.

She had him.

Only now . . . what was she going to do with him? As she studied his face, clasping the heavy gun in her hands, Cady noticed a subtle change taking place somewhere behind his eyes.

It was like facing down a rattlesnake. True said they always got very still just before striking.

'You're crazy,' he said slowly. 'You got no proof. Nobody'll ever know what happened to Laura Lynn. *Nobody.*'

'You took care of that, I guess, didn't you, Joe?'

'Mebbe I did. Mebbe I didn't. So what? You cain't prove it either way.'

'I wouldn't be too sure about that.' The handle of the Beretta was getting sweaty. Cady tightened her grip.

He crossed his arms over his chest, a much more aggressive and confident stance than a few minutes earlier, when he'd been holding shaking hands high in the air. 'Didja ever thank it coulda been Zach? Huh? That mebbe your big cowboy hero got rid of her hisself? Makes a helluva lot more sense, don't it?'

She narrowed her eyes at him. 'I don't know, Joe. As I recall, *you're* the one who was the most afraid I'd show that skull to the cops.'

He stared at her.

'I heard you talking about it in the saddle house one day. You said something about Zach not being able to . . . how was it? Control his wives?' She waggled the gun at him.

His jaw clenched. 'You're somethin' on a stick, you know that lady? You're not a'tall what I thought you was.'

'No, I'm not,' she said. 'I'm your worst nightmare.'

Shaking his head, Joe chuckled. 'You got t'at right. Ain't no other woman *ever* put a gun to my nuts before.'

'Maybe they should have.'

He narrowed his eyes at her, making an appraisal, trying to figure out if she was serious or not. Her arms were getting tired and she lifted the gun a couple of inches. Just a little reminder.

'While we're having this little discussion,' said

Cady. 'Why don't you tell me about the day you killed Rex Zimmerman?'

He shook his head slowly from side to side. 'Oh, you got t'at all worked out, have you? Well, sorry, lady. I ain't tellin' you *nothin'*. You got 'way too many cop friends.'

'You've always hated Zach, haven't you?'

'Nope.'

'But you were jealous of him.'

'I'll grant you that. But that's *all* I'll give you.'

Trying not to betray her nervousness, she swallowed. 'You're the one who's been stalking me, aren't you?'

He laughed, a nasty, mean-throated laugh. 'Crazy as a bedbug. You really are.'

'No,' she said. 'You're the crazy one, for thinking for one moment that you are one-tenth the man Zacharia Ralston is. For thinking – even for one second – that I would ever choose you – or anybody else – over him.'

He curled his lip. 'You always did thank you were better'n ever'body else. Come up here on your high horse, wearin' your fancy clothes, acting like your shit don't stink. Well, I got news for you, sister. We was *laughin'* at you.'

That stung. She hid it.

'Even Zach. He couldn't believe he'd brought home such a ridiculous little city slicker.'

'You're a liar, Joe. And that's just your first problem.'

A pretend heart.

'Seems to me like *you're* the one got a problem. Your old man's in jail for murder, and you're out here all

372

by your lonesome.' He leered at her. He was getting more confident, testing her.

She dare not lose her resolve. 'I can take care of myself.'

The phone rang.

They both jumped. It rang four times, and the machine gave its spiel, then came Georgia's voice; it sounded bizarre, floating out from the other room into this scene of deadly tension.

'Cady? Are you there? Pick up. It's Georgia. I just wanted to make sure you're all right . . . Cady? I know you're home. Okay. You must be asleep. I'll talk to you tomorrow.'

Joe pushed his hat back down over his forehead, shading his eyes. 'Guess I'll be headin' on back to the house,' he said, stretching his arms high over his head.

Cady stepped back, eyeing him warily.

He turned to go. 'It's been nice chattin' with you. I hate to leave, but I don't want to wear out my welcome.' Over his shoulder, he said, 'Sleep tight.'

And he left, leaving the back door gaping wide. Cady slammed and locked it, then slumped against the counter, shaking from head to foot. Her palms were so sweaty she could barely hold onto the gun. She let go of it, first with one hand, and then the other, wiping each hand on her shirt.

Then, she set down the gun within quick reach and made a pot of coffee.

Suppose she went to the police with her suspicions? All she had was the skull (on second thought, she didn't even have that anymore), and even if she did . . . the likeliest suspect would indeed be the man who was already in jail, accused of murder.

There really wasn't a damned thing she could do. There would be no more sleep tonight.

Cady was still awake, sitting in the semi-dark living room with Radar in her lap, when a car pulled around the drive and a second pounding sounded at the door. She had the Beretta in her hand when she answered the door.

'I knew something was wrong,' said Georgia, brushing past Cady. 'I had this awful feeling. I couldn't stand it. I just had to come and make sure you were all right.'

Cady gave her friend a one-armed hug and set the gun down on the cabinet. 'How about a cup of coffee?'

'You know me. Up all night anyway.'

'I'm glad to see you,' said Cady. She told Georgia about the scene with Joe, leaving out the part about Laura Lynn.

'That *asshole*! He could have raped you!'

Cady grinned. 'I don't think he'll try again.'

Georgia said, 'God, what I would give to have seen his face when you threatened to blow off his balls.'

'It *was* worth the price of admission.'

Their eyes met, and suddenly they were howling, holding their sides, laughing until the tears came.

'I can't remember which one to call you, Thelma or Louise!' cried Georgia.

'Stop it. I'm going to wet my pants!' It was a classic relief of tension, and Cady was so grateful to Georgia for providing it. Soon enough, the gloom drooped over her again.

They carried their coffee mugs and some cookies into the living room. 'Ever since Zach got into trouble,

I thought I'd forgotten how to laugh,' commented Cady.

Georgia grimaced. 'Zach didn't get into trouble, Cady. He got *himself* into trouble.'

Cady shook her head. 'He didn't kill Rex Zimmerman, Georgia. I'm sure of it.'

'Oh, Cady. I don't mean to hurt your feelings, but I have to say that I think the light of love has gotten into your eyes. It's just so obvious to everyone but you.'

'That's just it.' Cady leaned forward on the couch. 'It *is* obvious. That's why I believe that Zach was set up.'

'Who would want to do that, Cady? He's well liked in this community.'

'Joe Fenton, for one.'

'Aren't you forgetting one little fact?'

'What?'

'Joe has an alibi. Zach himself sent him over to the Rocking A that day to work cattle. Must be a dozen witnesses who saw him there. Check it out.'

A cold hand grasped Cady's heart. She'd forgotten it completely.

Joe couldn't have killed Rex Zimmerman.

She looked down into her lap at her crippled hand, and began rubbing it absently.

Georgia got up from her chair and came over to sit beside Cady on the couch. 'I'm sorry, Cady, but I think you're going to have to accept the fact that Zach is not what he seems to be.'

Stubbornly, Cady shook her head. 'That's not true. I don't give a damn how things may *look*, Zach did not kill Rex. He's the finest, kindest, gentlest man in the world.'

'Who rotted in a Viet Cong prison for years, who came home with a drinking problem, wild mood swings, and a sudden, violent temper.'

Cady raised her head. 'How do you know that?'

Georgia shrugged. 'You've let on in little ways. Plus, I've observed.' She sighed. 'I also know he had two other wives. Not the best track record for the finest, kindest, gentlest man in the world.'

Cady's cheeks stung. 'His first wife left him when he was overseas, Georgia. You know that.'

'And what happened to his second wife?'

Cady's stomach went cold. 'What do you mean?'

'I *mean*, what happened to her?'

'He divorced her,' Cady hedged.

'After how long?'

'A few months.' She took a nervous sip of coffee.

'She left him, didn't she? Vanished, as a matter of fact.'

Cady jumped to her feet and walked across the room, her back to Georgia. 'What makes you such an expert on Zach's life?' she said crossly.

Georgia said quietly, 'People talk of little else in town these days.'

'Yeah, well, *people* don't always know what they're talking about.'

'But she did disappear, Cady.'

Cady sniffed. 'Yes.'

'So? What happened to her? My God, Cady, didn't it ever occur to you that Zach could have *killed* her?'

Cady put her hands on her hips and turned back to face her friend. 'No. It did not occur to me.' That wasn't entirely true, but Cady was damned if she was going to admit it, even to Georgia. 'I don't know what happened to her, Georgia. And I don't think it's anybody's business, to tell you the truth.'

'It might be the sheriff's business, if he decides to dig deep enough.'

Cady felt sick. She couldn't believe the direction the conversation had taken. 'I don't want to talk about this anymore, all right?'

Georgia held up her hands. 'Fine! Don't shoot.'

Cady scowled. 'Very funny.'

Georgia got up and came to stand by Cady, putting a warm hand on Cady's stiff arm. 'I'm just worried about you, my friend. It's just . . . like you're *obsessed* with this guy or something. Like you're deaf to all the warning signals that are just screaming at you.' She sighed. 'Look, I'm no psychic or anything, and I don't know auras from dog shit, but every time I look at you, I see danger. It's like you're just surrounded by it, you know? Only you're just as blind to it as that little cat.'

'I can take care of myself,' said Cady. 'And I can guarantee you that there isn't any danger coming at me from my husband.'

'Of course not. Not as long as he stays locked up.'

Cady crossed her arms over her chest. 'I love my husband, and I will stand by him until my dying day.'

'I know,' said Georgia quietly, 'and that's just what scares me the most.'

Chapter Thirty-Six

The next morning, Cady paid a visit to Molly Maguire. Though Georgia had begged Cady to let her spend the night, Cady had refused. Something had shifted in her heart toward her friend; something subtle. It had to do with Cady's determined loyalty to Zach. Maybe it *was* an obsession of sorts, but as long as Georgia refused to support Cady in her quest to free Zach, then there would be this intangible barrier between them.

Molly lived in one of the remotest outposts of the Davis Mountains, some fifty miles from the town of Fort Davis, in a magnificent, forbidding setting of eagle-dangling crags and sweeping cattle-dotted ranges. Her house, from the outside, was a slapdash, piecemeal affair of awkward angles and sharp lines.

'I built it m'self,' she bragged to Cady as she greeted her, closely followed by a small sea of mixed-breed dogs. 'That is, me an' my husband, we got it started, then he died and I finished it. It was slow goin' though, doin' it alone and all.'

'Molly,' said Cady with a smile, 'you really are somethin' else.'

'Ain't I though?' She gestured toward the dogs. 'Most o' these are highway strays. I'm like a one-woman animal shelter. They're all worthless, but they won't hurt you.'

Cady patted a head or two as she followed Molly.
Like most ranch homes, this one was entered through
the rear. Molly led the way up to a faded back porch,
spurs jingling, long gray braid swinging down her
back. They, and about half of the smaller dogs, entered
a utilitarian kitchen, crowded with the same kind of
clutter Cady had found in Zach's home her first night
there. She now knew that ranchers were far too busy
holding things together outdoors with spit and bailing
wire to spare much time for sweeping and dusting
indoors.

Unlike the kitchens of most women, this one
contained no plants, no refrigerator magnets, no
matching potholders, no frills. Thumbtacked to the
walls were yellowed newspaper clippings announcing
the graduations and weddings of various kinfolk.

'Want somethin' to drank?' asked Molly.

'Sure.'

'Help y'self.' Molly left the room, followed by five
or six trotting little dogs. 'There's some Co'cola.'

Cady got a Coke from the refrigerator and trailed
after Molly to a big, comfortable room any cowboy
would be proud to call home. A tree trunk, complete
with branches but stripped of bark, was the room's
centerpiece, extending from floor to ceiling. Various
cowboy hats and leather chaps dangled from it, some
from branches, some from nails.

The floor was unfinished plank, worn smooth by use.
The walls were paneled with plain wood-chip particle
board, and virtually covered with rusty antique tools,
horseshoes, veterinary instruments, and other ranching
supplies no longer in use, along with a baronial long-
horn cow skull with a span of more than six feet.

A massive, paperwork-piled roll-top desk dominated one corner, but the delight of the room was a huge wagon-wheel table, glass-covered, resting on a pedestal. Within each triangular spoke space was a small, fascinating collection of antique keepsakes, nestled on red velvet: a pair of round wide-rimmed glasses, pillboxes, fountain pens and ledger books, medicine bottles, cosmetic cases – a virtual museum display of family history.

'Come over here some night, git me drunk, and I'll tell ye what ever' one o' them thangs means,' said Molly.

'If I had time, I'd love to hear now.'

'Trust me, you ain't got time.' Molly grinned. 'Now, what kin I do for ye?'

'Okay. I believe that Zach was framed for the murder of Rex Zimmerman.'

Molly nodded. 'Had to be. But I jist cain't figger out who'd do such a thang. I mean, we got our old farts out here, jist like anyplace else, and our nasty little church ladies, but none of 'em would be that mean. Not to Zacharia, anyway.'

'They might if they wanted to get to me,' said Cady. She told Molly about her trouble with the stalker.

'Whooo-weee. Bless yore little heart. How long's this been goin' on?'

'Since this happened.' Cady held out her crippled hand.

'You have any idea who could be doin' it?'

Cady sighed. 'I hate to go around making accusations without any kind of evidence.' She took a sip of her Coke.

'I ain't no judge. And I ain't no gossip, neither.'

'Okay . . . I think it could be Joe Fenton.'

'*Joe!*' Molly retreated into herself, leaning back on the worn sofa, thinking, one hand stroking a Chihuahua-looking mutt in her lap, the other stroking a beagle-mix curled up beside her. 'But you said this started back in Dallas. How could Joe have known you then?'

'I think he saw me on TV. And besides, he had only just started working for Zach again when I first met him.' Cady allowed a terrier to make a nest beside her.

'Don't it seem like an awful big coincidence that he'd be attracted to you from a TV show and then, lo and behold, you turn up out at Zacharia's?'

'I thought about that. And I wondered if maybe he'd been in the process of looking me up when he noticed that I was seeing Zach. Maybe his jealousy couldn't handle it and he became obsessed.'

Molly nodded slowly. 'Wouldn't be the first time.'

Cady took this as an opportunity. 'Molly? What do you know about Laura Lynn Baker?'

Molly snorted. 'I know she was born trouble.'

'What do you mean?'

'She come from a no-account family in Alpine. The daddy run off when she was little, and she had three or four little brothers and sisters that all had diff'ernt daddies. She an' her mama never got along. I thank she ran away two-three times. Finally, her mama moved away and she kinda looked after herself a year or two until she spotted Zacharia. Took after that boy like a coyote on a rabbit. He never had a chance.'

Molly leaned her head back on the sofa. Without her big hat, her face was surprisingly soft and unlined for a woman her age. It was her eyes that showed the years, and her waterfall of silver hair. 'Hell, I thank she and Joe was foolin' around soon as she got back from the honeymoon. She was jist a little gold-digger, was all.'

'So when she disappeared, nobody thought to call the police? Nobody asked after her or missed her?'

Molly shrugged. 'She didn't have no friends or family. Her and Zacharia got along like oil and water. We all figgered she jist took off to find somethin' better somewheres. Guess she found out thar's such a thang as bein' *land-poor*.'

Cady leaned forward. 'What about her clothes and things?'

'What about 'em? She took 'em with her, far as I know. Why would she leave 'em behind?'

'But she didn't leave a note or anything?'

'Shoot. You never heard of somebody goin' out fer a pack of cigarettes and never comin' back? That's kinda what she done.' Molly narrowed her eyes at Cady. 'What diff'ernce does all this make now? I thought we was talkin' about Zacharia's situation.'

'We were. Sorry. I was just curious, is all.'

'Goin' back to what you's sayin' earlier. Do you thank it was Joe who killed Rex?'

'No, I realize now that it couldn't have been. He was working cattle at the Rocking A. But I do think he could have hired somebody to do it – maybe even Pablo Romero.'

Molly rubbed her chin, where a few gray whiskers sprouted unplucked. 'Then why would the wetback say it was Zach?'

'I think he was paid to do it.' In her excitement,

Cady gestured grandly with her hands. 'I've been thinking about that sketching session. See, most people are afraid of making a mistake. They're unsure. Sometimes they didn't really see the face clearly, usually because they were concentrating on a gun shoved in their faces. Or they've blocked out the trauma. Either way, they tend to be hesitant at first in their descriptions. They have to gain confidence in what they think they saw – that's usually my job.'

Molly inclined her head in thought.

'But Romero was so bullet-sure.' She set down her Coke. 'He picked out each feature from the FBI Catalog with no hesitation. And there's just no way, if he was watching this event through a knothole in a barn some distance away, that he could have gotten that clear a view of the killer's face. No way, anyhow, that he could have been that *confident*.'

Molly's dark eyes sparkled. 'I see what you mean. So, you thank he knew Zacharia?'

'Either that, or he was shown photographs of him.'

'And you thank Joe's the one paid him off.'

'Maybe Joe. Maybe not. But somebody damn sure did.'

'You tell that airhead Dub Garner all this?'

'No. But I've hired Zach a new lawyer. He's a friend of mine from Austin. He's flying in tomorrow. I'm picking him up at the Midland airport.'

'Who is he?'

'A man named Jacob Goldberg.'

Molly let out a long whistle. '*Wildcat Goldberg?* I heard o' him! Honey, I don't mean to tell you your bidness, but Zacharia cain't afford the kinda fees that man would charge.'

384

Cady smiled. 'He used to be my mother's boyfriend. I don't think we have to worry about his fee.'

Molly rolled her eyes. 'Lord, the luck some o' you city folk seem to have.'

'Well, not really. I tried to get him out sooner, but he was tied up with a trial down in Houston. I'm sure he could get Zach a new bond hearing and get him released.'

'I don't know. Country judges don't like to feel manipulated by city slicker types.'

'Don't worry about Jacob. He blindsides 'em with the law.'

'So!' said Molly, slapping her hands down on her knees and interrupting the naps of at least three dogs. 'You want me to go with you and question this little runt Romero, huh?'

'If you wouldn't mind,' said Cady.

'Mind? Why, this is the most fun I've had since I rode a greenbroke horse into a cactus patch.'

Pablo Romero lived in what could only be called a shack, located so close to the barn that Molly surmised it must once have been a tool shed. 'Trust that horse thief Zimmerman to treat his wets like animals,' she said in disgust. 'Prob'ly cheated him on his wages, too.'

'Maybe that's why he didn't mind participating in Rex's murder,' said Cady.

They knocked on the warped door, then pushed it open. Slants of dust-flurried sunshine showed through the cracks between the boards of the one-roomed building. There was a filthy cot against one wall, a cardboard box containing some clothes and shaving things, a hotplate in one corner, and a few cans of beans and commercial tortillas stacked on a cement block shelf. A thick yellow extension cord ran like an umbilical to the barn. A blackened kerosene lantern provided light.

'I guess the boy goes home during the winter months, or works someplace else,' commented Molly. 'He'd freeze to death in here.'

'Where does he shave or get cleaned up?' asked Cady, looking around the eight-by-ten-foot room.

'Thar's prob'ly a sink in the barn.'

'Why would he *stay*?'

Molly shrugged. 'It's work. Some of these wets are no-account drunks or drug traffickers, but most of 'em send nearly all thar money home. All they want to do is brang thar fam'lies up here to a better life.'

'*This* is a better life?'

'If you been livin' on a garbage dump, yeah.'

Cady sighed. 'What will happen to him?' She had mixed emotions about the man. On the one hand, he had falsely accused her husband of murder. But on the other, who knew how much money he had been offered, or what kind of threats had been made? She was certain he was a mere pawn in this game; by no means the major player.

Molly said, 'They'll prob'ly jist send him home. And he'll walk on back across the river some other day. He'll be all right. Let's go check the barn.'

They found Romero in one of the stalls. Molly explained that he was patiently trying to get one of the docile milk cows, kept for just that purpose, to take on a maverick calf. Cheeks stuffed full of hay, the cow didn't seem to mind. It was the calf who was

386

stubbornly resisting Pablo's efforts to put him with a new mama.

'He's frisky now,' said Molly. 'Wait 'til he gets hungry. That Holstein'll make more milk than that little feller kin handle.' She spoke to Pablo in his native tongue, and after a few moments he came out to join them.

'I told him there was a problem with the drawing,' Molly told Cady. 'I asked him to show us the knothole.'

'Good going.' Cady grinned.

They followed Pablo around to the hay-storage area, and he pointed out the hole.

'Ask him how far away the men were standing,' said Cady. 'Have him take you out there.' She positioned herself in front of the hole.

Molly did so, and she and Pablo exited a barn and presently appeared about twenty-five feet in front of it. Cady peered through the hole and her heart skipped a beat. Even if this guy refused to admit he'd been paid off, ol' Wildcat could still rip him to shreds on the stand.

Cady went out to stand where they were. 'Ask him why he's lying.'

Molly spoke Spanish. Romero's black eyes grew round. He began shaking his head vigorously and protesting, pushing his hands out in front of him.

'Ask him how much he was paid to lie.'

Molly and Romero argued angrily.

'He says on his mother's grave, he's telling the truth.' She spoke sharp Spanish, and Romero began to cry.

'What did you tell him?'

'I told him we knew he was lying, and we were

going to tell the sheriff, and the sheriff was going to put him in jail until he was ninety-nine years old. And he would never see his children again.'

'*Molly!* Don't scare him to death. We don't want him to run off.'

Trembling now, Romero asked Molly a question. Molly shot a glance at Cady. 'He wants to know what will happen to him if he tells the truth.'

Cady's fingers began to tingle. 'Tell him we will take very good care of him. Tell him we will try to get his family out of Mexico. Tell him he won't get into any trouble.'

Molly spoke lengthy Spanish. After Romero spoke, she said angry words, but he closed his mouth and would say no more. Heaving a sigh, she turned to Cady. 'He said the truth is that he *was* paid to lie, but he will never, never tell us who paid him because, if he does, this person will find his family and murder his children in their beds.'

'*What?*'

Molly gestured toward the trembling little white-eyed man. 'Look at him, Cady. Have you ever seen anybody more terrified in your whole life?'

'Tell him it's okay,' Cady insisted. 'Tell him nobody is going to hurt his family. It was just a threat used to control him.'

Molly spoke to the man, but he shook his head stubbornly and said something very, very quietly.

'What'd he say?'

Molly gave the man a long look, then said, 'He told me that whoever it was who paid him . . . is the devil himself.'

Chapter Thirty-Seven

Cady was just letting herself in the back door from her visit to Molly when the phone rang. Fearful that it might be Jacob, calling to say he couldn't come after all, she picked it up on the second ring.

'Where have you been, my beautiful Cady? I couldn't find you all day long.'

Cady's hand gripped the phone. Carefully controlling her voice, she said, 'I'm glad it's you.'

'You are?'

'Yes. I've been wanting to talk to you.'

'You have? How wonderful. I've always known—'

'I've been wanting to tell you that if you ever step foot in my house again, if you ever send me one more godforsaken white rose, if you ever touch my things again . . . I'll hunt you down, whoever and wherever you are, and I'll kill you.' She was breathing shallowly. She took a deep breath.

'Why would you want to do that? White roses are so beautiful, they are so pure. Just like our relationship.'

'We don't *have* a relationship.' God, she felt like Jodie Foster talking to John Hinckley.

'But we do. Don't you know how long I've waited?'

'For what? What have you waited for?' Cady strove to keep the talker on the phone, so that she might mentally analyze the voice and see if there was any way she could place it.

'Why, for us to be together. I want to take you away from all this, to a beautiful place. Our own garden of Eden. We will marry, and live there in peace and harmony. You like the ocean, don't you?'

'What ocean? What are you talking about?'

'About us, my darling. Our life together. I'm thinking of the Caribbean, or maybe even the South Seas.'

There it was. Something. There was something so vaguely familiar about this voice. But she couldn't be sure . . .

'I've got it all planned. You can bring your art things, and we can live in a house by the sea. And at night—'

Cady let out an abrupt, bitter laugh, a pure sound of derision. 'You've *got* to be kidding! Look – I don't know who you are. But I want you to know, once and for all, that there can be no future for us. No *relationship*. No nothing. I am married already. I love my husband. I am going to spend the rest of my life right here, with him.'

'No. Surely you must see by now that he's a murderer. He's in jail, out of the picture. Gone forever—'

'Let me make this perfectly clear: Zach Ralston can spend the rest of his life in prison, and I will still be waiting for him. There can never be a life for you and me together. Do you understand that? Never. I want you to leave me alone – I want you to leave Zach alone – just get out of my life.'

'But we are so close, don't you understand that? Your old, miserable life is over. Your new one with me is about to begin. I can make you so happy, if you'll

just give me a chance!' A frantic note crept into the voice. *'My beautiful Cady . . . open your blinded eyes and see once and for all that your husband cannot be a part of it. He's gone.'*

'My husband will be free very soon. He didn't kill Rex Zimmerman, and we are going to prove that.'

'But I've been so patient,' the voice whined. *'I've waited for you and loved you. I've—'*

This was going nowhere. 'Look,' Cady interrupted, 'I'm not going to discuss this with you any longer. I do not know you. I do not want to know you. I want you out of my life. And if you don't get out of my life, I'll find a way to *force* you out.' Cady slammed down the phone. She was shaking, but she felt triumphant.

The phone rang again. She let the machine get it, and the caller hung up.

She clasped her hands over her head and did a little dance in the middle of the floor. Two points for Maxwell. She was taking charge, and things were going to change.

Cady noticed the television camera crews from various statewide newsteams while she waited for Jacob at the Southwest Airlines terminal in Midland, but she didn't pay any attention to them, assuming some politician must be flying into the city. She hadn't slept well the night before – there was so much riding on Jacob's visit, and she couldn't get Pablo Romero's face out of her mind.

It occurred to her that maybe she shouldn't have been quite so cocky over the phone to that guy. Whoever had paid off Pablo and had Zimmerman killed was obviously somebody very dangerous.

She thought about the LoverBoy Rapist and shivered. She'd seen his video-taped confession after they caught him, so she had heard his voice before. Could that be her stalker? If so, then she had to be careful. There was no doubting the man's ability to harm. So far, Georgia hadn't found anybody who'd seen a man resembling the LoverBoy's mug shot, but it was seven or eight years old; with a beard and longer hair, maybe some shades, he could fool a lot of people.

Passengers began disembarking from the plane into the airport. Cady searched for Jacob, but it wasn't until the crowd thinned out that she spotted him. Trust Jacob to be the last one off the plane.

Jacob's stilted body towered over most of the others in the terminal as he scanned the faces with his big, hooded eyes, looking for Cady.

As Cady started toward him, smiling and waving, she was rushed and eclipsed by the camera crews who surrounded him like ants to a drop of jelly. In spite of white lights in his eyes, he spied Cady and somehow managed to grab her with one spidery arm as he strode rapidly along, deflecting questions like so much machine-gun fire:

'Mr Goldberg, is it true that you're doing this case pro bono?'

'I'm doing it as a favor to an old friend.'

'Hey – Wildcat! They say an eyewitness squarely places the suspect at the scene of the murder.'

'Is there a question in there?'

'Yes, er, sir . . . How can you dispute eyewitness testimony?'

'Just watch me.'

Someone shoved a microphone into Cady's startled

face. She was following the whole scene numbly. How could she have forgotten just what a big showman Jacob 'Wildcat' Goldberg really was? She wanted to kill him.

'Aren't you the defendant's wife? Do you have any comment?'

'Uh—'

'No. Mrs Ralston has no comment at this time.'

'Do you believe Zach Ralston is innocent?'

Goldberg came to a sudden halt, sending reporters and camera people bumbling together like bowling pins. He pulled his cadaverous body up to its full, intimidating height, and fixed one hapless young reporter with a withering one-eyed glare. 'Young man, I wouldn't be here if I didn't believe Zach Ralston was innocent and, besides, in this country, I always thought *everyone* was innocent until *proven* guilty.' He took Cady's arm and steered her, almost in a run, down the corridor.

'Where's the car?' he mumbled.

'Right out here. Don't we need to get your bags?'

'If you can't carry what you need in a garment bag, you got no need to carry it,' he said, waving away the press like mosquitoes.

Still, they weren't free of them until Cady pulled the Lexus onto I-20, heading west. She gave him a sideways, accusatory glance. 'What was that circus, Jacob?'

He grinned. 'That was the opening statement for the defense.'

'But I thought jurors were chosen who knew nothing about a case.'

'Bullshit. No such animal. Every juror has some

opinion about a trial going in, I don't give a good goddamn what they say. The trick is to pick a jury with more folks on your side than on your opponent's.'

Cady drove in silence for a few minutes, struggling with emotion. Being with Jacob put her so much in mind of her mother.

As if reading her mind, he said, 'I still miss your mother, you know. There was no one like her.'

'I know. Me, too.'

He reached over and patted her knee in an awkward, grandfatherly way. Then, getting down to business, he said, 'Talk to me.'

'I already told you over the phone—'

'Tell me again. And don't leave out one single detail.'

They talked about the case for the rest of the drive. Every now and then he would look out the window, as if seeing it for the first time, and say, 'Jesus Christ, Cady, how can you stand it out here?'

'It's an acquired taste, Jacob.'

'My God, who do you talk to, the cows?'

'I'm making friends.'

'Who with? Rodeo queens?'

She smiled, thinking of Tammilee.

'What do you do for fun? Pitch cowchips?'

'There are dances, and barbeques, and events in town.'

'In *town*? That sounds so quaint.'

'It's nice, Jacob.' She shot him a glance. 'There's not much crime. Wouldn't be very much business for you.'

'But there's no *culture* out here. It's a wasteland.'

'Well, there are no pretentious artsy-fartsy types, if that's what you mean. You know, the kind of people who put a shower mat down on the floor in the museum, call it art, and charge five thousand dollars for it.'

'Ten thousand.' He grinned.

'Yeah, and you probably paid that much, too.'

'Only if they threw in the bathtub.' He gazed out the window. 'I just never would have placed you out here. Not in a million years.'

'You haven't met Zach Ralston. He's one man in a million, Jacob.'

'Well, he damn well better be Superman, to drag me all the way out here to the goddamned *tundra*.'

'Wait 'til you see the mountains.'

'Do they have cable out here? I don't like to miss CNN.'

'Gosh, Jacob, I don't know. I tried to call the motel in Alpine to find out, but their tin can and string was broken.'

He rolled his eyes, looked out the window, and said, 'God, how can you stand it out here.'

Well, all I can say is . . . it was the worst day of my entire life. I just sat there in a state of dumb shock, watching the six o'clock news. There, for all the world to see, was Cady Maxwell, walking along with that go-to-hell look on her face and Wildcat Goldberg on her arm.

Shit! She'd said she was going to get Zach free, but how could I have known she'd hired the richest, most successful Jew lawyer in the whole goddamned state?

She was probably sleeping with the old fart. How else could I she possibly afford him?

I remember I punched off the television with such

force it nearly fell over backward off its stand.

The bitch.

After all I'd done for her ... all the sacrifices I had made for us ... all the plans ...

I'd been so patient. I'd waited so long.

And for what?

To be the victim of treacherous deceit?

She'd lied from the beginning. I had always wondered about it, of course, but now I knew it for a fact. And she had obviously been plotting against me, just as I had suspected all along. Now I found out she'd been sleeping with an old peckerhead three times her age and who knows how many more?

Oh God – I felt so STUPID! So humiliated!

She just took my love and crushed it, like some kind of loathsome insect.

After all I had done for her, all the love I had shown her ... why, I'd given her my life!

I had killed for her.

And for what?

For nothing. All for nothing.

I had put her on a pedestal, lifted her up like a saint ... a goddess!

Nobody had ever cared for her like I had, and all along ... she was playing me for the fool.

And now she was laughing at me.

LAUGHING!

Nobody ... but nobody ... laughs at me and gets away with it.

So you can see that everything that happened was Cady Maxwell's own fault.

With me ... she could have had it all. Hell, she DID have it! She had my love – the purest form there ever was on this earth – and she laughed at it. She poisoned it with her laughter. She betrayed it.

From that point on, I hated her with the same passion with which I'd once loved her.

It wasn't my fault that this had to happen.

I was willing to give everything. It was SHE who had nothing to give.

You can't imagine how bad it hurt, like fingernails clawing on the inside of my skin. It made me want to die!

But in the end, I knew I would get the last laugh, because I was taking her with me.

Chapter Thirty-Eight

Cady hummed a happy little tune to herself as she steered the Lexus on the dark and winding mountain roads that led to the ranch turn-off. In the two days that Jacob had been in Alpine he had accomplished miracles. He'd convinced the prosecutor (and in all fairness to the prosecutor, it hadn't been hard to do), that Zach had been very poorly represented at the bond hearing and deserved another one. The prosecutor had convinced the judge and, this being a small town, he had arranged for the hearing to be held on Jacob's third day in town.

That meant that Zach could be on his way home *tomorrow*! Cady couldn't believe it. She hadn't let herself realize just how much she missed him until she had a real hope that he could be coming home. She ached for her husband.

But there was so much to do! For one thing, the house was a mess. She'd been so busy and, truth to tell, so depressed, that she'd hardly touched it in the time Zach had been in jail. And she wanted it to look really nice for him. She wanted him to feel welcome and glad to be home. And there'd been the shopping for his favorite foods, and an invitation to dinner for Jacob. Not to mention the sexy new negligee she'd bought. (Her breasts were swelling so that none of the others fit very well anymore.)

She couldn't wait! She'd never been so happy.

The Lexus seemed to point its own nose down the drive and around to the back of the house. Cady got out, took a bag of groceries under her arm, and stopped a moment. There was a nip of autumn in the fragrant mountain air, the moon was on the wane, and the stars . . . the stars canopied overhead like silver glitter dusted over midnight velvet. Somewhere over the nearest ridge, a pack of coyotes set up their spooky yippity-yip-yap singsong; Kip and Mutt returned howls. Gradually the song of the wild faded away, and the gentle lowing of a cow to her calf drifted on the soft night air.

Cady smiled to herself, remembering her first night on the ranch. The moanings and cryings which had sounded so foreign and frightening to her then, she now understood to have been the lowing of the cows down in the barnyard that had been gathered up for shipment that next morning.

Collecting as many bags as she could carry, Cady headed on into the house, noting as if with new eyes the cluttered sink and dusty table. She put away the cold things and headed upstairs, where she changed out of her 'town' clothes and into a tee shirt and a pair of sweat pants – her tummy was a little too big now for her jeans. As soon as Zach got home and settled, she would go shopping for some blousier clothes.

Since she could no longer carry around the heavy Beretta in her waistband, she laid it on the dresser while she changed the sheets on the bed, started a pile of laundry in the corner, and pulled out the cumbersome old vacuum cleaner. As she was pushing it over the bedroom floor, Cady's nostrils prickled. She lifted her head, sniffing.

Was that . . . *gasoline*?

From down below came a sudden *whoosh*. Cady snapped off the vacuum and headed for the stairs, where she stopped, her mind taking in two confusing facts at once: little Radar was clamboring straight up the stairs as if they were ten-foot walls, as fast as he could go, desperate to find her; while smoke trailed after him like a malevolent ghost.

Horror froze Cady.

Sudden, shrill screaming from the house's two smoke detectors stunned her into action. Stumbling down the stairs, Cady stooped to pick up the little cat, whose heart thumpety-thumped against her hand, and emerged to find the living room already engulfed in flames.

Radar clawed at her, his panic driving him to run, and she clutched him hard against her chest. Cady dove for the phone, dropping it in her own panic, then fumbling with the phone book as she turned to the emergency numbers. But it didn't make any difference. The phone was dead.

Unbelievably, the flames were everywhere, on all four walls, gobbling up the old wooden house with a voracious appetite that stopped for nothing, munching on the stairway and chewing on the ceiling, belching great gobs of smoke that stung Cady's eyes and choked her throat.

Shock rendered her momentarily stupid. All she could think about was retrieving her mother's shadow-box from upstairs, but when she tried to climb them, flames licked down from the ceiling and singed her hair. Radar struggled mightily against her, drawing blood. It brought her back to the urgency of the moment.

She bolted from the room, through the smoke-suffocated dining room and kitchen, and out the back door, coughing and spluttering. She jumped into the Lexus, tossing Radar onto the seat beside her, and drove it straight across the back yard and barnyard toward True's house, coming to a halt in a spray of gravel in front of the pens.

Leaving Radar in the car, Cady tore across the last yards toward the house, screaming Joe's name, pounding on his door, flinging it open, staggering into the living room where he sat in old True's recliner, staring straight at Cady with the only eye he had left in a face half-gone.

She blinked. 'Joe?' she asked stupidly. What had once been his face was now a mangled, bloody hole. His head was resting on True's blood-soaked recliner back. He still held a half-finished beer in his right hand.

It was the last thing she saw before her world went black.

The tall cowboy and the even taller big-city defense lawyer picked their way through the hot, blackened rubble that had once been the Ralston family home. Fire investigators huddled nearby, while sheriff's deputies and Texas Rangers clustered near True's house.

'I told Dub Garner that there was no need for you to identify the woman's body they found in the house,' said Jacob, clearing his throat. 'I had 'em send off for

Cady's dental records back in Dallas. If they don't have good X-rays there, then I'm sure she's got some in Austin. She had braces on her teeth as a kid.'

Zach leaned down and kicked aside the blackened remains of the horseshoe headboard his dad had welded together as a wedding present to his mother decades before. It looked as though it could be salvaged. He looked around for any surviving mementoes of his mother, but could see nothing. He spied a molten mess. It burned his hand, but he recognized it as Cady's mother's shadow-box. Squatting before it, he buried his face in his hands and sobbed like a child.

Jacob put a hand on Zach's shaking shoulders and looked away, his own eyes bleary. 'I remember when Jessica went to that march on Washington. She was weak from chemotherapy, but she traveled the whole distance. Cady has . . . had that kind of spunk.'

I couldn't protect her!' cried Zach. 'I feel so helpless! If I could have been here, I *know* I could have protected her. God help me, this is all my fault.' Agony laced the words with bitterness.

'No point in blaming yourself for this, son. Whoever blew away Joe could just as easily have caught you by surprise.' Jacob sighed, a world-weary sigh that spoke of sorrow and frustration and too much sadness. He said, 'Since Pablo Romero seems to be missing, that removes the prosecutor's main witness against you. I can probably get them to drop the charges altogether – especially after all this.' He gestured toward the wreckage of the broken man's life who stooped beside him, and let his hand fall limply to his side.

'Did she suffer? I have to know. I mean, did he kill her quick or did he leave her to burn?' Zach tangled his fingers in his hair and yanked. The pain felt good.

'They've got to ship the body off for the autopsy. It'll take a few days.'

'That's not a body, you son of a bitch, that's my *wife*.' Zach got up and stalked away, his shoulders rounded.

Jacob said nothing.

Zach's hands were covered in soot, his jeans ashy. He stank of fire.

He no longer cared what happened to him. He no longer cared about anything. He'd lost the only woman he'd ever really loved, and he'd lost his first and only child. He'd lost his home and his family.

What else could possibly matter? What else was worth living for?

Suddenly he took off at a jog for the barn. One of the horses was corraled, a big gentle bay named Luke. Zach took a halter and caught the horse, leading him to the saddle house, where he put a bridle on, but he did not waste time saddling. He sprang onto Luke's broad, strong back and kicked him into a run, first down the road and then across the open range.

The wind in his face caught his hat and blew it off but he didn't care and he didn't stop. The blue-green landscape blurred as the wind stung his eyes and the horse began to pant as Zach leaned forward, squeezing with his legs, lifting the reins just over the horse's neck, kicking him faster and faster, moving in rhythm as one, leaving behind the lawyer and the fire investigators and the sheriff's deputies and all their startled faces, leaving them behind until it was just

Zach and the animal and the wind and sun and the land.

And then he started to scream.

Cady opened her eyes to the sound of the ocean pounding the shore. She struggled to sit up, but her hands were securely bound behind her back and her ankles were taped. Duct tape covered her mouth almost up to her nose, but she was not blindfolded. She could smell smoke on her clothes.

It felt as if a steel spike had been driven into her skull and, with each thrust and thump of her heart, the pain throbbed behind her eyes and nausea surged into the back of her throat. Her mouth was too dry to swallow. The room seemed to be slowly swirling around her.

She was lying on a bed on her side, her knees drawn up. Directly in front of her were folded closet doors, propped open. On a table in the center of the small closet sat Laura Lynn's skull, glaring at Cady as if the whole thing were her fault. On either side of the skull was the forensic sketch Cady had made, framed, and the portrait of Laura Lynn as a high-school senior.

Cady slowly, painfully turned her head, saw something unbelievable and, with the sudden clarity of thought peculiar to small children and the dying, Cady Maxwell Ralston understood everything.

Chapter Thirty-Nine

The blue grama grass was beginning to mature. In spite of himself, Zach noticed this as he trod slowly through the range grass, leading his sweaty horse behind. Life did indeed go on, but he couldn't see much point in it without Cady.

He couldn't believe she was gone, couldn't accept it. In such a short time, she'd become welded to him; without her, he felt like half a man.

Zach felt as if Cady had awakened him from a long sleep. Made him feel alive again.

How could she be gone so soon?

He thought about killing himself.

It would be easy enough, getting his hands on a gun. He could just take that gun out into the middle of a pasture somewhere – that way nobody'd have to clean up any mess – and simply blow his brains out. And that would be that.

But it would be True or Dusty who would find him, and Zach couldn't bring himself to do such a thing to either one of them. Same with hangin' himself in the barn. None of them had any pills to speak of, and Zach figured if he drove off the side of a cliff, with his luck he'd just wind up paralyzed or something anyway.

But killing himself didn't ring true either, really. He was a survivor, and survivors somehow found a way.

But one thing was for damn sure. He was going to find out who'd destroyed his family, and he was going to make him pay.

He owed Cady that much.

Cady heard footsteps. Quickly, she turned her head back and closed her eyes again.

Someone slipped into bed behind her, pulling her close, spooning her body, caressing her hair. Though Cady tried hard not to – she flinched.

'*Oh, how I've longed to do this,*' came that same hoarse whisper she'd heard over the phone so many times before. The body writhed up against her, running hands down her side and over her hips. Goosebumps broke out over Cady's body.

'*So? You like this, do you? I always thought you would. I knew you would.*'

Cady started to shake her head, thought better of it, and lay very still.

'*I can send you places you've never been before. Places no man ever dreamed of. Let me show you, my beautiful Cady.*'

Cady mumbled against the duct tape.

'*Of course. How foolish of me. I can't kiss you with duct tape over your mouth. I guess we can take it off now. Nobody could possibly hear us. Now, I'm sorry, but this is going to hurt just a little bit.*'

The tape was ripped off Cady's face, and she gasped. Strong hands took hold of her body and turned her over onto her back. Cady looked over her attacker's shoulder, and there, right beside the bed, stood the telescope.

Georgia looked into Cady's eyes, then glanced back

408

at the telescope. 'Figured it out, did you? You don't know how many hours I spent sitting right here on this bed, focusing that telescope on the ranch – I could always tell when you went somewhere in your car or just wandered down to the barn. I only wish I could have seen into the house, that would have been something.'

Cady cleared her throat. Her mouth was so dry she had trouble speaking. 'All this time,' she said, 'I thought you were a man.'

Georgia nodded. 'I wanted you to think that. You see, in many ways, I *am* a man. I always wanted to be one. I always *felt* like one. Always. I never identified with my girlfriends in any way except to fall in love with them now and then.'

'But the telephone voice—'

'*You mean*, this *voice?*' Georgia's voice dropped to a deep, gravelly resonance. 'That's my *George* persona.'

'You're not . . . one of those multiple-personality people are you?'

Georgia laughed her deep, throaty laugh. 'Nah. Those people are crazy. They don't know when this other person takes over their lives, see. Me, I always know exactly what I'm doing. Like in Dallas, the mall shooting? Here, let me show you.' She bounded up from the bed and rooted around in the top of the closet, finally withdrawing a black pageboy wig in triumph. Jamming it on her head, she sat on the edge of the bed, dropped her eyes, and said in a whispery voice, 'Oh, Ms Maxwell, the man was so *scary*.' She twisted her hands in her lap, suddenly the very picture of a painfully shy, traumatized victim who would rather be anyplace else in the world.

Cady's eyes rounded. 'You mean, that was you?'

'The very same.'

'And you had me draw a sketch of a man who didn't exist?'

'Oh, he existed. I just got lucky. I'd been driving around town with my police scanner, listening for a violent crime I could claim to witness – so that I could meet you, of course – and lo and behold, the mall was very close to where I was. I just got there very quickly, blended with the panic-stricken crowd, asked a few questions, and *voila*! You had yourself a mighty fine witness, if I do say so myself.'

Cady's cheeks burned. She felt like a complete idiot. 'So I guess you're not an astronomer either, are you?'

'Nope. But I was pretty convincing, wouldn't you say? All that SST bullshit. It all came from a brochure I picked up at the observatory.' She gave Cady a smug grin. 'I always was a fast learner. Smarter than anyone else I knew. Until I saw you on television.' Her voice took on a wistful quality. 'I think it was your obvious intelligence that first attracted me to you. You were so ... *earnest* ... about your work. So serious about life. And so very beautiful ...' Her voice drifted, as though she were no longer speaking directly to Cady. 'Oh, you were so magnificent ... I knew we were destined to be together.'

Cady's thoughts were racing. She was trying to think of some way to escape. Asking questions might buy her time until she could formulate a plan. 'How do you ... live? Obviously you're not a graduate student.'

'Car wreck a few years ago. Sued the manufacturer.

I was so damn convincing I even fooled the private dick they sent to follow me around. So we settled for an as-yet-undisclosed figure.' She grinned again. 'See, I've been adopting these little "personas" for so many years now that I can move in and out of a role as easy as . . . Who's that film star? The one who went to Yale University? That guy Hinckley tried to assassinate President Reagan to impress her. Ah yes – Jodie Foster. Ironic that I should think of her now, don't you think?'

Cady studied Georgia's face. She did not appear to be insane. Yet, at the same time, she seemed to have no conscience. Nothing she had done struck her as extreme or wrong. There was one thing Cady *had* to know; even if she was going to die, she had to know. 'Georgia . . .'

'What, Cady-did.'

The sound of Zach's nickname for Cady almost did her in, but she made herself ignore it. 'Did you attack me in my apartment? Was it you who tried to destroy my hand?'

Georgia's mouth dropped open. 'How could you accuse me of such a thing? I'm the one who *saved* you.'

'What are you talking about?'

'I'd been following you for days, trying to think of some way to get your attention. Oh, I considered disabling you, you know, so that you would *need* me. And I would be there for you, just as I always have. But I never would have done such a thorough job. No, I didn't know who did it until you gave me that mug shot of the LoverBoy Rapist. That was him, all right. That was the one I saw shove you into the apartment.'

'Why didn't you call for help? How could you let him get away with it?'

Georgia shrugged. 'It all happened so fast, for one thing. And besides, it really dovetailed with my plans so well. I figured you'd be all weak and vulnerable and everything, and that would give me just the opportunity I needed to make my move. Would have too, if that stupid shit-kicking asshole Ralston hadn't done it first.'

Cady was panting as if she'd been running. 'Let me get this straight. You stood around outside, and waited for that maniac to *finish*? How did you know he wasn't going to kill me?'

'I peeked in the door a time or two. I couldn't see a gun or a knife, so I figured I'd just let him do what I'd been thinking about doing anyway.'

Cady closed her eyes. There was no limit to the outrage that washed over her. She remembered – only too vividly – how dark it had been in her apartment that night. It occurred to her that Georgia had to be lying. She must have hired the Rapist to do what he had done to her. Nothing else made any sense, regardless of what she said.

Cady tried to think clearly. Although Georgia appeared reasonably sane, there was something not-quite-right about her. She was a pathological liar, a consummate role-player, an arsonist and – thinking of Joe – a *murderer*. Cady shivered involuntarily. The woman had a wide sadistic streak, that much was certain, and Cady did not want to set it off.

She strained to remember what she knew about the psychopathic personality. They had no ability to feel any real human emotions, only to mimic them.

412

They felt entitled to whatever their hearts desired, no matter what. They often had superior intelligence. And they were master manipulators.

God knew, *she'd* been manipulated. Played like a harp.

'You know,' Georgia mused, 'we were so close, my beautiful Cady. At first, I was horrified when the shit-kicker showed up. I thought I'd blown it – I even considered killing him. But then I hit on this genius plan. I'd, like, be your *best friend*, right? While I made subtle little arrangements to help Zach dig his own grave. You wouldn't have anybody else, see, but me. And then, once I'd gotten Zach out of the way for good, we'd be together forever. I *thought*, anyway.'

'How did you ever find me out here?'

'Oh, that was easy. That lady who rented your apartment? She never would have given your phone number and address to a stranger, but she was glad to do it for your cousin Jackie.'

A little bolt of alarm stabbed at Cady. 'Jackie? How did you know about her?'

'Paid off a nurse at the hospital to get a list of your visitors. I'm telling you, it was a piece of cake. That lady had never met Jackie, and I can be so very convincing, don't you think? Too bad I can't qualify for any acting awards. It would be fun to hang out with Jodie Foster and share stalker stories.' She giggled.

Cady felt herself beginning to hyperventilate, and she struggled to breath deeply and calmly. It was important that she keep her wits about her, learn everything she could, and not let her emotions get in the way. But this woman had so completely infiltrated

Cady's life that it was almost beyond comprehension. Hearing how it had been done was almost as terrifying as living through it.

None of us are safe, she thought. Not against someone determined enough and devious enough.

Her mind working rapidly, Cady said, 'You set Zach up, didn't you? You killed Rex and paid off Pablo.'

Georgia raised her eyebrows. 'You know about Pablo? Hmmm. I must have been careless. I thought I had that little Mexican runt scared into keeping his mouth shut.'

'You did. We just figured it out.'

'Who's *we*?'

Cady bit her lip. She was damned if she was going to give this monster of a woman any reason to track down Molly. 'Zach's lawyer and me,' she said.

Georgia waved her hand in the air in a dismissive gesture. 'Whatever. Anyway. Would you believe I showed Pablo those snapshots I took at your wedding reception? *I love it!* All that lovely irony . . . Anyway, you were supposed to realize what a mistake you'd made marrying the shit-kicker. And I was going to be there, the ever-loyal friend. And when you realized how it was *me*, how it was always *me* you could count on, *me* who would always be there for you, *me* who really loved you . . . well, then, we would get together.'

Cady sighed. 'Surely you knew I was straight, Georgia.'

Georgia laughed, a big, hearty laugh. 'This doesn't have anything to do with straight or lesbian! Don't you realize that? It makes no difference to me one way or the other. This is about *love*. Real love. The kind of love that comes along once in a lifetime.' She stretched out her body, full-length, on top of Cady's, breasts crushing breasts.

It felt very strange. And very frightening.

Taking Cady's face in her hands, Georgia said, 'Why don't you give me a chance, huh? I can show you what real love is. I can make you forget all about that cowboy. I can make it so you'll never want another man.' She leaned her face down and kissed Cady full on the lips, her tongue searching Cady's mouth.

Trying with all her might not to flinch or cringe, Cady closed her eyes and tried to block out what was happening, without conveying her total disgust at the same time. She suppressed a shudder. When Georgia lifted her head, Cady whispered, 'How can I respond to you with my hands and feet tied like this?'

Georgia narrowed her eyes suspiciously.

Heart pounding, Cady said, 'You may be right. I mean, I've never made love to a woman before. The thought is . . . kind of exciting.'

'I can feel your heart, thrusting against mine,' murmured Georgia, leaning down to kiss Cady again.

Cady moved her body awkwardly. 'My hands are digging into my back,' she said plaintively. 'My bad hand is throbbing . . . Please?'

Georgia propped her body up on one elbow. Reaching underneath Cady's tee shirt, she fondled Cady's breast, teasing the nipple which, much to Cady's shock, actually stood erect.

'I'll think about it,' Georgia whispered.

'I could take my clothes off,' volunteered Cady desperately.

Georgia's cheeks were flushed, her eyes sparkling. 'Yes,' she said. 'Let's take them off.' She stood up and stripped for Cady, who strove mightily not to glance modestly away from the blonde thatch of pubic hair.

'Wait a minute!' breathed Georgia. She hurried over to the bureau where, to Cady's astonishment, she pulled forth a pair of Cady's own underwear.

'It smells like you,' she explained.

Cady wanted to scream.

'One more thing.' Georgia reached down to the back of the closet and pulled out a long, white satin peignoir, which she held out toward Cady, her eyes wide and gleaming.

Remembering the morning after the attack and all those white roses, bile rose in Cady's throat.

'I want you to wear this,' said Georgia. 'My mother used to wear one just like it.' She pulled Cady into a sitting position on the edge of the bed. 'You would have liked my mother. My mother loved me more than anybody else in the whole world.' Fumbling a little in her excitement, she fetched a pair of scissors and cut loose the tape from Cady's hands. 'All the other kids hated me. Everybody hated me. Teachers. Everybody. But my mother would fight for me. Like that time my hand slipped and I accidentally set fire to the school – Mother knew it wasn't my fault.'

Cady flexed her fingers, willing the circulation back into them.

'And when I ran over the neighbor's dog? Mother told that fat cow next door that if the dog hadn't been off its leash in the first place, it never would have happened. It's not like I didn't warn it, you know, when I was pulling into the drive? I honked the horn but it just sat there. So I ran over it.' She shrugged.

416

'The lady started screaming, called me a murderer. Again, not my fault.'

Georgia set the scissors down on top of the bureau. 'Mother was the only person in the world who really understood me.' She withdrew from the top drawer a .357 Magnum. 'She knew I had nightmares too, and I was afraid of the dark. I would have been frightened to sleep alone. She understood that. We never spent a night apart until she died two years ago. Now,' she said, gesturing toward the gun, 'this is loaded with hollowpoints.' And then, 'I want you to put on that gown.'

'What about the tape around my ankles?'

'No scissors. Use your hands.'

Cady bent over and picked at the tape around her ankles with trembling fingers, her mind racing.

'I'm going to tell you this one time, and one time only. Either you cooperate with me fully, right here, right now, and give our love a chance to blossom the way I know it can ... or I'll blow your head off.'

Cady, who had spent a lifetime studying faces, lifted her chin and looked into the eyes of a woman who had killed before. There was no overt aggressiveness there, no hatred, no fear. Excitement simmered beneath the surface, but it had not taken control.

What chilled Cady to the bone was the simpleness of Georgia's gaze; it was matter of fact. She might just as easily have been discussing gardening with Cady on her front porch at the ranch.

She'd never seen anything more terrifying.

The pounding surf of the ocean came to a sudden stop. The silence was eerie. Without taking her eyes off Cady, Georgia calmly stepped over to the tape

417

player and flipped the tape over. Once again, the ocean's waves beat on the walls around them, drumming against Cady's pulse.

'It's just a shame I don't have any white roses around just now. They were my mother's favorite flower.'

Laura Lynn's skull stared sadly at Cady. *Do what you have to do*, it seemed to say. *Just stay alive.*

Chapter Forty

Cady lay flat on her back, naked, on the disheveled, blood-spattered bed, her hands, feet, and mouth once again taped up, her body bruised and sore, her soul battered and bleeding.

Ropes secured her arms to the headboard.

Once again, Georgia had manipulated her. And she had fallen for it.

Georgia had feigned interest in making love. Then, when Cady pretended to go along with it, Georgia had plucked her strings once more, for the sole purpose of making Cady think that she might use the opportunity to escape.

Cady did not know much about lesbian love, but she did have a lesbian friend who had told her once that women tended to be very tender and gentle with one another, because so many of them had been hurt by men. What Georgia had done to her had not been tender or gentle. It had been savage, sadistic, and shameful.

It had been a rape and, as soon as Cady had realized what was happening and started to fight, it had turned nasty.

She felt like a miserable failure, because she'd been unable to get away, had found herself bound again before she knew it, and was sick with fear that the baby had somehow been harmed by the maniacal objects that Georgia had shoved deep inside her. (*'You wanna dick?'* she'd snarled. *'I'll give you one you'll never forget.'*)

Cady turned her head to the side, staring at Laura Lynn's skull. *She's going to kill me*, she thought.

Even when the attacker had smashed her fingers with a hammer, it had never occurred to Cady that she might actually be going to die. She realized now that she had come very close to it – which would explain the vision she'd had of her mother – but the whole experience had had an unreal quality to it, as if Cady were apart from herself, watching. Like it wasn't really happening at all. She hadn't even felt all that much pain at the time of the assault – that had come later, when she awoke.

But this was different. Shock could only protect her for so long. Now she had plenty of time to think, to trace her mistakes, to regret, to feel the pain of her wounds, and to face death.

For a few uneasy moments, she let herself dwell on wondering how Georgia planned to do it; whether she would be shot with that .357 Magnum, or stabbed, or bludgeoned, or tortured. She wondered if she would die quickly, and if there would be a great deal of pain.

And then she thought of Zach.

The image of his face pierced her heart. *I want you to start thinking of yourself as a survivor*, he'd said. He had come to her when the whole world seemed hopeless, and had taught her courage.

Love and longing for him gripped her so tightly she could hardly breathe.

Love.

That was it, then. That was what gave anybody

the heart and soul to live when all around them screamed only death.

Cady thought of True and his crippled hands and feet, and Molly with her dead husband and her handmade house, and even little Radar with his stubborn refusal to accept anything less than life at its fullest.

A tear crept from the corner of her eye and rolled slowly down her temple to mingle in her hair.

There was the child, too. If Cady died, so did the baby.

You haven't yet fulfilled your purpose, her mom had said as Cady had stood on the threshold once before, ready to step over.

Who knew what future lay before the little one whose heart beat within Cady?

Cady's mother had marched on Washington, DC to protect the freedom of choice for women, so they could decide for themselves whether they wanted to bring new life into the world. Cady had been raised prochoice, and had marched in a few rallies of her own.

And Georgia wanted to take that choice away from her.

Georgia wanted to remove from her her own right to decide whether to live or die.

NO! screamed a voice within her. *It's MY decision. And I choose to live.*

Cady would bide her time. She would trust nothing the manipulator said to her. She would watch everything and miss no more opportunities.

Above all, she would fight.

Okay, so maybe I did lose control a little with Cady

421

*that first night. I told you before that I really don't
like to lose control.*

*It's this little problem I've always had with my
temper. Anytime anybody defies me, well, I get mad.*

*Like the time that English teacher flunked me just
because I missed too much school. Mother knew I
hadn't been feeling well that semester. Besides, she
liked for me to stay home from school – we'd play all
kinds of games together then.*

*Anyway. I only missed two or three days a week,
and IT WASN'T MY FAULT!*

So, she flunked me.

And then her house burned down.

*They couldn't prove I did it though. Mother swore
I was home that night.*

Zach was standing in the barn, stooped over a couple
of sawhorses, sawing a two-by-four with a handsaw,
assaulting the wood with all the vengeance of a man
possessed. Sweat poured off his face, making mud of
the sawdust coating his boots and the barn floor below
the sawhorses. He'd driven True and Dusty relentlessly since their return, as they silently assisted him
with every hard-labor ranch job he could think of. He
would work late into the night by barnlight, until he
was so tired he could finally stretch out on True's
living-room floor with a sofa cushion under his head
and sleep.

Even then, he dreamed of Cady.

He wanted to leave, to escape the memories, but
there was nowhere to go.

Even the barn haunted him. He could almost smell
her perfume, thinking of her writhing beneath him

while ol' True unsaddled his horse that day.

He'd give anything – everything – he owned, just to touch her one more time. He sawed ferociously.

Her scent came to him – this time for real – wafted on the breeze from the open barn door. Heart hammering, Zach left the saw where it stuck jagged through the board and stepped toward the door.

Georgia was silhouetted in the sunlight.

Zach blinked. He took off his hat and wiped his forearm across his forehead. Sawdust had gathered in the rolled-up sleeve of his denim shirt and it stung his skin.

'I heard about the fire and . . . about Cady,' said Georgia. Her voice broke. 'I didn't know. I'm so sorry.' She began to cry.

'Thanks,' he mumbled, and took hold of the saw handle.

'Why didn't you *call* me?' she sobbed.

Push, pull. Push, pull. Back and forth across the grain of the wood. 'There was nothing you could do.' The board split at the last few fibers and the two pieces fell with a clunk at his feet. Zach set the saw on a bale of hay between them and tossed the boards over into a pile.

'And Joe,' said Georgia, dabbing at her eyes with a tissue. 'Do they know what happened?'

Zach sorted through the lumber, looking for another board to saw. To his frustration, he found that he'd already cut them all in half. He looked up at her. 'I don't think they know what the fuck's been happening since Rex Zimmerman got shot. They sure as hell jailed the wrong man for that one.'

'I never believed for a minute that you could have

423

done such a thing, Zach,' she said, her voice sympathetic and gentle.

He shrugged and stood there, lost.

'There's something I need to tell you,' she said, twisting the tissue in her hands.

Zach looked at her as the sweat began to cool on his body. Wariness raised the hairs on the back of his neck.

'Cady didn't want you to know. She thought you'd get mad at her.'

He folded his arms across his chest.

Georgia sighed. 'Cady thought that the LoverBoy Rapist might be the one who was stalking her, you know?'

He nodded, his eyes narrowing. 'And?'

'And so she gave me these mug shots, or reference photos, as she called them.' She smiled.

Zach frowned.

'Anyway. I've been showing them around town to people, to see if maybe anybody has seen anyone around here who might look like this guy.'

Zach shook his head. 'Why didn't she give these photos to Dub? That's his job.'

Georgia shrugged. 'I guess she didn't trust small-town law enforcement.'

Zach snorted and shoved his hands down into his pockets.

'The reason I decided to tell you now, is that somebody *did* see someone who looked like this around here.'

Zach crossed over to Georgia in two strides and snatched the photos from her. 'Who?' he demanded, glaring at them. 'Who saw this guy?'

She lifted her hands in abject apology. 'I wish I could say. I showed them to so many people, and I don't know that many folks in these parts, but I do remember that they said somebody like this was camping out around here. They thought maybe in the state park.'

Zach's whole body went hot. His hands began to tremble.

'They said the guy has a beard now, and long hair down to below his collar. But they felt pretty sure it was him.'

'Where in the park?'

'I'm not sure. They didn't say.'

Zach whirled and strode toward the door.

'Where are you going?' she called.

'None of your goddamn business,' he shouted, climbing into the pick-up and slamming the door. Gravel sprayed out behind him as he put the vehicle in gear and sped away.

Georgia smiled after him, giving him a saucy little wave he would never see.

The overhead light sprang on, jolting Cady from a jittery, shape-changing sleep. Georgia stood in the door, grinning. 'It's time for us to take a little drive,' she said. Humming a contented tune, she untied the ropes which bound Cady's arms to the headboard.

Cady's hands were completely numb – she had lost the feeling in them hours before. Her feet tingled, but she could still feel her toes if she wiggled them.

'Old Harley,' said Georgia, as she looped the length of rope around Cady's neck, 'taught me a whole lot about the fine art of hog-tying. You remember Harley,

425

don't you? The cops called him "LoverBoy", and he liked it. Too bad I had to shoot him. Hmmm-hmmm, hmmm-hmmm – you ever hear that song, "Don't Worry, Be Happy"? I figured the most exquisite torture I could devise would be to leave you with that song running through your head.'

Leave. She said, leave. What did it mean? Cady winced at the sound of more duct tape being yanked from the roll, and took in her breath sharply as cold steel cracked against her skull.

'A shotgun,' explained Georgia good-naturedly. 'I wouldn't move around too much, if I was you. I tell you that for your own good, because I'm going to untape your feet now so that you can walk. Now, as you probably know, a shotgun is quite heavy, and I've got to juggle it while I bend down to cut loose your tape so, if I were you, I'd stand very, very still.'

She wrenched Cady to her feet, where she stood, wobbling helplessly, her heart in her throat. Georgia cut between her feet but left the tape in place on each ankle, which sent little darts of pain up her calves every time Cady took a step. She longed to be able to put her hands out to steady herself.

'Don't forget the sta-irs,' sang Georgia. 'Could be a nasty fall. Oh, by the way, I went to see your husband.'

Cady stumbled. The barrel of the shotgun banged sharply against the back of her head. She felt the blood rush from her face and took deep breaths to calm herself. To faint would be disastrous. Like Radar, she placed her feet carefully, one after the other down each step.

'I was really good. You should have seen me. I cried and everything! Then I told him I'd seen the LoverBoy out at the state park. Actually, I did see some poor slob who resembled him. I figure, by the time Zach Ralston gets through with him, they're just going to *have* to lock that boy up again, don't you think?'

One foot in front of the other. Step down. Feet come together. Step down again.

'The wisdom of my plan is to throw the boys off the trail. I figure, it'll take about one more day for the autopsy results to come back on the body they found in Zach's burnt-up house.'

Cady stood stock-still. *Oh God, what body?*

'They'll figure out it's some hooker from El Paso who's gone missing, see. Or maybe they won't – if I'm lucky, they won't. Would you hurry up?' She cracked the shotgun barrel against Cady's head.

Step down. Feet come together. Step down again.

'Anyway, they'll know it's not you. So they'll call out the cavalry. And Zacharia Ralston will take them galloping off into the sunset, after some poor fucker, which will give me all the time I need to take care of you, and finish my business.'

They reached the bottom. Cady let out a grateful sigh through her nose. In spite of herself, her naked body was shivering. Georgia shoved her across the living room and out through a side door, into an attached carport, and over to her car. The concrete floor was cold on Cady's bare feet.

Snickering, Georgia said, 'It's ironic, isn't it? How they called the great Cady Maxwell the trap door? What a laugh. Because you, my precious, just fell through a little trap door of your own.'

It was twilight, but this was a hunting cabin. There were no neighbors. Maneuvering Cady sideways to the car, Georgia released the shotgun, quickly jamming the barrel into Cady's stomach. 'Get in,' she said.

Those eyes. She could just as well have been lifting the skim off a cup of hot chocolate.

Cady backed up to the trunk, positioning her body on the rim and trying to lift her feet, one after another, inside, but she lost her balance and fell, hard. Before she could adjust her position, the lid slammed down.

As the car backed out of the carport and took off rapidly down a bumpy road, Cady kept saying two words to herself, from deep behind the duct tape: *Stay alive. Stay alive. Stay alive.*

Chapter Forty-One

Zach had cruised every camp site he could find, and night was drawing close, whispering over his shoulder. Most of the camp sites contained families, but a few of them were obviously occupied but empty. He made notations to himself as to which ones to double back and recheck.

At the top of a twisting switchback mountain road which overlooked the old fort, Zach brought the pickup to a halt by a rest stop constructed of stone. He took a water jug, perched on the rock ledge of the building – which was open on all four sides – and gazed out over a rugged valley, the canyon walls of which were stair-stepped by jagged volcanic boulders. The fort was not readily visible from this site; he'd have had to take a hiker's trail up to the peak of the mountain to see it.

The wind up here had an edge to it, just a hint of oncoming winter. Dusk drifted over the valley and settled darkly. Shadows sneaked up the hillside toward him. He took a long drink of water and tried to make sense out of what he was doing.

But he couldn't, because there wasn't any.

But then, his wife was dead and his home was burnt – where was the sense in that?

He searched his heart, looking to see if he could find any remnants of the man who'd stood on a hilltop overlooking his own valley, his arm around the waist of the woman he would marry, at peace, maybe for the first time in his life. But that man was gone, buried in the blackened rubble of his former self.

In fact, the more he probed his heart, the more uncomfortable it made him, because he recognized the man he found residing there now.

It had all come back, just like that.

One thing war does, he thought, the taste of it bitter in his mouth, *is take a boy . . . and make a predator out of him*.

Cady was feeling thoroughly disoriented and sick by the time the car came to a stop. She couldn't remember when she'd last eaten, and she knew she was dangerously weak. The trunk was claustrophobically dark, and she could smell her own fear.

She heard a car door slam, and her heart set up a hammering so rapid it skipped a beat or two, leaving her woozy. Cady struggled to remain calm, not to hyperventilate, not to pass out.

The trunk lid swooped up, its little light bulb strobing painfully in her eyes. They were in a desolate area, and it was almost dark.

Georgia was standing over her, the mother of all demons, a little smile on her face. 'Get up,' she said, aiming the shotgun at Cady.

Cady floundered to get up but, with her hands behind her back, she had no way to prop herself. She lay back, panting.

Georgia shook her head. 'I said, get up.' She waved the barrel of the shotgun in Cady's face.

Cady lay back, drew her knees up to her chest, and

kicked both feet with all her might against Georgia. The shotgun arced up in the air and went off with a mighty blast. Georgia, off-balance, fell backward and the gun tumbled to the ground.

It was a single-shot, which meant she would have to reload before she could fire it again. While Georgia grappled for the rifle, Cady hooked her legs over the side of the trunk, pulling herself up with a mighty effort of her abdominal muscles. She scrambled out and kicked Georgia again, this time hard to the head, snapping it back to the ground with a *thunk*.

Cady maneuvered her foot beneath the stock of the shotgun and kicked it aside, and then again, until it slid down a ravine, barrel-first.

She turned and Georgia was upon her, tangling fingers in her hair and dragging her to the ground, preventing Cady from kicking her again. Cady felt a sickening *thud* against her upper right shoulder from the back, and a searing hot pain. Pulling hair out by the roots, Cady twisted her body around, to find Georgia crouched over her with a knife. Instinctively, Cady pulled her knees up to her chest to shield the baby.

Georgia was panting, but her eyes were no longer aloof. They blazed from her face like fiends from hell, no longer a part of the Georgia who could charm, the Georgia who could trade wit, the Georgia who could play any role she wanted.

This, then, was the real person.

She jammed the knife blade against Cady's skin, just beneath the jawline. Cady felt something hot trickle down her throat.

'I'm not leaving your body out here,' she snarled.

431

'Get the fuck up, or I'll slit your throat and drag you.'

Cady rolled over to her knees. The ground was covered with sharp rocks and stickers, which speared and clung to her body. She paused a moment to catch her breath, ignoring the pain, striving to keep her brain clear, her thoughts uncluttered.

Georgia jabbed the knife in Cady's hip. She screamed against the muffling tape.

'I *said*, get the fuck up, you stinking little cunt.'

Cady rose to her feet. Dizziness assaulted her and she fought it back.

'Start walking,' said Georgia. 'Head due west, right into this nice romantic sunset.'

Cactus plants clawed at Cady's legs. Thick brush scratched her, while sharp rocks cut her feet. She tried to look around, out of the corner of her eyes, to see if she could recognize where she was.

It was the desert, not the mountains.

Despair clutched at her heart. She beat it back.

'Keep going.' The knife point pricked her back. Cady flinched, but she didn't stop. She was bleeding all over. Sweat-drenched hair hung down in her eyes. A chill wind blew in from the north, chattering against her bare skin with icy teeth.

'You treacherous little fuck. After all I did for you, you couldn't wait to stab me in the back. And *laugh* about it! Now let's see who gets the last laugh.'

Pebbles embedded themselves in Cady's feet. She began to limp. She could barely see in the encroaching darkness, and stifled a whimper. Her foot caught on a rock, and she fell headlong, her face scraping across the ground.

'We're here.'

Cady got to her feet as quickly as possible and glanced down. It wasn't a rock that had tripped her. It was a four-by-four, outlined against the scrubby earth, dark on dark.

She swung her head back around. Flat rocks had been laid out in a pattern on the ground, almost like a walkway. She squinted. It *was* a walkway. It led to the foundation of a small house, long since gone. Over to the side of the house stood a rock cistern. A cast-iron slab with a hole cut in it for a handhold had been laid across the top of the cistern.

Georgia walked over to the cistern and lifted the lid.

Cady ran.

Zach was waiting, silent as a guerrilla, in the trees beside the camp site when the Blazer pulled up and the man got out. He was slight, about five-six or seven, and wiry of build. A dingy beard covered his face, and he had a Texas Aggies cap pulled down low over his eyes. His hair was collected at the nape of his neck in a rubber band. Most of it had come loose and strayed into his beard.

Humming under his breath, he got out of the Blazer and walked over to the tent, where he went inside and lit a lantern. Then he came back outside and rummaged through a knapsack which was leaning against the tent.

Zach melted through the trees until he was close enough to the man to breathe on him.

He went back inside the tent.

Like a crouched mountain lion, Zach waited.

When he came back out, Zach sprang, wrestling the man to the ground.

'*Help!*' the man screamed. '*Somebody help!*'

He fought powerfully. His body was stronger than it appeared. While Zach struggled to get a chokehold around him, he doubled over, throwing Zach off balance. He curled over the man's body and hit the ground, giving the guy just enough room to spring to his feet, screaming for help at the top of his lungs.

Zach gave chase.

Terror-driven, the man made a zigzag path through the brush, leaping over obstacles, screaming every step of the way. He was smaller and tidier of build than Zach, which gave him somewhat of an advantage in running – that, and about twenty years' age difference.

The man hit the open road and tore straight down it, startling neighboring campers, one of whom grabbed a CB mike from his pick-up dash.

Fueled by rage, Zach had the greater endurance in spite of his bum leg and, as soon as the man started to flag, he came into his second wind, gaining on him with each hobbling sprint. Finally, he was close enough to lunge the full length of his body, arms out. Zach grasped at the man's jeans, holding on for dear life, bringing him down. Then he was on him, pinning him with all fours, growling like a maddened Rottweiler. '*You killed my wife, you son of a bitch!*'

'*What?* What wife? I never saw you before in my life.' He turned his head and screamed some more. Zach pulled back his fist to knock the holy shit out of the guy, and felt iron hands grab his wrist and yank his arm so hard behind his back it felt as if it had come out of the socket.

More hands took hold of him and pulled him off the cowering man, and he heard the voice of one of the park rangers say, 'Call the sheriff.'

Tears of pain blurred Cady's vision as she sprinted headlong through the cactus, rock, and brush that was the cruel Chihuahuan desert. It was too dark to tell what direction she was headed, but she ran like a wounded rabbit.

A sudden sharp pain knifed through her midsection and brought her stumbling to a halt. She doubled over, fighting for breath through her nose.

She could hear Georgia crashing through the brush toward her. She straightened up and took a couple more steps, but she couldn't run anymore. Another cramp clutched at her. She bent over, sucking air through her nostrils, shivering in the wind and dark, weeping the fruitless tears of the hopeless.

'Good thing I stayed in this godforsaken hole in the wall an extra day,' grumbled Jacob Goldberg. 'You seem to have a rather remarkable knack for fucking up.'

They were talking in the Texas Ranger's office in Alpine. Zach was no longer cuffed, but Jeff Jenkins eyed him suspiciously from his place by the door. Dub Garner took a loud slurp of coffee.

'You assaulted a college kid,' said Dub. 'Scared the shit out of him. Only reason he's not pressin' charges is 'cause we talked to him a little bit and explained the situation. But it was strictly his choice, and it

435

seems he's got a little more common sense than you.'

Zach leaned his head back against the wall and closed his eyes.

'I called Peter Stanton at the Dallas Police Department,' continued Jacob. 'It seems the body of Harley Jefferson, a.k.a. the "LoverBoy Rapist", was found floating in the Trinity River three days ago.' He cleared his throat. 'Stanton didn't know about Cady. Came as a big shock to him. He said he'd been trying to call the house, and kept getting rings and no answer. That happens sometimes after a fire.'

Zach lifted his head and gave a sharp glance at Jacob. 'Then if the LoverBoy is dead . . . who killed Cady?'

The three other men exchanged looks. Jenkins said, 'We don't know. Could have been somebody she never thought of.'

Zach leaned forward, every muscle suddenly tense. 'But why would he kill Rex Zimmerman? Why Joe?'

'I guess he thought Joe was in the way.'

'But why *Zimmerman*?' Zach got up and began to pace.

Jenkins took a step forward. 'Settle down, now.'

Zach turned on him. 'A stranger could not have come into this town and figured all of this out.'

Dub shrugged. 'It's a small town, Zach. Folks talk.'

'Yeah, but not to *strangers*.' He turned suddenly to Jacob and said, 'Am I free to go?'

Jacob peered at Zach as though he were a specimen in a microscope. 'I guess so, as long as you stay out of trouble.'

Zach looked at Dub. 'Give me a ride back to my pick-up? It's still out at the park.'

Dub nodded.

Jacob said, 'I'm going to stay in town a while longer – at least until the autopsy results come in. If you're thinking about committing any violent crimes, please give me a call first.'

Zach nodded, but absently, as though he had barely heard. He grabbed his hat and strode from the room, dragging his bad leg a little more than usual. Even so, Dub still had to hurry to catch up.

Cady's mind was beginning to drift. She wondered if the devil could see in the dark. Georgia did not have a flashlight, but she prodded Cady straight ahead as though lanterns were strung in the trees.

Cady almost fell over the cistern.

'I ought to kill you now,' Georgia said. 'I thought about it. The thought does appeal to me. But the whole idea, see, is to make you suffer – just the way you made me suffer. I *loved* you. I *worshiped* you. I was your *friend*. We could have been lovers. We could have been so good together.' She made a noise of disgust. 'So many people had to die, and it was all your fault.'

Cady's mind was growing dull. She wanted desperately to think of a way to escape but, without her hands and in the dark, what could she do?

'Did you know that?' said Georgia sharply.

'Hnnh?' Cady said through the tape.

'That it's your fault those people had to die. I never would have had to kill Rex Zimmerman if you hadn't married that moron shit-kicker. I wouldn't have had to kill Joe – hell, I wouldn't even have had to call in Harley in the first place, if it hadn't been for the fact that you wouldn't even consider getting to know me on my own terms. That's all I wanted to do, you know. All the hell you had to do was say yes.'

Musing to herself, she added, 'I'm not going to jail, you know. You'll not get the last laugh on me. See, I was locked up once before. In an institution. After Mother died. They *said* I was depressed. Stupid fucking doctors. They couldn't figure me out any better than you did. They're so damn easy to fool. All it takes is a little knowledge of psychology and a little game-playing.' She chuckled softly.

Cady tried to think, but her thoughts were all muddled.

'Anyway.' She sighed. 'This whole thing is your fault. Nobody had to die. Nobody. I'd even have left Zach alone, if you had just *once* responded to me. Was that too much to ask? *Was* it?' She poked the knife blade into Cady's side.

Cady jerked, then slowly shook her head.

'Now look at you. I could have killed Zach too, you know. But see, *he* has to suffer as well. See the brilliance of the plan? I want him to cry for you, just like I did.'

Cady's eyes were getting used to the dark.

'As for you, well, you can cry for hubby, and you can cry for your own little lonesome, and you can even cry for me, as you get all dehydrated and starved and your sores get infected. You'll go out of your mind at the end. You'll even think people are coming to help you, but I want you to understand something *perfectly*.' She reached out and yanked a handful of Cady's hair, which she casually sliced off with the knife. 'The thing is, Cady-did . . . *nobody's* going to come for you. Nobody will ever find you. Nobody but the buzzards. And by the time they do, guess what? All they'll find is a bunch of bones.'

She threw back her head and laughed. 'You see the justice, don't you? They'll have to send your skull off to some ghoulish artist just like yourself, see, to get all reconstructed and everything, so they can figure out just who the fuck you are. But by then, *nobody* will care.'

Cady slammed her body into the woman and they both fell to the hard ground. Lacking any other weapon, Cady used her head as a hammer, pulling back and pounding whatever she could as the two women writhed together in the dust and scrub.

Then she saw a quick, pale flash beneath the hangnail sliver of a moon, and it was over.

Chapter Forty-Two

She shouldn't have fought me.

Things would have gone much easier for her if she just hadn't defied me.

I didn't want to hurt her, you see. That honestly was not part of my plan. I was just going to dump her in the well and leave her.

She was stronger than I expected. (Yet one more thing about her that was different from what I thought.)

My instructions were perfectly clear. If she'd just done what I said, it wouldn't have gotten nasty at the end. She really had nobody to blame but herself.

Well, that's neither here nor there, as my mother used to say.

I'm not mad anymore. There's just this, I don't know . . . VACUUM inside. It's more than emptiness. It's nothingness.

Deadness.

It's the same way I felt that time I strangled my kitten. (It should have known better than to scratch me.) I mean, I liked my little kitty. It was soft and it would curl up in my lap and purr.

And then it turned on me for no reason.

Just like Cady.

'I'm tellin' you, Dub, it's the only person it could be.'

Zach had been arguing with the man since Alpine.
They were almost in Fort Davis now.

'You're crazy. Gone nuts with grief.'

'Hear me out. She came down here about the same
time Cady did. Once they became friends, she was a
frequent visitor to the house. She befriended the dogs.
She learned our ways. It had to be her.'

Dub shook his head vigorously. 'Now, Zach, I may
look like a podunk hick, but I've taken classes up at
Quantico – you know, the FBI Academy? And they
say most ever sangle one o' them serial killers is a
man.'

'She's not a serial killer. She's an opportunist.'

'*Now* what are you talkin' about?'

'She wanted Cady, and she set out to eliminate
anybody who got in her way.'

Dub lifted his hat and scratched his head. 'I don't
know. It sounds screwy to me. Besides, if she's the
kinda girl that likes girls, then what use would she
have for Cady?'

Zach was silent for a moment. 'I'm sure she was all
ready to find out, and then I got in the way.' He sighed.
'Look, it would be easy enough to check and see if she
really is an astronomy doctoral candidate from UT,
right?'

'I suppose so.'

'First thing in the morning? Promise me.'

'Okay, okay. Anythang to git you off o' my back.'

I think people are starting to get suspicious.

*They're looking at me funny. And the guy at the
drugstore? I could swear he was whispering about
me behind my back as I left the store.*

It's Zach Ralston. He's been spreading lies about me. Plotting to get revenge because Cady was closer to me than to him.

Him and that hotshot lawyer – I bet they'd just looove to see me locked up. They're probably trying to set me up with the sheriff right now. Blaming me for everything, when I didn't do anything!

I mean, I LOVED Cady! I'd never do anything to hurt her.

SHE'S the one who lied to me, and plotted against me and defied me. I thought she was different.

I thought she was like Mother.

But it turned out she was just like all the rest. That's why I've gone to the trouble to make this video tape. Everybody on TV'll be fighting to air it first! It'll be an exclusive!

I want you all to hear my side of the story before everybody else starts spreading their lies.

Because I'm not going to jail. Criminals belong in jail, not me.

Surely you can see that.

Honestly, I'd rather die.

They drove in silence for a moment, Dub's headlights boring into the darkness. Like many law enforcement officers he tended to drive too fast, and came up suddenly upon a blue Chrysler. He was about to pass when Zach grabbed his arm. *'That's her!'* he hissed.

'What?'

'Stop her!'

'What the hell—'

'It's Georgia, I'm telling you! I know her car. I can see her head there. Pull her over.'

'I cain't just pull a citizen over whenever I damn well please—'

'Pull her over for speeding, for *something*, for God's sake, man, don't let her get away!'

'All right, all right! Honest to God, you're drivin' me crazy. I'll tell her she was speedin'. Would that make ye happy?'

'*Just do it!*'

Dub hit the lights and, when the car failed to pull over, squawked his siren a time or two.

Then all hell broke loose.

In a screech of tire rubber, the Chrysler peeled out ahead of him, gobbling up highway like a funnel cloud.

'Well, I'll be damned.' Dub floored it, and the chase was on. '*Shit!*' he cried, as they barreled past the old fort and the Chrysler careened up a mountain road. 'I haven't got no back-up out here. They're all over in Alpine. Oh, shit.'

The Chrysler skidded around one perilous corner and just missed a Suburban on another. Their headlights bounced against solid rock and then jetted out into space as he barreled after the Chrysler, both hands on the wheel.

White crosses flashed before them once. The turn was too sharp; Dub overcompensated and the sheriff's car fishtailed. Zach grasped the car door. His seat belt snapped against his ribcage. The car went into a spin, which Dub was just able to control, and then they took off again. His foot never left the accelerator for the brakes.

Zach thought about Dub's family. He started to say something, but just then, they caught the Chrysler in their headlights and Dub floored it. Just as he came

444

up close enough to pull around and maybe slow the other car down, it tilted on its side wheels and slid almost slowly over to the edge of the mountain road. Dub pumped the brakes and the air was filled with screeching and the smell of burned rubber.

Then the Chrysler careered over the edge and began a surreal flipping, over and over until the darkness eclipsed it and all they could hear over the screaming of their own tires was the nauseating crunch of metal as it twisted and glass as it shattered.

Dub found a tiny pull-in area in the lee of the mountain. He slammed the car into gear and jumped out, followed closely by Zach.

There was no other sound then but the wind.

When Cady opened her eyes, she was wadded on her knees, encased in a tubular coffin. Stinking, nasty water floated up to her hips. It smelled overpoweringly of something dead. Her world would have been utter blackness, were it not for a tiny circle of sunlight which sliced through the dark and bounced off her hair. She lifted her face to the light, and waited for her eyes to adjust.

She'd been dropped, feet first, into the cistern, which was about ten feet deep and about three feet wide. The circle of sunlight came from the hole in the lid. The walls were made of stone, and rocks littered the bottom of the cistern, along with a dead field rat. Cady shuddered, swallowing bile. Her mouth was still taped; if she vomited, she could choke to death.

Her tomb was silent, and cold.

She tried to get up, but her leg was twisted beneath her and she couldn't get into a position to hoist herself.

She managed to jam one leg against the opposite wall, with her buttocks against the back wall. She pushed, depending upon isometric leverage to lift her. But the walls were slimy, and all she did was slip and slide, though she did manage to rearrange her leg a little more comfortably.

Her mouth burned with thirst. In a way, she was glad her lips were taped after all, for she would eventually be tempted to drink the foul water, which would surely kill her.

Uncontrollable shaking set in. Her body was very cold and very weak, but there was no more cramping, so she had hope that she had not lost the baby.

The cold and pain from her cut feet and battered body mixed with hunger and made her mind wander. Desolation swarmed around her like clouds of summer gnats, hissing, *Georgia was right. She won, don't you see? No one will ever find you here. Never. Ever.*

At times she would find herself weakening, and then she would conjure up Zach's face in her mind and focus on it. She made up little games, imagining what their baby would look like and playing with names.

When the despair would seize her, she'd move her swollen tongue, as if anybody could hear her saying, *Stay alive. Stay alive. Stay alive.*

And the little circle of sunlight crept all around her tomb.

'*Zach?*' It was Jacob's voice, dragging him out of the sleep of the dead at True's house. Zach cradled the receiver against his chin and tried to come awake. He'd been out most of the night with Dub, waiting on the tow truck and the ambulance, waiting on the answer they both already knew: Georgia was dead.

'I called as soon as I heard. The autopsy results are in. Son, the body in the house. It's not Cady.'

Zach sat bolt upright, clutching the phone, his heart hammering in his ears. He cleared his throat. 'Say that again.'

'It's not Cady. They proved it conclusively.'

Zach was standing now. 'Then she could still be alive.'

'Now son, I don't want to get your hopes up. Everybody else connected with this case is dead. We could turn up a body—'

'I'm not dead.'

'What?'

'She didn't kill me when she had the chance. *I'm* not dead. She's got Cady somewhere, I *know* it!'

Hope – pure, clean, fresh cold *HOPE* – surged through Zach with all the force of a rushing mountain stream.

'Don't do anything crazy. Zach? *Zach!*'

But Zach had hung up. He struggled into his boots, slammed out the front door and sprinted toward his pick-up. True was standing in the barnyard between Zach's truck and the barn. He was instantly alert. 'What's goin' on, Zacharia?'

Zach jumped behind the wheel. 'The body in the house? It wasn't Cady. She might still be alive.'

True began hurrying toward the house. 'I'll git up a mounted search party. You call, soon's you got any idea a'tall whar she might be hid.'

Zach paused, staring at the old man out the pick-up window. There was so much he wanted to say.

'Go on,' said True. 'Git. We'll take care o'this end.'

Zach nodded, jerked the pick-up into gear, peeled rubber, then slammed it back into 'park'. He ran past a bewildered True, into the house, and came out clutching his hat. 'Can't think without it,' he said, almost giddy with exhaustion and hope.

But twenty-four hours later, they still had no idea where Cady might be.

Cady's mother came to visit her again. She told her about the baby and they chatted awhile. (Even with the duct tape, her mom understood her completely.) Some of her cop friends came by. Then other people came, but she did not recognize any of them. They soon left. In Cady's more lucid moments, she called them 'the shadow-people'. Most of the time, she knew they were not real.

Other times, she wasn't so sure.

Her tongue was swollen so badly that she was beginning to have trouble breathing. She could no longer feel her hands, but she had scored a major accomplishment. She'd managed to get her feet out from under her. She could pull her knees up to her chin or fold them sideways.

A very exciting development.

Then the buzzards came. They wore little white crosses around their scrawny necks, and they shook their beaks sadly at her and said, *'Hurry up. We're tired of waiting.'* But she would stare them down. No, she would say. *No.*

Then reality would swoosh in upon her like a gust of wind. She found that it was not wise to cry, because crying only stuffed up her nose. She couldn't remember the names she'd chosen for the baby, couldn't remember anything. Even Zach's face was getting hazy. Only the shadow-people were clear.

So she would repeat to herself in her mind, *Stay alive. Stay alive.* It became a mantra, a chant, a rhyme in rhythm to her breathing. *Stay alive.*

Five days after Cady's disappearance, and the third day after Georgia's death, came the first big break in the case. A real-estate agent from Alpine had seen the news reports and remembered a woman fitting Georgia's description who had come to her, interested in buying some land. She'd shown the lady four different areas for sale.

By noon, hundreds of volunteers and a helicopter sent by the Texas Rangers began combing the countryside in the areas delineated by the agent.

They had to call off the search at dark.

Cady did better when she had her little round yellow friend with her, but at night, her mind seemed to take flight. The utter blackness, the cold, the pain, the hunger, the thirst, the stench, the horror, the putrid water, the *aloneness* . . . all combined after dark to send Cady to the teetering brink of madness.

She tried to scream, but couldn't.

Sometimes, there was nothing left to her, nothing at all, but the words, *Stay alive. Stay alive. Stay alive.* She would stare up through the little hole at the tiny collection of stars which twinkled down at her – her only night-time reassurance – and she would think: *Stay alive.*

* * *

Zach was riding with those he trusted most: True and Molly Maguire. It was True who spotted the first droplet of blood.

Dismounting, he tracked the blood, the crackled brush, the crushed cactus.

Zach found the shotgun.

True said, 'Now, Zacharia, I don't want to say this, and I know you don't want to hear it. But we don't know what we're gonna find. If thar was shotguns involved, it might be pretty rank. I thank you need to ride on back to Dub's car and tell him what we've found.'

'No.'

'I'll go with ye,' volunteered Molly. 'C'mon, Zacharia. Ain't no need you puttin' yourself through this.'

Zach stared steadily at his old friend. 'Lead the way, True.'

True and Molly exchanged looks, then the old cowboy turned and continued tracking. The trail was sporadic. 'Looks like she run off a time or two,' True mumbled. 'See here? They had 'em some kinda skirmish.'

'Whod'a thought t'at little ol' gal from the big city would turn out to be such a scrapper?' marveled Molly.

'I did,' said Zach bleakly.

They moved on.

'What's that up yonder?' cried Molly.

True climbed back up in the saddle and squinted. 'Looks like a old homestead.'

Zach kicked his horse into a trot. *'Cady?'* he screamed. *'Cady! Darlin', it's me! Where are ya, honey?'*

They came up onto the site.

'Look here,' pointed out Molly. 'She took off runnin' agin.' True followed the newer, bloodier trail. Molly started to go after him, then glanced over her shoulder to see if Zach was following.

Zach was dismounted and was standing in front of the old homestead. He cupped his hands over his mouth and screamed his wife's name, over and over again.

The little circle of light was shining down just onto the top of Cady's head when she first heard her name.

It was Zach, calling her.

No, she told herself. *More shadow-people. They're not real.*

But he kept calling, and he sounded so near!

Cady tried to answer him, but she could get no sound out of her parched and swollen throat. Her knees were drawn up to her chin.

Then she spotted a smooth round stone at her feet. Using her feet like hands, she clasped the slippery stone between them, lifted her legs, and started cracking the stone against the side of the cistern.

Zach paused, his gaze following True.

The sound of tapping came to him. He shook himself. Could it be a woodpecker? No, not here in the desert.

Then, his body clenched together in one gigantic spasm and he almost doubled over. Tears flooded his eyes as he turned and raced toward the cistern.

'*What?*' cried Molly. 'What is it?'

Weeping, stumbling, Zach grabbed the cast-iron

cover of the cistern and flung it aside, yelling at the top of his lungs: *'Oh sweet Jesus, Molly – it's "God Bless You, See You Later"!'*

Chapter Forty-Three

Cady was airlifted directly to an emergency trauma center in Midland, where she was treated for dehydration, hypothermia, multiple lacerations and abrasions, superficial stab wounds, various infections, and vaginal scarring. A team of surgeons worked on her hands, repairing damage done to constricted blood vessels, while another team labored over her feet, removing pebbles, rocks, stickers, thorns, cactus spines, and ground-in dirt from flesh swollen and infected.

A psychiatrist specializing in Post Traumatic Stress Disorder counseled Zach, warning him of the upheaval of emotions that Cady was likely to experience in the coming months. He was smooth-shaven and smooth-talking, and Zach decided that the man had never experienced any great traumas in his own life.

'Statistics show that she may very well be plagued by nightmares and flashbacks to her ordeal,' he said in a monotonous tone.

'Oh really? Is that what statistics show?'

The doctor scowled at him. 'She may have to deal with guilt and shame, rage and frustration. Depression is almost a given. She may not respond to you sexually.' He extended a card toward Zach. 'If she has any problems – and I'm sure she will – give me a call.'

Zach only grinned. 'I don't think we're gonna have many problems, Doc,' he said.

'But you don't understand, Mr Ralston—'

'Now, there's where you're wrong. I think I understand better than you do. In fact, I think *Cady* understands better than you. She's not a textbook case, Doc. She's a gutsy fighter who's been through hell and back. We'll face this thing together.'

'You may need professional help—'

'Maybe. But I don't think we'll be callin' you.'

Most of the doctors had similar frustrating experiences with Zacharia Ralston. Said one gruff-voiced surgeon, 'She may never recover the full use of her hands. Gangrene is a worry, but I think we've caught it in time. Still, she will require hours of physical therapy, and she may never draw again.'

As before, Zach grinned broadly. 'You know, that sounds awful familiar, Doc, but the truth is, she carries a mean red rubber ball.'

'What?'

'Never mind.'

The obstetrician was a thin-lipped black woman who peered at Zach as though the damage to Cady's innards was somehow his fault. 'It's too early for a sonogram yet,' she said, 'but the cervix is undamaged and the fetus emits a strong heartbeat. I have every reason to believe that it is healthy. However, the lacerations on her vagina need time to heal. Otherwise, infection could set in and threaten the fetus.' She narrowed her eyes at him. 'I want no sexual intercourse for at least four weeks.'

Zach's smile was especially strong this time. 'Doc, you can cut me off for a year, for all I care. That lady's *alive*, the kid's *alive*, and as far as I'm concerned, nothin' else matters.'

The police, however, felt very differently. They found Zach's 30-30 in Georgia's apartment, her fingerprints were on it and the bullets found in Rex Zimmerman's body matched the boring pattern of the rifle's barrel, which the authorities took as the final evidence clearing Zach Ralston of Rex Zimmerman's murder. They felt comfortable in surmising that she had stolen the rifle from Zach's pick-up and had used it to kill Zimmerman, after bribing Pablo Romero to positively identify Zach as the murderer.

But not everything they found in Georgia's apartment was good news for Zach. They also found Laura Lynn's skull and Cady's forensic sketch, and had quite a few questions for Zach to answer, most of which he met with complete bewilderment.

As soon as Cady's situation stabilized, she was able to give a statement, and she told a number of different uniforms about Joe Fenton's incriminating comments concerning Laura Lynn's disappearance.

Clearly, Zach never knew that his wife had been murdered. He was astonished and horrified to learn that the skull in his footlocker had been hers. Still, Zach took a lie-detector test – twice – and passed both with flying colors. He and Jacob gathered in Cady's room five days after she was rescued to discuss the case.

'Goddamn, Ralston, am I going to have to *move* out here in order to keep you out of trouble?'

Zach only brushed Cady's hair and grinned.

'I convinced those bozos that without any hard evidence, and with Cady's statement – although it is prejudiced – and with the lie-detector results, then they might just as well eliminate you as a suspect. In light of what the two of you have been through recently, I have to say it wasn't very hard to do.' He frowned. 'You've got a lot of friends out here.' He made it sound like an accusation.

The door swung open and Molly Maguire swept in, unlit cigar clamped firmly between her teeth, boots clunking, long gray braid swaying.

Zach introduced her to Jacob.

'Wildcat Goldberg! This is truly an honor, sir,' she said, pumping his hand. 'I've follered ever' case you've done in recent years. I still got the *Newsweek* that profiled you a year or so ago.'

Somewhat taken aback, he said, 'You read that article?'

'Hell yeah! You thank I'm ig'nernt jist 'cause I got cowshit on my boots? I take *Time* and *Newsweek* and the *Dallas Mornin' News*. I got a satellite dish. I wouldn't miss CNN for the world.'

'I know what you mean,' said Jacob, smiling warmly. 'I'm a self-confessed news junkie.'

'Ain't it the truth? Hours I work, I cain't ketch the network news. I come in at sundown, crack open a beer, and watch CNN. I like PBS too.'

Their eyes met across Cady's bed.

'Have you had dinner yet?' asked Jacob.

'No, but I know a Meskin place'll blow steam out yer ears.'

'Jacob,' murmured Cady, 'I thought you were flying home tonight.'

'Plans change,' he whispered, leaning down to kiss her cheek, and added, 'I know your mama's proud of you now, wherever she is. She was a woman with moxie, and she passed it on to you.'

Cady swallowed. Her hormones seemed to have gone haywire and, especially since her rescue, tears were always just beneath the surface.

He grinned broadly and glanced up. 'Yep. I always did like a woman with moxie.' He walked around Cady's bed and took Molly's arm. 'Lead the way, ma'am. I'm ready to start steamin'.'

They left, and Zach kissed Cady. He deadpanned, 'I guess there's someone for everybody.'

She giggled, and he sat on the edge of the bed, looking as though he were about to say something, when Cady suddenly sat up and said, 'The remote! Grab it for me and turn it up!'

He obeyed.

Georgia's A-frame was shown on screen and, over it, the voice of the same newsmagazine hostess who had introduced the story on Cady Maxwell that had attracted the attention of a stalker: 'What drives a woman like Georgia Eldridge to commit multiple murders, harass and attempt to murder someone else, and generally leave behind her a wake of havoc and destruction? We consulted Dr Charles Suttenburg, Dean of the Harvard Medical School's Department of Psychology.'

The next scene depicted a bespectacled, neatly bearded man who spoke in slow, measured tones.

'Of course, I must make it clear that I never had the occasion to examine Georgia Eldridge, but from studying the medical records of her brief previous hospitalization, and by examining the nature of her various crimes, I would have to say that she displayed classic symptoms of the Narcissistic Personality Disorder, with strong sociopathic overtones.'

As the doctor began to describe the symptoms of Georgia's psychopathology, Zach glanced at Cady several times to make sure she was handling the program all right. When Georgia's face filled the screen, he encircled a protective arm around Cady's head as it nestled on the pillow.

'I'll never forget the first time I laid eyes on Cady Maxwell,' said the TV Georgia, her eyes lit with an eerie inner light. 'I felt this instant and powerful magnetism to the woman on the screen . . . Oh, I was so certain that she would be good for me! It makes me sad to think of it now.'

Cady's wan face flashed on the screen next, pale against the starched white hospital pillowcase. 'I thought Georgia was bright and funny and I was so glad to have made a woman friend. It never crossed my mind that I had anything to fear from her. Not once.'

Georgia's home-taped face appeared again. 'Okay, so maybe I did lose control a little . . .' Her face jerked as segments were edited together. 'Things would have gone much easier for her if she just hadn't defied me . . . She really has nobody to blame but herself . . . I'm not mad anymore . . . There's just this . . . deadness . . . inside.'

The video-taped image froze, and Cady's voiceover said, 'This may sound crazy, but sometimes I miss the old Georgia, you know? The one who'd sit out on the front porch with me and laugh over a glass of iced tea . . . I thought she was my friend.'

'Perhaps we will never fully understand what would

drive a person to torture and leave for dead another human being,' commented the announcer as cameras focused on Georgia's bizarre little shrine with extreme close-up. 'Or even to drive off the side of a mountain. But I think we can learn something from this about the power of the human spirit to fight – against all odds – for the precious privilege of just being alive.

'Who knows. Maybe Georgia Eldridge knew all along that somewhere along the line, that spirit was lacking inside her. Maybe that is what she hated, all along.'

Cady was quiet for a long moment.

Zach turned off the set. After a while, he said, 'I've been meaning to talk to you about this. I've had phone calls from no less than twenty-five Hollywood film producers who want to make a movie about your experience. I'm not sure what to tell them.'

She frowned. 'I just want some *control* over the story. There are some things I want to say about courage and survival. Zach – the way I feel today is nothing like the way I felt after the assault in my apartment. I feel glorious, euphoric, overjoyed ... I feel *alive*! It feels so damn good just to be alive! I fought to live and my baby and I both made it and I want to *dance*!'

Zach gave her a tender smile. 'Now you are thinking like a survivor.'

She nodded thoughtfully. 'That shrink came to see me. He said depression was inevitable.'

'He's a cheery guy, isn't he?'

She rolled her eyes and grinned. 'It's just hard for me to imagine going through what I went through before.'

'Well, you may not, darlin'. You'll have your up days and your down days, that's for sure, but people who have been through rough times come out of them much stronger, better able to handle the next wave.'

I wonder if Georgia's mother robbed her of that ability by handling everything for her, Cady asked herself.

Zach leaned forward, gesturing earnestly with his hands. 'Remember Max Cleland?'

Her brow crinkled. 'Wasn't he the head of the Veterans' Administration under President Carter?'

'Right. He was also a Vietnam vet, who came back with both legs and one arm gone.'

'I remember him.'

'He wrote a book called *Strong in the Broken Places,* in which he explained that when a steel pipe breaks and is welded back together, it is actually *stronger* at the welded place.'

'Really?'

'It's true. I do welding around the ranch all the time, and he's right. The way I see it, Cady-did, you are stronger today than you were after the apartment assault, because you *survived* it, you see? You know that you made it before, and you can make it again.'

She considered this. 'Sometimes I think that I only made it because you were there for me.'

'Nah. I like to think I helped, sure, but you had the ability to bounce back already within you. It was there all along. We've all got it, really. A gift from God, if you want to call it that. The human spirit, the will to live – whatever – hidden underneath a little trap door to the soul. Once you made the decision to live, you'd have found it eventually.'

*And if you decide not to live, like Georgia did, then
you'll never find it at all,* she thought. *Or maybe the
TV announcer was right, and she just never had it in
the first place.*

Zach was watching her. She would be glad when
he stopped worrying so much. Finally, she said, 'You
think?'

'Absolutely. I knew that from the beginning.'

'And of course, fell madly in love with me as a
result.'

'Of course. But that body of yours didn't hurt any.'

She feigned a punch with her bandaged hand. 'That
body's getting fat.'

'And I love every ounce. By the way, I've been
thinking.'

'Uh-oh.' She mock-cringed.

'Very funny.' He went on. 'With the money from
the fire insurance, and if you decide to option your
film rights or even write a book about what happened,
well, the extra money could enable us to build our
own dream home.'

'Oh Zach. I loved your parents' old house.' She grew
serious, her voice quiet. 'We both lost everything. I
lost all my professional materials, the things of my
mom's . . . and you lost your home. Even all your little
treasures. It just breaks my heart, every time I think
of it.'

He touched her cheek with the back of his hand.
'Listen. We did not lose everything. We've still got
each other. That's all that matters. Most of the
rest can be replaced. Besides, the townspeople have
been terrific. You wouldn't believe all the pots and
pans and dishes and blankets and stuff they've

brought out – including three Bibles!'

She smiled. 'I didn't know!'

'Oh, listen, you wouldn't believe it. Anyway. I'll miss the place, and all my stuff but, the truth is, it *was* my parents' home. We can build one of our own.'

'It couldn't possibly have the same character.'

'Why not? A new house doesn't necessarily have to *look* new.'

Cady's artist mind began racing. 'We could do up some Victorian plans. Have a wraparound porch.'

'I always wanted a fireplace in the bedroom.'

'Oh! That sounds wonderful!'

'And what the hell, it's hard to fit a jacuzzi into an old house.'

'Zach. I love you.'

He touched the tip of his forefinger to her nose. 'That's what it's all about, Cady-did,' he said. 'That's what it's all about.'

A sharp winter wind whipped around the corner of the mountain as Cady and Zach huddled together at the edge of the highway-lined ravine.

'Are you sure you want to do this?' he asked.

'I'm sure.'

He shook his head. 'I don't get it. After all she did to you . . . all the torture . . . all the grief . . .'

Plunging her hands deep into her coat pockets, which barely stretched over her growing belly, Cady sighed. 'I don't expect anybody to understand, Zach. Not even you.'

He frowned at her. 'She was no friend, Cady-did.'

'I know.'

'I don't think you do. You've got this idea in your

head that it was George who was mean to you and Georgia who was nice. Well, it wasn't a friendship, darlin'. It was a seduction.'

A gust of wind thundered around the lee of the mountain and funneled down the ravine, leaving Cady shivering. Zach put a protective arm around her.

'Let's go.'

'No. I want to do this, Zach.'

'Why? It's crazy. She was a lunatic and she nearly destroyed us.'

'Because. I will never be completely healed – never be a true survivor – until I am able to forgive.'

He was quiet a long time. Gray clouds scudded low over the mountains, carrying frost and snow – necessary moisture for the pregnant earth as it carried the seeds of spring.

Finally, he said, 'Then I must not be healed as a POW. I can't forgive those gooks for what they did to us. I know – "gook" is a derogatory term – but that's the way I think of those bastards who tortured and starved us.'

In a calm voice, Cady said, 'Well, if I'd been tortured by Georgia for years instead of just days ... then I might have a harder time forgiving her. I mean, it might take me longer than it has.'

'You're saying you think I'll eventually be able to forgive them?'

She gave him a gentle smile. 'We consider Japan an ally now, don't we? It will happen in time.'

'I don't know,' he said. 'You're a stronger person than me.'

'Oh, I doubt that.' She snuggled closer into the crook of his arm.

After a moment, he said, 'There were no skid marks, you know. She took herself over the edge of this mountain.'

'I know.'

A single fat snowflake drifted down right in front of Cady. 'My first mountain snow!' she cried. 'I can't wait!'

'Oh yeah. It's great fun. Chopping ice off the water troughs and stock tanks, shoveling it out so they don't refreeze, driving slippery roads with chains, hauling hay out to the pastures for the cows. Great fun.' But he was grinning at her, his eyes sparkling.

'I can beat you any day in a snowball fight,' she said.

'Ha! I'd like to see you try.'

Suddenly, flakes of snow were everywhere. 'Just give me a few minutes,' she said. 'I can do it pregnant. Can't we, Jessica?' she murmured, patting her stomach.

He looked around in wonder. 'Hell, if I don't get started, the damn ground'll be frozen.' He walked to the edge of the ravine, took a pick, and gave a few powerful swacks to the hard soil. Then he walked over to the pick-up and wrestled an object out of the back end, which he pounded into the earth, using the blunt end of the pick.

When he'd finished he joined Cady, and they locked arms around each other's waists. Cady gazed long – her soul, at last, at rest.

Swirling, dancing flakes of snow served as a gentle backdrop to the plain white cross as it stood solitary and stark on the drop-off edge of the world. Sugar-frosted boulders tumbled down behind it and stretching beyond were the valleys and craggy peaks of the snow-swept mountains. Pewter clouds hugged close, promising more, and everywhere was the talking wind.

Acknowledgments

Although this book is lovingly dedicated to my mother, it actually belongs to my agent and friend, Meg Ruley. It was Meg who first read the journal pages I'd kept as a city-girl bride – married to a cowboy and setting up housekeeping on a sprawling West Texas ranch – and begged me to take those pages and make them come to life in a novel. That journal was kept nineteen years ago. I'm still married to that cowboy, and I hope from the bottom of my heart that I did those pages justice.

Meg, this is your book.

One of the unsurpassed joys of my work is that, in the course of doing research, I not only meet some of the most successful and fascinating women in law enforcement, but I get to make friends with them. This book could not have been written without the expert guidance of two extraordinary women: Karen Taylor, forensic sketch artist and skull reconstructionist with the Criminal Intelligence Division of the Texas Department of Public Safety in Austin, Texas and Lois Gibson, forensic sketch artist for the Houston, Texas Police Department. Karen – thanks for your scads of professional slides, your careful answers to all my questions, your encouraging reading of the manuscript, your drive and dedication, and your friendship, which I will always cherish. Lois – thanks for allowing me the unprecedented honor of accompanying you during a crime sketching session, for sharing with me the heart and soul of such demanding work, and for extending your friendship, which I also treasure.

It has been a rare privilege of mine that I have been honored with the friendships of some very fine men – men who measure life by the soul, not the calendar, and who once rode the free range from sun-up to sunset. Just about the greatest cowboy I ever knew was a man named Roland Sullenger. Cancer stole him from us some years ago, but I tried, in my own clumsy way, to bring him – and others of his character and integrity – back to life in these pages. If I have failed, please don't blame Roland.

An expression of appreciation is long overdue to the fine staff at the Scurry County Library in Snyder, Texas. There is a misconception that small-town libraries are inferior, but every resource material I ever needed they had, and if they didn't, you can damn well be sure they got it for me. Thanks, many times over.

My work often demands many long hours of reading accounts of the most grisly of crimes, of interviewing emotionally drained officers of the law and sad victims of violent crime, and of immersing myself, overall, into the vagaries of the criminal mind. That sort of life does things to a person, after a while. Thank God for my two kids, Dustin and Jessica, for bringing me exquisite balance, laughter and love.

And for Kent, my love and my life, that tall, sexy

cowboy who can still turn my knees to jelly, thank you for the emotional foundation to work without fear, and the freedom to take wing.

TELL ME NO SECRETS

THE TERRIFYING PSYCHOLOGICAL THRILLER

JOY FIELDING

BESTSELLING AUTHOR OF *SEE JANE RUN*

'People who annoy me have a way of... disappearing'

Jess Koster thinks she has conquered the crippling panic attacks that
have plagued her since the unexplained disappearance of her mother,
eight years ago. But they are back with a vengeance. And not without
reason. Being a chief prosecutor in the State's Attorney's office
exposes Jess to some decidedly lowlife types. Like Rick Ferguson,
about to be tried for rape – until his victim goes missing. Another
inexplicable disappearance.

If only Jess didn't feel so alone. Her father is about to re-marry; her
sister is busy being the perfect wife and mother; her ex-husband has a
new girlfriend. And besides, he's Rick Ferguson's defence lawyer...

Battling with a legal system that all too often judges women by
appalling double standards; living under the constant threat of
physical danger; fighting to overcome the emotional legacy of her
mother's disappearance, Jess is in danger of going under. And it looks
as though someone is determined that she should disappear, too...

'Joy Fielding tightens suspense like a noose round your neck and
keeps one shattering surprise for the very last page. Whew!' *Annabel*

'The story she has to tell this time is a corker that runs rings round
Mary Higgins Clark. Don't even think of starting this anywhere near
bedtime' *Kirkus Reviews*

Don't miss Joy Fielding's *See Jane Run* ('Compulsive reading'
Company), also from Headline Feature

FICTION/GENERAL   0 7472 4163 5

More Compelling Fiction from Headline:

JOHN T. LESCROART

HARD EVIDENCE

'A GRIPPING COURTROOM DRAMA...
COMPELLING, CREDIBLE'
PUBLISHERS WEEKLY

'Compulsively readable, a dense and involving saga of big-city
crime and punishment' *San Francisco Chronicle*

Assistant D.A. Dismas Hardy has seen too much of life outside a
courtroom to know that the truth isn't always as simple as it
should be. Which is why some of his ultra-ambitious colleagues
don't rate his prosecuting instincts as highly as their own. So
when he finds himself on the trail of a murdered Silicon Valley
billionaire he seizes the opportunity to emerge from beneath a
mountain of minor cases and make the case his own. Before long
he is prosecuting San Francisco's biggest murder trial, the
accused a quiet, self-contained Japanese call girl with an
impressive list of prominent clients. A woman Hardy has a
sneaking, sinking suspicion might just be innocent...

'Turowesque, with the plot bouncing effortlessly between the
courtroom and the intraoffice battle among prosecutors...The
writing is excellent and the dialogue crackles' *Booklist*

'A blockbuster courtroom drama...As in *Presumed Innocent*, the
courtroom battles are so keen that you almost forget there's a
mystery, too. But Lescroart's laid-back, soft-shoe approach to
legal intrigue is all his own' *Kirkus*

'John Lescroart is a terrific writer and this is one terrific book'
Jonathan Kellerman

'An intricate plot, a great locale, wonderfully colourful characters
and taut courtroom drama...Highly recommended' *Library Journal*

'Breathtaking' *Los Angeles Times*

FICTION/THRILLER   0 7472 4332 8

A selection of bestsellers from Headline

HARD EVIDENCE	John T Lescroart	£5.99	☐
TWICE BURNED	Kit Craig	£5.99	☐
CAULDRON	Larry Bond	£5.99	☐
BLACK WOLF	Philip Caveney	£5.99	☐
ILL WIND	Gary Gottesfield	£5.99	☐
THE BOMB SHIP	Peter Tonkin	£5.99	☐
SKINNER'S RULES	Quintin Jardine	£4.99	☐
COLD CALL	Dianne Pugh	£4.99	☐
TELL ME NO SECRETS	Joy Fielding	£4.99	☐
GRIEVOUS SIN	Faye Kellerman	£4.99	☐
TORSO	John Peyton Cooke	£4.99	☐
THE WINTER OF THE WOLF	R A MacAvoy	£4.50	☐

All Headline books are available at your local bookshop or newsagent, or can be ordered direct from the publisher. Just tick the titles you want and fill in the form below. Prices and availability subject to change without notice.

Headline Book Publishing, Cash Sales Department, Bookpoint, 39 Milton Park, Abingdon, OXON, OX14 4TD, UK. If you have a credit card you may order by telephone – 0235 400400.

Please enclose a cheque or postal order made payable to Bookpoint Ltd to the value of the cover price and allow the following for postage and packing:
UK & BFPO: £1.00 for the first book, 50p for the second book and 30p for each additional book ordered up to a maximum charge of £3.00.
OVERSEAS & EIRE: £2.00 for the first book, £1.00 for the second book and 50p for each additional book.

Name ....

Address ....

....

....

If you would prefer to pay by credit card, please complete:
Please debit my Visa/Access/Diner's Card/American Express (delete as applicable) card no:

Signature .... Expiry Date ....